Adele Parks MBE was born in North Yorkshire. She is the author of 24 bestselling novels including the recent *Sunday Times* bestsellers *Just Between Us* and *One Last Secret*. Over five million copies of her work have been sold in English and her books have been translated into 31 different languages.

Adele's *Sunday Times* Number One bestsellers, *Lies Lies Lies* and *Just My Luck*, were shortlisted for the British Book Awards, and Adele has also won two Nielsen Bestseller Awards, the RNA Outstanding Achievement Award, a Capital Crime Fingerprint Award and the Quick Read Learners' Favourite Award.

Adele has written for a variety of national newspapers and magazines, and was an Executive Producer on Paramount's feature film adaptation of her novel, *The Image of You*.

She is a proud, long-term ambassador of the National Literacy Trust and the Reading Agency: two charities that promote literacy in the UK, and appears regularly on TV and radio to discuss matters relating to literacy and the publishing industry. She has lived in Botswana, Italy and London and now lives in Surrey.

In 2022 she was awarded an MBE for services to literature.

X: @adeleparks
Instagram: @adele_parks
Facebook: @OfficialAdeleParks
www.adeleparks.com

Also by Adele Parks

Playing Away
Game Over
Larger Than Life
The Other Woman's Shoes
Still Thinking Of You
Husbands
Young Wives' Tales
Happy Families (Quick Read)
Tell Me Something
Love Lies
Men I've Loved Before
About Last Night
Whatever It Takes
The State We're In
Spare Brides
If You Go Away
The Stranger In My Home
The Image Of You
I Invited Her In
Lies Lies Lies
Just My Luck
Both Of You
One Last Secret
Just Between Us
First Wife's Shadow

Short story collections

Love Is A Journey

OUR BEAUTIFUL MESS

ADELE PARKS

HQ

ONE PLACE. MANY STORIES

HQ
An imprint of HarperCollins*Publishers* Ltd
1 London Bridge Street
London SE1 9GF

www.harpercollins.co.uk

HarperCollins*Publishers*
Macken House, 39/40 Mayor Street Upper,
Dublin 1, D01 C9W8, Ireland

This edition 2025

1

First published in Great Britain by
HQ, an imprint of HarperCollins*Publishers* Ltd 2025

Copyright © Adele Parks 2025

Adele Parks asserts the moral right to be identified as the author of this work.
A catalogue record for this book is available from the British Library.

HB ISBN: 9780008586379
TPB ISBN: 9780008586386

This book is set in Sabon by Type-it AS, Norway

This novel is entirely a work of fiction. The names, characters and incidents portrayed in it are the work of the author's imagination. Any resemblance to actual persons, living or dead, events or localities is entirely coincidental.

All rights reserved. No part of this publication may be reproduced, stored in a retrieval system, or transmitted, in any form or by any means, electronic, mechanical, photocopying, recording or otherwise, without the prior permission of the publishers.

Without limiting the author's and publisher's exclusive rights, any unauthorised use of this publication to train generative artificial intelligence (AI) technologies is expressly prohibited. HarperCollins also exercise their rights under Article 4(3) of the Digital Single Market Directive 2019/790 and expressly reserve this publication from the text and data mining exception.

Printed and bound in the UK using 100% Renewable
Electricity by CPI Group (UK) Ltd

For more information visit: www.harpercollins.co.uk/green

For AJ Riach
aka Legend.

For Mum and Dad
who have nurtured, valued and encouraged me.

What will survive of us is love.
PHILIP LARKIN

Do not stand at my grave and cry,
I am not there; I did not die.
MARY ELIZABETH FRYE

THE END

'I could just shoot you in the leg. People think that's a kindness, a chance, but they're wrong.' The voice was deep and clear. No-nonsense, South London, civil. It took her a moment to process the words. They couldn't be right; they couldn't be real. They didn't fit in her world. 'See, if I hit the giant artery that runs down your leg,' he paused, waved the gun to indicate the length of the artery, the target, 'then you're dead in a matter of minutes. Even if I just nick the femoral artery but don't apply a tourniquet, there'll be a rapid drop in blood pressure, and combined with the inevitable blood loss, again, you'll be dead in minutes.' He paused and added, 'I'm not gonna apply a tourniquet.' He laughed at the thought. She was struck by the theatre he was providing. He wasn't panicked. He was practised. He knew about death. He'd killed before. 'Or, I could shoot you in the arm. The brachial artery. That takes a bit longer. I'd watch you go into decompensated hypovolemic shock.' He said the words quickly, confidently. Sniffing, he added, 'Ugly, that.'

Connie thought she was already in shock. She'd frozen. She had to do something, she knew that, but what? *What?*

'It's a lot of money.' He shook his head, almost regretful.

'I can pay it back.'

'Can you though? Because now I'm looking at you and I'm thinking, cheat or liar? You see, if you can pay it back but haven't when I've asked, and asked so nicely, then you're a cheat. If you can't pay it back, liar.' He paused. 'I don't like cheats or liars.'

Connie had expected the conversation to go on. To buy her a little more time to get her thoughts together, to act, but then *bang*. Sudden and irretractable. The sound of gunshot ricocheted around the warehouse.

One moment there was something – hope, possibility, a chance. The next, there was a lot of blood. She pressed her hands over the wound. An actual hole, in flesh, it was inconceivable. She couldn't think, she couldn't breathe. The blood spluttered through her fingers. She thought she was going to be sick or faint. There was screaming, *she* was screaming. Her vision began to sway, she felt sweat prickle up all over her body from the soles of her feet to the crown of her head. Her body felt like liquid but was also convulsing; a jarring, jerking electric solidness. Someone turned down the volume, dampened it, stretched out the tape recording of her life. The seconds lengthened and struggled. How long did she have?

She thought of the blood that she had encountered in her life to date, all of it to do with her children. Her periods, their births, their childhood injuries, their periods. Now this. A gunshot wound.

ELEVEN DAYS BEFORE THE END

1

Connie

Christmas Eve

'I am so excited,' Connie said with fierce determination, as she placed another vintage glass ornament on the tree. Ornaments that had not been in her family for generations, although over the festive period, if asked, she would pretend that they had been. She would not admit to the hours nor pounds splurged on eBay; part of an eternal effort to create the impression of stability, legacy.

'Situation normal, Mum.' Sophie yawned; she was forever styling out a penchant for appearing world-weary. She was wearing faded denim overalls and a white vest top beneath with the sort of confidence that suggested she'd invented cotton. Her mother remembered wearing the exact same outfit with DMs when she was at university, but she knew better than to say as much. Such a comment would be met with disinterest, scepticism or worse, borderline revulsion. Sophie wasn't even sixteen yet; was it possible she was already world-weary? Connie supposed it was. Young people were so burdened nowadays. There was the stress of performing in exams, that seemed to start when a child was aged about four, plus the stress of being awesome, living life to the full, as suggested by TikTok, looking like a supermodel or what have you. It was exhausting to witness, let alone live through. Although, honestly, Connie was unsure how hard Sophie ever worked at her exams, and as she was the youngest of three, Connie didn't have the oomph or inclination to enquire.

Flora, her middle child, wasn't offering much in the way of joy and goodwill either. She had just come back to the nest after her first term of university and had clearly been burning the candle at both ends. Her skin did not boast the youthful glow that it had in the summer; she was sallow, gaunt and at the same time puffy. She hadn't moved from the sofa throughout the dressing of the tree; she simply picked at the spots on her chin and occasionally let out a deep, lethargic sigh. She was missing her newly made uni friends and making it very clear that being back home was now dull in comparison to being at Durham.

'Why don't you go and have a lie-down if you're tired? What do you call it? A tactical nap.' The suggestion was rather more of a plea. Flora's presence was actively working against the Christmas spirit that Connie was diligently trying to foster. She had rejected the offer of hot chocolate – 'I'm spotty enough' – and champagne – 'Are you, like, an alcoholic, Mum? It's not even lunchtime.' She objected to her mother's music choice, not on the grounds of boredom at having to listen to the songs that had been piped out of sound systems in every shop, café and service station since October, but because she declared 'Do They Know It's Christmas?' to be 'imperialist, racist shit, born from white saviour syndrome' and 'It's Cold Outside' as 'basically a handbook on date rape'.

'Gosh, I've never thought of them that way.'

'Just listen to the lyrics, Mum,' Sophie chipped in. She rolled her eyes at Flora, clearly wanting to throw her lot in with her sibling rather than her mother. Connie felt a sting of betrayal. She was glad her daughters were close; she just wished it didn't mean they ganged up on her, colluded to make her feel outdated and irrelevant.

Instead of reacting to the suggestion of a nap, Flora asked, 'Do we even have a right to put up a tree?'

'Excuse me?'

'Or even, maybe, celebrate Christmas at all. It's not like we go to church or anything.'

'Speak for yourself. I believe there's something,' Connie argued vaguely. She had a feeling she'd be sending up regular prayers to God Almighty this Christmas, when she was surrounded by her friends and family. She placed another ornament on a branch that was already sagging under the strain of being overdressed. 'I don't remember everything being so complicated when I was your age.'

'That's because you're prone to being nostalgic. Nostalgia is a cultural tool designed by the patriarchy to control us and to keep the status quo that serves them best. It was probably shit in your day too. You're just brainwashed.'

'Possibly, darling, but it really doesn't help anyone to dwell.' Connie beamed and tried to somehow thaw her daughters' miserable cynicism by radiating happy-Christmas energy. Surely the order of the day.

'God, Mum, how do you fail to see it? Why are you always so oblivious?'

It frustrated Connie that Flora and Sophie, who were pretty, clever and wealthy, who had enjoyed a damned near-perfect childhood (hadn't they? Certainly that was what Connie and Luke had tried to provide, lavishing all their girls with an abundance of care and attention and every material advantage available), always seemed to be struggling with something. Real or imagined, Connie wasn't quite sure. She felt sad and sorry for their generation. It seemed that they saw everything as hard and gloomy. Difficult. Then she thought about global warming, and the internet, which provided not only round-the-clock bad news but also an abundance of easy-access porn, and she admitted that maybe it *was* hard and gloomy. Difficult.

'Can you pass me the angel? The blue one. It's Fran's year to be top of the tree.' Thank God for Fran. Connie's eldest. She'd be here any minute and she would bring with her that uplifting, unifying *je ne sais quoi* that she reliably oozed. She'd contribute to the Christmas spirit, no matter what her thoughts on holiday song lyrics.

The Baker family had three treetop angels, each of which had been made by the girls when they were in reception class. Connie strictly rotated which angel got top billing. Her daughters teased her for having a system to keep the tree fair and equitable, but she knew that if she was ever to slip up, they'd be the first to complain. While close, they were fiercely competitive with one another. Connie spent a lot of time and concentrated vigour avoiding attracting complaints or causing arguments. She liked things to be pleasant. None of her girls, nor her husband, Luke, had any idea as to how much energy it took to appear so bloody happy, eternally positive and upbeat in your mid-fifties.

The truth was, Connie didn't always feel like a contender

for Little Miss Sunshine; it took effort. But she was glad they didn't have any idea. That meant she was doing her job well. She was supposed to be steadfast, optimistic, productive and *there for them*; it was her job. Well, it was one of her jobs; she was also a photographer and she worked two days a week in a local art gallery. Yes, of course she could be irritable, angry or downright mean if she chose to be. She knew plenty of people who were, but she'd chosen to be the sort of person who counted her blessings instead. She embraced the perky posts on her Instagram feed that encouraged her to *Carpe Diem* and 'Choose Happy'. She was in good health, she loved her husband, daughters, friends and wider family, they could comfortably manage their bills, she often had two holidays a year, and she had a Sage Barista machine. She was living the dream.

She'd come a long way and she knew it.

She really didn't understand why so many people in her position found something to complain about (the indie baker selling out of sourdough bread, the 'endless wait' for the electric Audi to be delivered). It was a shame. A waste of good fortune. She was sometimes tempted to tell the complainers to get a grip, but she never did. Generously, she considered the possibility that complaining about a near-perfect life came from a 'touch wood' mentality. Maybe the beautiful, healthy and wealthy believed that if they openly declared their happiness, they'd invite bad luck. Perhaps in their deepest psyche, they were insecure.

Or maybe they were just spoilt twats.

She really didn't know.

Either way, she was *not* going to complain about her sulky

daughters or the stress of hosting her nearest and dearest over the festive period. She was the entertainer, the host with the most open arms, open heart, open purse. It was not an act; she considered it a genuine privilege (damn, that word had been ruined with overuse).

As the eldest of four daughters herself, Connie was used to big, noisy Christmases. Although her mother had never quite managed active excitement, or even peace and joy. The vibe she'd exuded was at best frazzled panic and at worst outright exhausted resentment. But then Connie's parents had operated within considerably tighter financial parameters than she enjoyed, and her grannies were both acerbic types and pretty offensive towards her mother no matter how hard she'd tried. Added to that, her mother didn't have a dishwasher. Of course she was stressed. Connie had it so much easier.

Luke was also one of four, and he too remembered Christmas as an exercise in logistics, sibling rivalry and careful fiscal policy. In the early years of their marriage they'd used the fact of their big, chaotic families as an excuse to drop below the radar. They'd opted for quiet celebrations, just the two of them, or noisy drunken ones with their friends, reasoning that they wouldn't be missed from their respective homes. When their babies came along, they'd started to host, initiating a complicated system whereby they invited both sets of parents and all of their siblings on various dates over the festive period, and more often than not, they managed to see most of them.

Christmas in the Baker household was undoubtably a magical time of the year. Exhausting, expensive, but above all exhilarating. Connie was looking forward to a noisy, squabbling, funny family Christmas. Luke kept joking that he was looking forward to the day when they found themselves on a Caribbean beach without any of the kids, friends or rellies. Connie laughed when he said as much. 'I don't believe you. You're just trying to make the idea sound appealing in case it ever happens. Which it never will while I have breath in my body.' He wasn't entirely joking though. She knew Luke would like her to himself and could live without the chaos of a family Christmas. That was vaguely uncomfortable for her, the fact that as they'd aged, they didn't always think alike on everything. She didn't like to dwell on that. So she chose not to.

Choose happy!

For the first time ever, Fran had said she was bringing someone home with her. *Someone special?* Connie had texted. Her hope palpable even digitally.

TBD, was Fran's response.

It was obviously someone special, though. It didn't need asking. He was no doubt the reason Fran had wanted to spend the summer in her uni flat, the reason she wasn't coming home until today, Christmas Eve! Not for a moment did Connie buy into the excuse that her daughter wanted to remain near the uni library. Fran, age twenty-one, had never brought a boyfriend home before. The house was often brimming with her friends, both male and female, but she'd never introduced a romantic interest to her parents. Connie realised that was possibly because she called them romantic interests. Publicly, Connie referred to Fran as her 'independent one'; mentally, she thought of Fran as her 'flighty one'. There was no judgement, just a realistic recognition of Fran's discontent: her idealism and her romantic nature when all mashed together tended to lead to fleeting entanglements only. Fran looked like Connie, as did Flora, while Sophie resembled her dad. But it wasn't only Fran's physicality that reminded Connie of her younger self. Fran was adventurous, fluid, open to everything, which tended to mean commitment was a struggle – finding it, giving it. Connie had been in her thirties before she became anywhere near as content as she was now. It was only after she'd married and almost lost Luke that she fully committed to him.

It wasn't a near-death thing. She'd had an affair. Risked it all. Rolled the dice and lost.

She hated thinking about that, what she might have thrown away, how she might have ruined everything due to nothing other than a lack of discipline and an irritating (but sadly inherent) impulse to play with fire. When the memory of her behaviour came to her, invariably her skin itched with shame and something darker still. Fear.

Connie was glad there was someone Fran wanted to introduce to the family. It was great news, and she hoped he'd be wonderful: clever, charming, caring and conscientious. But she was also prepared for the fact that he might be a total disaster. There was always a chance that they'd find him snorting something in the downstairs loo or shagging one of their friends' daughters in the spare room under a pile of winter coats; she'd had boyfriends who behaved that way. She shook her head and tried to dislodge that distinctly unfestive thought. It made her shudder. How little she had thought of herself. How easily disrespect was doled out, disguised as daring.

Ancient, long-buried history.

Since her daughters had started their own various romantic entanglements, Connie had noticed that her mind occasionally drifted to her past; she found herself comparing their experiences with her own, or simply reflecting on how she'd ended up where she was. It was a great place to be, so she figured if she could draw any conclusions about her own path, work out what she'd done well and where she'd gone wrong and then communicate those learnings to her girls, she might help them navigate their lives too. Perhaps allow them to avoid some of the most glaring and painful mistakes that she'd made. She wanted to guide, protect, accelerate, improve things for her daughters. Of course. However, the more she thought about it, the more she tended to believe that her ending up in a fine place was a matter of good luck rather than good management, and little could be drawn from being gifted a lottery ticket that just happened to have the winning numbers. This thought was frightening.

She wished she believed humans oversaw their own destinies in a clear-cut, unequivocal way, but throughout her life she'd seen misery rain down on the nicest people and extreme good fortune fall into the laps of some heinous beings. She'd seen grafters rewarded and grafters going without, she'd witnessed the idle hit the jackpot and the idle languish in poverty. There were no rules. Life had a cruel arbitrariness to it. Illness, death, redundancy, infertility, divorce, addiction, accidents all occurred with horrible indiscrimination. The best she could offer her daughters in terms of advice, or perhaps solace, was that shit happened and all that could be managed was our response to that.

Two of her three girls were officially adults; Sophie would be too in a blink of an eye. Out there, independent, in the huge, confusing world. It was another terrifying thought. She wished she could always keep them with her, Sophie in a stroller, Flora on a buggy board, Fran holding the handle. All three under her wing. Protected. People told you that them being babies was the frightening part, but that she had largely managed, even controlled. She'd fed them, bathed them, changed and dressed them. Most often she'd averted disasters, and then comforted and soothed when she couldn't. The school years were frankly torturous; she couldn't regulate many external factors. Injustices and disappointments were rife and abundant: broken friendships, being dropped from teams, bullying, tricky exams. They say you are only as happy as your unhappiest child; a mother of three school-age children couldn't expect to be dancing a cha-cha every day. But now she was beginning to realise that proper fear, an ice-cold terror of the unpredictable, *really* kicked in when they were adults. When every aspect of their lives slipped from your control. It had been a long time since Connie had had an idea about what they were ingesting or who they were playing with or since a 'quiet word with a teacher' solved their issues. Now it was up to them to fall and flounder or fly and flourish. She was powerless. When parents reached this stage, all they could do was stand back and trust that they'd given their kids enough guidance, resilience and basic common sense to get through.

'Mum, Mum! The angel,' Sophie barked at Connie, who had lost track of the conversation as she'd fallen into her own thoughts. Sophie held an angel out towards her mother and shook it with an air of impatience. She was offering the yellow one. Hers.

'I said the blue angel. It's Fran's turn.'

Sophie tutted, but dug around in the decoration box, retrieved the blue angel and handed it over. Connie carefully reached up and placed the paper doily skirt over the utmost tip of the tree. The angel's head scraped the ceiling; she looked like she'd indulged in a little drink. Connie climbed down the ladder and stepped back to inspect her handiwork.

'There,' she pronounced. 'It's perfect.'

'You really do have a very generous interpretation of that word, Mum. There are way more decs on the left side and hardly any at the top. It's really not balanced,' grumbled Flora.

'Yup,' Connie grinned. 'Just how it looked when you kids decorated it when you were young. Perfect.'

2

Fran

'So this is it. Bougie.' Zac pauses outside the smart black and white reclaimed Victorian tiled path that leads up to Portland stone steps and the entrance to our white stucco townhouse, sitting squarely in a quiet tree-lined street. He looks hesitant. Intimidated. My dad's an architect. They bought this place when I was really young. I can't remember much about the renovation, other than scooting through rooms on my pink tricycle, careless and carefree, while all around me there were builders, electricians and plumbers sweating and swearing, my dad calmly project-managing, my mum heavily pregnant and looking frazzled. I consider trying to downplay; telling Zac that when we bought it it was dark and dank, that it hadn't been renovated since the early 1980s and we got it for a song. But our obviously elegant home is spread over four floors and we're in Notting Hill. Any attempt to downplay would be patronising.

'Yup. You can't curve now. I promise you, my mum is hovering behind the curtains and has already clocked you. So there's no reasonable means of escape. If you do a runner, she will chase you down the street and drag you back. Possibly by your pubes.'

Zac laughs and pulls me towards him, leaning in to kiss my forehead. I'm a bit weirded out by the public displays of affection that he seems so into. I dip away from him and make out I'm grabbing my suitcase. He immediately tries to wrestle it off me, which is stupid because it's on wheels and I can easily manage it; plus he has his own bag to pull; plus, I'm not like a frail Victorian woman restricted by a whalebone corset or anything. 'I'm perfectly capable of pulling my own bag,' I mutter. Then I feel bad because he looks wounded and I know he's only trying to be kind. The thing is, I don't like to be fussed over; it makes me feel claustrophobic. He's nervous about meeting my parents. So am I, which is why I'm being a bitch. Mum saves me from having to apologise as she flings open the front door.

'Hello! Hello! Hello!' she shouts with the kind of enthusiasm that is generally saved for the return of soldiers who have seen conflict. Although it's only a couple of metres from me to the doorway, she can't contain herself: she dashes forwards and flings her arms around my neck, kissing my cheek over and over again. This is why I don't like public displays of affection. My mum loves them, and has throughout my life delivered them with alarming frequency and flounce – to me, my sisters, my dad and just about anyone she takes a passing interest in, no matter how often I've asked her to back off. She really is a hugger. It's pretty cool, I suppose. The fact she puts herself out there and makes herself vulnerable. I value it on an intellectual level. It's just IRL it's overwhelming. I should have grown out of being embarrassed by my parents, but I think my mum sees it as a personal goal to keep bringing the cringe.

She gestures towards Zac, but her gaze is still on me. My mum's eyes are always on her own kids. 'And this must be . . .' She inclines her head towards him, a none-too-discreet gesture. Embarrassed, I realise I haven't actually told her Zac's name.

'Zac,' I chip in now, cheerfully, with a better-late-than-never mentality.

She covers her blunder (or mine) by pulling Zac into a huge hug too. She hugs with her whole body. He's not a tall guy, so she folds her head under his chin. It's totally inappropriate and over the top. I know her full-body hugs are not meant to be sexual, but somehow they are. I notice Zac's cheeks flare. He's probably fighting a hard-on. My mum is hot. She's not especially aware of it, which is endearing and a bit dangerous. I should have warned Zac that she can be a lot.

Dad rescues the situation by hugging me briefly and shaking hands with Zac, asking about our journey down from York, telling us to get inside quickly as we're 'letting out all the heat'. Dad's job in life is to swiftly re-establish proper norms following my mum's almost pathological destruction of them.

As we all make our way through the open-plan house and head towards the kitchen zone, I notice Mum repeatedly checking out Zac. She is staring at him with weird obsessive intensity. I mean, I know it's the first time I've brought a guy to meet the folks, but back off, Mum. Stay proportional, yeah. My grandpop and granny slowly emerge from somewhere; they look a little frailer and older than when I last saw them at the beginning of summer. Sort of whiter. I sometimes think that's what ageing is. They'll get whiter and whiter until they are finally transparent. The thought of my grandparents disappearing creates a hiccup of horror and grief in my gut. My nose squeezes as though I'm suppressing a sneeze. I'm glad when my sisters bounce into the room; they are both talking at once and are a distraction from my own emotions. Dad introduces Zac to everyone, obviously unsure that I'll manage the job properly on my own. Mum is surprisingly quiet. I expected her to have fired like a million questions at Zac by now. She's been in his company for five whole minutes. She isn't saying anything, in fact, she's just staring at him. She almost walks into a breakfast bar stool. This really is a new level of embarrassment. What is wrong with her?

Dad does his best. 'Can I get anyone a cup of tea or coffee?'

'Can you do a decaf?'

'Do you have mint?'

'Mine's a flat white.'

'I'd like a frothy one.'

No two people request the same thing, and Dad repeatedly checks the orders as he does his best to accommodate. Every surface in the kitchen is heaving with food: mince pies, chocolate log, pretzel wreaths, Nutella Christmas tree pastry, but Mum hasn't offered anyone anything to eat. Weird, as normally she's a feeder, happiest when we are all munching something she's made.

Instead, she says, 'Take your coat and scarf off, Fran. Make it look as though you're staying.' It's one of her many familiar and vaguely annoying phrases. She stares at me. Steady.

Here's the thing, she's embarrassing and full on and all of that, but she's also my mum, right. And she is the total epitome of 'means well', 'good heart', 'got my back', all that.

I'm depending on it. I don't know how, but I think she already knows. I feel it in the connection we have; a connection that, I suppose, all women have with their mothers, to a greater or lesser extent. I unwrap my scarf from my neck and then slip out of my big bulky coat. I try to place them on the stool next to me, but the coat slips to the floor.

'You're pregnant,' she says.

3

Connie

'Surprise!' Fran placed her hands on her curved stomach and sent a wide smile to her mother. Connie recognised that her beam wasn't entirely authentic; she was apprehensive. Her stance, arms curled around her mass, communicated protectiveness. Something in Connie's heart fluttered. Her daughter was already protecting her own baby. Connie recognised it as one of those dividing moments: before and after, when things were never the same again. A second ago her daughter was a child. Now that was all behind her.

Done with.

The kitchen had fallen silent. Something that rarely occurred in the Baker household. The sight of the round belly had sliced through the various demands for coffee. Connie and Fran held eye contact; everyone else held their breath, waiting for Connie's response.

Zac stepped forward and said, 'We're both very happy. We're amped about being parents.'

Connie's head jerked backwards an infinitesimal amount.

She respected his move. He was making it clear he was in this, that he was with Fran. That was good. That was decent. Of course Connie respected that.

But she also wanted to kill him.

Literally. In that moment, she would have liked to efficiently, forcefully shove him off a bridge, or onto a railway track, off the edge of the planet, out into orbit, because he was claiming Fran.

'You're just twenty-one,' she said.

'I know how old I am, Mum.'

'You're still at uni.'

'I realise that too.'

'I take it that this isn't a matter of planned parenthood.' Fran glared at her mother. 'How far along are you?'

'Connie,' her mother and Luke chorused simultaneously. She heard the caution they were issuing. Connie had basically asked if it was too late to do anything to stop the pregnancy. Could they make this go away?

Fran didn't answer the question, or maybe she did. She said, 'I'm sorry you missed the twelve-week scan, Mum. Maybe you can come to the next one, we're close to that.'

'Well, forget the tea and coffee, Luke, we should open some champagne,' Grandpop said. 'My first great-grandchild. Well, I never, isn't that a lovely Christmas gift? The very best.'

Connie felt an inappropriate nip of irritation that her father had settled so swiftly into declaring this a moment of celebration. He'd have killed her or any of her sisters if they'd come home pregnant aged twenty-one and unmarried. Most likely throttled them with his bare hands. He'd changed. Mellowed. It was a good thing that he'd moved with the times. Usually she liked that about him, but just now she wanted him to shut up. Champagne, a toast, that would cement things. There was no going back once the cork popped. A pronouncement had been made.

Was this a good thing? A lovely gift? It didn't feel like it.

What was the proper response to this news nowadays? A generation ago it would have been cause for bitter recriminations and a row, two generations ago a shotgun marriage. Now, she couldn't think of what to do or say, so she opened the fridge and pulled out a bottle of champagne.

'We have fizzy elderflower too, Fran,' she offered. She was working on automatic pilot. She was probably in shock. As she reached up to the cupboard where the champagne flutes were kept, she felt Luke gently squeeze her arm. She was unsure as to exactly what he was trying to communicate. Was he supporting her or silencing her? It surprised her a little that she was unsure as to what he was thinking about this monumental news. Surprised and saddened. True, he never charged in with a less than carefully considered comment, but generally she could read him before he had to open his mouth. Often, he'd forget to take his reading glasses to a restaurant, and rather than borrow hers he'd simply say, 'Will you choose for me?' He was always happy with what she picked because she always knew what he'd fancy. She knew what he would want to watch on TV and he knew the same about her. They knew what to expect from one another around the house. They knew how one another ticked in bed. It rarely had to be spoken of; instinct and experience combined so that they knew the most efficient way to reach orgasm or when they both wanted to take their time or even not bother at all. Offence was never taken if it was the latter. There would always be another day. They knew that too.

But now? What was he thinking? Connie told herself it was unreasonable to hope she could guess his thoughts when she couldn't even process her own.

'Sophie, pour your sister an elderflower,' she instructed.

'Actually, I'll have champagne,' said Fran.

'Oh, I thought that you'd . . .' Connie didn't finish the sentence. It was obvious that she thought Fran would be abstaining.

'Half a glass of champagne isn't likely to be a problem, Mum. French women drink red wine throughout their pregnancies.'

'Do they? Even now, or is that a myth?' Connie challenged. Luke took the bottle off her and began to pour.

'If they're born alcoholic, then you can say I told you so,' muttered Fran.

Connie was about to tell her daughter not to joke about being an alcoholic, it wasn't a funny thing to be, but instead she gasped, 'You're expecting twins?'

'No.'

'But you said *they*.'

'I'm not going to mindlessly fall into restrictive patriarchal labelling, simply because it's inherited.'

'What do you mean?'

'I don't want to say he or she. Because that's creating expectations.'

'On whom?'

'On them.'

'But the baby doesn't understand what we're saying.'

'We don't know that, and anyway, I don't want to create expectations for everyone else by suggesting they will definitively be a he or a she.'

'Couldn't we just talk about "the baby"?' Connie asked.

'No.'

'I don't understand how saying "the baby" is patriarchal or restrictive.' She could hear her own voice rising, not in volume but in tone. She sounded squeaky, shrewish. Why was she picking this battle?

Fran rolled her eyes. 'You need to move with the times, Mum.'

Connie felt a flare of offence. She didn't need to do any such thing, as it happened. She was perfectly happy ensconced in her own part of geography and history, or at least she had been until about three minutes ago, when this news broke. She was stunned, scrambling for evidence of the *je ne sais quoi* her daughter was supposed to deliver. The excited, unequivocal, simple Christmas spirit.

'Will they have gender-neutral names when they are born?' Luke asked. He laid emphasis on the word 'they'. Was he being mindful or mischievous? Connie wasn't certain.

'We're going to wait and see what they look like they'll suit,' replied Fran.

'Are you expecting twins?' asked Connie's mother.

'Cheers,' said Luke quickly, raising his glass and then swallowing down the champagne in one gulp.

4

Fran

No one plans to have a baby in their final year of university with someone they don't know well enough to have established their zodiac sign. So thanks, Mum, for making that point, as though I might be unaware. Take several seats. Unplanned, yeah, but he's not unwelcome. It's a boy. I'm just not telling them that yet. That can be another announcement at a different time. I've given them enough to think about for one day. He *is* wanted.

I think.

I'm pretty sure.

Wow, I don't know. I want this most of the time and I don't think anything much in a consistent all-the-time way, so yeah, he's almost certainly wanted. Maybe it's bullshit to think anyone really knows whether they want a kid or not. How can you know that you want to take a massive gamble on the future. I might be growing the next Lamine Yamal or Barack Obama, but then I might be growing the next Hitler. None of us have crystal balls.

Truthfully, the only two things I'm absolutely sure of in life are: A, that if there was a world where I had to eat one thing for ever (while somehow serving all my nutritional needs), it would be chilli-flavour Doritos; and B, Taylor Swift's lyrics make her a modern Shakespeare. I find I have fluctuating opinions on nearly everything else in life. People who know what they think about everything terrify me. Inflexible opinions lead to wars. Really, a lot of the time.

I like men and I like women and can imagine having sex with either gender. I also dislike them both, quite intensely at times, because my experience is that the more interesting, beautiful or trusted a person is, the more likely they are to screw you over, no matter what gender or how they identify. Believe me, I have tested this theory with a wider than normal sample. It's exhausting. For months in my life I've followed a policy of not getting too involved with anyone, just, you know, trying different things. But then I flip-flop because I long for intimacy and I go deep. Being one of three and having a million cousins, I love having people around me all the time, but that feeling when I find I'm constantly negotiating other people's shit is pretty exhausting, so I hibernate. I'm totally pissed off at the boomers; ruthless, myopic consumers who have mindlessly expended the earth's resources and were totally spoilt because it was simply so damned easy to get a mortgage in their day. Yet I'd have hated to live at any point other than now because frankly, hair products have never been better and I just don't know how people filled their time before the internet was invented. Blue is my favourite colour, but I also like yellow and orange and honestly could imagine myself living in an entirely white house. I change my hair colour about once a month.

But since discovering I'm pregnant, things have hit differently. I've been settled in my thoughts. I've been happy approximately ninety per cent of the time. I'll take that as a win.

When I was fifteen, I was diagnosed with endometriosis. The doctor said that besides the chronic pelvic pain, which worsened during my period or when I went to the loo, and feeling constantly sick, suffering from constipation, diarrhoea and having blood in my shit, I could anticipate pain during sex and complications trying to get pregnant. Yay me, right. In an effort to console somewhat, the doc said, 'Don't worry about it. By the time you want children, there will probably be a number of medical advances that will make it possible.'

What I derived from that was that as things stood, getting pregnant would be impossible. I remember telling my mum she'd better look to my sisters to push out the grandkids and that it was a good thing she'd had three of us. Mum simply laughed and told me not to worry, insisting, 'Everything will be fine.' Vague, right? So Mum. She believes that shit because look at her life: everything for her always *is* fine. In the absence of any specific guidance as to how exactly that might be the case for me, I consulted Dr Google, and yup, most of the things I read pretty much definitively agreed that I was going to struggle to conceive. It was a scary thing to know at fifteen. Sad. Sort of an ending even before I got started. Yeah, I might have been too young to know if I really wanted kids, but I was definitely too young to be told I wasn't going to be able to. It was a lot. Vibe check, totally fucking bummed.

Yet in some ways I'm my mother's daughter. I looked for a silver lining. I realised that if I was infertile, at least I didn't have to bother with boring contraception. I didn't have to take pills that would play with my hormones or have a coil fitted, which I understand to be painful. I didn't have to have the awkward putting-the-condom-on moment. And I'd be fine. Sidebar. I know I should have been using condoms anyway. STIs are a thing. What can I say? I know stuff in my brain that doesn't always make it to my reality. Am I alone in this?

Anyway. I was fine for four years of sexual activity.

OK, retrospectively, I see that I didn't really fully comprehend what Dr Google was saying to me. Those articles that gave percentage chances were not entirely digested. I guess if there was a ninety per cent chance of me needing help to conceive, that did mean there was a ten per cent chance that I wouldn't. I wasn't too concerned when I skipped my period. The endometriosis means I'm irregular, and usually I bleed more often than other girls, so I thought I'd finally caught a break when my normally heavy period was skipped. Even when I missed the second month, I wasn't concerned. I was eleven weeks pregnant before I thought to take a test.

The way I see it, this baby is a miracle. What if he is my one chance?

I met Zac in the last term of my first year of uni. I thought from the get-go that he was one hundred per cent snack. We hung out together a bit, had a laugh, hooked up. It was a mutually satisfying arrangement. An energetic stress release after exams. He's in the year above me, and so my second year was his third year. He had to do an industry placement in London, and while we occasionally texted, whatever we had sort of petered out that year. I was a little sad about that. I liked him. I had briefly thought we might hook up in the holidays, but he didn't reach out. I'm aware enough to know that all the sitting around waiting for your phone to light up crap is a waste of time. We weren't officially boyfriend and girlfriend, far from it. We weren't even seeing one another. We didn't owe each other anything. I saw other people. I guess he was dating too.

I stayed in York for most of the summer between second and third year. Rip-off landlords of shitty student properties coin it in by insisting contracts start in July, even though they know we don't need the place until September. Like, how is that allowed? Whatever. As I had to pay rent, it made sense to live there rather than come back to London, where my parents offer me a very comfortable home but still feel entitled to ask what time I'll be returning to said comfortable home every time I pop out for a coffee. Boring.

I needed to earn some cash, so I picked up a job at Boots, on a make-up concession counter. I spent my summer advising women ten, twenty, thirty years older than me how to stave off the ageing process. They'd ask me which products I used and then buy them with hope that was so intense it was delusional. I wanted to tell them, it's BB cream, not a time machine. It's depressing if you think about it. I'm basically propping up the patriarchal norms that have unfairly dominated society and reinforcing the power of the male gaze. Or maybe I'm just selling lipstick, earning for a few spends. I don't know. I have all these ideas and just nowhere to put them.

It was a slow Wednesday afternoon in late July. I spotted Zac as soon as he walked in the shop but I didn't bring attention to myself. I just idly watched him mooch around, noting what he was picking up. Nearly everything anyone buys in Boots is embarrassing. It's not a great place to try to chat. He'd cut his hair short. He used to wear it in a topknot. I missed the topknot but also admitted that the new look suited him.

I mentioned Zac is hot, right?

He's not perfect. But egotists are the worst people to date. They think they're doing you a favour and so don't try hard in bed. I never swipe right on gym bunnies.

Zac's got a fantastic smile. Properly wide and willing. He cracks it out more or less continuously, revealing not unnaturally white, straight teeth. He has notably luminous skin and a shy smattering of freckles. His eyes are his best feature. Massive, glinting, blue, framed with thick dark lashes. He's lean and toned. He has this particular, deliberate air, as though nothing about him – either physically or mentally – is unnecessary, or excessive. This is remarkable in a world where so much is too much. He's short, though. Many would see that as a drawback, but I see it as his saving grace, given how I feel about perfection. He'd have probably been a total fuckwit if he'd been tall too. Just too hot for his own good. Short, dark and handsome works for me.

He came to my checkout point because there is rarely a queue at the skincare concession counters. He asked the usual question. 'Can I pay for these here?'

'If you want me knowing you use athlete's foot spray, you can.'

'Good to see you again, Fran.'

'I bet.' I'm not especially profuse in my praise or flattery. Men who look as good as Zac don't need to be indulged.

'How've you been?'

His question was uninspiring, but anyway we ended up in bed together within five hours of him asking, so I can't imagine he'll bother working on his chat. We were only driven from bed when hunger set in. Then we quickly tumbled back there. The days turned into weeks, term started, lectures were attended and some were missed, the lure of the squeaking IKEA bed proving irresistible. My student room, previously regarded by me as a dingy, slightly dank pitstop, became a haven swilling with pleasure and intensity. Laughter. From my bed I watched the world keep turning, blue skies, grey, white, black; the neighbours' treetops rushing from a verdant green to a show-off burnished gold.

And we made a baby.

5

Connie

Connie felt exhausted. It had been one of the longest days of her life. They'd waded through everything she'd painstakingly planned, slugging through the motions rather than revelling in them as she had imagined they might. They'd eaten chilli and jacket potatoes for lunch, then taken an afternoon walk to see their friends, Rose and Craig, who appeared to welcome the news of Fran's pregnancy with total joy. If they were shocked or disapproving, they hid it well.

'The first of our crowd to become a granny!' said Rose with a big smile. Her twin boys from her first marriage were twenty-six; Connie thought that Rose ought to have been the first in the crowd to be absorbing this news. The urgency of heating mince pies and prepping vegetables for tomorrow was enough to distract Rose, and the conversation moved on, or rather, petered out. Connie and Rose had known one another for thirty-seven years; silences could rest between them without either woman feeling uncomfortable. Connie watched as Rose peeled parsnips, carrots, red cabbage and Brussel sprouts. The incessant chop chop chop was somehow hypnotic, easier to think about that. She watched as the veg was scooped into freezer bags and popped into the fridge. She tried to help. 'Not the potatoes, Connie. Leave those in water,' said Rose firmly.

'Oh yes, of course. What am I thinking?'

Rose chose to see that as a rhetorical question and turned her attention to the matter of when her sister, Daisy, would be arriving. Daisy and Connie had studied at university together and were close. Daisy had moved to Leamington Spa about seven years ago. Connie missed her and had planned to wait for her, had expected to spend the evening all together. However, when she heard that Daisy wouldn't be arriving until after 9 p.m., she knew she didn't have the requisite staying power. Rose checked her texts. 'Traffic is awful. She says it's like a car park on the M40.'

'Shocker on Christmas Eve,' mumbled Connie.

'Right.' Rose rolled her eyes; she had advised Daisy to come yesterday. As the older sister, she wallowed in a perpetual state of knowing better.

Connie secretly felt a slither of relief that the slow traffic meant she wouldn't have to cross paths with Daisy. Daisy had suffered with endless fertility issues; it had taken years for her to conceive, as a result she greeted the news of any pregnancy with evangelical excitement. Connie wasn't up for endless conversations about birthing plans, stretch marks, spider veins, bra size or any of the other related subjects that Daisy was bound to revel in. A step at a time was all Connie could manage. Baby steps.

Oh God.

'We might head off now then.'

Early evening, the family walked home together. Rose's twins, Henry and Sebastian, tagged along. It was a crisp, cold night, the Christmas Eve of Connie's imaginings. The kids wanted to stop at the local for a drink. Connie had expected they would, she'd planned to join them at least for one. She had, for months now, imagined the three generations sitting around a wooden table drinking mulled wine: her parents, her husband, their offspring. She'd thought they might play cards or dominoes. One glance inside the pub confirmed that was not going to happen. The place was already heaving with rowdy crowds, pulsing with an excitement and a particular determination that she vaguely remembered from her twenties. She felt uncomfortable, exhausted by the obvious hunt-mentality. The people in the pub were pursuing sex, friendships, alcoholic oblivion. Connie craved quiet, time alone with Luke.

'We have to wet the baby's head,' said Henry. He'd said that about three times during the afternoon.

'That's what you do when the baby is born,' Connie snapped. God, these kids knew nothing. 'I think I need to get Granny and Grandpop home. You guys go ahead. Sophie, you can stay until nine, but only if someone walks you home, and you can't drink alcohol.' She knew she wouldn't be served it, but that was different to whether she might drink it or not.

'I'll walk her back,' offered Sebastian.

'I'm not a child,' Sophie snapped.

'That's exactly what you are,' chipped in Luke. 'You have to leave the pub at nine, that's the law, but if you – as a group – decide to go elsewhere, a café or something, you can stay out later.'

'We'll look after her,' promised Henry.

Rose's twins behaved like big brothers towards her girls. Connie was confident that Sophie would be fine, but she was also sceptical that they'd follow Luke's instructions about leaving the pub at nine. Law or no law. Normally she'd have insisted that she collect Sophie personally. Today she let it slide. She didn't want to be with them. She didn't want to say anything she might regret in the face of their exuberance. She needed to think carefully. Tread carefully. Everything she said or did now would be remembered for ever. Families were like that. Words intended as jokes or spilt through embarrassment became folklore. Connie thought parenting was a little like being placed under arrest. You do not have to say anything, but anything you do say may be given in evidence against you. *Ad infinitum.*

She wanted to find the right words. She didn't know what they were.

She linked her arms through her mother's and father's, felt glad that they were there, not only as an excuse to bow out of the night in the rowdy pub, but because they formed a wall around her, making her feel a little steadier. She didn't dare look at Luke. He might opt to stay and drink with the kids, keep an eye on Sophie himself. She hoped he wouldn't. She hoped he'd know she needed him and would come home with her, pour her parents a glass of wine. Talk. Her body sagged with relief when she heard him ask if the kids had keys and add, 'Have fun, but don't wake us up when you come in.'

Before the announcement, Connie had planned that after an hour together in the pub, they'd all come home and then she'd intended to prepare a charcuterie board. She'd kept a story from Instagram that demonstrated an incredibly artistic way to display the food in the shape of a Christmas tree. She'd bought four types of cheese, three hams, salami, crackers, olives, black and green grapes, goldenberries and starfruit. She'd been excited about impressing and delighting people, making the evening special. She'd imagined them all tucking into it, standing around in the kitchen, lots of chat and laughter. Fran would have to avoid the soft cheese now, and salami too.

She showed her parents what she'd wanted to prep.

'Oh, don't go to all that trouble for us,' said her mum. Being apologetic for the space she took up was not a habit she was likely to break in this her eighty-third year, even on Christmas Eve.

'I'm happy with a ham sandwich. We've eaten so much all day,' added her dad.

Normally she'd put up a fight, insist that they should all make an effort at this special time. She didn't have it in her. She made the sandwiches, watched the clock; when the hands finally dragged around to 9.30, she faked an enormous yawn and made her excuses to get off to bed.

Upstairs, she checked the temperature in the bedrooms. Fran's room was in the attic and was often the coldest, no matter how high they turned up the radiators. The rest of the house benefited from underfloor heating, but they hadn't been able to install that up there. She slipped a hot-water bottle in between the sheets, but then felt a sting of embarrassment that she'd done so. Fran had Zac to keep her warm now. She hesitated, unsure whether to take it out again. Her eyes slipped to the bookshelf, where Fran's favourite childhood books still nestled, whispers of a time gone by. But only just, surely yesterday.

She sensed Luke in the doorway before he spoke.

'Is she ready?' he asked.

'I don't know,' she replied, sighing, overwhelmed by how much she still didn't know about parenting, even though she'd been doing it for years.

She was glad when he articulated her thoughts. 'Peculiar, isn't it, that legally it's her decision, but . . .'

'But she still feels like a child to us.' Connie finished his sentence.

'Exactly. Do you think we need to sit her down and talk through the options?' Luke asked.

'On Christmas Day?'

'No, but at some point.'

'Yes, I suppose, but I believe she knows the options. She's clearly committed to having this baby, so we must support her, because the alternative is heartbreaking. We'll lose her.' Connie's voice creaked a little, emotion swallowing her tone. She couldn't imagine a world where any of her daughters did anything she disapproved of enough to abandon them, but she could imagine a world where if she offended her daughters, hurt them, they might choose to remove themselves from her. Wedge distance between them. She didn't want that, and she was old and wise enough to know it wouldn't be the best path for Fran, who would never manage on her own, financially, emotionally or physically. Fran needed Connie; she didn't know how much yet, but she would.

'Of course, a baby is a wonderful thing,' added Luke. The same sentence she'd heard her mother, father and friends say on several occasions today. The same sentence she'd uttered herself. She listened carefully to his tone, trying to see how much conviction his words held. 'It's just a little sooner than expected. They have no money.'

'No. They don't.'

'This isn't what I saw for her. For any of them,' Luke stated with a sigh.

Connie thought of him picking up the girls, playfully swinging them onto his shoulders. Their delight in him manifested in shrieks and giggles. She thought of him patiently sitting through cute but inexpert ballet recitals and dreadful school plays, noisy pop concerts. She remembered him learning to tie French plaits and allowing the girls to paint his fingernails. She wondered if he was thinking about all of those moments too, or was he thinking about the days he'd gone to work, dealt with difficult clients who didn't know what they wanted, who dismissed his expertise as he built his practice and reputation? He'd put bread on the table. Was he regretting all the time he hadn't spent with them? Or worse, any of the time he had? Was he blaming Connie for this? Did he think she'd failed to instil proper rules and guidance, botched articulating life plans?

'No. It wasn't what I had in mind either,' she admitted.

'I keep thinking about what an idiot I was at twenty-one. How incapable I was. I knew nothing then.' Luke shook his head, his face creased with concern.

Connie had her own misgivings. Plenty of them. But she also recognised a need to protect and prepare her husband, her family for this transition. It was what it was, so she had to do the best with it that she could; for all of their sakes, even though she wasn't ready. Even though her thoughts and feelings were still in flux. Sometimes, adulthood meant faking it until you were there.

'Really? Or is that just something we tell ourselves so that we feel better now in our fifties, so we have a sense of progress?' she asked. 'I think I was then who I am now. Just more stuff has happened to me since. I suppose this is just the beginning of the stuff that's going to happen to her. But we both need to remember it is happening to *her.*'

'You're saying she doesn't belong to us any more?' Luke looked shocked.

'No, she'll always be ours.'

'But she's more his now?'

'She's just her. This is her story. I think really this is what people mean when they talk about main character energy. Our twenty-one-year-old is having a baby and that's her story. We are being relegated to bystanders. Maybe that's what we're struggling with.'

Luke moved his weight from one foot to the other. When his eyes met his wife's, he was smiling. 'When did you get to be so wise, Connie Baker?'

'I know, right. I hardly recognise myself.'

'So you're happy with this situation?' He was clearly surprised.

'I'm undecided. I'm trying not to be unhappy with it because who would that help?'

'Parenting is a lot.' They both let out a short, sharp laugh. This was a certainty they could always agree on.

She was aware that they were trading their usual roles. She was soothing him, reassuring and calming him. He needed her to. Luke was usually the calm one. The logical one. He was also the most indulgent one with the kids. Neither of them was particularly draconian, but he got to be the good cop when they parented. It sometimes secretly irritated Connie that she was the one who always had to point out that homework needed to be done, that bedrooms needed to be tidied, that allowances needed to be stuck to. The girls had soon learnt that they could count on their dad to give the nod that allowed them to leave the last spoonful of peas or to bung them an extra twenty quid to visit the local ice cream parlour. It wasn't a play for popularity on his part, or an agreed strategy between them; their parenting styles had resulted from the respective hours they spent with the children – as main caregiver, Connie had to oversee routines – and, more decisively, from their personality types.

That was what upset Connie the most, the reality that instinctually she couldn't be as relaxed as Luke, as much as she might long to be, because she had always seen the consequences of slackening off or being distracted. She had always feared it. He really didn't see the harm in allowing the girls to neglect their revision plans, to buy the shoes in both colours if they liked them a lot and couldn't choose. He didn't think they could be spoilt. He didn't believe anything could ever be ruined. He believed with every iota of his being that everything would always be wonderful for all of them, all of the time. Connie thought things only worked out wonderfully as a result of careful management, graft and vigilance.

Now she didn't know what to think.

Luke had never wasted any of his time worrying about food additives leading to cancer, and so he occasionally let the girls eat fast food; when they didn't secure swimming lessons at the local pool, he hadn't immediately jumped to scenarios where they might drown; he'd never spent time drafting elaborate B plans in case exams were tricky and chosen unis were unreachable. He'd lived by a philosophy that they would all have tremendous lives; happy, healthy and successful. Connie had always envied him his conviction, but right now she almost pitied him for it. This must be a bigger shock to him than even her. She wondered whether he thought she'd let him down. If in some deep part of his mind or heart he was angry that for all her foreshadowing and insuring, she hadn't seen this coming, hadn't prevented it. Her years of being bad cop had been an attempt to future-proof their lives, to prevent disaster, but it obviously had not worked.

Of course, a baby was not a disaster.

Connie adjusted her internal thoughts. Embarrassed at having them. They seemed so ungrateful and cruel towards the tiny being, her grandchild. A baby was a blessing. But truthfully, if there was a sliding scale with disaster on the left-hand side and blessing on the right, an unplanned baby as an undergraduate felt closer to the left side. She could and would pretend otherwise, but she was struggling to believe that these two young people were likely to stay in love for ever, that they'd never regret limiting their options by creating a baby with a relative stranger and that they'd be fulfilled human beings as well as parents. She wanted to nestle into her husband's chest, feel his big arms wrap around her, but she was concerned about ratcheting up the emotional moment.

'You can't save them from everything. Or maybe anything,' she admitted.

'Right, but it doesn't stop you wanting to.'

'They have to live their own lives.'

'Do you like him?' Luke asked.

Ah, him. Zac. Connie's efforts to find clarity immediately crashed, her thoughts turning opaque once again. 'He's good-looking. The baby will be beautiful.' She straightened the duvet cover. Refused to meet Luke's eyes.

'That's all you have to say?'

'Well, we don't know anything about him.'

'That's never stopped you judging the girls' friends before. What's your gut feeling?'

Connie hesitated. 'He reminds me of someone, so that's a bit disconcerting. You know when someone reminds you of someone else, you imbue them with all the same qualities of the other person. The original person.'

'Who does he remind you of?' Luke asked, interested.

'Oh, someone who comes into the gallery.' This was a lie, but one of those lies that Connie considered justified because telling the truth in this case would cause upset, pain.

'And do you like the person Zac reminds you of?'

How to answer that? Like? Like wasn't an adequate word. She tucked herself under her husband's arm, buried her face in his chest. Breathed in his smell. Washing powder on his jumper, traces of body wash on his neck and his skin. Not sweat, nothing discernible or identifiable, something that she thought of as simply him. She couldn't answer his question. Instead she murmured, 'Come on. We'd better get to bed or Santa won't come.'

6

Fran

The worst thing about being pregnant is not the morning sickness, the ballooning body, the sore tits or even the shocked looks that my parents fired my way when I announced it (admittedly looks that they quickly suppressed as they grasped that the supportive and understanding route is the only way to go on Christmas Eve; a family set-to is a little primitive for my parents). No, none of that. The worst thing is being in a pub on Christmas Eve and being stone-cold sober when everyone else is absolutely pissed. Alcohol is complicated now.

I feel guilty about the fact I drank when I didn't know I was pregnant. I worry about that a lot. And I feel guilty about the half-glass of champagne I had earlier. I don't know why I asked for that. It was just some stupid response to the fact that my mum had elderflower as an option, proving that even me coming home pregnant couldn't quite throw her. She's so bloody together, I just wanted to rattle her a bit. I could feel Zac's glare burning into the back of my head as I sipped. I didn't even enjoy it; it gave me heartburn. I don't miss drinking; I miss being part of the gang that can drink. I miss the heady, weightless, floaty feeling of being pleasantly not quite there but also absolutely and one hundred per cent in it. Dad calls it the two-beer buzz.

Zac is being really all over what I should and should not be doing, eating, drinking throughout this pregnancy. He's read countless online articles; he even bought a book about it: *The Expectant Dad's Survival Guide: Everything You Need to Know*. A book is a basic fanfare, announcing to the world how seriously he's taking being a daddy-to-be. Which is cute and adorable and a bit pointless because ultimately he's not going to be the one pushing the baby out, is he? He is supporting me by avoiding the foods I can't eat (not that we'd eaten a lot of shellfish, shark or quails' eggs before I got pregnant) and he has cut down on his coffee drinking, but there has been no offer to give up booze. Right. Which proves that I didn't hook up with an idiot, because why would he?

He, my sisters and Henry and Sebastian are all going to have hangovers tomorrow. I guess I at least avoid that. Lots of fam have joined us as they spotted us on Snapchats or because we sent out word of our whereabouts. I know half the people in the pub and it's a very packed pub; no cap, they have *all* put their hands on my belly and hiccupped in my face. The baby is probably drunk on fumes anyway.

'OMG.'

'OMG!'

'OMG!!'

The heat of so many bodies is making me queasy. It's harder than I imagined, this en masse announcement. I thought it would be fun, but it's sort of wearing. I'm bored of explaining to everyone that yes, I'm having a baby, and yes, I'm still at uni, and yes, I plan to finish my degree, and yes, this is Zac, so at about 9 p.m., I wiggle my way through the cram in the hope of finding some peace and quiet in the snug. It's a tiny, tucked-away room with space for only one table. Some old blokes, my dad's age, are there and so I stick out my belly and they immediately leap up, offering their seats. I am so hyped about feminism – it's a goal, obvs – but this is a medical-based requirement not a gender thing, except of course only women can have babies, so there's that. I gratefully accept their sacrifice, slump into a seat and watch as they shove their way back into the main bar. I breathe. It feels good not to have anyone pushing up against my bump or slurring nonsense in my ear.

Zac, Flora, my bestie Auriol and Henry notice I have a table and come to join me. I guess Sebastian is babysitting Sophie. He's good like that.

'I just can't believe you're pregnant,' says Auriol.

'It's like a Christmas miracle,' adds Flora, she's glassy-eyed and emotional.

'Not a Christmas miracle, actual cock was involved. You're drunk, so I'll forgive you that banality.' Although I deliver my put down in a droll, none-aggressive way, I note the others raise their eyebrows and share a look. I think I see Zac mouth the word 'hormones'. I sip my lemonade. Flora is going to die of jealousy when I'm inundated with attention and gifts and stuff. She always got weird at our birthday parties when we were kids. Also, she'll be thinking I'm out of my mind. My sister is the sort to have a life plan. It does not involve getting unexpectedly pregnant. She will marry at twenty-seven, have her first child at twenty-nine, second two years later. Stop there. She's had it mapped out for ever. I've never really had a plan as such, which is perhaps a good thing, considering.

But besides all of that, she'll be really worried for me. Because she loves me like crazy. We are all tight. 'I'm tired,' I say by way of an apology.

Zac squeezes my hand. The conversation quickly moves on. Henry tells a funny anecdote about his boss and Flora tells another about her talking her way out of a parking ticket. Auriol shares a story about some creep from her gym sending an unsolicited dick-pic and her responding with the magnifying glass emoji. Away from the crowd, everything seems more coherent, and my fam are entertaining, like a live-action Reddit post. I'm engrossed and it feels normal. Nothing much has felt normal since I went for the scan and got told how soon I'd be a mamma.

Time zips by, when I check my phone and realise it's 11 p.m., I say I'm heading home. 'Santa won't come unless we get to bed,' I say with a grin. Flora beams back at me, recognising our family motto, which Mum and Dad have repeated every year for as long as I can remember. My sis pulls me into a huge hug. 'Where's Sophie?' I ask, suddenly concerned that we really haven't done as our parents asked and there's a high chance she'll be off her tits somewhere.

'Over there with a snatched girl. I think she's planning on coming out this Christmas, just to steal your thunder,' says Flora. I'm glad she's obviously kept one eye on our baby sis. That's normally my job, but I'm so distracted.

'I'd be glad to share the heat.'

'There is no heat. Your mum and dad are cool. They'll support you through this,' says Auriol.

'Yeah.' I nod. I know they will. I'm lucky.

'I bet they're dying to help out and stuff when they are born. You know, with money and with babysitting,' adds Flora. She sounds a tiny bit pissed off. Nothing big, just sibling-rivalry level.

'When are they due?' Auriol asks.

I feel flushed, the sort of heat that scalds, and I'm so bone-weary tired and achy that I am tempted to lie on the sticky pub floor. I just want to get home and to bed as quickly as possible. 'Spring,' I respond. It sounds cool not to be too hung-up on an exact date. People obsess over that shit. It's an invasion of privacy. Is that the deal when pregnant? Basically people are now entitled to ask me when I had sex just because it was fruitful sex? That's so weird if you think about it.

'Where is Zac?' I ask impatiently.

'Probably having a piss,' says Henry.

'More like a pissing contest.' My sister points to a corner, where Zac is embroiled in what looks like some beef with two other guys. They are way taller than him, built and older. I immediately feel panicked and protective.

'I better go over,' says Henry. He glances around the pub, probably hoping to locate his twin so that they can even up the numbers. He doesn't look too confident about following up on his offer. The guys Zac are talking to look a hundred per cent like trouble. Henry used to play rugby at school and was a bit of a bully as a kid, but as an adult I don't imagine he's ever thrown a punch.

'Maybe. I don't know,' I mutter. 'We don't want to escalate things.' The crowd between us suddenly seems to expand, as a bunch of people start singing a cringey but enthusiastic rendition of 'Last Christmas'. I temporarily lose sight of Zac. I'm relieved and grateful when I spot Seb threading his way in Zac's general direction from the opposite side of the pub. Before he gets there, however, Zac emerges, slicing through the singing crowd.

'What was that about?' I ask.

'What?' He's a picture of serenity. I'm beginning to see that not much rattles him.

'Those guys you were talking to. It looked heavy.'

'No, not really. I accidentally knocked the guy's elbow and spilt his drink. He got a bit arsey about it.'

'Jesus, Zac, you're bleeding.' He's got a dirty-looking bar towel wrapped around his hand.

'Yeah, I broke the glass. That's all. I bought him a new pint. All good.' He kisses my lips. No tongues, but meaningful.

He leads us out of the pub into the cold night air and I think how cool it is to be with someone whose mindset is to calm things, avoid conflict if possible. I value that so much more than someone who wants to throw his fists around and prove what a big man he is.

Zac is the sort of man who will make a good dad. That's important.

7

Zac

They fell out of the pub door, but the street was almost as lairy. Someone was puking, someone was crying, another group vaping, everyone was laughing and chatting, being loud. It was doing his head in. The street light seemed like a spotlight. He quickly put his hand in his pocket so that Fran wouldn't keep worrying about the cut. He probably did need a stitch or two. Had that just happened? In his girlfriend's local on Christmas Eve? In his worst nightmares, he hadn't imagined they'd find him so quickly. Fuck.

London was never completely dark; he had learnt that last year when he'd done his placement down here. Last year, a lifetime ago. He had been so totally stoked about the placement. Proud, borderline insufferable, his flatmate had half joked. It hadn't been easy to secure the year in industry. The university were supposed to help you, had promised all sorts, way back on the open day, but when it came to it, you were on your own. Loads of his friends had never got anything and had to skip that year, go straight to finals without the salary or experience they'd banked on. He'd thought he was the lucky one. He'd been a smug twat. Just went to show. You never knew what lucky was. Not this, though, that was for sure.

London simmered twenty-four/seven. There was always a pub, a nightclub, a kebab shop open somewhere. Many of them. Some streets seemed to only come alive after 11 p.m., and when they did, they throbbed and pulsed. It was like living inside a slot machine: glaring neon lights, constant flashing, insistent alarms, whiny sirens. Londoners knew this was the deal. Some people drew their curtains, tried to carve out a bit of peace and space, others didn't bother. They accepted the inevitable forced congregation of the city, the impossibility of privacy, so they left their curtains wide open. Brazen. Zac was fascinated by the little squares of life in the walls of buildings; they put him in mind of doors on an Advent calendar. Although the tableaus didn't reveal pictures of snowmen or mistletoe, he had witnessed people zombified in front of TVs, guys lifting weights, a mother pacing the floor with a baby in her arms, couples hooking up. At first, he'd enjoyed playing voyeur. It was exciting to know life was bubbling, buzzing all around him, all the time, and that he was a part of it. Even at 2, 3 or 4 a.m., the streets streamed with a constant flow of people going to clubs, bars, to work, to shops, to cafés. He felt elated by the industry, the activity and purpose. He'd metaphorically looked over his shoulder, a little disdainful of his own sleepy village of origin, and even his university city, which generally fell silent by midnight.

But then, after what had happened – what he'd done – he quickly reappraised and decided living inside a slot machine was not exciting. It was frightening.

He tried to tell himself that the constant noise and activity was at least a help, some level of insurance. He reasoned, if people were everywhere, he was never alone, and bad things only happened if you were alone, right? That is the perceived wisdom. The threat is in the dark when you're isolated.

But the more he got into it, the more he'd had to reappraise his view. Downgrade his optimism about the city, about his place in it. He was learning that the neon lights, the constant activity didn't offer comfort or provide protection. The sort of people who were in the streets in the early mornings taught him it was possible to feel most alone when people were close by. The thing that just happened in there, it was unbelievable, no one had intervened. He supposed to onlookers it just appeared to be a standard tussle, some argy-bargy about who was next to be served, maybe. Did anyone see the knife? They'd dropped the packet in his coat pocket; he'd felt the weight of it instantly. He'd tried to bluff it out, show he wasn't to be controlled or intimidated, so he'd taken it out of his pocket and slammed it on the bar, next to them. Everyone around them had turned away at that point, an elegant wave of abandonment and disinterest. Like synchronised swimmers, it seemed they'd collectively agreed not to get involved.

One of them moved quickly, scooping the package up and plonking it back in Zac's pocket, and faster than that, the other drew his knife. He jabbed it sharply into the back of Zac's hand. The bit where his thumb met his forefinger. He didn't hit a vein and he didn't go deep. It was a coolly controlled warning. It fucking hurt and bled a lot.

It turned out he could be controlled and intimidated.

Of course he could.

No one asked if he was OK as he grabbed the beer-sodden bar towel and wrapped his wound. The other revellers staunchly stared at their phones, glanced the other way, looked through him as though he wasn't there at all. People didn't keep him safe.

The opposite.

The clubs, bars and pubs that were open late just offered these men a comfortable waiting room until they paid him a visit.

8

Connie

Luke was snoring heavily, which annoyed her in a petty way that she wasn't proud of. When they were younger, if he had slept peacefully as she lay counting sheep, she might have turned on her side and simply gazed at him. She'd have examined the contours of his face and plump lips, fought the urge to kiss them so as not to wake him up. Now, she often prodded him in the ribs, not caring if she disturbed his sleep. But then, when they were younger, he didn't snore. She did not love her husband any less now than she did before – she probably loved him more as the years passed – but she was less dazzled by him, more prone to accept and expect everything he had to offer. That was what contentment was, she supposed: a surrender of the heady, exhausting days when emotions ran high and reactions couldn't be predicted or counted upon.

Anyway, his snores were not the reason sleep eluded her. She never could sleep until she heard the girls arrive home. It was nonsensical, because of course, the oldest two lived elsewhere now, and it wasn't her house they generally returned to. She had to assume they were often out late, sometimes not home until the morning. Occasionally she woke in the middle of the night and felt compelled to track their whereabouts on Find My iPhone. The girls were aware of this and generously allowed it. Sometimes she found out they were back at their student digs, other times not. It was out of her control. Tonight, was different though. They were all expected back here to the family home, and she needed to know they were in and the door locked behind them before she could sleep. She supposed her mother-hen traits had been reignited with Fran's news.

It was past 11 p.m. Not late, exactly, but far past Sophie's curfew. She got out of bed. Looking out of the window, she saw some of the distinct and peculiar magic of Christmas Eve. There were far fewer cars parked on the street than usual – many of her neighbours had country homes and stayed out of town over the festive period, although every house was lit up by garlands of twinkling lights. Most were tasteful white lights; only the new family across the street had plumped for cheerful coloured ones. They also had an inflatable snowman in the garden and an inflatable Santa on their roof. He swayed gently now in the breeze; he looked like he was dancing. Connie imagined the street's housing association might have something to say about these decorations at next month's meeting. Residents were gently encouraged to conform, but she secretly hoped the tacky, joyful inflatables made an appearance again next year. Ed, who lived two doors along, was out walking his Labradoodle. He stood near the lamp post, checking his phone as he waited for the pup to finish peeing. The dog was wearing a Christmas coat and reindeer headband. Connie didn't know if she absolutely approved of people dressing up their pets, but there was no denying it, the Labradoodle looked ridiculously cute.

She craned her neck, pushed her cheek up against the cold window pane to get a view along the street. There was a couple walking at speed, holding hands. Connie wondered if they were rushing because it was cold or because they were eager to get one another to bed. Another couple were arguing, their friends were trying to intervene: too much of the wrong type of Christmas spirit. The revellers all looked so young and so underdressed. Connie could barely recall a time in her life when she chose short skirts and high heels over practical trousers or jumpsuits and flats. Had she ever? She watched the bickering group walk under her window and then out of sight. The street settled, but instead of enjoying the unusual peace and calm, Connie felt uneasy. She couldn't pinpoint exactly why. Fran's announcement, Zac's arrival in their lives, the girls not being home all combined, left her feeling tense, not in control. Her breath steamed the window. She shivered, but didn't want to abandon her post to grab her woolly bathrobe. She didn't feel cold exactly. It was something closer to spooked.

Then she saw them turn a corner. Her clan – her three girls – glorious and giggling. She let out a sigh. She noted that Auriol, Fran's best friend and practically Connie's fourth daughter, was with them. Henry and Sebastian were walking with Zac. They were all there. Safe and accounted for. Of course. Internally she chastised herself for imagining anything other. Countless nights had been marred by a brief worry that they might not return to her, but it was silly. They always did. Yet experience simply couldn't triumph over Connie's maternal worst fear.

Auriol was not only Fran's best friend, but the daughter of Connie's own best friend, Lucy, and half-sister to the twins. Lovely Rose had been married to Peter before he met irresistible Lucy. He'd left her for Lucy. It had been officially nasty at the time. Armageddon. The blast of the betrayal had lodged splinters in the friendship group, fractured it, temporarily torn it apart. It had taken a huge amount of discretion, tact and compassion to negotiate both friendships and remain loyal to both women, but Connie had managed it. Rose and Lucy had eventually found a way to co-exist in a civilized manner, both accepting it was better for the children. Rose had Craig now, Lucy and Peter were happy. People changed and moved on. Connie knew that nothing was for ever.

It was a great comfort and a great horror.

Auriol must have joined the others at the pub and was now being walked home by her brothers. Seeing her children with her friends children caused Connie's heart to lift in a moment of relief and joy, as it always did when she saw them all together. It was one of her favourite sights.

The girls were walking in a two-by-two bundle, arm in arm, laughing, singing. She wondered what they might be singing: a Swiftie anthem or a Christmas carol, most likely one or the other. Fran's coat wasn't fastened, it flapped wide open like a bird trying to take flight. Connie thought of the gifts she'd bought her daughter for Christmas. Wrapped so beautifully and currently nestled under the tree. At least three items of clothing would probably need returning; even if they fitted her right now, they would not in a few weeks' time.

Connie would take her shopping for a new coat straight after Christmas. The twins and Zac walked behind the girls. As her eyes rested on Zac, her joyful relief was elbowed aside by something considerably more complex. She tutted to herself. Shook her head sharply, just once. She was being ridiculous. She had to get used to including him, expecting him. Not being surprised by the sight of him. Henry was holding court as usual, Seb seemed to be nodding along. It didn't look as though Zac was listening. Well, she couldn't blame him for that, Henry did tend to be a little opinionated. Zac's head was bent over his phone. Who might he be texting when he was out with Fran? Connie shook her head again. That was a silly thought. He could be texting his parents, his friends. It was Christmas Eve; what could be more natural, more normal. Yet she felt uneasy, untrusting.

Her attention was grabbed by two men walking behind the group. Something about their energy immediately felt off, hostile. Connie had lived in the city long enough to know how to spot trouble. These two didn't seem like the other Christmas revellers she had watched. They were not swaying, or laughing or chatting, or even rowing. They were silent. Menacing. They wore big black puffer jackets, strode forward with a determined strut, heads up, necks out, knees loose and wide, as though their balls were too big to accommodate a more regular gait. They didn't glance at one another or share a word, yet there was a sense that they had a uniform purpose. They were watching her family as intently as she had been. For a panicked moment, she feared that they might be about to jump the boys, snatch their phones, maybe relieve them of their watches, but then she dismissed the panicked thought.

Why would two jump three? Even if they were tougher. They'd be looking for someone on their own, surely. Yet there was something threatening about their swagger. She felt sure the threat was towards her kids and their friends. Did she imagine it, or had Zac just looked back as though he too sensed danger? It seemed to her that he curled in on himself when he spotted them; his shoulders, up around his ears, were a shield.

A knife would mean two could jump three.

The men walked at a rate that meant they quickly overtook the twins and Zac. As they did so, she thought one of the guys shoved his shoulder into Zac. Zac stumbled, quickly righted himself. The guys did not apologise or even acknowledge the bump. Was it deliberate? Were they looking for trouble? Sensibly, Zac did not react. Connie's heart quickened as she realised the men were now walking very close to the girls. Not giving them a normal amount of social distance on the pavement. Most likely they did not realise the guys were with them; were they trying to intimidate the girls? A standard and hideous practice. She braced herself as she waited for . . . what? Something. A catcall, a pathetic attempt at flirting, an unwanted touch. Something worse?

'Luke, Luke, wake up.' She alerted her husband before she knew what help might be needed, just in case. She stayed by the window to see what occurred. But nothing happened. The men continued to walk right behind the girls, but from what Connie could gather, they did not speak to them or bother them with any unwanted attention. The girls turned onto the path, stood by the door, laughing and chatting, two floors below where Connie hovered, fraught. They were unaware of her, unconcerned by the strange men who walked on by. One of them glanced back over his shoulder, but maybe he wasn't trouble; maybe the group of pretty girls had simply caught his attention in the usual way. Zac, Henry and Sebastian caught up. They all stood in a merry gaggle. Connie could hear them debating whether they should have a nightcap or call it quits. She sighed, relieved. She had nothing more to worry about than the probability that Luke's malt whisky might get finished off tonight and the kids would all be grumbling about hangovers tomorrow.

Except for Fran, of course. She wouldn't have a hangover.

Despite her calling to Luke, he had not stirred, and now Connie was glad of that. She felt slightly silly that she'd let her imagination get the better of her. She slipped back into bed, put her freezing cold feet on Luke's legs. He jumped and sleepily murmured something. Intuitively snuggled closer to her. Night-time thoughts. Never rational. Always bloated with imagined threat and panic. How many times had she lain awake imagining a problem, only for it to completely disperse the morning after?

Except for Fran, of course. The same thought drifted into her head.

That worry was not going to disperse in the morning.

9

Fran

'Mum's acting weird, right?' The night air is nippy but disappointingly not freezing. I feel cheated that it isn't cold enough to wear bobble hats or gloves this Christmas Eve. If not now, when? No sign of snow. I am hot, incubated by the baby. When my sisters and friends mumble something about global warming, I am stung with irritation, more than usual. What sort of planet will my baby inherit? Will he ever have the excitement of lying on his back, flapping his arms and legs, making snow angels in inches of snow, as I sometimes did as a child? Or is that a thing of myths now in west London? I realise that when I think of him, I internally monologue 'baby' and use the pronouns he/him. I do not use 'they' in my head; I only did that to prove a point to my parents. What point? I'm unsure, exactly. Perhaps that I am going to do this my own way, perhaps that I just needed to underline that things have moved on, changed, since they had us. I like the names Arlo, Leo and Luca, but really I'm undecided. Luca is kind of a nod to my dad. Is that cool or patriarchal shit? I don't know.

Apparents there's a lot to think about now the theoretical is moving to the real. I said to Zac that I'd know what suited him when he arrived, but what sort of baby might suit the name Arlo and what sort might not? How might I distinguish an Arlo from a Luca? Does that sort of thing just come to a parent?

Flora is focused on my comment that Mum is acting weird. She replies, 'Not notably weirder than expected, considering her, considering everything.'

'She is, though,' I say. 'The thing that's usually cool about Mum is she always tells us what she's thinking. No matter how bat-shit crazy her thoughts are. I've always found that oddly comforting. You know where you stand with her.' She isn't *absolutely* honest with *absolutely* everyone. I do sometimes see her bite her tongue, swallow her fight. She says not everyone is worth the effort. I have seen her choose politeness over honesty when making small talk at a parents' night, and I have seen her choose kindness over honesty over small matters; like if Sophie or Flora ever look really gross in some daggy outfit and they ask her opinion, she'll lie about that.

But with big stuff, *real stuff*, with her family and close friends, honesty is first.

So many other people are deceitful, manipulative or just too damn weak to be honest. My mum tells it as it is – always kindly, because she is kind, but always with absolute sincerity. It's pretty cool. People overuse so many chill phrases and people talk a lot of crap, at Christmas in particular, but I just want to say, for the record, Mum has always been my true North Star. She shows me the way.

'But today,' I add, 'she's just been so . . .'
'What?'

'Careful.'

'You're right, that does not sound like Mum.'

'She's in shock or something,' offers Sophie.

'She's like a handbook on what you should say to your knocked-up kid, so obviously, she's checking her vibe. She hasn't really said much at all; she just stares at Zac, watches him like a hawk as though he's going to steal the Patrón tequila or something.'

'Well, naturally she hates him, since he's the baby daddy,' chips in Auriol. I utterly love my bezzie to the stars, and she's nailed it.

'Right, but she hasn't *said* she hates him, and you know usually she lets us know if she disapproves of our friends or whatever.' She has never told us who we should or should not mix with, but since we were kids in the playground bringing friends home, we've had to get used to Mum's pronouncements. She's the epitome of judgy. Sometimes she would say, 'What a sweet child, I like her,' or she might say, 'I don't trust her, so watch your back.' My sisters and I used to find it annoying, but we soon came to rely on it; Mum's character assessments (or assassinations) are always spot on. Also, she is a very self-aware person, and she once told me it starts there. 'If you know all your own failings, Fran, it's easier to see them in others,' she laughed. 'I was expecting her to say something about Zac, but when I asked if she liked him, she just replied, "The important thing is that *you* like him."'

'Well, she's not wrong.'

'Yeah, but that's not very *her*, is it?'

'We're in uncharted waters,' comments Flora. She starts to hum 'Silent Night'. She has a great voice, but I talk over her anyway.

'I'd prefer it if she just said, "You should abort."'

'You really wouldn't. You'd be in therapy for ever if she said that,' points out Sophie.

'*Have* you thought of getting rid of it?' asks Auriol.

'I don't want an abortion.'

'You're sure? If it happened to me, I'd rather take a bullet to the head than bring up a baby.'

'Sensitive,' mutters Flora, who doesn't get Auriol's sense of humour and anyway has always been a bit jealous of her because as kids I always chose my friend over my sister.

'You are very young,' adds Sophie.

That's from my baby sis. I respond in the age-old manner. 'I'm way older than you.'

'*I'm* not the one who is pregnant.'

'There are options other than abortion,' chips in Auriol.

I glance behind me to see if Zac is in earshot. When my sisters and Auriol and I talk, we don't filter. I filter with Zac. He's new. 'What? Like giving it away?' I shake my head. 'I think everyone has a right to choose, but I couldn't live with the thought of knowing my baby was out there in the world somewhere, but not by my side. Adoption isn't for me.'

'Right.'

'I want my baby,' I say firmly.

'OK. Well, obviously we'll be the best aunties in the world,' says Flora in her matter-of-fact way.

'Totally the best,' agrees Sophie. 'I can't wait to meet them.'

'And me,' adds Auriol. She's not my sister by blood, but she will definitely be his aunty. He'll be very loved. He'll be OK. I squeeze her arm. 'But I'm not doing nappies. Not ever,' she adds. 'Never ask me.'

I don't think I've ever heard her be as serious about anything.

TEN DAYS BEFORE THE END

10

Connie

Christmas Day

Christmas lunch passed off without incident, which was Connie's newly revised goal, downgraded from the goal of having the Best Christmas Ever. She drank less than she usually did, to keep Fran company, because she remembered how tedious it was to be the only sober person around a table of drunks when pregnant. It seemed unlikely her daughter noticed the sacrifice, but it did mean that, possibly for the first time in the Baker household, they sat down to a Christmas lunch that was not interrupted by Connie sporadically jumping up as she remembered the crackers, cranberry sauce, pigs in blankets, etc. She had stayed focused on the lunch, not allowing herself to think about anything else, and as a result it was delicious, coordinated and complete. Lucy, Peter and Auriol had, as usual, joined them.

Once again, the news of the pregnancy was discussed and digested. Auriol did not refer to the baby as 'they'; she called it a 'smol'.

'Smol?' asked Luke.

'Small and adorable,' chorused everyone under twenty-five. Connie was glad of the info, not that she'd have asked for an explanation herself. While Gen Z vocab was a foreign language to her, and she found it just as incomprehensible as Luke did, she had a hangover from being their age herself, and she always liked to pretend she understood cool talk. She was embarrassed to note this. Hell, she was about to be a grandmother; she ought to have grown out of a need to appear cooler than she was.

Lucy said nothing at all; she just smiled and dispensed a brief, rare and efficient hug to Fran, her god-daughter. Elegant. Connie was grateful for her verbal restraint, because Lucy was not known for valuing fecundity. It was unlikely she thought this was good news but had resisted saying so in front of Fran and Zac. Connie couldn't wait to be alone with her friend so they could have a frank exchange.

When everyone had overindulged, gorged on turkey and trimmings, so needed a pause before pudding, Connie grabbed her coat and Lucy's too. She flung it at her friend, 'I need to show you our log pile, at the bottom of the garden,' she said by way of an excuse for them skipping out of the overcrowded, overheated room. It was a faulty diversion if anyone had considered it. Lucy was not the type to take an interest in anything domestic, not even something as elite as drying logs for the burner, but no one was paying either of them much attention.

The moment they were alone, Lucy laughed and said, 'Well done! I was thinking all lunch that I wished I still smoked. It was always a decent excuse to get up and leave the room.'

'Have you ever thought of vaping?'

Lucy seemed offended. 'It looks ridiculous, Connie. The

main reason for smoking is to look cool. Vaping is an abomination.' Then, conscious that they wouldn't have long before, most likely, someone joined them, she said, 'So, she's pregnant and she's keeping the baby.' She hummed the tune of Madonna's classic 'Papa Don't Preach'. Connie was strangely comforted by the cultural reference, which she knew her daughters would deem outdated. She had been quashing the urge to sing it since Fran had announced the news, in case she appeared flip. Now she felt understood.

'Yes and yes.' Without being asked, because she was with her best friend, she was able to say the things she was trying not to say to Luke or Fran. 'I'm still trying to digest it. This is not what I wanted for her. My baby is so clever and interesting and young. She has it all stretching out in front of her. This changes everything. She hasn't even finished university. I feel it was just a blink of an eye ago when I was bringing her home from hospital, a newborn in rompers. How can she possibly be going to have a baby of her own?'

Lucy squeezed Connie's shoulder and said nothing. Which was, Connie found, the perfect response. What could be said?

'I can't pretend I think this is the ideal time.'

'When would be?'

'Oh, say when she's twenty-seven-or-eight. Ideally with a long-term partner. Not someone she's dated for such a brief time.'

'No, you misunderstand me. I mean, there really isn't an ideal time,' clarified Lucy.

Connie smiled. Lucy had initially struggled with being a mother. She hadn't liked anything about the job. She'd found the whole process smelly, tedious and disappointing. Lonely, tiring and competitive. Her biggest competition had been with Rose, naturally, as she was Peter's first wife. Or maybe she had simply been in competition with herself, normally so incredible at everything. Either way, she hadn't enjoyed early motherhood. She'd only got into the swing of things when Auriol was about seven. They were very close now. Which demonstrated that it was never too late. Connie wondered whether that meant it was never too early either. Was that the point Lucy was making? She perched on the wooden garden bench. It was damp, but she felt the need to slump. The cold slipped through her coat. Lucy remained standing. Ramrod-straight posture as always. The fresh air and total honesty was a relief after the heat and flippant chatter over lunch.

There was something else. Something Connie was dying to discuss, and it could only be discussed with Lucy. 'You were next to him at lunch, what do you think?' she asked. She had wanted to sit next to Zac herself and had gone to the trouble of making a seating plan and putting out home-made festive dried orange-slice name cards, but by the time she'd brought all the food to the table, everyone had sat wherever they pleased and ignored her plan. She could hardly ask them all to change seats.

'It's more important what you think of him, and most importantly what she does,' said Lucy. Connie recognised this for the dodge it was. Hadn't she used the same line on Fran?

'He seems . . . pleasant. He's not what I expected for her.'

'Why not?'

'Well, doesn't inherited wisdom have it that all little girls marry their fathers?'

'That Freudian stuff has always struck me as frankly weird.'

'Maybe, but generally accurate all the same.'

'Well, perhaps Zac *is* like Luke.'

'He's not. Luke is tall and blond with green eyes. Zac is short and dark with blue eyes.'

Lucy let out a hoot of laughter. Not unkind, but certainly mocking. 'God, I sometimes forget just how shallow you are. I didn't mean physically. I meant, maybe his temperament is similar. Is he hard-working, calm, honest, loyal?'

'I don't know. I don't know him.'

'I can see how that would be a worry.'

'He hasn't done anything to make me mistrust him. Other than have a spectacular lack of understanding about how contraception works. He hasn't shirked in any way. There's no sense that he wants to leave Fran to this.'

'I suppose the advantage of having a kid when you are still one yourself is you don't know what you've missed out on,' observed Lucy.

'Are you trying to be comforting?'

'Yes. What do you want me to say?'

'Should I be angrier?'

'What's done is done, I suppose.' Lucy shrugged. Her gesture summed it all up.

'That's where I'm at. And people manage. They make a go of it. Don't they?' Lucy didn't answer. They both knew Connie's ambition for her daughters expanded beyond them making a go of it. She had wanted them to have spectacular careers, to travel extensively and have many interesting love affairs before settling on the person they wanted to commit to for an eternity. It was pointless saying as much. Life was more to do with making a go of it. Connie knew what else she wanted to talk about. The thing that was niggling at her and that she couldn't share with anyone other than Lucy. Her concern seemed silly and selfish. But unshockable, unflappable Lucy would understand. 'Does he remind you of anyone?'

'No.'

'You sure?'

Lucy flicked her eyes towards the house and through the large Crittall-framed windows appraised Zac, who at that moment was clearing the table of the debris of paper crackers. Someone said something that made him laugh. His wide grin cracked across his face a fraction of a second before he threw his head back and laughed out loud.

'He's very good-looking,' she murmured with approval.

'He is,' Connie agreed.

'Dazzling. A little short.'

'Yes. So I ask again, does he remind you of anyone?'

Connie watched as the thought slithered into her friend's head. 'Oh my holy fucking God.'

'Lucy, it's Christmas Day. I don't think—'

'John Harding.' Lucy stared at Connie, her eyes wide and incredulous. 'He's the absolute double. Now I see it, I can't unsee it. How did I miss that?'

'Right. I was hoping it was in my imagination,' Connie said with a defeated shrug.

'It's not. He's the image. How weird.'

John Harding was Connie's most beautiful mistake. The life-defining affair that she'd had in the first year of her marriage. When Luke found out, he left her. Not an unsurprising consequence. For a while, it looked like they would divorce, that they couldn't recover and correct their path. Connie had been an archetypal example of 'you don't know what you have until you've lost it'. She'd fought to get Luke back. She worked on herself; became the person he deserved her to be. Eventually he returned to her. The wound she'd inflicted on their marriage slowly healed, but it had left a scar. People thought scars were a blot, an eyesore; they tried to get them removed. But Connie knew scars were part of the body's healing process, a mark where the skin had repaired itself by growing new tissue to pull together the wound and fill in any gaps caused by the injury. They faded but never quite disappeared, and perhaps they shouldn't. It was sometimes best to remember the hurt. The affair had happened twenty-five years ago. It was ancient history. Very, very occasionally she allowed herself to think of him – John Harding. She recalled meeting him, having sex with him, eventually letting him go. These memories were among her most vivid and perfect. Not perfect in the sense of wonderful – often they caused her to internally squirm – but perfect in the sense of entire, precise and whole. She could not forget him. She still considered him one of the best and worst things that had happened in her life.

'I had no idea a child could be attracted to the same type as a parent. Is that inherited, then, what one finds attractive? What a funny coincidence,' commented Lucy.

'You think that's all it is? A coincidence?'

'Well, what else?'

'You don't think Zac's his son or something?'

Lucy laughed out loud. Which Connie found reassuring, if not a little belittling. 'Wow, Connie, even for you that's a big leap. Are you mad? Oh God, yes you are. You always were whenever it was anything to do with that damned man.'

She shook her head. She was wearing a paper crown, which was surprising; when she was younger, she used to refuse to do so. She considered them ridiculous and complained that they weren't flattering. She needn't have worried; she suited the crown. She looked regal, it didn't slip or slide. Connie felt her own crown fall over her eye; she snatched it off her head and scrunched the tissue paper in her hand. She felt awkward, ashamed. 'You're obsessed.' Lucy looked disappointed.

'I'm just finding it disconcerting.'

'Zac talked to me about his parents. They're called Clare and Neil. Neil, not John. Stop this. We can't have this. Not after all these years. You can't hold a grudge against Zac because he has a resemblance to your ex-lover. Get the hell over it.'

'I'm not holding a grudge. What made you think that?'

Lucy rolled her eyes. 'Fact. You can't fool all the people all the time and you can never fool me.'

'I'm *not* holding a grudge. I've been very supportive and accepting. Not a single reprimand. It's just that I'm worried. It's not a passing resemblance. He's the absolute double.' Connie sighed. 'They have the same eye colour, freckles, mannerisms, stature.'

'Connie, do you have a crush on your daughter's boyfriend?' Lucy demanded.

'No, don't be ridiculous. I'm just terrified that they're related. What if Zac's mother had an affair?'

'Don't judge everyone by our standards. Not everyone has affairs. Only the very brilliant and the very stupid.'

Connie definitely did not want to ask which category Lucy thought she fell into. 'Well, maybe he's an uncle or something. I think John has a sister; maybe that's Zac's mother.'

Lucy moved her head from side to side, slowly. 'Why are you doing this to yourself? You're looking for trouble in that way you have.' Connie felt stung. It wasn't fair. Her friends often implied she was a handful, hard work, a little much. It all stemmed from her one transgression, the affair. She didn't look for trouble. It found her. 'Have you spoken to Zac? Asked him about his relatives?'

'No.'

'Well, isn't that the logical thing to do? That or your therapist. They'll unpick why you are indulging in this fantasy.'

'I don't have a therapist.'

'You should get one.'

'It's not a fantasy. If he is in some way related to John Harding, it's a total and absolute nightmare.'

11

Zac

After Christmas pudding but before charades, Zac took the opportunity to slip away, nip upstairs to find somewhere quiet so that he could call his parents. He perched on the end of Fran's bed. He felt a bit uncomfortable in this room, which had fairy lights hung over the dressing table and curtain rail, there were a lot of fluffy cushions too. The room was grey and lilac. There was a daisy thing theme going on. 'A motif', Fran had called it. It was girlie. He was surprised at that; she had always appeared sophisticated to him. He felt nipped by the reminder of her youth, her vulnerability. She knew the names of ski resorts and how to pronounce French words that popped up on a menu. She was pregnant. Yet she seemed innocent, certainly in comparison to him. Her childhood bedroom was a big fat reminder of that. As if he needed a reminder.

It felt good to be alone, away from the roomful of strangers who he had to think of as family now. That blew his mind. His concept of family morphing, moving like a shoreline on a beach. His family had been his mum, his dad and his sister, and now there was Fran and her entire clan. Soon there would be a baby. Wow.

He could hear their laughter and chatter drifting up the stairs; barks of merriment sounding weirdly aggressive from this distance. A little intense, shrill. He'd drunk too much. But not enough.

His mother picked up before the second ring. He imagined she'd had her phone within reach all day. She'd have wanted him to call earlier. 'Hello, love, how's it going?'

'Yeah, good. Really good.'

'It doesn't sound it.' Her voice was a mix of concern and accusation. Zac stared at his phone in annoyance. 'You sound quiet. Are you OK, really?'

'Yes, of course. Why wouldn't I be?' he snapped, and then, trying, 'Happy Christmas.'

'Happy Christmas,' she repeated on rote, then yelled, 'Neil! It's our Zac. You're on speaker, Zac, your dad's listening. Where's Celeste? She won't want to miss his call. Celeste!' Zac moved the phone away from his ear as his mother had obviously failed to move it from her mouth when she called to his sister.

'Happy Christmas, son.' His father's voice caused his chest to tighten. His dad exuded good natured, no-nonsense simplicity; that should have been comforting, but somehow today, it wasn't. It made Zac feel a little lonely and adrift. Distant.

'He's not having a good time,' stated his mother.

'Oh, that's a shame. Why not?'

'What? No, I never said that. I said the opposite.' Zac flipped the bird, not exactly at his mother but at the irritation he felt at her overwhelming compulsion to catastrophise, to expect the worst for him. From him? Her pessimism made life less sparkling. She'd always been that way. He could tell her three good things, maybe even amazing things, and one not so good, and she'd focus on that one; inflate it like a balloon so the not-so-good became a total disaster. The good things were forgotten. Why did she always think total disasters were what he had in store? What did she know? Sometimes he thought she caused it, this crap he was in. He knew that wasn't fair. Not on a rational level. But it was like her years and years of expecting the worst had somehow manifested just that. Why couldn't she trust him to be brilliant, or at least mediocre?

Zac thought of Fran's parents. Their confident chatter thrummed through the floorboards, and even though he was high in the attic room, he could hear their trust and certainty that everything was fine and everything would work out. Not just with him and Fran, but with all things. He thought of their clear skin, straight teeth, their seemingly endless supply of impressive friends. They oozed assurance and poise. Not surprising really, a chicken-and-egg scenario. The skin, the teeth, the friends – Fran was buoyed up on all of it.

'I am having a good time,' he insisted. He was, but he knew that he sounded defensive and wouldn't be believed.

'It was always likely to be sticky. Considering everything,' said his dad, carefully.

'It hasn't been. They've been very relaxed about the announcement,' Zac reassured him.

'Oh, liberals, are they?' His mother sounded critical, which made no sense.

'They took it much the way you did. They're being very supportive.'

'Pleased, are they? At becoming grandparents?'

Zac didn't know exactly how to answer that. They weren't *dis*pleased, or if they were, they were putting on a polite face. His head ached. It was possibly because he'd drunk an espresso martini, a beer, three glasses of wine and two of champagne already today; he wasn't good with mixing. But the tightness might also come from the fact that he too had been putting on a polite face. It was an effort. He was twenty-two and about to become a dad. He didn't even know if *he* was something as simple as unilaterally pleased, so it wasn't easy to process everyone else's reactions. He loved Fran, she was amazing. Funny, clever, beautiful, different. From the moment he'd met her, he'd thought she might be the sort of someone that one day he might want to be with in a permanent way. He imagined them at one another's graduation ceremonies, holidaying afterwards in Ibiza, clubs, drinks, music, sunshine, maybe moving to London together, not in the same flat, separate flats with their own mates, but nearby. He imagined work, commutes, brunches, enjoying that for a few years. He hadn't got further than that. Now they were having a baby together. It was a fast leap.

'Do they like you?' his dad asked.

He didn't get a chance to answer, as his mum interrupted. 'Of course they like him. They must love him. And if they don't, I'll get straight in the car and drive there to tell them exactly how lucky they are.' He could hear the quiver in his mother's throat. The outrage, the upset. He recognised it and was grateful for it, but also a bit shamed by the insistence. It was too much. She was fiercely protective, always had been. Zac and his father had learnt to glaze over her intensity.

'Yeah, I think they do like me.'

'And do you like them?'

'They're really nice.'

'What's wrong? There's something. I can hear it in your tone of voice,' his mother said. She knew him better than anyone else did, which used to be comforting but had become a big problem. Sometimes he avoided calling her to swerve this sort of thing.

'It's just weird, you know, Christmas Day and not seeing you lot.' That was not untrue. It was not entirely true either. He glanced out the window. Checked up and down the street. There was an old bloke walking his little puffball of a dog. Zac watched as the guy stooped to scoop up the crap. He loved dogs but couldn't imagine scooping crap off the street and then carrying a little green sack around with him. There was a father-and-daughter combo, the little girl wobbling on a big red bike, presumably left by Santa and in need of a test drive. He tried to imagine that scenario. It was as tricky to reach as the crap-scraping. No one else in view. He sighed, relieved.

'So, what are they like?'

'Posh. Loud. Sweary. Clever.'

'Well, we're three of those,' said his dad, laughing.

'What you talking about? We're posh,' insisted his mother, convincing no one. Zac didn't know much about social class structures, but he was pretty sure no one in the history of ever who was posh had to state it.

'Clare, love, be realistic. I'm a town planner, her dad is an architect. Her mum is a famous photographer, you work in WHSmith. Plus, they're from down south.'

Zac chipped in. 'Actually, her mum works in a shop too and she's a northerner. Born in Sheffield.'

'There you go,' his mum declared as though her point had been proven. 'What sort of shop?'

'Well, it's more of a gallery. They sell art.'

'We sell art supplies in Smith's. We're not that different. You hold your head up, son, you have nothing to be ashamed of. You're good enough for anyone.'

'No one is suggesting anything other,' said his dad.

Zac really wanted to get off this call. He knew his mum always battled a misplaced sense of inferiority that manifested in bolshie aggression. He couldn't stand it.

'Has anyone talked about money?' she asked.

'Mum, it's Christmas Day. All we've talked about is food and the King's speech.'

'Well, you do need to talk about money. Having a baby is expensive.'

'I know.' He sighed.

'We've got money, Zac. Not a fortune, but we won't let you go short. We'll help out.'

The suggestion, while well intentioned, just made him feel grubby, restricted. He imagined his parents doling out cash like pocket money. They'd want to know what it was spent on. He remembered lying as a kid, pretending he'd bought books when in fact he'd bought Pokémon cards. They'd offer ugly furniture and second-hand pushchairs that friends of his mother's didn't want any more. They'd say the stuff was 'perfectly good, still serviceable' even if it was blatantly otherwise. They'd always had a make-do-and-mend attitude. He didn't want to be a dick about it, but it wasn't what he wanted for his own kid, for himself. 'I'm fine. We're fine. I've got to go. We're going to play charades. They're waiting for me.'

'Don't you want to talk to your sister? She's just com—'

'Happy Christmas. Love you. Miss you all.' He spoke over

his mum and then pressed end as though he hadn't heard her request. He'd text his sister. She'd be OK with that. He just had to get off the call; it was dragging him down.

His phone buzzed. He read the message. Sighed. Glanced out the window again. He'd hoped they were bluffing. But no. While there was no sign of the little girl and her red bike, or the dog-walking guy, there, parked just across the street, was the dark grey Beemer. Such a cliché. They were too close. What if they got out of the car and walked up the little path, banged on the door? That would bring the Christmas festivities to an abrupt halt. He dreaded it so much that the vision grew in his head, large and looming. Real. He was surprised when the banging didn't happen. He double-checked. They were still in the car. He ducked behind the curtain. Had they seen him watching them watching him? His heartbeat had speeded up to a crazy rate. He could feel it clobbering his chest.

They were waiting for him. They would wait as long as they had to. They'd said so. He believed them. He'd be an idiot not to. He'd tried ignoring them, like his mother used to tell him to ignore bullies at school. The advice didn't stretch. It hadn't worked. His muscles ached and resisted as his thumbs danced and he sent a message back. He bit his thumbnail as the grey ticks turned blue. They didn't respond instantly. But after two or three minutes, the car's engine started up and they pulled away.

Thank fuck.

But it wasn't over. He knew that. It was a stay of execution, not a pardon.

12

Connie

Connie and Lucy came in from the garden just as another cork sprang from another bottle, the pop and the clink of glasses chiming through the house. 'Don't worry, mine is apple juice,' said Fran. It was impossible to ignore her touchy tone.

'I wasn't worried,' Connie replied with a quick smile. 'I was just wondering if there was a glass for me.'

'I thought you went outside for fresh air because you were feeling a bit drunk,' commented Sophie. She sounded vaguely accusatory. She didn't like her mother drinking. She didn't like anyone over the age of thirty drinking, but this was very hypocritical, as she believed that the moment parents turned their backs, anyone under the age of eighteen was absolutely entitled to secretly chug hundred-per-cent-proof vodka from a flask until they vomited or passed out.

'I've hardly had a sip all day. We were looking at the log pile,' Connie reiterated her lame excuse. Everyone was perfectly aware that she and Lucy were having a gossip; she should have just said so.

The idea of playing charades was shelved as the younger generation all wanted some time on their phones so they could send their mates memes and messages. Connie tried to take an interest, but when Sophie showed her a few things she'd sent and received, she found the greetings to be on a scale of offensive to incomprehensible, so instead she turned her attention to stacking the dishwasher, while Luke ensured that their guests were furnished with drinks and chocolates and that her father had the remote control. While clearing the decks, Connie took the opportunity of cornering Zac. Like her daughters and Auriol, he had his head bent over his phone. From a distance it looked like the kids were all praying, and indeed they were worshipping, but at the altar of technology. Zac would probably have preferred to be left alone with his phone, but Connie was newly invigorated with the intention of getting to know him, so she asked if he'd give her a hand in the kitchen. He could hardly refuse, and to his credit, he managed to accept with a level of grace and charm. His smile caused her insides to churn. So familiar. So strange.

They made small talk about lunch. He was extremely polite, repeating that it was delicious, that he was so glad to be spending Christmas with them. She expressed mild concern that the parsnips were a little charred, and wondered aloud whether there had been enough purple cabbage to go round.

'There was more than enough food. Everyone's stuffed.'
'Oh good.'
'My mum is just the same. Always sweating the small stuff,' he commented. Connie wasn't sure she liked being called out for having petty concerns, but she saw that his comment was well intentioned; he was comparing her to his mum, that had

to be a compliment, didn't it? And anyway, it was certainly a way into the discussion she wanted to have.

'Tell me about yourself, Zac.'

'What do you want to know?' he asked. Connie wondered if she'd heard a smidge of defensiveness, but she supposed that was to be expected. It was such a long time since she'd had to be apprehensive about impressing anyone's parents, but she could still, just about, recall that pinch of stress at having to prove yourself to someone who mattered to someone who mattered to you. He was clever enough to know she was grilling him.

She wanted to know everything, but specifically she wanted to shoo away her hunch – no, that was overstating it, surely: her niggle. Lucy was no doubt right. It was most likely a passing resemblance, nothing at all to worry about. What were the chances that her daughter had met John Harding's son or nephew and fallen in love with him, fallen pregnant to him? Infinitesimal. Once that thought was out of her head, she would be able to think about the pregnancy properly. Focus on what it meant for Fran and Zac. What she could do to help and support. She just needed to put the idea firmly to bed. She was aware that her subconscious had picked an ironically poignant idiom. Whenever she thought of John Harding, she thought of beds. She always had.

'Anything, everything. We're family now. Right?' she replied with a beam.

'Well, I'm from Cheshire. I'm studying at York Uni. Like Fran, as you know. My degree is in business management. I'll graduate this year. I did a year's work placement as part of my degree last year with ZapionTec, developing BI software that performs tasks such as data mining, forecasting and reporting.' She had no idea what any of that meant but felt asking would appear as a challenge; it sounded like something he was proud of. 'They've already offered me a job on their graduate programme. I start in September. In London. Of course the salary isn't huge, at least not to begin with, but it's a great company. I have prospects, if that's what you are asking.'

He had practically straightened his shoulders and squared up to her. She felt sorry for him. He was just a kid. Her own experiences with the girls meant she was very aware that this generation spent the first quarter century of their lives being tested; jostling for positions, places and prizes and having to constantly prove themselves. As a parent, she had been horrified to witness the level of pressure young people endured now. There were copious exams, endless interviews, trials, tests, levels and league tables. It was exhausting to witness, let alone endure. This boy was telling her he was a success. That he had endured everything that was required nowadays to bob to the top of the pile. A Russell Group uni kid, with a job lined up before he'd even graduated. A baby probably hadn't been part of his life plan either.

'Oh no. That wasn't what I meant. Well, yes, yes, I suppose it was.' She smiled, gently. She didn't ask him what his salary was. Whatever it was, he and Fran were going to struggle financially if they were planning on living in London. Everyone, other than trustafarians and nepo babies, struggled. 'Tell me about your family. I'm sure we'll all be meeting soon.' Maybe, hopefully. Hopefully not. She didn't know which to wish for yet.

'Well, I consider myself extremely lucky because I grew

up knowing that I had parents who love each other. I think that's important.'

'Yes! That sounds wonderful. Yes, it is important.' The relief was intense, meaning she was far too enthusiastic in her response. Connie was often far too enthusiastic in life. She'd tried to rein it in because people found it unnerving; they tended to doubt her sincerity. But she was *so* glad to hear he came from a stable home. Him leading with that was very sweet.

And it meant he was not John Harding's son.

Oh, thank God for that.

Of course he wasn't. How utterly silly of her to ever have imagined such a thing. Lucy was probably right: she should consider seeing a therapist. How could she have conjured up this problem? Was she just avoiding tackling the real issues arising around the unexpected pregnancy? Fran's prospects, their financial security, their emotional well-being. His parents had *always* loved each other. How marvellous! She hoped Fran would say the same of her and Luke. He'd grown up knowing that. He thought parents loving each other was a goal. Hurrah. She rolled the thought around her head, allowing it to softly massage away the stress she had been harbouring.

'I was unplanned. A mistake. They told me often enough. Not to hurt me, simply a fact.'

Connie laughed, giddy on relief. 'Well, yes, I think if you asked Luke, he'd say Sophie was a surprise, but she absolutely wasn't, at least not to me.' She winked, happy to take Zac into her confidence, happy to make him one of the family now her silly fears had been allayed.

'No, I was a surprise to my mother too,' Zac insisted with

a firm smile. 'The situation was exactly like it is between me and Fran. I'm the product of an enormous attraction and a careless, full-on, caution-to-the-wind one-night stand.' Connie stared at him. He checked himself, no doubt realising that how he'd just described the conception of her grandchild was perhaps unpalatable. He coloured, high in his cheeks. 'Sorry. I mean, obviously we're more than a one-night stand now. I just mean that, looking at the dates, it was probably the first or second week after we got together this time when we, you know . . . when she . . . when . . .' He stopped talking. It was an impossible sentence to finish while talking to Fran's mother.

They stayed in an embarrassed silence for a moment or two. Connie was vaguely aware of her father asking if there was a glass of port going, the sounds of the TV blasting through from the sitting room. The Christmas tree lights were flashing. Who had switched the settings? The flickering was so distracting. Connie processed the fact that he had made the exact same mistake as his parents. Wasn't that the sort of lesson that people ought to learn from? But on the other hand, all these years on, Zac's family could only be glad of that first wild and careless encounter. They were still happily married, Zac was a son to be proud of, there was a sister too, she'd heard. She considered that the lesson his parents offered was an example of how it could work. She was not looking for Fran and Zac to marry, but she did want her daughter to be loved, supported, helped by the baby's father. She grinned, letting him off the hook. He was a nice boy. From a nice family. Yes, they were young, but that meant they'd have energy and find the fun. This was far from the disaster she'd feared.

'I'd love to meet your mum and dad.'

'They feel the same.' He smiled back at her, relaxing too now. 'I'm proud of us, you know. We're like this perfect example of a blended family.'

'Blended?' Connie thought for a moment that she'd misunderstood the word, that there must be a trendy update on its meaning. She'd always understood a blended family to be one with step-parents, step- and half-siblings. She'd loved the term, really liked the idea that people smudged together in all sorts of ways to become a family. But it probably meant something completely different now.

'Well, that's what we are, technically,' said Zac. 'My dad is the only dad I've ever known, and I just think of my sister as my sister, not half-sister or anything pedantic, but as I just told you, my mum had me after a one-night stand.'

'So you're saying . . .' Connie's world shuddered and slowed. She lost her grip on the plate she was holding. It dropped onto the kitchen surface. It didn't break, but gravy and other food debris splashed up the sleeve of her dress. She didn't reach for anything to sponge it off.

'My mum and Neil met when I was about four. My biological dad was never on the scene.' And suddenly she was struggling for air. Zac clocked her panic and interpreted it as confusion. 'Sorry. I'm not being clear. I think I'm nervous. Talking too much and not giving you the details in a chronological way.'

'Your biological dad, tell me about him.' The words squeaked out of her mouth. There was still a chance that this was not what she feared. A chance, a hope, she told herself as much over and over again. But she knew that there wasn't a chance. There was no hope. She had always known that this mistake of hers was going to come home to roost. Sooner or later her past would catch her up and shove her over.

'He'd never been in my life. Irrelevant really, until recently. But now we've reconnected. I'm pretty excited about him being in my life. You know.'

'What's his name?'

'Sorry?' Zac looked vaguely confused by the odd and abrupt question.

'I'm just thinking of baby names,' Connie lied. Her breath high in her chest.

'John. But we won't be calling the baby after my biological dad, that's for sure.'

'What's his surname?' Clutching at straws now, Connie spoke with the sort of force that drew the attention of other people in the other room. They couldn't hear the exchange exactly but they could probably pick up on the increasingly frantic tone, or maybe it was something about their body language that gave it away. Zac gazed at her with puzzlement and concern.

Fran wandered over to where they were standing. 'Mum, stop it, leave him alone. We probably can't afford to scare him off at this early stage.' She smiled and wrapped her arms around his waist, dropped her head onto his shoulder. The gesture was natural and protective. They were a unit. A family. This was real. 'I'm getting pretty used to having him around.' She was blooming, glorious.

'Harding. My bio dad is John Harding.'

13

Connie

No, no, no, no. Inside her head, the F-bomb exploded time after time. She wondered if the harsh, guttural word slamming around and around her skull was going to split her head wide open. She imagined everything splattering out. Her brain and blood, her thoughts, secrets and shame would be splashed all over the walls. She tried to take deep, calming breaths. She had to form a plan, think what was for the best. What were her options? But she couldn't, she was frozen. Her palms were clammy, her intestines roiling and her heart racing. She wondered if she was having a panic attack. Was this it? She rushed to the loo. Locked the door behind her, leant her head against the cool glass mirror. Sweat gathered under her arms. Uncomfortable. For a brief moment, she hated herself. Her past self. The mistake she had made so long ago. It wasn't fair. Life wasn't.

On balance, Connie was a good person. A loving wife, mother, daughter, sister, friend. She'd paid for this dalliance when Luke left her, and a hundred times since when the thought of it came back to her and she was just sad and ashamed that she'd caused so much pain. She knew Luke had never quite got over her infidelity. She was so sorry. Sodding karma had nothing more to do here, the debt was collected.

And yet. It appeared not.

EIGHT DAYS BEFORE THE END

14

Fran

27 December

In retrospect, announcing the baby at Christmas was possibly not the most Zen move. People are weird at Christmas, properly hyped and intense, and people are weird about unplanned pregnancy, also hyped and intense although more justifiably. To me, it's a no-brainer. In terms of life's big questions, 'Should I ask for the receipt so I can take it back?' just does not provide stiff competition when stacked up against 'Will they go ape and throw me out?' Slayed.

TBF, Mum and Dad are holding it together well enough. We've skirted the drama. But now Zac's met my lot, he wants me to meet his. Fair enough, but couldn't we just slow down? He's just kicked off his relationship with his bio dad, who hasn't seen his mum since the night he was conceived, and now he's got a mad idea of asking them down here – *all of them*, at the same time.

Mum is really against it. She says we should wait to meet his bio dad. She wants me to 'talk sense' into Zac. I'm not sure if that's a dynamic Zac and I have negotiated, but also I can see it's a lot, so I give it a shot.

'It will be so intense,' I warn him. 'My mum says it will be a shitshow. I quote.'

'She's probably right, so we should just get it over with, rip off the Elastoplast,' says Zac with his easy-to-come, easy-to-love smile. 'I talked to your dad; he suggested the twenty-ninth. No one ever knows what to do with the limbo days between Christmas and New Year. We're doing everyone a favour. Fact proven, 'cos everyone is up for it.' I must still look less than chill, because he wraps his arms around me and says, 'I don't know if any of them are especially happy about this, but I don't care. They should be. We're brilliant and we're going to make them a brilliant grandchild. Can you imagine how cute he will be?'

He sounds high. He starts to kiss my neck and I feel my body respond to his. His lips, cheeks, fingers are freezing cold. He's just got in after taking the dog for a walk. He's made that his thing, these past couple of days, slipping out with Asti, our Airedale terrier. I offered to go with him on Christmas Day, but he made it really clear he fancied a bit of alone time. I'm not the clingy type and I can appreciate that my family are full-on and a little bit of silence is covetable, so I've stopped even suggesting I join him when he goes for a stroll. Now, I lie back on the bed and he nestles so close to me it's like we're zipped together. I study him. His nose, mouth, chin. His lashes, long and lush. I love the dip of his collarbone, the rise of his Adam's apple. Our baby *will* be the cutest thing ever. Fact. I'm hoping he gets Zac's eyes and head for numbers but my musical ability and my dad's height. We kiss for a long while and he does inexplicably brilliant things with his cold fingers and hot tongue.

It kills me to break away, but I really want to talk about this family meet-up and, any second now, someone will call us downstairs and offer us another meal or suggest we watch a Christmas movie or play cards. I'd forgotten how much my family love organised fun. We're not getting much time alone. It feels like my parents are chaperoning us. News flash, Mum, the horse has bolted.

'Why bring your bio dad into this now? Don't you think we're already dealing with a lot here? I don't want to make your mum uncomfortable.' I'm parroting my mum's argument here. I sort of guess she has a point. She's usually spot on with room-reading.

'My mum will be fine,' Zac assures me. 'They didn't have feelings for each other; they had sex together, that's all. And it was a really long time ago.'

'But there must be feeling associated with him because he made you.'

Zac shrugs and sits up. He scoots to the edge of the bed and reaches for his phone. He keeps his back to me. I don't think he's angry, I think he's just bored of the conversation. He's made up his mind and so doesn't think any more discussion is needed. I wonder what it will be like to live with that trait. Hey, maybe he's right. Maybe he knows better than my mum. It is his family after all.

Zac and his biological dad have only been talking for a few months. He told me that when he first started to track him down, he expected to be disappointed. But he wasn't. The search wasn't at all tricky, or convoluted, he didn't encounter endless dead ends, his perseverance wasn't tested. There was a friend of a friend of his mum's who was still in touch with

John Harding via LinkedIn or something. It was a matter of an email, a few texts and a WhatsApp message. Not at all difficult. This has made Zac flip-flop between saying glib stuff like 'It was meant to be', 'It's a sign I've done the right thing' and getting moody and depressed about how many years they'd wasted and asking why, if it was so easy to make the connection, hadn't any of the adults thought to reach out before.

His bio dad agreed to meet straight away. He'd had no idea that his one-night stand had been so fruitful. He couldn't quite place Zac's mother, but he didn't deny the possibility that Zac could be his son; in fact, he welcomed it. Zac bottled the first time they planned to meet, but his father persevered, showing understanding of his nerves or anger or whatever. When they eventually met, he apparently commented that it was 'like looking in a mirror'.

'Was it?' I asked Zac.

'Well, he's like thirty-something years older than I am, so no, he's deluded, but he showed me a picture of himself when he was young, and yeah, I look just like he did.'

'What were the feels when you saw the photo?'

'It was weird. But good weird. To fit somewhere so completely. Don't get me wrong, I've never felt like I don't fit with my fam. I do. We're tight. But I don't look like my mum and of course I can't look like Dad. My sister does, so it was just different seeing the biology pop up. You know. It matters.'

John Harding has made it clear that there's room for Zac in his life. He doesn't have any other kids and he isn't married. Zac is hyped that everything is rolling so easily. He told me, 'Other kids might have been awesome but they'd also be an extra complication, further relationships to negotiate. It's going so smoothly. We really get on. It's defo as good as I could possibly have imagined.'

You think? I just hear disaster whenever Zac talks about this guy. He's in his fifties, twice divorced and no kids, sounds like a total prick with commitment issues. What if Zac gets hurt? What if this John bloke is all in and then not, and he just disappears? I study music, not psychology, but it doesn't take a shrink to work out that Zac's obsessive need to stand by me is because this man spectacularly failed to do as much for his own mum. Hmm, thinking about it like that, in a perverse way maybe I owe this John Harding dude. Maybe I should agree to meet him.

'Look, it's going to be a bit awkward, but I need to have him there,' says Zac now.

'Why?'

He shrugs. Although he has good shoulders and forearms, his back is scrawny. Even through his T-shirt I can see the bumps of his spine, standing out like crustaceans on a rock. Curved away from me. I trail my finger up each vertebra. They rise and fall as he takes deep breaths. This is when I feel our age, or lack of it. Twenty-one, right, is older than anything I've ever been before, and I'm no longer a teenager, so ancient in some ways, but not really. When I see his scrawny back, he looks lost. Like, even younger than me. He's a year older, but right now he seems as though he's in Year 6 and just lost his favourite Pokémon card.

He sighs. 'Honestly, I don't know. Maybe to shame him. Maybe to give him a second chance. I want him to see me do what he didn't.'

'To prove you're the better man?'

'Just to prove it can be done.' He turns to me and holds my gaze, his eyes slicing through me. Intense. I have to look away. The moment depresses me; it feels like the one when the day sinks and the light is swallowed but night-time with its excitement and possibilities has not emerged, the bars, music, laugher, loving. We sit in the limbo. A no-man's-land. It's sad, airless. But it passes; the raw, difficult, exposed moment dissolves. Time strides on. You just have to get through it.

From what Zac tells me, since his mum married Neil, they've been a happy family, a strong unit. He says he can't remember much about when it was just him and his mum, he was too young. However, Clare made the decision to fill him in on the missing years. It wasn't that she wanted to remind her boy of the poverty, struggle and insecurity they'd endured; her recounting of history came from a good place. I get it. She wanted her son to be grateful to Neil, glad of him, and to bond with him. Neil came through with a big heart, a steady income and a willing commitment to show up at the side of a football pitch, at parents' evenings and cub camp. He's done the heavy lifting for years. He *is* the dad. Zac says Clare always maintained that the one-night stand was insignificant. A sort of unrequested sperm donation. But the thing is, her narrative, the one where things were bad and bleak until Neil turned up – a knight in shining armour – did leave Zac with a fear of poverty, struggle and instability. I know he's worried about money for us. He's brought it up a few times, so I'm not surprised when he adds, 'Besides, John is worth something now, I think. He seems minted. You know that when they meet, they are all going to be focused on the practicalities.

Where we'll live, how will we afford it, et cetera. He's never paid my mum a penny for my upkeep. The least he can do is cough up something now.'

This makes me feel a bit icky. I hate people obsessing about money or faking it with people who have money for some sort of gain. It's vulgar. Dad says my position is right, but also privileged. I consider that Zac might be just saying this crass thing to look less emotional about wanting his bio dad involved in his world. Admitting to needing money is less exposing than admitting to needing love, I guess. I try to make him feel better about coming from fuckwit genes. 'To be fair, he didn't know you existed, so he could hardly contribute,' I point out. 'I guess that's on your mum.' Zac just stares at me and doesn't reply.

You know, Philip Larkin got it dead right. 'They fuck you up, your mum and dad. They may not mean to, but they do.' I studied that poem at A level. It got a lot of buy-in from the entire class of Year 13s.

Preach.

SEVEN DAYS BEFORE THE END

15

Connie

28 December

She had to tell Luke, she couldn't put it off any longer. She knew that, and yet Boxing Day had come and gone, absorbed in an urgent demand for food and entertainment, a complicated criss-crossing of guests and relatives that she was glad to hide behind. On the twenty-seventh, Luke met up with his friends to play golf. He came home late and a little inebriated; he'd won the game. She told herself it would be mean to spoil his day. Fran had not been able to persuade Zac to delay the inevitable, so she had to bite the bullet. There had been about fifty occasions today when she'd tried to find a way into the conversation. And failed. She'd barely slept since Christmas Day. She'd spent the nights lying awake staring at the ceiling, listening to the percussion of the house, the floorboards groaning when someone got up to go to the loo, someone coughing, someone else snoring. Normally she loved everyone being here, under one roof – her husband, offspring and parents. Normally it made her feel secure and full. Now she simply felt aware that if anything should go badly, everyone dear to her would witness her humiliation.

Her night-time worrying had led to further concerns. She suspected one of her daughters had started smoking. She'd heard the back door open and shut at about 2 a.m. last night; she'd found a stub on the path this morning. She'd need to tackle that issue too. Fran was pregnant, so she'd ruled her out (please God!). Sophie probably wouldn't have the nerve to leave her room – much more likely to lean out of the window – so Flora was the most credible suspect. How much control could Connie wield over her eighteen-year-old? If she wanted to smoke, could she stop her? They were so desperate to grow up. She wanted to tell them that adulthood wasn't the finish line they might imagine. It was when exams were over that the big tests of life would begin. An awful thought occurred to her. Was their desperation to grow up because they wanted to leave her behind?

She slipped between the sheets, and while she waited for Luke to finish in the bathroom, she rubbed cream into her hands and tried to silence her internal monologue, which bounced from noting the dark spots and prominent veins to wondering whether there was any possible way she could just avoid telling Luke this awful news about Zac's parentage. Luke would never directly ask her if she was OK, if anything was the matter. It wasn't his style. He expected her to tell him if there was a problem. Usually she spewed up her every thought as she formed them. He often teased her about her stream of consciousness and suggested she use her internal voice more. He wasn't a fan of open-ended questions or discussing emotions, and since Fran had announced her pregnancy, he'd doubled down on his commitment to avoiding both. Was there a chance that he might fail to recognise John Harding? They'd only met once, as far as she knew, and that was a quarter of a century ago. But she couldn't manage to be self-delusional enough to think that was a realistic course. It was ludicrous. Even if she happened to get lucky and Luke didn't recognise his face, he'd recognise the name in an instant. Besides, the moment John walked through the door, he would give the game away.

John was going to love this.

He used to thrive on drama and chaos. Especially of his own making. It was just a matter of how much damage he would want to inflict. Would he take a sniper's aim just at Luke, or would he want to lob in a grenade and blow everything apart by telling everyone of their past? She had to silence him. Fran must not find out that her mother had had an affair, let alone that she'd had an affair with Zac's father. Hell, no.

As Luke got into bed next to Connie, he said, 'Do you want to read, honey? Or get an early night?'

Connie launched in. 'She loves him now, but it will turn sour. Everything always does.'

'Wow.' Luke looked startled and a bit amused. She found his amusement vaguely patronising. 'That's a very un-Connie Baker thing to say. *We* haven't soured. We are still madly in love twenty-nine years after meeting one another.'

'Oh, Luke.' She envied his certainty. His clarity on the matter. His childlike belief in the phrase 'madly in love'. What did that even mean at their age? She did love him. Of course she did. And yes, they had almost three decades under their belt, but that wasn't a guarantee. It wasn't enough. Nothing ever would be. She feared that what they had was about to sour.

'You seem agitated, Con. You haven't been yourself for

a few days.' He'd created an opening. She could tell him if she wanted.

'Well, it's Christmas, it's stressful. People can't be expected to be happy at Christmas,' she muttered.

'Actually, I think that's exactly what they are expected to be.'

'You know what I mean. Not all the time. We're dealing with a lot here.'

Luke rolled onto his side, so that he was facing her. He propped himself up on his elbow. 'I thought you were on board with this.'

'It's not the baby. I am on board with that. I want to be supportive and there for them. But— it's John Harding.' She spat the name out like a curse. *Macbeth* in the theatre of their bedroom, a tragedy in their marriage. Luke's face immediately tightened. His entire being curled in on itself; an effort to shield, probably. So, he recognised the name. The years hadn't eroded its power. He tensed, waiting for whatever blow might rain down on him.

'What about him?'

'He's Zac's father.'

'What? No. Zac's father is called Neil. What are you talking about?'

'Biological father.'

'You have to be joking.' Luke slowly, deliberately pulled back the duvet and got out of bed. A stony rage. He stood statue-still for a moment, unsure as to what he was going to do next, just certain that he couldn't lie next to his wife. Normally he wore his age well. Slim, tall and blond, with just a smattering of silver in his hair and enough wrinkles to make him look wise, trustworthy, experienced. Now, suddenly, he looked aged and brittle. Grey, sunken and old, but somehow simultaneously like a child, fragile, lost. He shook his head, scrunched his face into an uncomprehending scowl.

'It's not ideal,' Connie admitted, running for cover beneath the understatement of the century. Even though she'd been torturing herself with this since the moment she'd feared it might be the case, she knew her job now was to minimise the size of the problem, to reassure and make light of it. 'Look, it's history. This doesn't have to be anything bigger than what we make it.' She wanted this more than she believed it. She doubted this situation would stay within their control. 'I just need you to have the facts.'

'Which are?'

Connie brought Luke up to date with what she'd learnt from Zac; when she finished, he groaned.

'The man's a bloody wrecking ball. Wherever he goes, there's destruction.' It was hard to disagree. She shrugged. Luke misinterpreted her gesture of acceptance of the sad truth of what he was saying, and instead thought she was being flippant. 'You seem OK with this. Pleased even. You're glad he's back, aren't you?' he accused.

'No. God, no. I've just had a little longer to process it, so I'm more resigned.'

'How long have you known this?' he asked angrily, his face a jagged piece of glass. 'More secrets, Connie!'

'No, I . . . There was . . . there *is* a resemblance.' She tried to explain. 'I've feared this from the moment I saw Zac, but I didn't want to say anything to you because you'd have thought I was obsessing about John or something.' Luke glared. 'I only had it confirmed when I spoke to Zac on Christmas Day.'

'*Three* days ago.'

'I was trying to find the best time to tell you. I didn't want to spoil Christmas. I don't see how you knowing sooner would have helped. I'm not OK with this, but I'm just trying to make the best of it, for Fran's sake,' Connie said.

'For your sake, you mean.' His words were snarled. She didn't recognise his tone. Certainly didn't like it.

'We need to contain this. I admit I would die of shame if the girls ever knew about my past. But also think how complex it would be for Fran.'

'You mean how complex it *is* for Fran. This is a reality.'

'Well, only if she finds out.'

'No, Connie, that's not how it works. It's a fact either way.' Luke shook his head. 'He's going to be in our life for ever.'

'Right. But nurture is a more dominant factor than nature, isn't it?' Connie was thinking about Zac being Fran's partner. Would he treat her well, or would he be an irresponsible, womanising bastard who brought her nothing but heartache and disappointment, attributes she couldn't help but still pin to John Harding? Her greatest concern was not that she'd be exposed and shamed, but that her daughter was heading for a lifetime of heartache. 'I'm worried for Fran.'

But she realised Luke hadn't got that far in his thinking when he said, 'That man is *my* grandchild's other grandfather. We're going to be related.'

'Well, not exactly. I don't know if there's a name for that relationship.'

'Blood.' One word, but a thousand connotations and contradictions. Blood: it meant so much, everyone agreed on that, even if they couldn't agree on it representing heart or hate, loyalty or war, vitality or gore. Life or death. She wondered which Luke meant in that moment. 'I'm going to sleep in the spare room,' he muttered sulkily.

'You can't, Luke, Mum and Dad are in there.'

'On the sofa, then.'

She held out her hand towards him. 'All the kids are home. You'll upset them. It's Christmas.' She didn't want there to be a scene, a problem. It was unfair. She'd worked for the last twenty-four years of her marriage to repair and build up what she'd damaged in that first year. Yet it might all still come crumbling down. 'Come back to bed,' she pleaded. She had planned to tell him everything, but he was making it difficult for her. She wasn't blaming him, exactly; she realised the fault was all hers, the responsibility, the mess, all hers. The reaction was his, though. If he'd been a touch more temperate, she could perhaps have found a way to tell him that this wasn't the first time John Harding had popped up in her life unexpectedly since the affair.

He'd re-emerged when Fran was almost five, Flora still in a pushchair. That thought made her burn with fury and embarrassment. She would always remember how Fran's first term of primary school – which was saturated with an almost debilitating sense of fear over whether her little girl would settle in and make friends – was further challenged by the chance that John would appear at the school gates and attempt to blow up her life. In a tricky twist of fate, he was lifelong friends with Mr Walker, the primary school headmaster, aka Craig, the man her friend Rose went on to marry. 'It's a small world after all' wasn't necessarily something Connie always revelled in.

Over the past day or so, she'd wondered about the fact

that she couldn't quite seem to shed him from her life. He always popped up. Some might think that was fate. Destiny. She shivered at the idea. Recoiled. She had to believe she was more in control of things than that.

The last time John Harding had stumbled into her life, he had been a lost divorcee, licking his wounds after a brief marriage and inclined to fond reminiscing about opportunities past. She'd fallen under that umbrella, and he'd half-heartedly flirted with her, talking affectionately of their affair, viewing it through rose-tinted glasses, although when it had been going on, he'd been significantly less romantic about it. Then, he'd viewed her through the sort of sharp but illusory vision that is created by alcohol, lines of cocaine and high-octane sex.

It was a matter of pride to her that she had not fallen for his charms at that second encounter; she barely glanced his way except with trepidation that he'd rock the boat. She loved Luke and her family too much to be sidetracked. But she had never told Luke that John knew Craig, that he had for a few months occasionally turned up at the school gates and other places in a vague attempt to pursue her or corrupt her or whatever. She'd begged Rose and Craig not to mention the connection either, and although both were scrupulously honest types, they were also realists and had accepted that it would cause unnecessary hurt and complications. So they'd agreed to keep shtum. Rose had insisted that it would come out at some point, but when John had been unable to attend their wedding because he was working in America, the imperative to come clean about the connection was put on the back burner. His name had never come up over the years, and Connie had let herself stop worrying that it ever would. She should have known her luck would run out.

It was too late to confess now. If she did, she knew they'd row into the night. There would be hiss-whispered recriminations, accusations of betrayal and deceit. She was too tired for that. It would only complicate things further and they both needed a good night's sleep. They had to support Fran to the best of their ability tomorrow; it wouldn't help if they were weary. It surprised Connie sometimes how practical and clear-sighted she could be if her daughters' needs were involved.

'He'll be here tomorrow,' muttered Luke, shaking his head slowly, sorrowfully.

'Yes.'

'In my house.'

'It's *our* house. I feel the same outrage as you do.'

'No, Connie. You don't.' Luke stared at her, his expression blasting shards of anger and hurt directly into her core.

'We don't need to rake it over. That's not going to help. Please, come back to bed. Please.' Pleading with her husband wasn't undignified. Perhaps it should have been, but a long marriage eroded that sort of thing: embarrassment, dignity, awkwardness, apportioning of blame; at least she thought a good one did. Those flaws no longer had a sense of disaster or gravitas. That was the majesty of marriage. And the tragedy.

He did return to bed, slowly, reluctantly. He flicked off the side light. Turned away from her. She didn't have the confidence to shuffle up to him, to press her body into his, but she was relieved when he said, 'Don't forget to set the alarm. We have an early start tomorrow.'

16

Zac

'Where are you going?' Fran's breath smelt of sticky sleep and pickles. She'd been craving pickles of all kinds: onions, dills, even walnuts. He was surprised that her iffy breath made him feel happy rather than off-put, although he hadn't wanted to wake her and felt disconcerted that he'd been caught sneaking out of bed.

'I thought I heard Asti scratching at the door. I was just going down to check on him.' His lie whispered into the air.

'I didn't realise you liked dogs so much,' murmured Fran.

'Yeah, I do.' Zac didn't elaborate. He and Fran locked eyes, both daring one another to say something more, both hoping they would not. If it wasn't said, it wasn't a thing. She gave a small, sharp nod and didn't offer to accompany him. Why would she? It was 2 a.m. and warm in bed. He hid behind the fact that there was still a lot they didn't know about one another, and neither wanted to draw attention to as much. In truth, he was slightly allergic to dogs; spending so much time with Asti was making his nose run and eyes sting. He was allowing Fran's family to think he had a cold. The dog was the only excuse he had for nipping out of the house, alone, at any given hour. In other families over the Christmas period it might be possible to pretend you were helpfully heading to the shops to buy a jar of cranberry sauce or more milk, but Fran's mother was like one of those uber hosts who had everything anyone might want. He couldn't work out how she did it. Henry, the slightly nerdy and arrogant twin, and Fran's grandfather had both amused themselves with testing the capacity of Connie's hospitality. On a few occasions they'd requested very specific foodstuffs, including but not limited to pickled gherkins, creamed horseradish and chocolate-covered dates. She'd been able to supply everything so far. Every time she dug around the cupboards or fridge and then triumphantly laid her hands on the requested goods, the girls and the twins laughed as though her devotion was something that should be ridiculed. Zac felt embarrassed for them all.

He sneaked downstairs quietly, carefully, his way lit by the torch on his phone. It was enough that he'd woken Fran; he didn't want to alert anyone else. He was getting to know the Bakers' house; he'd learnt which doors creaked and which floorboards groaned so he could avoid them. It surprised him how quickly he'd adapted to being sneaky. He didn't consider himself a sneak. He didn't consider himself shifty, dodgy, devious, dishonest.

Criminal.

Did anyone ever? He thought he was one of the good blokes. At least he had. But he wasn't. Not any more.

He slipped his feet into his boots. He wasn't wearing socks, but that didn't bother him. He tucked in the laces, didn't stop to tie them, never did. Asti let out one bark. It was sort of questioning. Zac hushed him. 'Good boy, quiet now.' The dog looked through him, as though he had the measure. Zac clipped the lead to his collar and dragged him outside, although he was reluctant to go out into the cold night. Walking the dog was his cover. He could say he thought Asti needed a pee, that was why he was unsettled. Besides the cover, a reasonably stocky dog was a bit of extra something. Protection.

Fuck. He needed protection.

They were waiting for him. They always were, even when he turned up early. Normally the person or people kept waiting lacked the agency, not in this case. They had all the power. They were showing him they were always ahead, always ready for him. He still didn't know their names. There had never been any level of formal introduction. It wasn't that sort of relationship. He knew who they worked for. A man known as Bear. It should have been laughable, but it wasn't, it was terrifying. Zac couldn't imagine anyone had ever laughed at Bear's name. No one called him Teddy Bear or Running Bear or even Grizzly Bear. People had told Zac stories. It was well known that Bear could and would pummel a man to death; urban myth would have you believe he'd rip off limbs, if he wanted. Chew your face, snap your neck. Not that he had to do anything so involved any more. His gang carried knives and guns. He could teach you a lesson from a distance. Punish you without getting blood on his hands. But if he chose to torture you personally, he was up to it. Up for it. Everyone knew that. It was a fact as cold and hard as a blade. And if that wasn't enough, Zac remembered that they knew his name, and hers, and now they knew where he drank and where her parents lived. They knew too much.

He thought back to the beginning of this year, when he'd first encountered them. He'd been working in London for a few months on his placement. The work was good but his social life sucked. He was feeling the pinch of homesickness after having a decent Christmas break with his family. He'd been bitterly disappointed that he'd arrived in London oozing excitement and hope, which was crushed because he couldn't make mates. That seemed such a bougie problem now. Thinking that he was missing out on what London had to offer, getting bored of the four walls of his tiny room in his scruffy flatshare. If only he'd been content to stay in every night and watch YouTube videos on his phone. Everything would be very different now.

The night he met them started so normally. Just ordinary. One decision leading to the next, nothing complicated, nothing ambitious. Just a slate-grey normality. He had been out trying to find that elusive good time. It was harder to make friends than people imagined. Everyone in his office was old and rushed home to the kids and their partners the minute the clock said 5.30. He was missing Fran. They weren't a *thing*, but they'd had something and even then he thought she was special, so killing time with Tinder dates just didn't appeal. Many nights he found himself going to pubs alone, nursing a criminally expensive pint and trying to strike up conversations with randoms. It was sometimes successful, sometimes soul-destroying. He felt like a scrape, which was not something he was familiar with. At school, college and uni he had loads of mates.

That night, *the night*, as he thought of it now, started off seemingly lucky. He met some Irish lads in a pub. They were a laugh. Noisy, fun, put him in mind of his mates at uni. It was close to midnight when they'd decided to move on to a club, but the problem was, they couldn't all fit in one Uber. He and one other bloke held back, tried to secure a second car. They'd left the pub, cut through an alleyway that opened onto a road in front of the river, hoping to get a clear pin drop for a pickup. They just had to walk through the smell of piss, the litter and rats. If only that had been the worst of it. Zac remembered his mood; he'd been a bit miffed to be left with this one dude, Rob, who didn't seem to be part of the core group either. He was trying to shrug off the feeling that they – the hangers-on – had been ditched deliberately. He didn't know if the bloke was just drunk or high, but he was crap company. He was jumpy and talked a lot of shit. Stuff about gangs and drugs. Zac tried to blank him out. He should have listened closely. Rob presented like a borderline conspiracy theorist freak, and the freezing-cold night was crashing his mood. He was debating whether to bother trying to get to Clapham and find the Irish posse or just call it a night and go back to his flat. The place was a pigsty: damp, tiny, smelly. If it had been one iota more charming, he might have turned round, headed to the Tube. He wouldn't have witnessed the mugging. That was what he'd thought it was at first. Some chancers trying to relieve the jumpy, annoying bloke of his expensive phone.

It wasn't that.

It all happened so quickly, he didn't understand it. There were two of them beating down on Rob. Kicking the shit out of him. Vicious. Christ, it was shocking. One minute Rob was standing next to him, the next he was lying on the floor curved into a question mark trying to protect his stomach, his head. He was bleeding because he'd been kicked in the face. There was a lot of blood. 'Give them the fucking phone!' Zac screamed. But they already had the phone, why weren't they running away? He didn't know what to do. Rob shouted, 'Zac, help me. Help. Zac, help.' Zac would never forget that. He did try to intervene. He'd pulled at the attackers, clawed and shoved at them, trying to get them off Rob. He'd even thrown a few punches. His instinctual physical response surprised him as much as it surprised the guy who took the blows. He'd never hit anyone since he was about seven, when he'd sometimes scrapped inexpertly in the school playground. Because he didn't know better, he made a fist with his thumb tucked inside; he hurt his thumb, thought for a while he'd broken it.

Later, he wondered if by fighting back they'd seen something in him. Would it have all landed differently if he'd just got away as soon as possible? Left them to it.

It didn't matter what he did anyhow. They were far more savage and expert than he was. They batted him away as easily as if they were swatting a fly and continued to lay into Rob. Zac wanted to stay and help, he definitely wanted to think he was the sort of person who might save the day, but he was as scared as shit and so he started to run. He could call the police from a distance, that was the best thing to do.

He ran hard and fast and his feet slammed into the pavement sending shocks through his core, making his brain rattle. He didn't dare head back up the lonely alley, the way they'd come: what if there were more of them? He didn't know for sure, but he already sensed that it wasn't a straightforward mugging. He ran along the river, towards a more touristy and therefore safer part of the city. As he ran, he bumped shoulders with people milling. After the fifth or sixth bump, he realised he was surrounded by lots of ordinary people who were simply going about their business, looking at the lit-up bridges, buying a burger from a van, vaping. He felt sick and yet strangely elated as the distance between him and the attack grew. While he was ashamed of running, he also felt something like triumph that he'd got the hell out of there. Whenever he remembered that brief feeling of relief now, he felt like shit. Two reasons: a) because people (himself included) weren't as good as they thought they were, and b) because he hadn't got out of anything; he was so badly mistaken about that.

When he stopped running, he bent double and fought the urge to vomit. He wasn't sure why he needed to puke, maybe the exertion. Maybe fear. Breathing heavily, sweating, he reached for his phone. He had to call for an ambulance and the police; the muggers had most likely left the scene now, but Rob needed help.

The message was the first thing he saw. It was from Rob.

Don't think of squealing Zac. We'll be in touch. We cud swing by ZapionTec.

He didn't understand it. It took him a second to realise that the message wasn't from Rob, but from the muggers. They had Rob's phone, of course. They wouldn't want Zac to call the police. How did they know where he worked? His brain seemed to be resisting piecing it together, as though on some subconscious level he already knew he was into something ugly but he didn't want to process it, accept it. Rob had asked for his number at the beginning of the evening, when they had all been talking about footie. He'd said he was in a local club, that he went to an organised session on Thursdays. Zac had just wanted to make some friends, take some exercise. He had told Rob where he worked, so they could decide on the feasibility of the kickabout. Rob had entered those details into his phone. Zac had felt a bit smug at the time, secretly proud when he gave the company name and address; both were impressive. He'd done well. Rob and the Irish blokes had taken the piss for a few minutes, the ultimate boy-compliment to show they were impressed with his placement. He felt ridiculous now. Desperate. If only he hadn't given his deets.

The image of their boots backwards and forwards, slamming into Rob, exploded in his mind. Rob's flesh splitting, the bloody boot prints on the pavement. He thought he remembered a tooth lying on the ground. It didn't feel standard. It was horrifying. His hand ached with throwing just a few punches. What state must Rob be in?

That was that, right? Rob would be making his way to a hospital now. He'd be OK.

No, he wouldn't, because how could he get to hospital? Without his phone, he would be in trouble, no chance of an Uber, unlikely to have cash on him. If he had, they'd have taken it. Would a cabbie pick him up? Doubtful. None of them wanted trouble, and a beaten, bleeding man was trouble.

Zac leant back against the wall of a building. He didn't know which building or how long he stayed there. Many minutes, he supposed, because the cold damp of the bricks seeped through his clothes, settled into his bones. He was frozen. He still felt shit about that now, thinking back to everything. That, more than anything, those minutes that passed. He realised now that, most likely, he was in actual medical shock, but still he felt like shit. What if he'd moved faster? Responded quicker?

Around him he heard people going about enjoying their night. Laughing, chatting, arguing; he saw them kissing the faces off each other or hurrying through the cold. It felt like he was watching them from behind glass. He thought about when he was a little kid and believed that the people on the TV were inside the box. It felt like that, like he was separate. And the funny thing was, he didn't know it then, but he *was* separate from normal life from that night on. There was a divide and he was on the wrong side of it. Eventually he started to process what had happened, he felt a sense of responsibility creep, and then pump and flow, through his body. It was as though his blood had slowed, as though he'd almost died but then he'd come back to life. If he wasn't going to call the police, then he had to go back and help.

And he wasn't going to call them.

Yeah, he'd been brought up with a healthy respect for authority but also a healthy fear of violence. In this case, the latter won out, hands down. They had his number. They had warned him. They could find him at his office. He didn't want any trouble at work. What if he got kicked off his internship? What if the uni heard and he got kicked off his course? This thing, whatever it was, could escalate.

And what was this thing? More than a mugging. They had the phone within seconds. Why didn't they just leave with that? Then it occurred to him exactly why not. They had come for Rob, not the phone. Why? This was bad. He told himself he didn't really know Rob, surely he didn't owe him anything. But he did, he owed him common decency. What if he was unconscious? What if no one found him? Zac knew he'd have to go back, offer help and support, however terrifying that prospect was.

He ran back to the alleyway. Well, he did a sort of scout's pace. Ran as much as he could, then jogged a bit. He definitely hurried but he couldn't get to full pelt, the way he had when he'd run away. He'd have to live with that for the rest of his life too. His legs were shaking. They wouldn't cooperate. He wanted to think it was from exhaustion or adrenalin, but he thought it was maybe fear.

He arrived to see them covering Rob's body with a police sheet. He was a body by then. Zac couldn't get close; the police were cordoning off the area and asking people to step back. A small crowd had gathered. A girl was crying on her boyfriend's shoulder; the boyfriend was talking to the police, confirming he'd called it in. 'We cut through the alley, we stepped on him,' the guy said, his horror and disbelief tangible. Infectious. Zac felt drenched in it. He watched as a police person in a white plastic suit took photos of the bloody boot prints and tagged the area. It started to rain; the police appeared concerned about that. Zac found himself feeling relieved. The police systematically made their way around the crowd. They asked the same questions of everyone. Zac explained he'd been drinking at a nearby pub, said he'd just arrived. No, he hadn't seen anything odd. No, he hadn't seen anyone run away from the scene. No, he hadn't seen anything at all. The words tumbled out of his mouth. He kept his bruised hand in his pocket and was glad it was dark. They didn't take his address. Across the cordoned-off area, he thought he saw one of the blokes who'd done the beating. A fleeting moment.

He almost pointed him out, almost called out to him, but he was gone in a second and maybe Zac had imagined him. Maybe he'd never been there.

Zac had walked swiftly to the Tube station, made his way home. It was a twelve-minute walk from his local station to his flat. He'd known he was being followed. Sensed it. His skin stung, his scalp shrank. There were eyes on him. He didn't turn around. He was pretty sure someone was there, but if he didn't turn, it wouldn't be confirmed, he could tell himself he was imagining it. As he put the key in the lock, he felt his phone buzz. Once the door was closed behind him, he leant against it and pulled the phone out of his pocket. A message from Rob's phone.

Nice place.

It wasn't. The comment was facetious. Simply letting him know they knew where he lived.

A second buzz.

Job opportunity has come up. Interview tomorrow @11

It wasn't an invitation, it was an order. There was the name of a café and a pin drop. The words felt like blows. Zac immediately googled the venue. It was a dive in east London, far from anywhere he usually hung out. His phone buzzed again.

Sleep well.

Yeah, right. As if. He didn't know it at the time, but he would never sleep well again.

SIX DAYS BEFORE THE END

17

Connie

29 December

Seeing him was awful. He'd aged, and she hated that. He was still twinkling, and she hated that too.

The morning prep had been torturous. Luke had watched her like a hawk, assessing if she was buoyant or trying too hard, noticing if she plumped cushions or plucked her eyebrows, judging it. She'd wanted to go to the hairdresser's for a quick blow-dry but hadn't dared mention as much to Luke who had barely said a word this morning and was struggling to stay civil to Connie, to Zac, to Fran. He hadn't yet picked his enemy; he hadn't decided who to blame for this mess so he was tetchy with them all. Connie told her reflection that she didn't need a professional blow-dry and tried not to spend longer than usual in front of the bathroom mirror. She hated that she cared how she looked to him.

Clare and Neil and their daughter, Celeste, arrived first. Connie was relieved about that. She had wanted to give them at least a few minutes of her undivided attention, and she knew once he arrived that would be impossible. Once he was in the room, she'd struggle to concentrate on them or anyone. She was a moth. He was a flame. She could already smell her wings burning. She hoped those few minutes with Zac's family might secure her some goodwill, allow her to create a favourable impression, something she might need to rely on later down the line. She was depending on his tardiness. She sighed, recognising again that the only thing that was ever dependable about him was how frequently he disappointed people. She held a hope that he'd fail to show altogether. Maybe he'd change his mind about wanting to get to know his son. He might step back into the shadows, disappear. Zac would be disappointed, of course, but in the long run it might be the better option.

She had these thoughts as she passed around the bowls of nuts and listlessly offered mince pies, aware that no one ever still fancied a mince pie this far into the season. She made conversation with Clare and Neil, tried to focus. They were a pleasant couple, willing to like what they found and to be found likeable. They negotiated the awkward moments of juggling food and cups of tea and conversation. They touched politely on matters of home decor and their journey to London. They didn't talk about the pregnancy. The mother seemed a little more on edge, the sharper of the pair. Connie thought the lacing of spikiness came from a determination to show she wasn't a fool, that she wasn't easily impressed, that she knew her worth and her son's. She recognised the other mother's vulnerability, which presented as aggression; she had spent time suppressing something similar on occasion.

'Lovely tree. Very traditional,' commented Clare, alighting on another safe topic. Connie started talking about where each ornament came from, then realised it was a dull conversation so stopped mid-sentence.

'We never bother with a real one,' chipped in Neil, no doubt desperate to avoid a silence.

Clare explained, 'It's hard enough lugging a plastic tree down from the attic. The idea of going to a garden centre or something.' She shook her head. 'I don't like the needles dropping. There's enough work at Christmas without causing it.'

Connie agreed that real trees did cause extra work, she remarked that plastic trees had a kitsch charm. Her comment came out sounding far from the compliment she'd intended.

Possibly to change the subject, Neil said, 'It will all be different next year, with a nipper about.' He shook his head – something like wonder, Connie surmised, but maybe it was shock or resignation.

'Yes.'

'Right.'

'Indeed.'

The room fell into the silence they'd all dreaded as everyone thought about just how different everything would be. Northerners, like Connie, they reminded her of those she had left behind when she came to London aged twenty-one. For this reason she felt close to them and could imagine calling them family. She wished she was meeting them in five to eight years' time. That would have been perfect.

At that moment the doorbell rang, sending an electric shock through the elephant in the room, and Connie realised with a sinking feeling that she'd frittered away her precious moments with Neil and Clare. She'd done little to endear herself, nothing to explain. Now her time was up. No one stirred. There was a second buzz.

Luke stared at Connie. His face a challenge and an accusation. The minute she stood up, he rose too, perhaps thinking better of allowing her to open the door to John Harding alone. He trailed after her. Zac followed behind.

'I'd better go too,' said Fran, shrugging apologetically at Clare, Neil and Celeste.

Connie flung open the door. He was not looking her way; he was gazing down their elegant tree-lined street. He'd rung the bell and then glanced about, taking in the surroundings, taking up the space. She would never have done that. When she visited anyone and rang their bell, her eyes remained trained on the door, waiting for it to open. She always wanted the host to know she was excited, expectant. He either wasn't those things, or if he was, he didn't care about his host knowing as much. His gaze rarely stayed fixed; she remembered that. He'd once said to her that he struggled to commit to anything, anyone, that he was easily distracted. He described himself as fickle, lazy and selfish. But she'd ignored him. Only heard the challenge, not the warning. He'd said he could be distracted by other women, football on TV, even a sweet wrapper fluttering down the street. Now, she glanced along her quiet road, expecting to see a cat or something that had caught his eye.

When he did turn to her, it felt like he moved in slow motion as the new image of him lodged in her consciousness. It was as though she was looking at him through a kaleidoscope that was being turned; the colours danced, morphed and then resettled into a new pattern. It took just a few fleeting moments for John as he was now to chase away the image that had secretly nestled in her head for many years. An image she very occasionally dredged up, to play with when she needed to. Not when she was masturbating, nothing as obvious, but when she was reminiscing, when she was drunk, when she couldn't stop herself.

She remembered his skin as thin, translucent, almost transparent, a sprinkling of freckles, raw and shiny. Zac had that skin. Now, John's skin was thicker, lined, tanned. A tan in late December said he was wealthy enough to travel. It suited him. She recalled Zac mentioning that his bio dad had been in the Caribbean for Christmas. Who with? she wondered now. She used to believe that John would only ever be at home in a nippy, bitter environment, chasing around a football pitch or energetically jumping up and down on the spot, waiting for a pub to open; he was a fidget, always clapping his hands together, tapping his fingers to the beat of whatever music was playing, or busy lighting a cigarette. Apparently he could settle on a sunlounger now. His hairline was receding; what was left was grey. Yet his five o'clock shadow was dark even though it was only lunchtime. She liked it that something about him still said rebel. He hadn't felt compelled to shave to meet his son's girlfriend's family. But maybe she should have been rolling her eyes for that exact reason. There were some other things that remain unaltered. She shouldn't dwell on them, but his lips were still full, turned up, ready to smile. His eyes were still too big, too blue. He stared at her, his perennial unfair advantage wide open with surprise. No one on the planet had eyes that sparkled the way his did, with mischief and fun and life. But right then, his eyes were not glittering with mischief; instead they were clouded with confusion.

'Connie?' He looked thoughtful and sincere. Adult. That confounded her. His demeanour was wary, hurt. He'd taken some hits. Who hadn't?

Before Connie could respond, Zac darted past her and threw his arms around his dad. Side by side, their height, stature, jawlines mirrored one another, but Zac did not look like his father now, he looked like his father had once been. How she remembered. John hugged his son with both arms, slapped him on the back. He oozed pride and excitement with his boy in his arms. The moments fluttered and the readjustment solidified. This new John Harding had completely ousted the old one. All she was left with was her daughter's boyfriend's biological father. Nothing more.

'This is Fran,' said Zac as he broke from the hug. He gestured past Connie, past Luke to where Fran was hovering in the hallway.

John turned to Connie's daughter but didn't seem to understand what was being said. 'You're Fran?'

'And these are her parents, Luke and Connie,' Zac added. 'Sorry, I should have said that. I'm making a mess of the introductions.'

'These are your parents?' John looked dazed. He clearly couldn't take it in. Connie considered for the first time what this must be like for him. He had been expecting to meet the woman with whom he'd had a one-night stand that had led to the birth of a son he'd only recently heard of; that must already be daunting enough. He no doubt was hoping to bond further with his son and make a decent impression on Zac's girlfriend and her family. Now he was faced with the fact that Luke and Connie were her parents. His eyes dropped to Fran's bump. Oh yes, and that too: he was going to be a grandad. Connie wished she could have given him a heads-up. 'Bloody hell,' he muttered.

'Well, that's not the usual greeting,' said Zac with a laugh. 'But I guess it's an icebreaker of sorts.'

John pointed to Fran's belly. 'Are you . . .?'

'Yes,' Zac pre-emptively answered for Fran. 'Fran and I are pregnant.'

John shook his head and looked at Connie. 'And you're . . .' His eyes were as wide as saucers. Connie feared he was so stunned he might blurt everything out, so she acted to try to avoid that.

'Yes, I'm Connie, Fran's mum. This is Luke, my husband. Fran's dad.' She spoke as though she was talking to someone learning English, slowly and with careful enunciation. She threw her hand out and waited for him to shake it. He didn't. His head simply spun from Zac to Fran to Connie. She felt vaguely irritated by him. Why was he acting like this, hamming it up? Just to make her sweat? She felt Luke's hand heavy on her shoulder. He was clammy.

'Bloody hell,' John said again.

By this time Zac had started to look awkward. So did Fran. Both of them were scarlet with embarrassment and studying the floor, no doubt wondering what was going on with their parents.

'Well, we've all had quite a shock,' said Connie firmly. Fran shot her a peculiar look, something like horror or fury. Connie quickly corrected herself. 'I mean surprise.' She held the door wide open and glared at John. 'Would you like to come in and get reacquainted with Clare?' She couldn't resist that little dig. He'd asked for it by behaving like a dick often enough and for long enough. But she did need him onside, so she added, 'Let's have a drink. It's so nice to meet you.' She hoped he understood what she was saying. They had not met before. He didn't know the sound she made when she came. She hadn't nearly trashed her marriage for him. That was a different woman; that was a lifetime ago.

18

Fran

Mum predicted a shitshow. But *this*. *This* I couldn't have conjured in my worst nightmare.

'What's your biggest fear?' That's what Zac asked me just after the first time we had sex. I didn't think it was weird. I thought it was original, so I told him the truth.

'Missing chances. Not filling up my life like I know it should be filled.'

'Filling up your life? What do you mean?' It was a warm summer evening. The window was open, but only a couple of centimetres. There was a security lock on it to avoid people hurling themselves onto the pavement below. The breeze made the gauze curtains flutter.

I was high on the great sex so rushed at my answer. 'You know, with like travel and mates and sex and success at work. *Everything*. I want my life to be so full it's overflowing, gushing, a deluge.' I decided to tell him the entire theory. It wasn't a big deal; I've told other people. I talk shit a lot of the time. Everyone does. Some guys get it, others don't, some pretend to. I hoped he'd get it. 'I think of life as a sort of basin or bowl. You know, a receptacle.' He nodded. 'Some people are born with small bowls, they just are, it's bullshit pretending we're all born with the same chances and opportunities and choices. A total fairy tale. Some people get like a cake-mixing-size bowl of opportunity, others get baths, others just thimbles. I think I got like maybe one of those pop-up pools that people buy in unusually hot summers and put in their gardens.'

'And how do you grade the size of receptacle you think people get?' He sounded interested, for real.

'There are lots of factors. Geography, the place you're born matters, as does time in history, socioeconomic environment, parental devotion, physical abilities, gender, colour, aesthetic appeal, intelligence. This list is far from finite.'

'Given that's the criteria, I'd say you were born with an Olympic-size swimming pool.'

I heard the compliment and smiled at him, and murmured, 'Maybe.' I didn't tell him about the endometriosis. Infertility is not a first-date conversation. I think my container was downsized by that limitation. I didn't want to think about it. I rarely did. 'Those pop-up pools are really big, though. I know I'm lucky. That's the thing, that's what I'm afraid of. It's my responsibility to make the most of all these opportunities I've been lucky enough to land. I need to put the shift in, you know, and be good at stuff. I need to think about things and change things and speak up, because I can.' I should've felt like a dick saying that, but I was deep in the afterglow and he made me feel interesting. 'You're not stuck with the size container that you're born with; people can be born with a thimble of opportunity but die with a swimming pool. Those sorts of people are amazing. The trick is to make sure that whatever size container you get, it overflows, or grows, stretches, you know? I haven't thought through the exact science of this. My biggest fear is that I don't do enough with my life, considering the wealth of opportunities. I hate waste. I'd be ashamed and furious with myself if I let my paddling pool deflate, right?' OK, so maybe I hadn't gone into that much detail before. Largely because most people would have tuned out long before I got to this point. He didn't.

He said, 'Wow. Interesting, the meaning of life as per Fran Baker.'

I shrugged. 'Well, yeah, I'm not saying I'm starting a cult or anything. I'm just saying it's my theory.'

'What about me? What size receptacle was I born with?'

My best guess was maybe a bath. Less opportunity than me. I lied because I liked him. 'Same as me, obviously.'

'Not bigger? I'm male.'

'You're short, though.'

He laughed, like I knew he would. It's another thing that's perfect about Zac. He gets my sense of humour. 'What's *your* biggest fear?' I asked him.

'Being poor.' He didn't elaborate. And I thought it was a bit basic, so I didn't probe.

I'd answer the question differently now. There are worse things than missing an opportunity. I'm just beginning to see that taking them can be toxic too.

19

Connie

The awkwardness mounted, expanded like foam, filling every space. John did not recall Clare and he didn't even pretend to. 'Well, it was a long time ago, we've all aged,' he said, making me wonder how I ever thought he was charming. 'Maybe if you had a photo of yourself back then, it would jog my memory. But.' He shrugged, not bothering to finish the sentence, believing it to be obvious. Connie knew there had been dozens of women, maybe hundreds. Most of whom he'd had when he was drunk. A one-night stand had very little chance of being recalled through the haze of years and blur of alcohol. 'I mean, would you have recognised me if we'd passed in the street?' he asked defensively.

Connie thought she heard Luke groan. Or it might have been Zac or Neil. 'I would have, yes,' said Clare with impressive brevity and dignity. Connie felt a gentle sympathy, empathy in fact, with Clare, the other woman in the room whose life had been defined by this man's sexual prowess. God, it couldn't boil down to that, could it? It seemed so base, so barbaric, but she thought that in the end, that was what it probably amounted to.

'Right, yes. Well, it was obviously more memorable for you than me,' he said. This time everyone in the room seemed to groan, to object to his arrogance, his callous indifference. Not entirely tone-deaf, John rushed to add, 'No, no, I just mean because of Zac. I didn't know about Zac. I wish I had.'

The feelings people had for John were on a scale from irritated annoyance to outright fury, but the honesty of this desire caused a discernible shift. It was true he'd missed out. Clare could have tracked him down but for her own reasons had decided not to. She had cheated him out of something priceless, there was no denying that. That would perhaps be unpicked another day; Connie hoped John wouldn't push the point now. She wanted Zac and Fran to have a pleasant first family lunch. That wouldn't happen if people were called to account for their past actions.

It really wouldn't.

Clare seemed to want to keep things positive too. 'I didn't bring photos of me when I was young,' she said. 'But I did bring some of Zac. I thought you, or Fran, might enjoy seeing them.' She reached into her bag and pulled out a small faux-leather photo album. Zac laughingly objected, but he looked secretly excited to be the centre of attention. Clare handed the album to John, who greedily flipped through the pages, gave it his entire focus. Fran had told Connie that according to Zac, Clare maintained that John Harding hadn't mattered that much to her. She said she believed in things 'happening for a reason'. She wasn't sorry she'd met Zac's biological father, even though their encounter had been brief and left her with an unexpected number of consequences and sole responsibility. 'I got Zac, the epitome of a bundle of joy. How could I be anything but grateful to the man?' That was a magnanimous stance to take. Connie thought Clare was probably a better person than herself. She often worried that people were morally better than her. When she wasn't doing that, she was dealing with the fury that people were so obviously morally worse than her. It never ceased to surprise her how difficult it was to be human.

Did things happen for a reason? Was there a reason John had appeared in her life for a third time? Connie didn't really believe in fate. She used to, but as she'd got older, she was more inclined to believe people made their own destiny through their choices, their effort, engagement and some unaccountable level of luck. Fate, believing things were reasonable, logical, was a comfort to people who largely had had to endure disappointments and misfortune, so not a dreadful thing per se, helpful really, but a bit passive for her liking. Who could say wars, murder, paedophilia happened for a reason? That was insane.

Looking at John now, sitting in the same room as Luke, Connie couldn't think of a reason why this was meant to happen. She tried to view it with a cool clarity, in the here and now, not burdened by or buoyed up with projection or reminiscing. John was small and complicated, Luke straight as an arrow, somehow clean and correct. John didn't appear to be coping with the social situation especially well. He was struggling to make small talk and there was no evidence of his fun, spirited side, the quick mind and confident tongue that Connie remembered. Two ex-lovers, a son he hadn't been aware of and the news that he was going to be a grandfather seemed to have taken the wind from his sails. He hunched over his glass, nursed it like a toddler clinging to a security blanket. It wasn't even alcohol; he'd asked for an elderflower and sparkling water. 'Watching my cholesterol, cutting back on the booze,' he announced. Connie wondered if she'd ever been confronted with anything so astonishing and depressing.

John Harding had grown up.

Her parents were out for lunch, meeting up with one of her sisters, and Connie was relieved about that. So they were ten for lunch in total. At least it was an even number, although that didn't seem to make the seating plan any easier. Normally she was very good at working out who might chat most convivially with whom to create the most fun time for all. Today she simply couldn't muster the energy to try to control the situation; she waited to see who would sit where. John sat at the end of the table, or the top of the table, it depended on how you looked at it. He'd simply dropped into the nearest chair, but Luke thought it was a pissing contest so sat at the opposite end. The other top of the table. Oh God.

Luke invited Neil to sit on his right and Fran plonked down to her dad's left, encouraging Sophie to sit on her other side. She didn't seem interested in making conversation with any of her new family which was a little rude of her since that was the entire point of the lunch. She looked washed-out, most likely suffering with morning sickness or heartburn, Connie decided to cut her some slack; she really couldn't be bothered to force her into conversation. Experience had often shown that if she did that with any of her children, the conversation would be sulky and stilted. Zac and Flora settled on that same side of the table. Opposite them Celeste nestled between her mum and dad. When Connie brought the mango chicken curry to the table, the only remaining free chair was between Clare and John. They were steadfastly turned away from one another, John talking to Zac, Clare to Celeste. Connie considered forcing Flora to swap with her, but the idea of allowing John to cosy up with one of her daughters sent shivers up and down her spine. Flora was astute and inquisitive, John was indiscreet and unreliable; her secret was likely to be revealed before the profiteroles were served. Reluctantly she flopped into the seat next to him.

He didn't bother with small talk. He dived right in.

'So my son and your daughter are an item.' There was a lot of chatter, people were asking for the salt, the naan bread, more wine, the rice to be passed one way and then the other. Everyone had sunk gratefully into the comfort of food. She heard Sophie say to Celeste, 'Can you believe we're going to be aunties, like before GCSEs? It's unreal.' Celeste started talking about the cutest little baby socks that she'd seen on Etsy and was definitely going to buy. Clare was piling food onto Fran's plate and saying eating for two was important. Connie knew this to be scientifically incorrect. Pregnant women only needed an extra 200–400 calories a day in this middle trimester, but she didn't interfere. She was just grateful for the chatter, the clatter of crockery and clink of cutlery, which masked her whispered conversation with John.

'Yes, apparently they are.'

'Well, that's a turn-up for the books.' He shook his head. She nodded hers. 'Yes.'

'Christ, this is bloody complicated.'

'Well, not overly. Not really.' Of course it was, but Connie thought admitting as much was somehow defeatist. She didn't want to give their history any import.

John wasn't having any of it. 'Oh, it is, Greenie.' Green was Connie's maiden name. She'd already cast it off by the time she met John, but throughout their affair he'd insisted on using the derivative as his particular name for her. It was his way of denying Luke, she supposed.

'Look, we're ancient history.'

He laughed. 'Yes, we are. I am not arguing on that point.'

'They want a crack at a future.'

'Do they now? So how often have you thought of me over these past twenty years?'

She stared at him, gobsmacked at his audacity. The assumption that she might have thought of him at all.

'Every day?' he suggested. Connie barked out a shocked laugh that was also a protest or a denial. He tempered his opening bid. 'Once a week, then?'

'No, of course not,' she snapped.

'Once a month? I bet you've thought of me at least once a month, Greenie.'

'I have not. Stop calling me Greenie.' She felt colour flash through her body, and he saw it; he laughed. 'Sometimes I have forgotten to think about you for months on end, probably years, and then other times you have drifted into my mind,' she admitted. And that was the problem. She wanted to be honest with him, she didn't want to lie to him. Although since he had come into her life, all she'd ever done was lie about him. To herself, to others. To Luke most of all. Oh Lord. The thought of Luke made her skin crawl as though it was trying to creep away from her mind and not be part of this betrayal. Luke would see this as a betrayal, her talking to John in this honest, intense way. She should be sticking to small talk.

'So we can agree that over the years your thoughts about me have averaged out to about once a month,' he said, clearly determined to establish the veracity of his point that the situation was complicated.

'Probably,' she admitted with a sigh. He nodded, looking satisfied, and Connie wanted to kick herself. 'What about you? How often have you thought about me over the years?' she asked. She dared to look him in the face. Her bravery went unrewarded. He was not looking at her. He was staring down the table, almost glaring at Fran.

Then, firmly, he said, 'Never. I don't do retrospection, Greenie. You should know that about me by now.'

And she believed him. The mortification was real.

She had to bring it back to the kids. She wanted to beg him not to spoil it for them. She wanted to point out that they had enough against them without layering on any extra mess. But before she got her words out, he said, 'This can't happen.' She followed his gaze to their end of the table. Zac seemed comfortable enough, laughing and joking. Fran was poking at her food; she looked a little pale and tired. This was a lot to manage at such a young age. Connie felt a spike of defensiveness on behalf of her daughter.

'Besides our history, what's your problem?' she asked.

'They're very young.'

'I agree with you on that, but some people do manage. With the right support.'

'It's very sudden.'

'I've made the same point,' Connie admitted. 'They both seem to think this is love.'

'Do they now?' His tone was doubting. He shook his head. 'Jesus, how did he get trapped by the oldest trick in the book?'

'Excuse me!' Connie snapped. She felt stung on Fran's behalf by the accusation. Fran hadn't intended to catch Zac; the baby was an accident, but she had a right to choose to keep it. He could walk away if he wanted. Like John himself always had. And anyway, what right did John have to object to her daughter for his son? Fran was kind, brilliant, beautiful, adored. He should be ecstatic. 'You know he's very lucky to have Fran. She's an incredible person,' Connie said firmly.

'Right.' He looked unconvinced.

It took everything she had to remain calm and polite, reasonable and sensible. She picked up her fork and carefully loaded it with food; she pushed it into her mouth and made herself chew slowly. She never talked with her mouth full; this was a way of ensuring she didn't say anything she'd regret. After she'd swallowed and drunk half a glass of water, she said, 'I think, as they are in love and determined to have the baby together, our only duty here is to support.' She was using the voice she used when she spoke with particularly difficult clients.

'Too late for an abortion, is it?'

'I'm not even going to answer that.'

'You have asked, though, right? You have had the conversation so she's clear what she is getting into. This isn't like playing with dolls.'

Connie had often thought she loathed John, almost as often as she'd thought she loved him. But in this moment, she felt a very clear steely dislike that was more determined and logical than any of the emotions that had ever gone before. 'How would you know what they're getting into, John?' she challenged. 'Really? You haven't a clue. You didn't bring up your son. And God knows how many other kids you've got out there that you've dodged taking responsibility for. I'm just very glad Zac seems to be nothing like you.' It was at this point that she noticed the conversation had died around her. No one was chatting about cute baby clothes or the delicious lightly oaked Chardonnay; everyone was listening to her. 'And for the record, Fran never played with dolls. She preferred Lego and crafting.' She should have stopped there, and would have, but he was smirking. 'We had very high hopes for her and this wasn't what we wanted either. Can you imagine my horror when I found out that you are—'

'Connie!' Luke interrupted sharply.

Connie was surprised to see she was on her feet. Her knees were shaking, sweat prickling under her arms. All eyes were on her. She carefully placed her hands flat on the table. It had been a wedding gift from Luke's parents. Touching it made her think of the many hundreds, perhaps thousands of times they had gathered around it. She recalled the girls in highchairs rejecting vegetables and smearing yogurt in their hair and faces, hours rolling play dough and building with Lego; she thought of the silent, sulky teen dinners they'd endured and the noisy, laughter-filled ones they'd enjoyed. She wanted to rephrase, somehow communicate that while this hadn't been what they had wanted for Fran, they were happy to readjust their ambitions if this was what she wanted. But she couldn't be as explicit. Possibly because it would reinforce what she'd just blurted, possibly because she wasn't quite sure she believed it. Connections in her brain darted and shot like popcorn in a microwave as she scrambled to think how she could possibly finish the sentence. *Can you imagine my horror when I found out that you are—*

Zac's father.

Back in my life.

Biologically connected to my daughter's baby.

Never going away.

None of them would save the situation. She coughed and said, 'Can you imagine my horror when I found out that you're allergic to nuts? That sort of allergy might be hereditary. Now, can I get anyone anything at all? Clare, do you need your glass filling up? Sophie, perhaps you can pass the bhajis to Neil.'

John stared at her, a hard look of disappointment and disbelief. He'd wanted to provoke her. Wanted to see if he still had power over her. If she was still the woman he'd seduced. She knew he was judging her for moving so completely into middle-class territory, hiding behind good manners and keeping up appearances, leaving behind the raw anger and honesty of her working-class roots that he'd tapped into, exploited as common ground all those years ago. She'd been brought up in a house where no one shied away from a rant, a row, even throwing plates against a wall. He was probably judging her as a sell-out for not saying what she really thought.

She was congratulating herself on a level of maturity that developed when your own needs came second to keeping the peace. To protecting the feelings of your child.

20

Connie

They probably would not have managed to stumble through the whole awful business of John Harding's visit if Lucy, Peter and Auriol had not turned up and saved the day by asking if anyone wanted to join them for a walk on Hampstead Heath.

'I thought we were doing that tomorrow?' said Flora.

'Really, have I got the date wrong?' Lucy had looked astonished. She never believed she did anything wrong. Nor did Connie, who suspected Lucy had guessed the parental meet-and-greet would be a nightmare and wanted to avert that. Or to witness it: Lucy was not above a little mischief. 'Well, let's all go for the walk today, since we're here now.' Lucy turned to Zac's family and asked, 'Have you travelled far?'

'We drove down from Marple this morning.'

'Marple?'

'It's a village south of Manchester.'

'Oh.' Lucy never really knew what to say to northerners about geography as, other than a single trip to Edinburgh, she hadn't ever travelled further north than Muswell Hill.

Connie was relieved that Lucy didn't feel a need to share that information and that Peter didn't say anything facile like 'It's rather beautiful "up north", not at all grim,' as he had done before when meeting people from north of Watford Gap in a misguided attempt to appear amenable. Instead Lucy said, 'Well then, you'll want to stretch your legs and see some of London. Not just the smog, but the parks too.' She said it in a way that didn't brook any opposition. 'I've known Connie since we went to university together. I'm Fran's godmother, so we're practically family too. You don't mind us crashing your afternoon, do you?'

No one ever minded anything Lucy did or said. She was too glorious to object to. Even at fifty-five, when, if popular opinion was to be believed, women vanished, Lucy still glittered. Zac introduced John. Lucy said, 'Hello,' in her most clipped manner and drank him in. She was fully aware of all the details of his relationship with her friend and yet her face stayed entirely impassive; even Connie couldn't discern whether she was impressed or underwhelmed. He drank her in too, Connie noticed. Still had an eye, then.

The walk was a good idea, although Connie would have preferred a different park. She'd first had sex with John on Hampstead Heath. The thought scalded her from the inside. She found it hard to process that she was once so infatuated with him that al fresco sex was something she indulged in, let alone adulterous al fresco sex. She couldn't expect Lucy to have remembered the location of their first tryst. She couldn't imagine that John would, but still it felt awkward. What if he did recall and assumed her best friend was pushing him down memory lane?

A party of thirteen managed to find enough subgroups and space to kill a few hours peacefully. John said very little to anyone, which considering the thoughts he'd expressed at lunch was a relief. He looked abashed. Cowed. Small. Sulky even. Connie didn't have time to worry about him. She had to keep the show on the road. It was important to her that conversations stayed general, that everyone stayed civil.

He did not come back to the house after the walk. He got back into his Range Rover; as he drove off into the distance, Connie considered that she hadn't heard anyone make a plan to see him again. She wished that might be a permanent thing. Zac's family came in for a quick cup of tea but said they were keen to get to their Airbnb. Zac left with them. There was a sense that everyone needed to be with their own tribe. Being on best behaviour was exhausting.

Lucy, Peter and Auriol lingered the longest. Lucy loitered in the kitchen while Connie put leftovers in Tupperware boxes, wiped surfaces and avoided her friend's eye. 'So the famous John Harding, in the flesh, in your home, after all this time.'

'Don't, Lucy.'

'Don't what?'

'Don't question my sanity. You don't have to, I already am.'

'Darling, you know me, I never judge. Besides, despite his brooding act this afternoon, I appreciate his charm.'

This pleased Connie, although it shouldn't have. There was something satisfying about having Lucy's endorsement of her long-ago lover, because Lucy was hard to impress. Connie couldn't judge it any more; she had lost all sense of clarity or perspective when it came to John Harding. She was fearful she'd been seduced by someone quite ordinary. Weren't they all, in the end, quite ordinary? Wasn't everyone? Herself included? After all the passion and longing and jostling for love, as time passed, everyone seemed quite happy to be in a bicker-free relationship with someone who shared their views on what to watch on the streamers and what to eat for dinner. It was an awful thought that ultimately it reduced to that, or perhaps it was a wonderful thing and could give a lot of people hope. Connie wasn't absolutely certain. Her opinions flip-flopped a lot on so many subjects now she had hit the perimenopause; sometimes she found that annoying, other times she thought it was progressive and open-minded. Thinking about what a knob he'd been at lunch, and in an effort not to admit she cared whether he was or was not attractive, she muttered, 'I'm surprised you think so. He's a shadow of his former self.'

'Aren't we all, darling,' laughed Lucy.

Connie felt a rush of love for her friend, who had not only articulated her own thoughts but had come to the rescue today, and on so many other days. Lucy knew Connie as well as she knew herself. Better perhaps. Connie wondered, if she'd been young now, would she have had a *thing* with Lucy. The thought made her flush internally, a woozy, complex thought. Lucy was breathtaking and certainly always the most interesting person in the room. Sexual-preference fluidity just wasn't spoken of when they were younger. It had never crossed Connie's mind to imagine being anything other than heterosexual and to hold the goal of being monogamous. But everything seemed to cross everyone's mind now. Connie thought that, on balance, most probably she would *not* have had a thing with Lucy, however attractive Lucy was; she couldn't imagine sex with another woman. Her basic barrier to entry was that she wouldn't know when the sex was finished, and that would be awkward. Being a heterosexual of a certain age meant her experience was that 99.9 per cent of the time, sex was finished when he came. Perhaps her daughter's generation would pity her for that, or judge her. But it was just the way it was.

'You know, today, I told him how often I think of him.'

'Dear God, Connie. Why?'

'I have no idea why I have this impulse to make myself vulnerable to him. It's humiliating.'

'You read too many Victorian novels at university. It might even go further back.' Lucy sighed. 'When you were a kid, I bet you watched all those black-and-white re-runs of tragic romantic films on Saturday afternoons, with your mother and your sisters. A veritable hotspot of yearning and longing and female servitude. Nothing other than desperate, doomed love affairs with moody, uncommunicative men.'

'You're right, I did. I also danced around the house with my sisters listening to my old spinster aunts' 1950s records. Along with Dusty Springfield, I did a lot of wishing and hoping.' Lucy muttered 'FFS' at this point. 'I'm surprised *you* watched the black-and-white movies,' Connie added.

'I didn't, darling. I went outside and roller-skated. That's why I have trim legs and a healthy attitude towards men.'

Connie thought her friend made a good point, and she was glad she'd encouraged her girls to do a lot of sport. Fran always seemed to have a healthy attitude towards men. Well, at least healthier than Connie's had been. She wasn't to be blamed for the fact that Zac's father was none other than John Harding. That complication was all on Connie

'Do you think the connection will stay buried?' she asked.

'He knows Rose's new husband too, doesn't he?'

'Craig is hardly Rose's *new* husband, Lucy,' Connie said with a gentle sigh. She didn't want to be sidetracked, but she always felt the necessity of defending Rose when Lucy was a little snippy about her. It was an odd impulse. Connie loved both her friends, but the truth was that while it was clear that Rose was a good person (it could be argued that she was the *better* person), Lucy was far more fun and beautiful and significantly cleverer, wealthier, more adventurous, etc., etc. It seemed obvious to Connie why Peter had chosen her over his first wife all those years ago. It was perhaps because Lucy was the obvious winner that Connie felt the incessant need to fight Rose's corner, even though Rose was never aware of her efforts and Lucy was always irritated by them. Perhaps it was an unnecessary gesture – the girls might even call it patronising – as Rose wasn't any longer a rank outsider or even a runner-up. She was very happy in her second marriage, but still Connie said, 'They've been married about fifteen years and I'd have thought you, above everyone, would want to up his credentials since you ran off with her original husband.'

Lucy shrugged and said dismissively, 'I adore it when you use phrases like "run off with", it's so quaint and un-London. Look, we're not talking about me here. I'm just saying there are a lot of loose ends. You only need someone to tug at one of them.'

'Aren't you, as my friend, supposed to cheer me up?'

'Darling, we are long past that. I, as your friend, am supposed to be honest with you. Be on your guard; this whole thing is precarious. The young lovers barely know one another, Zac barely knows his father, you know his father far too well.

It's a tinder box.' Lucy shrugged again. 'Don't worry about him. Concentrate on Fran. She looked very pale and drawn today. Is she eating properly?'

Connie thought how she'd thrown away the plate of food that Fran had barely picked at. Fran had been extremely quiet during the walk, and while she had, along with everyone else, got a hot chocolate from the fairy-light-adorned van in the park, Connie had watched her hand it to Zac untouched. Lucy was right: Fran was her concern, and today must have been a challenge for her. Connie ought to sit her down and ask what her impression of Zac's family was. They also needed to have a conversation about how she might manage her studies and money, as well as where they were going to live, short- and long-term. As annoying as John was, he'd correctly made the point that Connie hadn't had all the necessary conversations with her daughter. It wasn't a comfortable thought to admit that he, a completely inept parent, had still identified her lack. It was clear that it needed to be done. 'I'll talk to her.'

21

Zac

He could tell himself a lot of things.

People smoked and drank. Neither thing was good for you. Smoking was pretty crap for everyone around you too. Yet far from being illegal, society actively glorified both. Cool-as-hell people in movies always smoked, always had. And could anyone even imagine a western party – a wedding, a funeral, a graduation, a Friday night even – without alcohol? How many times had someone suggested opening a bottle of champagne since they'd announced the baby? It was celebratory. (Her family never suggested Prosecco, he'd noticed.) Even getting shit-faced and emotional or punchy or pukey was considered totally normal. Was it *that* different?

He could tell himself that it wasn't up to him how people spent their money or their time. It was a free country. Some people needed this. Whatever. People's lives were crap – not all of them, but a lot of them. People were in pain and needed to self-medicate, they were grieving, stressed and looking for an escape. You could argue that substances led to some level of gratification for the poor bastards who had nothing else sparkling in their worlds. No one was forcing anyone to take the stuff he delivered. And that was *all* he did. Hand it over. He didn't make it, sell it, profit from it. He just took it from one guy and gave it to another. People made choices. It was up to them. They were adults. It was a free country.

He didn't feel very free, though. He felt trapped. Scared.

The point was, while he could tell himself a lot of things, he delivered what they told him to because they might kill him otherwise. They really might. He lived in a world where that wasn't just a turn of phrase. What the actual fuck?

He heard the party way before he saw it. Predictable rap music was pounding down the street, polluting it with lyrics that were so obviously offensive but somehow slid by the Millennial wokes; it didn't catch their attention. He guessed wokes didn't like to tackle systemic sexism and inciting of violence in rap songs in case it was considered prejudicial to do so. That made him smirk a bit. As a Gen Z you had to laugh about how shit and hypocritical and limiting everything was for your generation. If you didn't laugh, it would depress you. Like, really depress you. He thought about the neighbours. Were they too scared to call the police and complain that it was close to midnight and the street was shaking, echoing with profanities and slurs? Most likely they'd have told themselves that twelve was the cut-off point; they'd do something then. Probably wouldn't, though. He thought about the neighbours' kids asking what a ho was and it made him feel a bit sad. He wondered vaguely how he'd answer that question when his own kid asked. He didn't know. He didn't know so much.

When he thought of the baby, he was slapped by a white,

blinding panic. He wanted it, this being, a baby that he'd created with the most amazing girl ever, but was he worthy of it? Current circumstances would suggest not. He worried whether he'd make a good father. What even was that? He thought of his dad and he thought of John. Conventional wisdom had it that a good father was someone who loved you blindly; well, he'd do that. Someone who provided. He could try to do that. Someone who offered you a path, a way to distinguish right from wrong. He couldn't examine that. If he did, he thought his head might implode, just cave in on itself. Done for.

Inevitably, the party had spilt into the street. The front door of the three-storey, seen-better-days terrace was wide open. Light, noise and people gushed out of every window and door. There was a couple going at it on the short path, too out of it to care that her left tit was on show to anyone who wanted to take a look. Not that anyone cared enough to be curious. Real live flesh wasn't all that exciting if you'd watched a thousand hours of porn before your sweet sixteenth. Other people were hanging about smoking weed; one girl was sitting on the step crying; a couple of guys were arguing. Everyone was high. They looked like wasters. They looked like normal people. They looked like he sometimes looked on some Friday nights at uni if he'd mixed drinks unwisely or started too early. The thought made him shiver.

The next morning, after he'd seen what happened to Rob – Jesus, he still struggled to say it, even to himself, in his own head: *the next morning, after he'd seen a man beaten to death*, for fuck's sake – he'd turned up at the café as instructed. He'd been sick with terror, didn't want to go, but they knew where he lived and worked; he thought he had to go to them or else they would come for him. He hoped he could explain that he didn't want trouble; he was happy to forget everything he'd seen. He wasn't *happy* with doing that exactly, but he was able to, or at least he'd hoped he would be able to. He thought it was his best chance. Wipe it away, pretend it had never happened.

When he arrived at the café, there was no one there. Not another single customer. It was a tiny place, white tiles yellowed with the fat from the fryer, sticky beige lino. He was distracted by the slight tug on his trainer soles as he walked towards the counter. He felt like he was trudging through quicksand. Sinking. There were three wooden tables with two or three seats around each. None of the furniture matched; the condiments on the tables were cheap, unrecognisable brands. It was far from the sleek places he'd imagined brunching in London. Avocado on sourdough was not an option here. There was a faded plastic menu pinned above the counter that showed photos of various combinations of white toast, fatty bacon and sausages, dried-out baked beans, fried eggs slick with grease. He ordered a black coffee. He couldn't eat. He waited for half an hour. Shitting himself. No one came in or out of the café. He thought that was odd. He tried not to look at the guy behind the counter. It might have been his imagination, but he thought the guy was avoiding his eye too. It was as though neither of them wanted to see or be seen. Eventually the guy asked, 'You Zac?'

'Yeah.' Zac didn't like it that this man knew his name or that he'd taken thirty minutes to use it. He was being played. Everything was a game. But a deadly one.

'I have something for you.' The man placed a padded envelope on the little wooden table. Zac sometimes looked back on that moment and wondered whether he could have just stood up, walked away. He hadn't, though. Life rolled on or out; there wasn't much point in looking back and wondering about the choices you'd made that landed you where you were. It was just a way to beat yourself up if you were in a self-loathing mood. His mum was forever saying, 'The why's not as important as the where.' Maybe.

Inside the package there was a phone and a note. The note had the number 135711 and the words *see photos* written on it. Zac followed instructions, tapped the code into the phone, went straight to photos. It was Rob's phone. He found it difficult to concentrate. He didn't know what he was supposed to be looking for. He randomly scrolled, letting images spill and stumble in front of his eyes. There were loads of Rob with his tongue out, holding a bottle of beer, arms flung around other guys or girls, sometimes he was flicking the V. Most of the time he wore an Aston Villa football top. In a few he was sweaty and bare-chested, posing to show the results of his gym sessions. Did he think he was tough? Did he think he needed to be? Zac had paused at one where Rob sat on a sofa between two women who were most likely his mum and his gran. He had an arm around both the women; there was no beer, no hand gestures. The women were beaming. Zac shifted in his seat. They wouldn't be beaming today, they'd be wrecked. There were also screen shots of adverts for protein drinks, trainers; video game stats and football leagues. The sort of photos everyone had on their phone. Their familiarity somehow scary as hell.

The last five photos taken were the ones that mattered. There were two that Rob had taken in the pub. Rob looked the same as he did in the other photos. Same desperate, exaggerated caricature of what fun was supposed to look like. Tongue out, eyes and mouth wide, beer in hand, a V to the camera. It was painful to look at him, to judge him for wanting to present so innocently and so enthusiastically when he probably already knew his life was a mess. The photos had a try-too-hard air to them. Who was he trying to convince? Himself? It was so odd to look at the image of him and know that just an hour after it was taken, he was dead. Zac was there in the pub shots, one of five faces. Zac felt sorry for himself too because that lad didn't exist any more either. The bloke who was just out to make friends, to have a laugh, get off his face, get a kebab on the way home. He'd vanished in the last twenty-four hours too.

The final three photographs were of Zac alone. They hadn't been taken in the bright, boozy and buoyant pub. They'd been taken on a dark, damp night and were streaked with frantic motion. He was running away from the beating, the scene of the crime. He hadn't remembered glancing over his shoulder, but apparently he had. There he was, caught on camera. He looked guilty as hell. He *had* felt such guilt about running. He was clearly recognisable to anyone who knew him. If this photo was circulated or put through one of those facial recognition scans, whatever, he'd be tracked. He'd be identified as one of the last people who saw Rob alive. He might be mistaken for the person responsible for his death. It could look as though he had beaten Rob and left him for dead, that Rob had taken these photos as a final desperate act as Zac ran away from the scene of the crime.

Zac sat in the grubby little café and worked it all out. It felt like he'd stepped into the Matrix or something. It was mental, but he understood what had happened. The men who had attacked Rob were not random muggers; this was the work of organised people. A gang? A mob? Rob had got himself mixed up with a shitty lot. Now, apparently, Zac had too. The thought shuddered through his body. Quaked. The attackers had obviously taken his photo to trap him. Quick thinking on their part. He needed to think carefully now, but he couldn't. His heart was beating so hard he could feel it in his throat, his head was pounding too; it was as though someone was knocking on the inside of his skull. The coffee cup in front of him distorted like a mirage. Was he going to pass out? Fuck.

The phone buzzed with an incoming message.

This is ur phone now. Photos r backed up.

So. There was nothing for it.

Over the next four months, Zac delivered nine packages. A location and meeting time would be texted to the phone. He'd go wherever they sent him. Mostly pubs. There, someone would give him a package and drop-off location. Mostly parties. He didn't understand why they needed him, a middleman. But he did understand what would happen if he didn't do what they wanted. They could leak the photos at any time. He'd be arrested for murder, tried and sent to prison. Or worse, they could do to him what they had done to Rob.

When his internship finished, he left London the same day. Fled. He didn't want to go back home; he felt soiled and was certain his mum would spot the change in him instantly. Because he had changed. He was dirtier. Internally wrinkled or shrivelled in some way, not quite as splendid and vibrant as he'd once been. Hope had been wrung out of him because he'd seen a murder and, however reluctantly, he had worked for a drug gang. He thought it was better to spend the summer in York, wait for term to begin. He just wanted to be a student, put all of this behind him. A fresh start. He cut his hair, planned to keep his head down.

That was when he hooked up with Fran again.

For a few weeks, he'd thought everything was going to be OK, that everything was brilliant, actually. He was ecstatic to be out of London, charged, like there was actual electricity running through him. Maybe that was one of the reasons his relationship with Fran had blazed so brightly. The total relief. He decided that the answer was to never return to London. He would decline the offer of a permanent position at ZapionTec. He could find another job away from London. No one had pursued him to York. Clearly he wasn't worth chasing up the A1. His guess was there was already some other sucker bribed, or tricked, or terrified into doing the job he had done. Maybe there were many of them. A network. With luck, they'd forget about him.

But then Fran told him her family lived in London. And then she said she was pregnant.

Initially, he'd tried to comfort himself with the fact that London was a big place. Her parents probably lived in a leafy suburb, nowhere near the places he'd done the drops. But the minute she told him they were getting a Tube to Notting Hill, he'd started to feel a slow-burn panic. He had walked those streets before. He thought it would be OK if they just hung out at her parents' house or their friends' place, but then someone suggested they stop off at the Duke for a drink. He'd known it was a risk. He'd tried to get out of it. He'd said it would be more polite to go home with her parents and grandparents, but

Fran had insisted. 'Mum and Dad need some time to process the baby news. I want you to get to know my friends.' Inside, he recognised the barman instantly and the barman recognised him too, apparently. Bear had people everywhere.

They told him they might not have bothered bringing him back into the game. 'But it's Christmas, right. A busy period. Lots of parties. So since you're here, you might as well help out.'

They'd presented it like a reasonable proposition, almost as though he was a mate and they were asking a favour, but it wasn't that. It was entangled and organised. He felt like he was in a maze, running full pelt to a dead end. He'd said no. Bullish on the few months' break from being in their power, buoyant as only people in love ever were.

'I'm not doing it,' he'd said firmly, confidently. 'I'm finished with this.'

The knife was jabbed into his hand before he'd completed the sentence. The blood oozed; the pain ran up his arm.

'We decide when you're finished.'

So.

They were right, Christmas was a busy time. This week he'd already delivered three more packages. It didn't help to think about the accruing number of crimes he was committing, how deep he was falling.

It was too deep.

It was too much.

22

Zac

Zac pushed his way through the sweaty, stumbling throng. The smell of bodies, alcohol, smoke, vomit and sex was overpowering. He noticed that the ceiling fire alarms were all covered in plastic bags. A planned party, then. He wondered whose house it was. It wasn't a student house; it was someone's proper home. There was a wicker basket full of trainers by the door, loads of coats piled up on a wooden bench in the hallway. He didn't imagine many of the partygoers had arrived in coats, despite the season. Whoever's house it was, he hoped they had insurance; the carpet was already pocked with marks where cigarettes and joints had been stubbed out. He had seen this sort of filth before. Someone might have urinated in the cupboards, ornaments would be broken, books torn, toilets blocked. Not actual vandalism, just a total lack of awareness. No respect, no care. Civility gone. Rules ignored. Laws broken.

He shoved his way through to the kitchen, which was awash with bottles and cans, full, empty and everything in between. Open, often upended. The tiled floor was slippery underfoot.

He was sort of relieved to note the pools of beer frothing on surfaces and dripping to the floor. He was at least stepping in alcohol, not piss or vomit. There was a plastic vat of purple punch. If it had begun life as a measured cocktail, it certainly wasn't that any longer. He saw someone pour two bottles of vodka into the mix, while someone else stuck his head under the flow. What he didn't swallow splashed onto his face and then into the vat. There were slices of fruit and joint stubs floating on the surface. Zac kept his hand in his coat pocket, covering the package. As the tips of his fingers touched it, checked on it, he felt a sort of shock through his body, as though he'd been burnt. Totally psychological, obviously. It made him think of his mother grumbling that 'Money burns a hole in that boy's pocket.' He didn't want to think of his mother right then.

He just wanted to leave.

His man wasn't in the kitchen. He hadn't really expected him to be. He'd be somewhere darker. Upstairs. Hanging about in a bedroom. Zac pushed his way up, past the partygoers. He tried not to look at them too carefully. Best to think of them as a crowd, a mass, rather than individuals. They were just anyone. He recognised some blokes huddled around a doorway. He knew who they were by sight. They knew him too. Their vicious faces had become familiar to him now. Unfortunately.

'Bear about?' he asked.

They were all huge. They didn't answer his question or even acknowledge it. Zac stood still and waited silently. What else could he do? He didn't know what would happen next. Whatever, it was beyond his control, that much he did know. It was important that he didn't look terrified or out of his depth. Even though, obviously, he was both. That was what he had to concentrate on, not letting them see him shake. They wouldn't be able to see the patches of sweat blooming under his arms because of his bulky coat. He hoped they didn't notice it bubbling on his lip.

One of them he hadn't seen before. His face was inked, but only his face, as far as Zac could see, not his arms or neck. Zac assumed it was to show some level of 'straight in there, no messing' mentality. Most people who got into inking worked towards face tattoos after they'd covered less painful parts of their bodies: thighs, back and chest. Usually a face tattoo was the result of some level of addiction to the process, which therefore showed a peculiar form of helplessness, as all addiction did. This man, who was bald and had every centimetre of his face and head inked with Celtic symbols, illustrations of medieval weapons, a dragon and some Chinese characters that said who knew what, was showing that he didn't need to work towards anything. He looked vicious. There was little doubt that his viciousness was more than just a look. He held out his hand. Zac dug out the packet and handed it over. Glad to see the back of it. Ink guy went into the room that they were guarding; through the crack in the door, Zac could see it was a bedroom. On the foot of the bed he saw piles of money. Notes, scattered. Loads of them. No one ever used cash any more. Well, no one legit. He supposed there was always someone who wanted funds to be untraceable, fast, untrackable.

'Wait,' instructed a second thug. Zac didn't need telling. He knew by now that these were situations where you didn't leave until you were dismissed. Besides, despite the increased regularity of the drops, he was not getting used to this – in a way he supposed he shouldn't want to; it wasn't a thing that should be normalised – and was paralysed with fear. He only hoped his legs would move once he was allowed; it was a fresh sort of hell to think that he'd be frozen to this particular spot for ever. Today's package had felt like powder, not pills. He knew they'd be weighing it, perhaps tasting it. Checking he hadn't tampered with it. As if. He'd never touch the stuff. Drugs disgusted him. They gave bastards like these power. The wrong people always seemed to have the power.

Another guy poked his head out from behind the door. Was it just a show of Bear's strength, a display of his numerous foot soldiers? 'Fuck off,' he said.

Zac quickly turned away, so didn't see which one of them added, 'See you soon.'

As he was coming down the stairs, he saw a girl standing on her own in the hallway. He noted her outfit first; it was in every way revealing. Too short, too sheer, too tight. Not just scant but somehow uncomfortable, inappropriate. 'Sophie? What are you doing here?'

'What do you think? It's a party. I'm partying,' she snapped defensively.

She did not look like she was partying if by partying you meant having fun. She looked awkward and lost. She looked like she'd tried too hard and that she knew everyone knew it. Her shoulders were curled around her own body as though she regretted choosing the short, strappy scrap of a dress, with a plunging neckline that almost dipped to her tummy button. He'd never seen her in anything so obviously sexy before. She normally wore jeans and hoodies. She was still a kid. He felt uncomfortable noting that her outfit was sexy. The scourge of the male gaze and all that. But how the hell else was he supposed to look at anything? He was male, unequivocally – physically and by how he chose to identify – and he had eyes. How he looked at an apple or a garden or a person – yes, OK, a woman or girl – could only be through a male gaze.

'You're too young to be here.'

'Who are you, like my dad now?'

'You should go home.' She rolled her eyes. He tried a different tack. 'Who do you know here?'

'My friend's brother invited us along.'

'Which friend?' She didn't answer. 'Where's your friend now?'

She shrugged. 'Maybe she's upstairs. Or maybe she left.'

Zac frowned, concerned. He'd been on enough nights out at uni to know that girls who got split from their crowd were seen as sitting ducks by some absolute dickheads.

'You can't stay here on your own.'

'Dude, when did you become so uptight? I didn't have you down as Mr Square, what with being a baby daddy at twenty-two and everything. Life goal right there.' She was holding a red plastic beaker half full of the purple liquid he'd seen being prepped in the kitchen. He fought the urge to snatch it out of her hand. Maybe she sensed as much, because she drank it down in one long, defiant slug and then deftly turned the tables. 'What are *you* doing here?' This was the last question he wanted to answer. 'Where's Fran?' Or maybe that was.

'At yours, I think.'

Sophie raised an eyebrow, as though she knew what he was up to. She didn't, of course. The betrayal she was imagining was ordinary, not seismic. 'So who do *you* know here?' she asked, hinting at her suspicion.

'No one,' he said quickly. 'I was just passing.'

'Just passing a party in Shepherd's Bush and you thought you'd pop in?'

'Yeah. My mum and dad's Airbnb is just along the street. I heard a lot of noise and was curious.'

'Sure.'

It was a pathetic lie, unconvincing, but Sophie wouldn't be able to call him out to Fran because she shouldn't be here either.

Their conversation was interrupted as a huge guy, in his mid-twenties, stumbled into Sophie. He was totally out of it. He put his hand on her neck, pinned her to the wall and kissed her. There was nothing about the kiss that suggested it was expected or welcome or even enjoyable. It was sloppy and brutal, entitled.

'Hey, hey, piss off, get your hands off her.' Zac pulled the guy off Sophie. His response instinctually angry.

'Sorry, mate.' The guy laughed, held up his hands in surrender. He was half a foot taller than Zac, considerably wider too. But then he was an entire foot taller than Sophie. 'She yours?'

'No, no, she's not mine. She doesn't belong to anybody. Just piss off.'

He didn't piss off. 'Well, if she ain't your ho.' He turned back to Sophie and started roughly kissing her neck. Sophie didn't push him away but nor did she offer any encouragement. Her eyes met Zac's; they were dead. He couldn't work out if she was into it or not. Had she taken something?

'We should leave.'

The guy took a momentary break from running his tongue over Sophie's collarbone. He turned and snarled at Zac. Bared his teeth like a dog. He put his hand on Sophie's thigh. High up, just centimetres from where her legs joined. She was frozen. 'Just fuck off, mate. This is nothing to do with you.'

Zac ignored him and spoke to Sophie. 'Come on. Let's go home.'

'I'm OK here,' she said, but her voice was a squeak.

'No, you're not.' Zac knew he couldn't leave her here. He turned to the leery, handy guy. 'She's fifteen, she's my sister.' The guy's hand worked up her skirt as though Zac's words were motivation, not the opposite. 'And I work with Bear.'

The lout immediately pulled away from Sophie. Let go of her as though she was on fire. He stepped back. His hands once again raised in that annoying surrender gesture, but this time the sentiment was genuine.

'Hey, hey, no offence. I'm not looking for trouble.' He turned and quickly walked away.

'No, come back,' yelled Sophie. 'None of that is true. I'm not fifteen, he's not my brother.'

'Bitch, those things weren't the problem,' the guy called over his shoulder. He didn't turn around.

'What the hell?' Sophie glared at Zac.

'I'll walk you home. Your mum would not be happy if I left you here.'

'As if she'd even notice right now if I was at home or not. I could get head-to-toe inks and she'd ask me what I thought of baby names.'

'Did you bring a coat?'

Sophie rolled her eyes but followed him out of the house.

FIVE DAYS BEFORE THE END

23

Connie

30 December

Connie felt that Fran was avoiding being alone with her. It was frustrating and concerning; it seemed an immature response at a time when her maturity most needed to be evident. As Zac was spending the day with his parents, Fran no longer had him to hide behind, but she stayed close to her sisters, and unless Connie officially requested time together to talk, she couldn't see how the moment might be engineered. If she did request a specific time, the conversation was obviously not going to be a cosy chat. She did not want to give scheduled conflab vibe. Flora had just left for Brighton to visit friends, so Connie offered Sophie fifty quid to go to the sales. Sophie was naturally suspicious. 'I thought you said I hadn't done enough revision this holiday for my mocks.'

'You haven't, but I thought you said you wanted something new to wear on New Year's Eve.'

'I'm not going to argue.'

'Why would you?' Her youngest daughter skipped out of the house on the quest for the perfect NYE outfit as girls had for generations. Luke was back in the office, and so when Fran finally stumbled downstairs at 11 a.m., all bleary-eyed and leggy, they were alone.

'House is weirdly quiet,' Fran commented.

Connie immediately hit her phone and selected a Hôtel Costes playlist to run in the background so the silence wasn't ominous. 'Everyone's out. I didn't want to wake you. You need your sleep.'

'You should have. I have uni work to do.'

Connie resisted pointing out that if that was the case, Fran ought to have set an alarm. She simply nodded, smiled. 'Yes, right, it's going to be a matter of balance. Decaf?'

'Can't you just call it coffee? Try and make it sound normal.'

It would be far too easy to comment that she'd got out the wrong side of the bed, but even Connie could remember that being an annoying thing for parents to say, so she simply made the coffee in silence. In front of her daughter she placed a fresh fruit salad and a bowl of oats that had been soaked overnight in yogurt and honey; this at least elicited a muttered 'Thanks.' Fran began languidly spooning food into her mouth, her head draped over her bowl, her hair trailing in her coffee. She was dishevelled but somehow still inherently beautiful, the way your own children always were to you.

'So how are you feeling?' It was a lousy start. Too wide. Connie should have avoided the open-ender.

'Peachy.' The word at odds with the averted gaze, sallow skin and hunched shoulders.

'Really? Because you are managing a great deal.'

'I'm aware. Mum, will you stop, like, policing my emotions.'

Connie didn't know exactly what she meant by that. Nothing

good. She hoped her next question was more acceptable. 'What did you think of Zac's parents?' She decided this conversation demanded a level of specificity. It was the only way to make progress. 'Clare and Neil, I mean.'

'They seem nice. Clare gets it. She's easy to talk to.'

Connie bit down the slight sting of jealousy that her daughter had found comfort in another woman, another mother. All that mattered was that Fran had someone she trusted and could confide in.

Sort of.

Not really.

That was the kind of thing Connie said out loud and even to herself, but really, in her core, she just wished Fran was talking to her as she always had. Until this. 'Well, yes. I imagine she is helpful. She's been through exactly the same thing.'

Fran's head shot up and she glared at her mother. 'Not exactly the same thing. She had it even worse. She was on her own.'

'Yes, quite. I didn't mean . . . I only meant that it must be great to have someone who understands.'

'So you don't understand?'

Connie decided not to take the easy route. The glib reassurances that she could imagine what Fran was going through. She couldn't and so admitted as much. 'Not entirely, no. You haven't talked me through your decision-making process and I've never been in your shoes. I *want* to understand, though.'

'You want to understand why I'm not getting rid of it like *that man* said.'

'That man?'

'John Harding.'

Connie could understand why she might not want to say his name. It had to be the most ungracious thing he'd ever suggested, and he'd once told her that every hole was a goal and that you didn't look at the fireplace when you poked the fire. Sometimes Connie couldn't understand how her generation had survived the endless humiliations, the ingrained misogyny that was considered dating banter. 'No, no, of course not. He had no right to say such a thing. To say anything. I would never suggest that. I don't want you to get rid of the baby.'

'I can't anyway. I've told you it's too late.' Fran dropped her spoon. It clattered against the bowl and an arc of yogurty oats leapt onto her pyjama sleeve. She didn't appear to notice.

'Would you have? If you'd discovered your pregnancy earlier.' Connie reached out and rested her hand on Fran's arm, careful to avoid the breakfast gunk. It didn't seem enough. She moved her hand to her daughter's cheek and felt the heat of her, the life in her, as she had since Fran was a baby.

'That's a pointless question, Mum. I hate it when you talk about theoretical situations.' Her daughter started to cry. Big, fat tears silently rolled down her face. Connie moved forward, arms open, but Fran abruptly stood up, dodging the embrace, and walked through to the sitting room. Snatching a tissue out of the box on the coffee table, she flopped down onto the sofa and pulled a throw over her legs. Connie trailed after, sat at the opposite end of the sofa, sensing she mustn't crowd, and waited.

'I want the baby,' Fran muttered. 'I just didn't have all the facts.'

'What do you mean?'

She shook her head. 'Not facts, just understanding, right?

I have my exams, so does Zac. I guess I'm just crying because of my hormones.' Connie thought too much was blamed on hormones. Fran was crying because her situation was scary, overwhelming and unknown. She didn't say so. It wouldn't help.

'It's OK to cry, it's good to let it all out.'

'And loads of my friends are applying for jobs already. How will I apply for jobs?'

'Well, you'll need some time. That's not for you this year, but maybe next year.' Or the year after, Connie thought. She kept this to herself too.

'Do you have to declare dependants on job applications?'

'No, I don't think so.' Connie wasn't absolutely sure. The job application process was, like so many other things nowadays, a mystery to her. She had heard stories that some companies insisted on blind applications, names and genders redacted. She understood this removed the chance of prejudice, but that 'blindness' had stretched to removing the name of the university the candidate had studied at, in case an interviewer had a prejudice for or against a particular institution. She found this frustrating, since her girls had worked so hard to get the grades to go to Russell Group universities; surely they should be able to say where they were educated. Shouldn't it be the responsibility of the interviewer not to have a prejudice? Plus, how did that stack with active encouragement of declaring your sexuality on applications? Something that confused Connie. Considering the #MeToo campaign, shouldn't everyone be working towards an environment where a person's sexuality didn't factor in any way, shape or form to the suitability of a job? It didn't feel like progress having to specify your preference between the sheets.

Anyway, all that aside, she was glad to hear that Fran still wanted to work after the baby was born. She'd had fears that her daughter might have given up on any ambitions to have a career. 'Don't worry about job applications, we can cross that bridge when we come to it. We'll get all the information we need then. Let's think about some of the things that are more immediate concerns. Have you thought about childcare?'

'Why are you pressurising me?' Fran yelled.

'I'm really trying not to, and I'm sorry if I am. But there are long waiting lists for nurseries, so it does need to be discussed.'

'I thought you could help with the baby's care. You said you would.'

'*Help*, yes, but not take over full-time. I have my work to think about too.'

Fran looked surprised. 'You work for yourself. You can be flexible.'

Of course she should have expected her daughter to quote those words back to her; it was exactly what Connie had said all her working life as she fitted her career as a freelance photographer around the needs of her three daughters. But it hadn't been that simple. Before the girls were born, her career had been promising, flourishing. There was the occasional exhibition and reviews in the papers; she'd sold her work in Germany, Sweden and America and there had been talk of a coffee-table book. But as her family grew, she'd increasingly found that she had to turn down assignments, particularly those that involved travel. She'd had no time whatsoever to network and those two factors contributed to limiting her progress. Or maybe it was just the invention of the iPhone. Everyone was a photographer now, right? AI was the final nail in the coffin.

She had never complained that her career didn't grow to Annie Leibovitz proportions; she was grateful that it had provided her with the sort of income that meant she didn't have to feel guilty for having a gym membership or treating herself to the occasional pedicure. Luke earned a great salary as an architect; his career had thrived. It was hard not to note that he had never had to turn down an invitation to travel abroad or meet a client somewhere glitzy late in the evening. She always considered herself privileged to have been able to spend so much time with her girls. She really had.

But she wasn't ready to do it all over again.

Not yet, not full-time.

Now, her photography work was mostly taking headshots of authors or B-list celebrities, and she enjoyed it. She met interesting people, she had a reason to dress up, buy decent clothes. To feel like herself. To suit herself. 'I can't take a baby on a shoot,' she pointed out.

'Well, you can give up the gallery work at least, you don't earn much there. It's basically the living wage, isn't it?'

'But I like being at the gallery and they sell my work there.' And I'm not the one who got pregnant, Connie thought. She said, 'I could look after the baby one day a week, maybe two, but you will still need to think about nurseries. You'll need to start looking.' Fran pulled the throw over her head and growled.

'What are Zac's thoughts on childcare?'

'Zac's thoughts?' Fran threw off the cover and emerged looking confused. She was far from used to being in a partnership, conferring with someone else, taking their views and wishes into account, that much was evident.

'Well, if he's in.'

'Why do you say *if*?'

'It wasn't meant to be loaded, just a turn of phrase. *As* he's in and you're co-parenting, he could perhaps work a four-day week. If you both did that, and I looked after the baby for two days, you'd only need to find the funds for one day of childcare.'

'Zac says I mustn't worry about money. That he'll look after me.'

Cost of living and feminism made that seem unlikely and – frankly – unsavoury. Connie couldn't understand how her slipping up and using the term 'chairman' might cause huge concern to Fran – which it had in the past – and yet the idea of being 'looked after' was totally palatable. 'So how much will he earn?'

'I'm not sure. We haven't talked about it exactly.' Fran shrugged. Her skinny shoulders seemed to creep right up to her ears and then slither away. She was glorious to look at, she always had been; she took Connie's breath away. She had all the luxuries of youth: big eyes, thick lashes, smooth long limbs, plump, dewy skin. Resplendent and terrifying. Connie had thought girlhood would last longer, be enjoyed more. Fran wasn't crying any more, but there was one single tear still on her cheek. She looked like a Pre-Raphaelite muse, tragic, lost. 'He will look after me. He promised. He's not the sort to break promises.'

'Right. Have you thought about where you're going to live after the baby is born?'

'Well, *here*. This is my home, Mum. Like, are you going to evict me?'

Connie hated her daughter's excessive use of the word 'like' and had hoped she'd have grown out of it; it was another thing that she had to swallow, the realisation that the time allocated to correcting her offspring's grammar had now most probably elapsed. 'No, of course not. You're welcome here, as is Zac. Obviously. I just didn't want to presume that's what you'd want to do.'

Connie had a sudden image of her home with plastic toys scattered everywhere, the particular smell of baby wipes and nappy sacks drifting through every room, ousting the Neom diffuser scent. She thought of stair gates and baby locks on the cupboards. It was a classic example of 'be careful what you wish for'. She'd been nervous about becoming an empty-nester, but that was no longer something she'd have to concern herself with, she thought ruefully. This hadn't just happened to Fran; it had happened to them all.

Mother and daughter sat in silence. It was solid and uncomfortable, like a bare arm grazing against a pebble-dash wall when playing hide-and-seek as a child; it stung. 'Have you even had your first row?' Connie asked.

'What?' Fran looked outraged, and Connie knew it was a stupid, top-of-mind question. She should have stuck with the practicalities.

'I mean, your relationship is so new. It's untested.'

'You have always said you knew almost instantly that Dad was the one for you.'

'Well, yes, but I tested my theory by being with him for three years before we got married and years more before we added pressure to our relationship by having a baby.'

Fran's jaw dropped and her eyes glistened; she was going

to start to cry again. 'So that's how you see being a parent. *Adding pressure.* As your eldest child, all I can say is gee, thanks, Mum.'

'You know what I mean. Financial pressure.'

'There's more to life than money.'

'There is, but money tends to take top billing.'

'That's a gross view, Mum. Really *old*.'

'I'm fully aware,' said Connie, sighing. She had no idea when she became so realistic. 'And marriage, have you even—'

'Look, I get it. Right. I understand what you're saying, Mum. Loud and clear. Money makes the world go round. Good talk.'

Fran jumped up off the sofa and stormed towards the door, out of the room. She slammed the door so hard the vibrations upset the plastic Santa that Connie's parents had bought in the late eighties. A vintage classic that Connie was always quick to explain was ironic. The Santa fell forward onto the button that activated its voice box.

'Ho ho ho. Merry Christmas.'

'Merry bloody Christmas,' Connie muttered.

24

Fran

We *have* had our first row, but I don't feel like telling Mum about it. I don't like thinking about it. It happened just two weeks after that day Zac walked into Boots. Honestly, the make-up sex might be when this baby was conceived. A detail Mum is unlikely to find an amusing origin story. Though it might not have been then. It could have been the day before or the day after. I didn't practise restraint, so I can't pinpoint exactly.

Following the meet in Boots, we'd hung out together more or less continuously, both pretending what was happening between us was no big deal. I certainly wasn't going to risk acknowledging that being with him hit differently, that it was cool, in case he didn't feel the same. There are rules and everyone in my generation is aware. Texting then chatting and seeing each other before dating, before exclusive, then bf and gf. The Boomers and Gen Xs don't get it; even the Millennials struggle with why it's that way and they created it, but I like it because it's clear-cut. No mistakes. The labels are designed so that everyone knows where they stand. It's crystal when and if we need to meet each other's parents, buy birthday gifts, say no to having sex with other people. I tried to explain that to my mum once, but she just said, 'I thought your generation liked fluidity and resisting labels?' which was a basic pop.

But Zac apparently doesn't give a shit about the rules. After two weeks of hanging out, he said, 'Do you think we're falling in love? I totally love loads of things about you.'

It was so naked. So raw. We were in fact naked. Slick with our own and each other's sweat and cum. He was drunk, which was a relief, so we could both ignore his outburst if we had to. I was shocked, sort of thrown. I didn't know how to respond. I mean yes, maybe. Clearly there were things to love about him. But also no, what? Who says that? I took the next day to process my thoughts and my plan was to tell him that maybe I could see us moving on to bf and gf. We could jump some steps. I wanted us to be exclusive. My silence wasn't a rejection. It was a process. But. Well, he didn't see it that way.

Before his total batshit-crazy declaration of love, we had agreed that the next day we would try out AUX, a cocktail joint. It was a new place and glitzy. We were supposed to be meeting there at 6.30, straight after I finished work at Boots. It's a bit expensive and not an obvious student hang-out, but I was kind of excited to do something novel. We hadn't texted much that day. I hadn't really known what to put in a text after the 'Do you think we're falling in love?' question; sending him pictures of my matcha oat latte seemed lame. I sent him a single text to confirm times. 18:30 cocktail emoji, question mark. He replied with a thumbs-up emoji, as though he was my dad. I didn't know what that meant after everything. It was pretty distant. A sort of retraction. A cooling? Maybe. Which wasn't an entirely bad thing. It's universally accepted that it's hot to be cool, but it had been something really different when he wasn't being cool. I already regretted the idea that he might start to play games. Or, I wondered, was the thumbs-up emoji just old-school? Like a literal 'yup'? Confused as possible, I squirted deodorant under my arms and changed out of my work uniform into a black top and leather trousers. No false modesty, I looked many sorts of good and was pretty sure me dressed this way was one of the things he loved about me.

Places do not intimidate me. I tend to strut into a room, rather than walk. My mum taught me how to manage that when I was tiny. I was about four, starting pre-school nursery, and the room seemed massive, chaotic and somewhere I did not want to be. She told me to take the time to look around. 'It's not scary if you know what's in all the corners,' she promised me. It's one of my first memories, her crouching down so she was eye to eye with me. She told me that knowing the room I was walking into would always be useful, for two reasons. 'Firstly, you can decide if it's somewhere you might want to stay and . . .' and at this point she leant very close to my ear and in a whispered giggle added, 'secondly, you can spot all the exits and find a way to get out of it if you really want to.' It wasn't a conventional thing to say to your pre-schooler, but it was respectful, honest and helpful. She knew I'd feel empowered and in control. She's always wants that for us. Then she pointed out the music box pushed up against the nursery teacher's desk. I already had a recorder and could play a few notes. Mum knew the music box would make me feel better. It did. Inside I discovered a ribboned tambourine and a pretty cool glockenspiel. Over the years, I've used her tip whenever I walk into a new room. I look about me and note that there's nothing to be intimidated by. A busy club, a school hall, the hall of residence at uni, a stage where I might be performing. It's a really useful tip in life and has led to quite the strut.

The bar was trying hard. Maroon-coloured curved brick walls scooped out areas of cocooned intimacy; there was dim lighting and lavish leather sofas to sink into. I admit I was more than a bit excited by the moody, rich feel, offset by splashy, glittering chandeliers. We didn't have anywhere else like it in York. I thought it was going to be the right place to say we'd move up a level or two. Notable, sexy, standout. I picked up a menu. It was a fake-leather-bound thing that told me before I looked that the cocktails would be overpriced. Fifteen quid each! I asked the guy who was waiting if there was a happy hour. He tried to do that shitty make-you-feel-small thing that servers do to show that the place they pour drinks at is special.

He winced, spoke in a tone learnt through watching TV that showcased NY waiters being rude. 'Er, no. We think they're a little tacky. Attract a daggy crowd. The soft drinks are only a fiver.' A Coke for a fiver, are you kidding me? The waiter was early thirties, so I guess a total knob, because at his age he shouldn't have to embarrass someone my age to feel validated. I gave him a withering look that suggested I ate boys like him for breakfast. My mum's friend, Lucy, taught me it. She's in her mid-fifties but I swear is the coolest woman to walk the planet. I wondered what she'd do in my position, but I couldn't imagine a world where she couldn't afford to buy a bottle of champagne if she wanted to. I ordered tap water, 'With ice and lemon,' I insisted. Making it clear I wasn't intimidated by his dick move. The place wasn't *that* cool.

I glanced around hoping that Zac would appear, because it was already quarter to seven and it was not like him to be late. The place was busy but not heaving. In the north, people don't go out straight from work as much. They go home, have tea, get dressed up and then come out. It was a Monday night; I didn't expect it would start banging any time soon. A bunch of people in their late twenties, laughing loudly, held my attention for a while as I casually assessed their attraction and duly gave them a digit. The girls were cute, averaging sixes and sevens, whereas the guys were coming in with fours, maybe fives, with just one exception. A guy with big thighs and a good smile, long eyelashes. A seven in the right setting. I know it's considered reductive and shitty assessing people and giving them scores, but surely women get to do it to men for a few years, considering men have done it to women for thousands. Social and historical justice, right? And anyway, the scoring thing is really only a problem when the score is less than six. People judge all the time, I'm just open about it. There was a gay couple to my right. They were in their thirties and possibly newly-weds: their rings were shiny and they were solicitous to one another. They were talking about home decor, which was a cliché but also lovely. I thought of chipping in, because I have lots of views on colour pops and the emergence of teal, but as time ticked by, I became more awkward about the idea. I didn't want to draw attention to my obviously waiting-for-someone-maybe-stood-up status.

I *was* drawing attention, though. There was a guy, I felt him staring. I was trying to avoid his gaze, but he had caught my eye twice. Through boredom and habit, I checked him out. He was wearing expensive-looking dark clothes; the sort of looks he kept floating my way suggested that maybe he had a dark heart too. My life at that moment was such that I thought to myself, 'Ah well, I will never find out. I haven't got the time or emotional energy for a thing. I have Zac.' I was that content. That *full*. Then something flickered, so briefly, just the most fleeting acknowledgement that it was a bit of a shame that I couldn't pursue or investigate the man with rizz, as I sort of like a dark heart. The feminist in me hates this about me, but also deeply respects my complexity. Look, to be clear, I had no real interest in him, it was just a butterfly-wing beat of a moment. Like everyone in the bar, he was older than me and clearly not a student. He sent over a drink, FFS, what century? But I couldn't afford my own cocktails and he'd sent a negroni. I like a negroni. I nodded my thanks but deliberately picked up my phone and didn't plan on talking to him. Then there was a second drink. He brought that one over himself.

'I'm waiting for my boyfriend.' To be clear, at that point Zac and I were not boyfriend and girlfriend. I've mentioned that, right? That's important. It's like the Ross/Rachel moment in *Friends*, but for my generation. Ross claimed the moral ground because he thought they were on a break. I guess whether you cut him some slack is dependent on whether you agree or not.

The guy was confident, unfazed. I do like confidence. 'I'm waiting for someone too. York is clearly a city full of tardy types. We might as well wait together.'

'No thanks.'

'OK. Sorry if I bothered you. Enjoy the drink anyway. I don't drink negronis.' And he just left it on the low table in front of me and went back to his seat. He didn't push me. He didn't try to talk me round. He didn't tempt or tease or coerce. If he'd tried to push himself on me, I'd have told him where to go, but because he had the confidence to walk away, I was more inclined to follow. I have kind of bought into the vibe that if a guy thinks he's a winner, he sort of automatically becomes one. Women too, I guess, but we employ the technique less often. I could have just picked up my bag and gone back to my flat. I don't think he would have stopped me. It's weird how many critical decisions can be rammed into just a matter of seconds and also stretch for ever. The negronis were strong and Zac had stood me up. Obviously a power play, after him talking about love and me not responding. He clearly needed to reassert himself and show me he wasn't in too deep.

So I fucked the negroni man just to prove I hadn't bought into his crap about love anyway.

25

Fran

I went back to Negroni Man's hotel. He said he was in York on business and his company were paying for it. It was the best hotel in the city, high ceilings, low light fittings, someone playing a piano in the lobby. The sort of decor that made me feel confident that the chances of him murdering me in his room were slim. He offered me another drink in the hotel bar. To help reduce the chances of the aforementioned murder in the room, I made a point of telling the girl serving at the bar that we were just hooking up and what our room number was. Negroni Man thought that was funny. 'Clever. But I'm really not thinking of killing you. I like my girls very much alive and kicking.' It was a creepy thing to say, but he had something about him that made me want to fuck him anyway.

So I did.

Technically it was very good sex, but I thought about Zac throughout and felt shitty rather than happy. It was at that point I knew I probably was in love with Zac. Lousy timing on the development of expressive intelligence, but the mechanically brilliant yet emotionally dull fuck with Negroni Man had tragically underlined that.

'You're not staying?' NM asked as I pulled up my knickers. 'They do a great breakfast here.'

'No, I'm not a sleepover sort.' I'd have thought he'd got that since I hadn't asked his name, and when he asked me mine, I just avoided answering by saying, 'You can call me baby.'

'Do you want some money for a taxi?'

'No, I've called an Uber.'

'Should I take your number and call you next time I'm passing through?'

'Call me? No.' He looked surprised and amused rather than hurt. 'It's been fun, but I can't see . . .' I broke off and waved my hand vaguely between the two of us. I can't see this going anywhere. I can't see a repeat performance. I can't see you again. I didn't finish the sentence.

'Fair enough.' He rolled onto his side. 'Hit the light on your way out, will you?'

And that was that.

Until my period didn't come.

I've read everything I can on the matter. This baby is Zac's. Most likely, statistically speaking. A one-off encounter (well, twice, technically) is far less likely to have got me pregnant than the sustained at-it-like-rabbits action that Zac and I had been indulging in for a fortnight and resumed after just a twenty-four-hour break.

I had put Negroni Man out of my head. I had not allowed myself to think about the possibility that the baby might be his. I want it to be Zac's. Zac wants the baby to be his (although he doesn't know that there's a chance it's anyone else's, so there's that). It never came up. I am in a relationship with Zac now. We love each other. Just the day after the thing with NM, we made up and told each other that was the case. As I'd slept with someone else while we were not official bf/gf, I didn't think it was worth mentioning. When I found out I was pregnant, I didn't know *how* to mention it. I said I was pregnant and Zac assumed it was his. Right? Our situation wasn't an ideal one, but thinking about the slight possibility that someone else might be the father was only going to make it worse. I just didn't allow for that possibility.

But after meeting Zac's parents, everything has changed.

The thing is, like Mum said, I may be in exactly the same position as Clare. A fruitful one-night stand. I shut Mum down because it's too much, I don't want to hear it. It's massive. What if it *is* NM's baby? Then Zac is Neil in this, sort of. The guy bringing up some other guy's baby, but far worse because Zac doesn't know. It's so messed. I can't get my head around the whole dynamic with Zac's complicated feelings about his situation, the position Neil finds himself in now John Harding is in their lives. It's all totally impossible. So messy and painful. And I'm in the same space. I've been doing a good job of ignoring that fact, but since I met them all – his family – I really can't ignore anything any more. It feels different now.

The morning after NM, Zac called me at 9 a.m. He didn't text like a normal person but rang, bang straight into it. I considered not picking up. But I couldn't not.

'I'm really, really sorry about last night. Really, really, really sorry.' He sounded stupid but sincere.

'I have a hangover, Zac. I don't want to talk to you.'

'But you took my call, so . . .'

'I answered just to tell you I have nothing to say to you.'

'You're more rational than that.'

'You don't know me enough to decide if I'm rational or not.'

'I think I do.' It's what we all want in the end, isn't it? To be known and liked anyway. I stayed silent. 'I can explain,' he added.

'Nope, you can't, because I'm not giving you the chance to.'

'How come you're hung-over? What did you do with yourself?' I stared at my phone, glared at it. Outraged that he dared to be checking up on me after standing me up. Then he added, 'I hope you had fun.'

'As previously mentioned, I don't want to talk to you. Now or ever again.'

'That would be a tragedy.'

I didn't mean that I never wanted to talk to him ever again, even as I said it. I already yearned for him. Think about that. The word yearn, the feeling yearn. It's massive. I'd already forgotten feeling pissed off with him or turned on by NM. I just wanted the status quo between us reinstated. I was too proud to admit that straight out, straight away. 'You're a prick. How do you go from "I think I love you" to no-show in twenty-four hours? I am genuinely curious.' My mum has always told me the importance of staying curious. She gets me to read wall plaques and news articles and stuff. I'd never been more curious about anything in my life than this question, though.

'Last night wasn't about you,' he replied.

'Gee, thanks.'

'No, that came out wrong. I mean me no-showing wasn't about you.'

'It felt like it was when I was sitting on my own in a bar waiting for you.'

'I'm sorry.'

'What happened?'

'Something came up.'

Obviously, and that's a shit response. I wanted to say as much to him, but a not insignificant part of me wanted to find a way back to where we had been. 'Like what?'

'A family thing.'

'Not good enough.'

'Please let me make it up to you.'

'This family thing. I'll need details.'

'OK, well if you meet me for lunch, I can tell you then.'

I was strung out with hangxiety. And, I guess, a little guilt. I maintain we hadn't talked about being a *thing*, monogamy was not part of the deal, so having sex with the bad-boy NM was within the realms of acceptable behaviour.

Except it felt bad. Dirty. I did wonder whether I should tell Zac. Just drop it into the chat so it wasn't a big deal. But I didn't dare.

I didn't say a thing. Mistake. Big mistake. Huge.

FOUR DAYS BEFORE THE END

26

Connie

New Year's Eve

'Hello. It's me.'

She swallowed the flirty auto response, 'Hi you,' and instead asked, 'You being?'

He laughed. 'Greenie, it's John. Aren't I programmed in your phone?' He chuckled quietly. Pleased with himself. He was always pleased with himself. It was one of the most attractive and repulsive things about him. He wasn't programmed into her phone, long ago deleted, but of course she had recognised his voice.

'I didn't think you'd still have my number,' she responded. Everything she said sounded loaded: resentful, accusatory or desperate.

'Well, I have.'

'I see that.' She squirrelled that fact away. She'd think of it later. Decide what it meant and how she felt about it.

'You could have changed your number if you'd wanted me never to reach you,' he pointed out.

'I didn't think that was necessary and for many years you have shown that it wasn't.'

'I'm ringing to ask what you're doing tonight. After all, it is New Year's Eve. I thought we could go clubbing.'

'Seriously?' she stuttered.

He laughed. 'No, obviously not.' She felt stupid. Why wouldn't her brain get into gear? 'Do you want to grab a coffee?' It was such a normal question. Something she asked one of her girls, her friends, her fellow yogis, someone or other, daily. Yet it felt like the most loaded question that had ever been put to her when he suggested it. She felt awash with panic and uncertainty. It was panic, wasn't it? That fluttering she felt. Not excitement? Not desire? The adult thing to do was say no to meeting up alone, and he obviously meant alone. But maybe she could use this opportunity to set out her stall, make it clear how she saw their relationship moving forward (strictly chummy, familial). She wanted him to see how serious she was about this being about Fran and Zac now, not about Connie and John. That conversation was best face to face, surely.

Or was she just kidding herself, the way she always did around him? Did she simply want to be alone with him? 'Where are you staying?' she asked.

'The Portobello. But we should go out. It's not a great idea for us to meet in a hotel.'

Heat flooded through her body. Mortification. She wasn't suggesting *going* to his hotel, she simply wanted to know which Tube he was close to so she could suggest a decent coffee shop. He was so arrogant. She wanted to avoid a dreary chain; she could fully imagine what they would look like at this time of year. Pasty, bloated people in big coats and woolly hats that had already lost their pizazz. Wet boot prints all over the floor, Christmas music still playing, almost mournful now. Everyone was pinning their hopes on the new year; the indulgence of Christmas was something people were regretting or resenting. No. That wasn't the sort of place she wanted to meet him. She suggested a chichi coffee house that she liked, a five-minute walk from his hotel. She sometimes went there with the girls. The baristas wore leather bibs and the clients wore heavy-framed glasses and Veja trainers.

She changed her top, put on mascara, stopped herself there.

The café was, as usual, busy. The black tiles and the convincing plastic greenery resisted any nod to the festive season, and it was refreshing for that; the smell of coffee beans offered a boost, a sanctuary, after the wet and windy London streets. At most tables, Gen Zs and the younger Millennials had their laptops open. They nursed a single cup of coffee and would do so for hours. They didn't feel in the least bit intimidated by the waiting staff, who tutted and repeatedly asked if they wanted anything else, or by the new customers who hovered awkwardly in the hope of getting a seat. Connie couldn't understand how that generation managed to often be confident to the point of bolshie but at the same time were so frequently held hostage to feelings of anxiety and imposter syndrome. She didn't know why they behaved one way and felt another, but she was vaguely guilty that they did. Was it her generation's fault? Could they have done more to pave the way or offer guidance? She didn't think so. Her generation had been so busy and trying hard to ignore the grabby hands up their skirts as they climbed the ladders and smashed the glass ceilings. It hadn't been the picnic younger people always assumed.

He was at a table in the corner. He did not have a laptop in front of him; he had an empty mug and a paperback. She was immediately curious as to what he might be reading. The old image of greeting him in scruffy bars and working men's pubs blasted into her mind; then, he'd waited with empty pint glasses and overflowing ashtrays. She had waded through cigarette smoke as she made her way towards him. Now, she cut through the coffee aroma and the steam from the elaborate espresso machine.

A different world.

'You managed to get a table, then?'

'I thought I'd walked into an office.'

'Our office was rarely this industrious.'

'Maybe you weren't, Greenie, but the rest of us put in a shift.'

She shrugged; it was too true. She hadn't been fulfilled in her work when they met. She'd thought at the time maybe it was boredom that had led to the affair. At least in part. 'I'll go and order. Do you want another?'

'Flat white.'

She went to the bar, ordered the drinks. It seemed to take ages for them to be prepped. She wanted to relax into the minutes. Concentrate on her breathing and rehearse the conversation she needed to have, but she found it was as it ever was. She resented the moments she was away from him. She willed the servers to be more efficient, couldn't focus on anything other than being with him. What was that about? When she returned to the table with her double espresso and his flat white, she nodded at the paperback and commented, 'No one reads novels or newspapers in cafés or even on the Tube commute any more.'

'This isn't mine.' He put it back on the shelf next to him, which was full of artfully arranged orange Penguin Classics. The sort of books no one read but that made a nice display.

Connie felt oddly disappointed. She pushed on. 'Do you remember, they once did?' She sat down opposite him. 'I miss that. The commitment to the time and even space that was required to read a paper. Now, at best, we scan curated articles on the media channels we've pre-selected. Echo chambers to our own thoughts. Most people simply play Candy Crush.' She was speaking too quickly, saying too much and nothing at all. Nervous. The girls would identify it as word-vomiting.

His eyes widened and he raised his eyebrows. The gesture familiar. Her insides pulled like a yo-yo coiling up a string. 'I think you're romanticising the past. Our world was narrow and slow,' he argued.

He'd often argued with her. They'd disagreed on a great number of things. That had been part of it. That, and the exquisite delight when they finally agreed on something, usually something deep and fundamental. She countered, 'I liked slow. Now everything is temporary, fleeting.'

'But vast. I'd have thought you'd be supportive of wider experience. You were always up for that.'

She ignored the innuendo, told herself she was reading too much into everything. She stuck to the argument. It was exciting enough, this debate. She didn't need flirtation. She and Luke shared opinions on most things, never spoke about anything they disagreed on. They'd been together too long to want to try to change one another's minds about anything much at all. Which was fine. Just fine. A path of hard-edged loyalty gave direction to many good marriages. Still, it was fun to spar. 'A few inches on a screen is not experience,' she said with a swift smile.

'Of course it is. Stop being so negative, it's boring and predictable. News flash: middle-aged beauty resents progress as it reminds her she's ageing.' Connie knew she should be angry – his comment was derisive, his tone combative – but he'd called her a beauty. She let the moment settle.

After a beat, he said, 'Weird, despite the oddness of this situation, it is good to see you again, Greenie.' He stared right at her. Through her. She nodded but couldn't bring herself to say the same back to him. It was certainly *something* seeing him again. But was it purely good? 'This' – he waved his hands, gesturing between them and, confusingly, more widely, perhaps indicating the situation in general, rather than specifically the two of them – 'this is complicated. It's made me feel very young and very old at the same time.'

'Yes,' she admitted. That much they could agree on.

'I'm not happy about it.'

'You made that abundantly clear when you came for lunch.'

'I know she said it was too late to do anything about it, but is that true? When is she due exactly?'

Connie forced herself to swallow down her fury with him for voicing this thought for a second time. What right did he have? Instead she concentrated on finding a path through it. 'They *are* having this baby. You need to get on board or get out of the way.' She stared at him, but he had dropped his gaze to his coffee. What was wrong with him? Surely he realised that this was a second chance for him. He'd missed out on seeing Zac grow up; now he could be a grandfather. Was he so stupid and selfish as to resent the fact that he'd found Zac and almost immediately had to get used to sharing him? That was part of being a parent, realising you didn't own your children, you didn't have an automatic right to their love or time. No claim. You were simply a launch pad.

Connie took a deep breath, summoned up some patience. Of course he didn't have a clue; he hadn't had years of practice as a parent. He wasn't in the habit of putting other people first, seeing things from their point of view, occasionally swallowing down your own thoughts as you scrambled about for the greater good, the bigger picture. She could help here. She could guide him. 'Look, I am absolutely certain that being a mother has been the most important, absorbing, rewarding thing I have ever done. But it's also been the most exhausting, time-consuming and limiting thing too. I'm glad I have three amazing daughters, but I'm very glad I had them in my thirties, when I was more financially and emotionally ready for them. I'm not an idiot. I see the potential issues; as a woman, I see them better than you do.' He looked uncomfortable, bit down on his lip as though stopping himself saying anything more annoying. She was glad he was showing some restraint. 'I tried to talk to Fran yesterday about some of the practicalities.'

'How did that go?'

'Not well,' Connie admitted with a grin. 'But I'll keep trying. We'll get through this. She had a lot of questions about her career and childcare responsibilities. I'm struggling to know how to advise her, but—'

He cut across her. 'You think *you* can advise *her*?' He seemed to be laughing at the idea.

'Well, yes.' He looked unconvinced. She couldn't expect him to understand. 'We're very close and—'

'She won't listen to anything you have to say,' he said emphatically. It seemed a brutally dismissive claim to make. 'And he won't listen to me. They are so young. Don't you remember knowing it all?'

'As opposed to now,' she said with a nervous smile.

'Right.' He laughed ruefully, meanly, rather than heartily. She felt there wasn't a need to articulate her fear that as she got older, she had become concerned that she knew less and less; he seemed to get it. Everything was murky now, a sludgy amalgamation of shades of grey; youthful invincibility didn't last for ever. He shook his head and said sadly, 'If you make a mistake when you're so young, you have to pay for it for a long time.'

'Yes,' she admitted. She wondered whether he was thinking about Zac and Fran, or about the mistakes he'd made. Or the one she had.

'The consequences roll and roll. They can't imagine that right now. It's weird, isn't it, because popular opinion would have us believe that having so much future ahead is a good thing.'

'It is, of course,' said Connie. She refused to admit anything other. It was too bleak, but she understood what he was saying. She had thought the possibilities were endless when she was young, but it was a fallacy, a fairy tale. Every choice taken closed another option down. Every opportunity seized voided a different chance. Life was a series of possibilities, yes. But not a limitless amount of them. She played with her coffee cup, turning it in around in its saucer. 'I remember thinking everything was possible and available when I was young, and maybe it was, but even so, I chose to do the same thing over and over again. Live in the same city, country. Sleep with the same man for nearly thirty years.'

'Greenie, remember who you're talking to. You *almost* slept with the same man for nearly thirty years.' He started to laugh out loud. People around them eyed them uncomfortably. Connie had often noticed that younger people were shocked by boisterousness from anyone over fifty.

'Stop it. That's not funny. You were a blip.' They both knew that wasn't true. They fell silent and sat in it. The air shimmered. Would they talk about it? She didn't want to. She believed now that she didn't have the energy to talk about it ever again. He might have been thinking the same, because he let it go. He stayed on point.

'So you agree? You also think they're too young.'

'No, that's not what I'm saying. They *are* young, true. But maybe not *too* young. I'm saying that even with the endless possibilities of youth, I chose stability and continuity, so maybe it's not a disaster that they are looking to do the same. They're just starting earlier.'

'Can I bring you back to the question of monogamy and your struggle with it.' Connie scowled at him but didn't respond. It was undeniable. Fran and Zac were twenty-one and twenty-two; it would be a struggle, fifty, sixty years of fulfilling each other's every need – physical, intellectual and emotional. Was it even possible? 'So you say you're close. You and Fran.'

'Yes, we are.'

'I wasn't sure. I didn't see much interaction when I was at yours the other day.'

'It was a difficult lunch. Obviously I wasn't at my most relaxed. Nor was she,' Connie pointed out sharply.

'Oh, don't be offended. Why are you always so quick to take offence?'

'Because you are always so quick to cause it.'

'No, that's not true.'

'I'm offended because I pride myself on my relationship with my daughters. I'm honest with them, rational, supportive, loving.' She wasn't sure why she felt the need to list her parenting credentials to him of all people. But as a people-pleasing perfectionist, she couldn't bear to be found lacking in any way, and especially not in this way.

'Honest?' he questioned.

'Yes, we are honest with each other.'

'So does she know about us?'

'Jesus, John, don't be a prick. Of course not. She's my daughter, not my best friend. Why would I tell her about a long-ago affair?'

'I see.' John winced, crossed his arms and sat back in his chair.

'That's what I wanted to talk about, that's why I'm here, actually, to make it clear that—'

'What?' He flashed his eyes at her. The blue, unfair ones. It didn't help her stay on track.

'I wanted to say that obviously, erm, that, us . . .' She felt around for the correct words. 'Our past must stay a secret. I mean, I can't imagine a world where you'd chat to the mother of your grandchild about having an affair with her mother, but just in case. Am I being explicit enough? For the avoidance of doubt. You must not say a thing to her. Or Zac. Or anyone.'

John shrugged, took a sip of his coffee. Scratched his cheek. 'She'll find out.'

His nonchalance irritated. 'No she won't. Not if you keep your mouth shut. I've talked to Rose and Craig. They've agreed they will continue to be discreet.'

'And what does Luke think about all of this?'

Connie sighed, glanced around the café; she'd hate for this conversation to be overheard. 'Obviously he's delighted,' she muttered.

'Really?'

'No, you idiot. He's concerned for the kids because, well, they *are* kids, and as for the fact that you're Zac's dad, he's . . .' Connie didn't know how to finish the sentence.

'He's what?'

Apoplectic. 'Unsettled.'

They sat in another silence for a moment or two. She marvelled about who it was that she was speaking with. How ordinary it was to be having a conversation with him about their children's welfare, as she had had conversations with various parents at the sidelines of netball matches, at parents' evenings, at DoE planning meetings, for many years. And yet, how extraordinary it was. John Harding and Connie Baker sitting at a table and not reaching for each other, tugging at one another's clothes or hearts. Not negotiating their mutual and individual wanting or willingness. Not giving a thought, or at least articulation, to the subject of their own love or lust. All of that had been left behind, grimy baggage in a faraway lost-property office. Faded, covered in a light cloud of never-to-be-disturbed dust.

John stared off into the middle distance so she was able to study his face. He looked perturbed, angry even. She never recalled him being angry. He'd always been careless, carefree.

One might argue oblivious. What had wrenched him into adulthood? she wondered. There was so much she didn't know about him. Missing years. Was it that the small things had snowballed, the usual jetsam and flotsam of life – final demand bills, missed promotions, parking fines, broken relationships, wet holidays – meaning that he'd finally been crushed by an avalanche of concern? Or was it this situation? Their particular situation. She was trying hard to appear positive, hopeful, but there was no denying it was a bloody disaster. Could he be as disturbed by it as she was?

'Look, can't we just go into the new year hopefully? Peacefully? We just need to find a way to manage being grandparents together,' she said with a sigh.

He looked pained. 'I'm not sure.' He broke off. Shook his head. The words stuttered out of his mouth. 'Maybe I can't fill that role. Maybe I'm not that man.' Connie felt a sudden and intense flare of dislike shimmy up her spine. Her good intentions and positive thoughts were ejected instantly. He hadn't been a father to Zac and now he was wriggling out of being a grandfather too, apparently. He sighed and brought his gaze to meet hers. 'I just don't think this should go ahead.'

'Well, you don't get to decide. She is having the baby.'

'I realise that's her intention. But my son, your daughter, they shouldn't be together.'

'What?'

'I know things.'

'About Zac?'

He stared at her, a hard look as though he was weighing something up. He had something he wanted to tell her. He was deciding if she would hear it, how she would digest it. She recognised the expression. In the past, he'd worn it just before he revealed something disappointing about himself; today he was about to reveal something unsavoury about Zac, she was sure of it. 'This isn't right for him.'

Connie didn't have much of a clue as to what Zac was like as a person, what troubles or ambitions, triumphs or secrets might have collided to create his personality, let alone what might qualify him to be a young father, or sit at odds with that possibility. She braced her body for a shock, while her mind flicked through the imaginary rotary card index of offences he might have committed. Debt, addiction, infidelity. Her active imagination charged on. Drilled down into some of the specific offences that she could begin to imagine might be applicable to a seemingly mild-mannered twenty-two-year-old. CV exaggeration, expulsion from school, cheating in exams, a bad trip at a festival, another impregnation, shoplifting. She leant a fraction closer to John to encourage him to spill, but he remained tight-lipped. Apart. He shook his head, just once. Obviously he was deciding to keep something from her that she wouldn't like. Protect his son. She'd wanted him to behave like Zac's parent and this act was exactly that, but she felt panicked. What did John know about Zac that might be an issue for Fran?

All he said was, 'She's not right for him.'

What? A pivot. His issue was not Zac's lack but Fran's unsuitability. Connie was ambushed by a sense that her daughter was being rejected in some illogical, nebulous way. Fran was a gift. Anyone would be lucky to land her. She couldn't keep her irritation in check. 'How would you even know what or who is right for Zac? You haven't exactly been a main character in his life, not even a bit part. And you don't know Fran at all. Are you just making this judgement because of me? Because of *us*?'

John slammed his hand down on the table, attracting the attention of other patrons in the café. 'Bloody hell, Connie, not everything is about you. I have unrelated concerns. Right.' He looked directly at her. 'I'm going to advise Zac to walk away from this.'

'You're going to do *what*?' Connie couldn't believe what she was hearing.

'I just thought it was fair to give you a heads-up and to let you know that if she still wants to proceed with having the kid, then I'll chip in financially. See her right that way.' Connie's mouth dropped open, but no words came out. 'She's not a moral fit for my son.'

'A moral fit?' Connie leapt to her feet. The chair legs let out a squeak that sounded almost like a howl as they resisted the wooden floor. What decade was this man living in? His phrases were ludicrous – 'chip in', 'see her right' – and his mindset was worse than his vocabulary. He was determined to pile shame on the unmarried mother but protect the father. It was like something out of a 1950s kitchen-sink drama. All eyes in the café were on them now. One teenage boy had pulled out his phone and was recording her, hoping she'd do something meme-worthy. Was that even legal, recording a private conversation? In that moment, she didn't care. She didn't care whether she broke the internet for all the wrong reasons. 'A moral fit? What the hell does that even mean?'

'I've nothing more to say. As far as I'm concerned, the matter is closed.' John's face was red. She didn't know if he was embarrassed or angry. She didn't care. She no longer cared what this idiot man felt, or did, or said about anything. How could she have ever?

She glared at him. 'I thought I could come here and have some sort of adult conversation with you. That we'd pull together to help them. More fool me. You are a fucking wanker. You always have been and always will be.'

'You tell him, lady,' encouraged the guy recording the outburst. It was obvious he was geeing her on to get more outrageous footage. Connie cast him a withering look too, and then strode out of the café. The door crashed closed behind her.

27

Zac

He loved her so much. Like, an overwhelming amount. He didn't know it was possible to be this involved with someone. That their happiness, their safety, their *being* was absolutely intrinsic to your own. He noticed everything about her. The hole in the heel of her sock (there always was one in every pair she owned; she must walk heavily on her right foot); what her pillow smelt like (shampoo and fake tan); how she lined up her toiletries in size order (biggest bottle on the right); which way she preferred the loo roll to sit on the holder (over not under). She sang in the shower and talked in her sleep. Her voice was everything. He loved the sharp correctness of her consonants and the gentle contrast of her vowels. He loved talking to her and also just lying around being silent with her. Her silence was like being in a hammock; it cradled.

He only felt safe when she was in his sight. Rooms and spaces where she wasn't felt like vacuums.

He loved tracing the shape of her lips: pouty plump, but naturally so, not bloated with chemicals and shit. He liked to trace her jawline, her neck with his finger; she often shivered when he did so, but in a good way. She coiled into him like a cat. He loved the feel of her collarbone, her arm, her waist. Her skin was soft, smooth, it grew hot when she was angry. Her buttocks were always cold even when she was on top. Her elbows, they were the epitome of defencelessness and might at the same time; crazy, right? They summed her up more than any other single part of her body. Vulnerable and tough. There wasn't anything he wouldn't do for her.

He didn't know if she felt exactly the same. Was it possible to quantify? Did it even matter? He didn't think too closely about any of that. Nor did he give any thought as to whether this feeling would last for ever, because it would, it was impossible to imagine it not being there, despite his mother muttering dark warnings about infatuation and lust. He thought that was pretty close to hilarious, his mother using a word like lust, his mother *thinking* about lust. And also, it was sad, right? Her inability to understand the enormity of what he was experiencing obviously meant she'd never known anything like it. But yeah, no, of course she hadn't. His dad was a good bloke, but he couldn't imagine him or John Harding inspiring the same sort of absolute immersive, devoted obsession in anyone that Fran inspired in him. He felt sorry that his mother had never had anything like this, although over this past week he'd started to think that maybe it was for the best.

Loving someone as much as he loved Fran was debilitating, it was a crazy risk. Not a weakness as such, but a vulnerability.

He didn't like to think of what Bear could do to him, but he couldn't bring himself to think of what could be done to *her*. If the thought crept up on him, he felt dizzy and sick.

He shoved it away; he just wouldn't allow it into his head. Couldn't. He shouldn't have come to London, got messed up in this again, but how could he avoid London now? This was her home; she was having his baby. He'd do anything for her. Go anywhere to be with her. But Bear must never get the chance to hurt her. Never. The thought 'over my dead body' sprang into his mind. An old-fashioned thing his nan muttered about five times a day. When she said it, it always seemed funny. Now that the thought landed in Zac's head, it didn't seem funny at all. He knew the reality: they could hurt her if he wasn't around to look after her, if he was to end up the way Rob had. He knew these people had no limits, no qualms. He felt breathless and anxious a lot of the time. *All* of the time. Admitting that was filthy. His nan talked about people 'living on their nerves, very panicky'. He used to think that was a funny expression too. Again, now he knew better. Now he understood the pain of it. He hadn't been sleeping well, he was struggling to eat, when he did, it gave him the shits.

'He's definitely in love,' laughed his dad when he turned down the offer of tacos at Wahaca. 'Off his food.' Zac had tried to smile, joke along. It was hard pretending everything was OK to those who used to be able to make it so.

But his parents couldn't help him now.

Everything felt in flux, like liquid, inside his body, inside his mind. He needed something to feel solid. Focusing on keeping Fran safe felt like a concrete thing to deal with. So he had no choice. He just had to keep doing what they asked. Unquestioningly. Not upsetting them was the key, the only answer. That was all there was to it. He could never let her be in any danger. And he could never let her know what he'd done. What he was.

He didn't like having secrets from her. Obviously. In an ideal world he'd tell her every thought that flittered into his head, and all his thoughts would be about sex and video games, uni work and food. But he no longer lived in an ideal world. She could never know the real him. Which was a total pity. That was why he knew she couldn't love him as much as he loved her – he had secrets, she was an open book. He had made it impossible for her to love him entirely because he was dark and shadowy. Unknowable. Undeserving. Those thoughts were too big, sort of too loud, for him to deal with right now. There was a lot going on in his world.

He knew one thing, just one, in a clear and focused way. Loving her was like sitting up close to something beautiful. It was real. Their love was an actual thing, a fact. Something good, something great. And now there was a baby. He couldn't process just how incredibly, awe-inspiringly fantastic it was that they had made a being. An actual human.

He wanted to buy her a ring.

It was the right thing to do. Not in the way his parents and grandparents meant when they talked about 'doing right' by a pregnant girl. He wasn't *saving* Fran; if anything, she was saving him. He wasn't even flagging an outward commitment so people took them seriously; it was more profound and central than that. She was his person, the person who made the world make sense to him. The baby they were having would be his reason for everything, for ever. It was almost too big to put into words. Which was why he needed a ring; which was why he needed her to marry him. He wasn't sure how other people managed to go about their daily business when something as extraordinary as these feelings he was having existed. They were so massive. It was a pathetic, embarrassing cliché, but if she agreed to spend her life with him, it would be a privilege.

He realised all the stuff that everyone was going on about was a huge deal – babies being hard work and expensive and all that – of course he understood the money thing. Arguably buying a ring wasn't the best use of money. On the other hand, he couldn't imagine spending it on anything more important. A bond. The three of them versus the world.

He'd seen a little pile of stiff card jewellery boxes in her room. Three of them were from Tiffany. She was quite dismissive when he asked about them. Brushed it away as though it didn't matter that she owned not one, but *three* pieces from the jeweller that was the epitome of 'made it'. 'Oh, they were just gifts for my twenty-first. A pendant from Mum and Dad, earrings from Lucy, a bracelet from my grandparents.' She shrugged. 'I know I'm a cliché, a girl in Notting Hill who was gifted a diamond Tiffany key on her twenty-first. Honestly, I'd have been happier with like a piece of art or cash or something, but Mum thought it was this whole rite of passage. I think she bought it for her as much as me.' Fran had laughed; he didn't know if she really was embarrassed that she was surrounded by flags and signals that marked her out as a girl of a certain sort or whether she was secretly very comfortable with being in the club. There was still so much he didn't know about her.

That thing she said, though, that her mum had thought a pendant from that particular place was a rite of passage. That made him think that it had to be a Tiffany ring. If not for Fran, then for Connie, if he wanted her approval, and he found he did. Connie didn't like him, he could tell. It wasn't that she'd said anything out-and-out confrontational. She was extremely polite whenever they interacted, but she watched him all the time. He felt her eyes on him following him around the room, as though she didn't trust him. Her scrutiny was the last thing he needed. He didn't like it, not least because he knew she was right not to trust him.

He didn't trust himself.

He'd had a look at the Tiffany website before he dared venture into a store. He'd seen a ring that spelt out the word LOVE. The gold version cost £720, but you could get a mini version in rose gold for less. He thought it looked cool. It would suit her. Say everything.

The shop was insane. Exposed. Bullish. He didn't belong, but he didn't let himself feel intimidated exactly. He'd rubbed shoulders with Bear and his men; how could a few heavily made-up shop girls alarm him? As it turned out, the assistant was chatty, pleasant, not patronising or snobby. He relaxed with her, which was a mistake, because that was when he spilt that the ring was 'sort of an engagement ring'. Her demeanour had changed instantly. She'd looked aghast.

'An engagement ring?'

'Well, yeah.' He felt strangely shy. Silly. He thought she was thinking he was too young to be getting engaged. She didn't know him, though. He was going to be a father. He felt very, very old. He coughed and said more confidently, 'Yes.'

'But this isn't an engagement ring. It's a beautiful ring, but it's a token.' Zac was unsure what else a ring could be, if not a token. It did not serve any specific purpose, like a car, or a laptop, or a kettle even. 'You need a diamond for it to be an engagement ring.' Because she hadn't been snobby or patronising, he did not feel hustled, he felt advised. He allowed her to lead him over to another glass counter. The rings laid out before him sparkled, fizzed. They cost way more than he was expecting. Five times more, even for the simplest one. But the assistant looked happier, so he handed over the credit card that his dad had given him when he first started uni, for emergency use only. He crossed his fingers that it wouldn't be declined. He'd find a way. He'd pay it off.

28

Fran

Since my talk with my mum, I've felt like shit. Or rather, even more like shit. Not the hoped-for result. I am so adrift. Lost. Normally I can find my way home when I'm with her, you know. She sorts stuff. Metaphorically kisses me better. But since she isn't being herself – since she's being all careful and weird – I just couldn't find the words to tell her what I need to. It's a first. Not a good one. Not so much a PB more of a PW. I miss being able to talk to her about anything and everything.

When I was fourteen and some fuckwit boys in my class wanked over her picture and mine then sent me a video of them doing it, saying I was a slut, I just told her, no shame, no embarrassment, just a 100 per cent belief that they were pricks and she would sort them. Which she did. Even when I was more to blame over something, I knew she'd have my back. Like when a teacher caught me and Auriol looking at porn when we were about twelve, Mum just talked to me about 'realistic sex versus performative, exploitative, misogynistic sex'. I kind of needed a dictionary to have a clue what she was on about, but she didn't judge my curiosity, she just wanted to protect me. I've always been able to talk to her about anything: friendship groups, exams, weird body stuff. She even took my pregnancy in her stride. But this.

She'd go ape.

She's so straightforward, she sees the world in a very cleancut, black-and-white way; she has no idea about how complex things can be. She likes to drop hints that she 'lived a bit' before she married Dad. Vom. She wants us to think she was once wild, but I know that means she went from one snoozy monogamous relationship to the next. It was all that was available in their day. She wouldn't understand my position. I guess Lucy might. She ran off with the husband of one of her inner-circle friends, so I think we can safely say she's a little more fluid when it comes to questions of fidelity. But if I talk to her before I talk to Mum, Mum will find out and feel hurt. I'd have to manage her feelings on top of everything. I just haven't got that in me.

Is staying silent an option?

Maybe. It's worked so far. What else have I got?

I've spent the afternoon with Auriol. I was wondering whether I might spill to her; again that would be situation normal. We are – or at least were – the definition of BFF; we have an AAA pass to each other's every thought and feel. But when it came to it, today, I just couldn't. I see that she's trying to stay involved since I announced the pregnancy – going on about smols and cute little Dior rompers that neither of us will ever be able to afford – but I know it's freaked her. She's not interested. Not really.

Up until this, we've managed logistics and experiences so that we grew together; more than that, we've grown intertwined. We went to the same schools, we learnt to swim, horse-ride and ice-skate together; we both had our first kiss on the same night at the same social (different boys), ditto first time we drank too much alcohol, smoked cigarettes, smoked weed. We even managed to have sex for the first time within a week of each other (for clarity, different guys). We never even learnt a TikTok dance separately. It's the first time ever that one of us has done something that the other doesn't feel compelled to do within the next five minutes. We have always talked about getting a flat in London sometime after we graduated. I guess that's off the table. I know she feels on some level that the baby has ousted her. Problem. Night before last, I asked her straight out.

'Do you think I'm making a mistake?'

We were at her house, watching some lame romcom where the protagonists were all wearing Christmas jumpers. I wasn't following the plot, not just because I had half an eye on my phone as I was texting Zac but because, as ever, my mind was chewing over my real-life drama, no room for romantic montage or the inevitable glow-up makeover scene on the screen. Auriol replied, 'Not a mistake exactly but it's certainly, like, a . . .' To her credit, she paused for ages, really searching around for the right word. 'It's a definite hiccup,' she said finally. 'You know, for our plans and, erm, generally.' She looked uncomfortable, but I got the sense that she was not uncomfortable with what she was saying, more that she was uncomfortable with me for making her say it.

A hiccup.

FFS

It's a two-way rift. Today we went to Oxford Street. Big

mistake. I wanted to go to the Selfridges sale because that's what I usually do on NYE, but then I remembered, nothing is usual. Blythe Carter came with us. She's our third wheel. Always has been, since Year 9. She knows it, we know it. We are never unkind to her, she's definitely a friend, it's just she's never been essential to our fun. We've always had each other. The vibe sucked. The three of us trailing around the clothes departments lacked energy. We were looking at delish Toteme tops, glittery corset dresses from House of CB and everything adorable at the Kooples, but I was pretty nauseous and feeling tired, and then I remembered it was a stupid idea looking at clothes because who knows what I'll fit into in even a month's time. It's not like I forgot I was pregnant, I just kind of wanted to pretend I might still be the same as everyone else. Auriol noted how green I was looking, on both a physical and emotional level, so she said we should go to the department that sells baby stuff. There, she and Blythe kept giggling and picking up tiny babygros and socks, doing fake orgasms over the unbelievable minuteness.

'This is everything.'

'Oh, tooooo much.'

But I wasn't looking at the dinky little outfits; my gaze was locked on the equipment stuff. Oh my God. I have no idea what most of it is for. Humidifier, baby monitor, nappy bin (gross). What the hell is emollient cream? Usually I'm so in on the beauty products – ask me anything you want about peptides or hyaluronic acid – but I've never heard of emollient cream. There are like a million different cribs alone – cot, travel cot, bassinet, carrycot or Moses basket. Like, there's only one baby! There was so much stuff. Most of it ugly or terrifying, all of it expensive, as my mum said. After twenty minutes Auriol suggested a coffee.

Today, Blythe seemed to be more centre-stage than usual. Offering up more opinions, making jokes, spilling the tea on the girls we went to school with but had already lost touch with, kinda sliding into my space. She and Auriol were both talking about who they're crushing on. I don't blame them exactly; they haven't changed, it's what we always talked about. I just found it very bloody boring. I hadn't realised that we talk about so much remote and pointless shit. For months now Auriol has been going on and on about this guy she was hot for, Ned; today I asked about him and she stared at me all vacant.

'Ned? Oh yeah, I thought I was . . . oh my God, I thought I was falling so in love. It was everything and now it's quietly just sort of something. But not, you know.' She paused and stared at me intently. I realised that usually this was the part where I chipped in, but my body ached with tiredness and my head was full of real problems I just stared at her. Dumb.

Blythe jumped in. 'Like a side dish, not the main meal. I hear ya.' She giggled.

I nodded, but felt a bit irritated at the thought of the many hours we've lost talking about Ned, and really exhausted at the thought of the many hours there will be in the future, talking about someone else that she's pash about, and then someone else, and then someone else.

'I thought you really liked him,' I commented a bit petulantly. I don't know why I was hacked off by her frivolity, but I was.

'Yeah, but now I think he's something like a faded picture, developed at the chemist's in the 1990s, blurred and tinged, evidenced but lacking in colour.'

I swear she rehearsed that line. I bet she's been dying to deliver it.

Blythe said, 'Wow, that's poetic. You should be a writer, Auriol. You really could. I'd buy a book you'd wrote.'

'Written,' I corrected, but I don't think she heard me. Anyway, all of this meant I didn't want to tell Auriol about my baby-daddy dilemma. My life seems so depressingly real compared to hers.

I got back to my house and went straight up to my room, ignoring my dad's offer to make a hot chocolate. Flora has gone to her friends in Brighton for NYE. I miss her. She's who I go to on the rare occasion that things aren't perfect between me and Auriol. Don't judge that, it's just how sisters work. Not always the first choice, but always the reliable choice. If she was at home, I might have told her about Negroni Man. It's not quite the same with Sophie. She's still a kid. She wanted to show me the dress she's bought for tonight, but I shut her down. 'I'm tired, Sophie. Show me it later.' I just wasn't up to a whole thing with her giving breathless, overlong recaps of events with her friends, all of whom I am expected to remember and be like involved with. Not right now. Mum is out somewhere. No one seems to know where.

I've never been more grateful for my room at the top of the house as I have been this last week. Once I'm up there and I close the door, my family tend to get the message. Back off, leave me alone. That's why, when the door opens and I'm dragged from my weird, dense half-sleep/half-awake state, I know it's Zac.

'Hey.'

'Hey.'

He sits on the bed and I feel the cold evening air on him. It sort of balances the overheated room and I feel awash with gratitude that he's here and he's mine. I want to crawl closer to him and lay my head in his lap. I don't, though. I'm questioning my right to do so. Spontaneous affection is kinda slayed when secrets and guilt and fear and all that shit comes into everything.

'What do you want to do tonight?' he asks.

'Am I allowed to say nothing?'

'Yup.'

I sigh. His understanding somehow triggers a sense of guilt or responsibility or something. If he'd been unreasonable, I could have stayed in bed fuming at him, but he's really lovely to me. If he's disappointed about my lack of interest in partying, he keeps it to himself. 'No, look, we'll go out. I'll get showered and dressed and . . .' I break off. The very thought of this exhausts me. But I should make an effort. There will be many NYEs in our future when staying in is the only option, I'd better not flick the finger at this one. I decide not to discuss the matter, to conserve energy. I start to haul myself out of bed. That's when he says, 'I've bought you something. I hope you like it.'

'As long as it's not a breast pump, I'll love it.'

He places a Tiffany bag on the bed between us and nudges it towards me. His bitten fingernails look raw and shy, young, next to the solid special package.

'No, Zac, you shouldn't have. We don't have the money.' I'm thinking a pendant, and even while I'm saying that he shouldn't have, I'm reaching for the bag and untying the crisp white ribbon, because this is *perfect*. Right this second, I don't care that we have no money and the cost of this undoubtedly went on his credit card and will have to be sorted, swallowed by the enormity of the student loan debt that he also has; I am just thrilled that we're behaving like a young couple, reckless, careless, in love.

I open the bag and see a little blue box. Iconic. I prise it open. Not a pendant.

He hasn't.

Has he?

'Is this . . .'

'I hope it fits.'

'Is there a speech to go with it?' I don't know why I ask this. To buy time, maybe. Or because I want to be sure. He is proposing, right? Maybe I ask just because I'm a bitch.

'I should have a speech. I had, up until about three minutes ago. I was going to tell you all the things I love about you, but now that seems pretty lame. Not right. Not needed.' He shrugs.

I don't know whether he thinks I know all the things he loves about me and don't want to hear them – what world is that? Then, for one awful nanosecond, I think he's found out and no longer loves anything about me. He's just showing me the ring to say he's not offering it any more.

To punish me.

The thought kills me. I can't breathe. I freeze and feel awash with panic and shame. It crawls up my spine, over my head, into my eyebrows and my ears. I want to cry. But then I clock the way he's looking at me, and I know he doesn't know anything bad or disappointing about me. His face is aglow with hope and excitement. Actually luminous. He believes I'm something special, possibly incredible. It just kills me.

'The speech is lame. It comes down to one thing. I'm in love with you and I'm in love with our baby. Everything will be OK if we're a unit.' His words are so straight and sincere.

Absurdly simplistic. Each one of them hits me like a hammer. The hurt shudders through my body. I'm not who he thinks I am. Not entirely. Or more pertinently, the baby may not be who he thinks it is.

'Falling in love is a fucking disaster. It's not for our generation,' I mumble. He sort of spurts out a sound that's a bit like a laugh, a bit like a howl. I think it's shock. I guess it isn't the response he was expecting. I look again at the solitaire diamond on a gold band, classic, classy. I haven't touched it. I wonder if it fits. Instead of slipping it on my finger, I must tell him. Everything. The truth. I can explain that it was before we committed, that it was just one night, that it didn't mean anything. Instead I hear myself say, 'We haven't been trained for it.'

'What do you mean?'

'Like in my parents' era, there were different expectations, different rules and . . .' I break off. I would never have been unfaithful to him if the rules hadn't offered me the option as a basic right. The rules say it wasn't infidelity; we had not agreed to be exclusive. I know that, but I also know that it *was* infidelity. A betrayal. Mum is always telling me that in her day, as soon as you'd so much as held hands with someone, or shared a pizza even, you were basically in a full-blown relationship, just a breath away from picking out the colour of the bridesmaids' dresses. It sounds archaic and restrictive, unrealistic, but also somehow sort of charming and attractive as a concept right now. 'The problem for our generation is there's too much choice and not enough parameters or consequences,' I say. Although there are consequences, obviously. I'm sitting in that right now.

He runs a hand through his hair, 'I don't understand what you're saying.'

No, why would he? 'And there's divorce. Divorce statistics are so depressing. You know that, right? You've thought of that?' I'm clutching now. Veering away from what's really on my mind. I do not have a fear of marriage in general; just an acute awareness that he wouldn't be asking me to marry him if he knew, so I'm cheating again.

'You're wrong. That's not true. Our generation are just as capable of falling in love as previous ones. Some people care too much. Some people care too little. Some not at all. It has always been that way. It always will be.'

'That sounds so chaotic,' I groan.

'It is all an experiment, I'll admit that.'

'So you're saying *I'm* an experiment.' I choose to take offence. It's better than taking my medicine.

'Yes, in a way. We have chemistry and now there's a catalyst.' He smiles, there's something in his eyes that's begging me to go with him, wanting me to relax and enjoy the moment. I ache to just lean into his silly dad humour, to be able to simply enjoy his sweet metaphor.

Instead, I say, 'That's really corny.'

'I am corny. But I think we should make a go of it. The marriage thing. At least give it a try.' He's starting to look awkward now. His body becoming jagged and defensive. No doubt confused that his proposal isn't going the way he'd hoped. He must have expected me to fling my arms around him, to immediately slip the ring on my finger, then to slip my body under his for celebratory sex.

'Do you?' I ask. The emotion swells in my throat and my voice is thick with the sound of the tears I'm swallowing.

'Don't you?' I just stare at him. The words won't come out.

If I confess what I must, my world will blow up. I'll lose him. The baby will lose him. What then? The silence screams into our history. Downstairs, I hear the shower running. Sophie must be getting ready to go out. I can hear Dad, Grandpop and Grandma in the kitchen. Their voices a soft smudge. It's inexplicable to me that these sounds of my family, my home are gently rumbling along, unaware of what I'm dealing with here. Then I see his phone light up and I'm glad of the interruption. I guess he is too, because he snatches it up. Reads the text.

'Who is it?' I ask. I don't really care, but I pretend to because I need to change the subject.

'No one.'

And that's weird. Because he sounds sort of angry. Off-key. But then I suppose his proposal was just interrupted, or at least my response to it. Or lack of it. Still, his reaction alerts me to something I can't quite pinpoint but I know is bad. 'Well, that's not true, is it. It's obviously someone.' I want to sound sort of witty, blithe, but I sound suspicious, untrusting.

'It's nothing.' I expect him to put his phone away, but he stands up, reaches for his jacket.

'What, so you've just proposed and now you're going out?'

'I sort of have to.'

I think about that and it makes no sense. Where could he *have* to be right now, in this exact moment? I can take a good guess as to who sent the text. John Harding. He must have clicked his fingers and Zac is jumping. The finding-my-father thing is all-consuming for Zac. It's a disaster. I think about the lunch and that man suggesting I abort. I feel sick at the thought of them meeting. John Harding wants to break us up.

It's dangerous to allow them to meet alone. 'I'll come with you,' I offer, although it's the last thing I want to do.

'No, you can't. That's a stupid idea,' Zac snaps.

'Excuse me.' I widen my eyes at him, making it clear that his tone is not helping us. He is being a twat and he's never been a twat to me before. But I guess I understand. He must have been expecting a fast-and-hard yes. 'Look, Zac, stay here, with me. Have supper with my parents and grandparents. Let's see in the New Year quietly and then talk about everything.' I make a deal with the universe. 'Don't go.' If he stays, I will tell him everything. I promise.

Suddenly he looks so sad and sorry. Weary, almost ashamed. Ashamed that he's asked me to marry him and I haven't given a response. But I'm the one who should be ashamed.

The air has a claustrophobic tang to it. It tastes as though we're breaking up.

'I've got to go and you can't come. It's cold and wet, and the baby and everything.' He's keen to be gone. He kisses me on my forehead. Like I'm his aunt or something. 'I won't be long.'

But I don't believe him.

He's out of the bedroom and running down the stairs before I can say anything else. I listen to the front door being pulled open and slamming shut behind him. A draught swooshes through the house, all the way up the stairs to my attic bedroom. I shiver as I fight the feeling that something is very wrong. Something really bad is going to happen.

29

Connie

Connie hadn't wanted to go straight home after her conversation with John. She'd felt a need to walk around the streets, partially to shake him off (would she ever?), partially to think about what he'd said. She had to plan what to do next. He said he was going to advise his son to abandon her daughter. The bastard.

Eventually, after she'd walked for so long the wet bite of the evening had settled into her bones, she arrived home to find the house surprisingly quiet. There was a note on the breakfast bar from Luke saying he'd taken her parents out for an early drink before the New Year's Eve revelry expanded into outright raucousness. They wanted to avoid the crowds but also celebrate the season; they wouldn't be late. She felt a rush of gratitude towards him. He was keeping the show on the road, entertaining her parents, ensuring they had a fun festive season, even while they were firefighting this crisis.

She went to find Sophie in her bedroom, but it appeared her youngest had already headed out too. There was a tsunami of discarded clothes, smeared products, empty shopping bags, never-to-be-checked receipts, packets of chewing gum, grubby make-up brushes, shoes and underwear left in her wake; not just littering every surface but also on the bed and floor. It wasn't clear what was clean and what had been worn, so with a sigh, Connie scooped up the clothes. She decided against giving them the usual swift sniff test, but instead dumped everything in the wash basket. She didn't want to smell her youngest's hormones, deodorant and that particular smell – something musky, often shadowy – that lingered under perfume. The flags of impending womanhood. She missed her girls smelling of classrooms, grass and soap.

She picked up an upended bottle of foundation and another of nail varnish. Thank goodness for wooden floors. Sophie was not usually so sloppy, and her carelessness irritated. Connie reached for some make-up wipes and cleaned up the spillages while trying to recall where Sophie had said she was going tonight. Which girl's house was she partying at? She felt a lick of shame that she couldn't quite recall. It would be Amelia's most probably. Sophie quite obviously had a gentle crush on Amelia's older brother, and she liked hanging out there, hoping to catch a glimpse of him. She'd been there a lot over the hols. There, rather than revising. Connie filed the thought as one she ought to act on. She needed to ask Sophie how her study was going. Was she feeling ready for her GCSE mocks that were timetabled for the first week she returned to school after the holidays? She thought of how she'd helped Fran and Flora construct revision timetables for all their big exams. Together they'd practised lists of French vocabulary, Connie had listened to endless music practice with Fran and mounted art projects with Flora, she'd printed off past exam papers in the sciences for both girls and marked them too. She had planned to do the same for Sophie. But time was getting away from her.

She would check with Luke. He'd know where Sophie was tonight. He'd have arranged to collect her either just after midnight or perhaps tomorrow morning. Connie didn't feel concerned about that. He was there to catch the balls she dropped when juggling. That was a partnership. Amelia's family were lovely; Sophie would be having a fun time. As would Flora, who had sent a decent number of texts since she arrived in Brighton and had promised to FaceTime tomorrow. The new year.

Whatever it might bring.

Connie stood in the hallway and looked up towards Fran's room. She wondered whether Fran was up there with Zac, and if so, what they might be doing. She wanted to check but inwardly debated whether it was an invasion of privacy if she knocked on the door and interrupted . . . well, whatever. Her daughter was an adult and separate now, a direct result of the pregnancy. She had always belonged to Connie first and most, but was that true any more? Now she belonged to the baby first, and maybe Zac. Where did Connie fit?

'Mum?' Fran's voice was hesitant. The small upper hallway was illuminated as she opened her bedroom door and light pooled around her shadow.

'Yes, darling, it's me.'

'Do you want to come up?'

Connie almost tripped on the stairs, she moved at such a speed to accept the invitation.

The moment she walked into the bedroom, she saw it. The

starchy bag, the open box, the glinting diamond. Not on her daughter's finger. Still in the box. She made instantaneous calculations as to what this meant.

'So Zac proposed,' said Fran flatly. Far from the giddy excited fiancée.

'And how do you feel about that?'

Fran glared. 'Who are you? That's such a damned reasonable question to ask.'

'Sorry, are you shouting at me for being reasonable now?'

'It's just not very you. Why aren't you yelling "No way, don't do it, you're a child"? Or *something*.' Fran slumped onto her bed, then wiggled so that she was sitting propped up against the headboard, the force with which she landed against it causing it to bang against the wall. Connie had been kept awake by the sound of the headboard banging against the wall for a very different reason nearly every night this past week, so the sound made her uncomfortable. She planned to Sellotape foam to the back of it; hardly a very robust DIY solution, but she didn't want to ask Luke to deal with it. While he'd have a better fix, he'd have to know that Connie had spent a week with her head under her pillow trying not to listen to the slow, rhythmic bangs and the faster, more frenzied ones. He'd slept through it. Unbelievable.

She sat on the edge of the bed. Her weight made the cardboard bag flop over. It seemed defeated. She asked, 'Is that what you want me to say? You want me to tell you not to marry him?'

'For fuck's sake, Mum, I just need you to be *you* right now. You could say that or you could rush to get a bottle of champagne to spray around the room. I don't know, but you should be doing something loud and dramatic. Not this stupid fucking textbook version of how an open-minded, eminently reasonable parent should be when they hear their child is up shit creek without a paddle.'

Connie could have taken offence or reprimanded Fran for swearing at her but she didn't. She absorbed the outburst, the way she used to absorb toddler tantrums, recognising the fact that it was motivated by fear and confusion. She was glad of her decision when Fran put her hand on her belly and said, 'Sorry, baby, cover your ears.'

'I think, considering the fact this baby is going to grow up in this house and spend a reasonable amount of time with Lucy, it might have to get used to the swearing.' She smiled gently at her daughter, hoping to get them on a firmer, more companiable footing. Fran's was a fair accusation. She was not acting quite like herself. How could she? She was usually straightforward and honest with her kids, but since her daughter was carrying her ex-lover's grandchild, that option seemed remote. Still she tried her best to offer support and a sounding board. 'So the ring is still in the box and Zac isn't here. I take it you said no.'

'I didn't say anything. So he left.'

The sentence punched. It was a biological advantage and a prerogative men had been exercising since time began. Leaving. 'Do you love him?' Connie didn't believe love was all you needed, but she did believe it was where you started.

Fran sighed. 'I do love him. And I think I want to marry him. Maybe, one day.' Despite her bump, which clearly announced she was going to be a mother, she looked slight and vulnerable in this moment. Possibly because of it. Connie thought this was a spat. A miscommunication. Something the young people could work through if they took a breath. It wasn't the irreversible disaster Fran most likely thought it was.

'There's no rush, darling. You can take your time. If he's serious about the proposal, then he'll ask again, and if you feel rushed, he'll wait.'

Fran turned away from her mother, looked out of the window. It was dark, there was nothing to see. Connie shivered and wanted to draw the curtains, but she didn't dare move. Years of parenting had taught her that these moments of confidence needed to be handled carefully. They could easily be lost through interruption or movement. Anything that drew attention towards the listener and away from the child who was speaking might bring a premature end to the chat. She sat still and silent, waited.

Fran sighed. 'No, you're wrong. I can't marry him, *ever*. I can't do this.' Her words were forceful but careful, considered.

'Do what?'

'Lie to him.' Then, in a blurted rush, 'The baby might not be his.'

'What?' Connie froze. She couldn't understand what her daughter had just said. She felt like you did when you tripped up in the street and fell flat on your face. Rare as an adult, therefore all the more shocking. Knees bloody, hands stinging. Dignity and certainty bruised. She'd been expecting a confession of fears or doubts, a general sense of not being ready for this level of responsibility or intensity, a concern at being too young to decide who she wanted to spend the rest of her life with. But this?

This.

Fran stared at her, defiant. 'I had sex with two people in

a very short period of time. Technically either could be the father.'

'I see.'

'It's not a crime. Zac and I weren't exclusive.' Her voice was haughty, insistent. 'I'm not the first person in history to do so and I won't be the last.'

'No, but . . .'

Fran glared. 'But what?'

'Does Zac know?' Fran's bravado was immediately punctured; she shook her head. 'Are you planning on telling him?' A small shrug. Her daughter shrank some more. Considering she was about twenty weeks pregnant and hadn't told him yet, Connie assumed that was not on Fran's to-do list. 'Have you told the other boy you're pregnant?' Silence. 'Are you going to?'

'Jesus, Mum, all these questions.' Fran leapt off the bed and violently tugged at the curtains to close out the ink-black night. As Connie hadn't wanted to move for fear of interrupting the conversation, she realised Fran's activity was designed to do just that. Connie wasn't going to be derailed. The baby might not be Zac's. Therefore John would not be the grandfather. A solution? For her, maybe. But for Fran? Perhaps a nightmare.

'Talk to me, Fran, I'm here.'

Something flickered over Fran's face. It looked oddly like defeat. A weary shame. Connie braced. 'I hate myself for the mess. I just wish it was clear-cut. This is a lot on top of everything. You know, like me still being at uni and stuff. I'm trying to work out what's best for me and for Zac, but for him too. I love him. I love them both.'

'You love both Zac and the other boy?' Connie asked, confused now.

'No! I love the baby.'

'But you said I love *him*.'

'Oh yeah, I'm having a boy.' Fran grinned broadly, despite the seriousness of the discussion.

'A boy. I thought you didn't know the gender.'

'Oh, I knew when I came home. I just wanted it to be a surprise for you.' And Connie swallowed this too. This tiny deception. This small – quite natural? – power play. Her daughter's secret. Another one. It irritated. But she took a deep breath. She told herself that her daughter had every right to keep the gender a surprise, of course. In the scheme of the bombshells that Fran was dropping, the knowledge of the baby's gender was more of a firework than a hand grenade.

A boy.

As a mother of three daughters, she couldn't fail to see the attraction of novelty in this news. The thought flittered into her head. She imagined big gummy kisses from a sweet toddling boy. She understood what Fran was saying. Connie loved him too. Even though he hadn't been born yet. Even though she hadn't held him. She wanted to find what would be best for him too. She patted the bed, an invitation for Fran to sit with her. Which she did.

'So you are committed to being a mum. What exactly are we looking at here?'

Fran shrugged, opting to be sullen and silent. Connie wondered whether she genuinely didn't know the answer to the question. Or whether she did, but just didn't want to articulate it. The mother had to do the heavy lifting.

'And what's your relationship with the other boy?'

'It isn't a relationship.' Fran spat out the word.

'Then what is it?'

'It was a one-night thing. He was in and out of my life before I learnt his name.'

Connie did not let her eyes widen or her mouth gape. She'd always considered herself open-minded, but seriously, she didn't know his name! There was a point when basic manners counted. An introduction before seduction, surely. She pushed the thought out of her head and leapt to what was important in the moment.

Her daughter's happiness. Her daughter's comfort. The baby boy.

Quickly, with the experience and practicality of a middle-aged woman, her mind worked at a speed of knots to selfishly prioritise her offspring's well-being. She had some hard questions to ask if she was to clearly navigate the situation. She must balance the factors, the people, the consequences with the expertise of an old-school greengrocer swiftly weighing and bagging up produce. Would Fran's life be better or worse with Zac in it? Would the baby's? There was a world where she could try to keep Zac in the picture if that was what Fran desired, and another where she might ease him out if that was what was needed. She liked the boy, very much, despite the complications of his own parentage. However, she loved her daughter, and twenty-one years of protecting and prioritising her child had wired her brain in a particular way. Later she would think about whether that was conscionable.

So she asked, 'Does it really matter which one of them is the father?'

'Well, I guess they'd think so,' snapped Fran.

'But to you? Does it matter to you? What I mean is, would you want to be with Zac even if the baby isn't his?'

'Yes.' Her daughter's voice was a squeak. 'But that's never going to happen.'

Stranger things had happened, Fran was just too young to know as much. 'I take it that you're worried you're going to lose Zac if you tell him the truth now.' Fran nodded. 'And the baby will lose him too, even if it turns out that he *is* the father.' She nodded again; big, fat, splashy tears fell on the duvet cover between them. Connie held her arms open, but Fran shook her head slightly. Too much sympathy at a delicate moment would be an undoing. It was likely to unleash a wave of tears. 'If it happened before you'd both committed to the exclusive thing—'

'It did!' Fran interrupted, hotly.

'Then surely the answer is to explain as much to Zac.'

'No, it's too late for that.'

Connie felt a nip of irritation. She'd always taught her girls to grasp the nettle. Face problems down as soon as possible. Obviously it would have been a far better situation if Fran had told Zac about the other boy on the day she discovered she was pregnant. 'Fran, my angel, you are going to have to tell him. Look, I can see the temptation of keeping quiet, and I know that in the past lots of women have gone down that route, but you are going to have to come clean. It's the right thing.'

'Don't make me tell him, Mum. You should have seen the way he looked at me when he gave me the ring.' Fran's face, wet with tears, softened at the memory. 'He is just so into me. In a real way.' She turned away from her mother and sighed, a realist at heart. 'But he doesn't know me, does he?

Not really. He doesn't know this massive thing. I want him to always look at me like that, and he never will again if I tell him what I've done.'

'That's not necessarily true, darling. That's not how love works.' Connie wondered if the boy had it in him to find a way through this. Past this. Was his love for Fran big enough, deep and mature enough to weather this early mistake? 'Fran, the fact is, telling him the truth is not only the right thing to do but it's the only thing to do. I don't believe you'll get away with keeping quiet. Somewhere along the line it will come out. There are so many genetic tests nowadays. Anything from a curiosity to check out your ancestry to an illness or blood group anomaly that can't be explained might catch you out.' Fran looked terrified. 'The most leeway I can recommend is that you wait until the baby is born and do a paternity test at that point. You can tell Zac you need a sample for something routine. I don't know if he'll buy it, but he might. If the baby is his, no harm done, maybe you get to keep your secret. If the baby isn't his, you'll have to speak up.'

In her head, Connie apologised to Zac for suggesting this route that might very well cause more pain for him. There was a chance that just at the time he believed he'd become a father, he'd have to find out that he was not quite that. Fran was now crying with renewed vigour. Regardless, Connie pushed on with what had to be faced. 'Plus, you'll have to give some thought to finding the other boy if he turns out to be the father. I know you don't know his name, but you can go back to where you met, ask around. He'll have a right to decide whether he wants to be involved with his son at that point.' The advice hung in the air awkwardly. 'I don't think I can suggest anything other.'

'I can't do that. It won't work,' Fran wailed.

'It will. Even without the other boy's DNA, you'll have Zac's. I realise this will be awful, but remember you'll have us – me, your dad, your sisters – whatever happens. This baby will be loved.'

'Nooooo.'

Connie was reminded of her daughter as a toddler refusing to eat whatever vegetable she was waving on the end of a fork. A grim, determined refusal. 'Look, darling, if Zac loves you as much as you think he does, even if he isn't the biological father he might still want to stay in a relationship.'

'No, he won't.' Fran shook her head. Her chest was rising and falling now with the force of her tears, her face transparent with fear but blotched red through crying. Connie reached for a tissue. She wanted to hold it to her daughter's nose and instruct her to blow. But that time had long gone. Instead she handed the tissue to Fran.

'I'll find out more about DNA tests. Maybe there's even something we can do *in utero*. So this doesn't drag on. Let's gather some information.'

Fran shook her head again. 'It won't work because the other man has the same DNA. You see, I slept with John Harding.'

30

Fran

Mum is speechless. Like absolute death silent. She just stares at me. Sort of through me. Then I hear her breathing; it's super heavy and raspy. I think she's having like an asthma attack, even though she's never had one before. Sophie gets them and it sounds the same. Jesus, is she actually having a heart attack? She's gripping her heart and sort of opening and closing her mouth like she's silently wailing. I try to read her lips. I think she's saying *Oh my God. Oh my God.*

'Mum, what can I do? Should I call an ambulance? Mum!'

She shakes her head. So I just wait. I think normally I'd be crying right now, but her reaction has actually shocked me into stopping. This is bad. As bad as I thought. A tiny part of me had hoped that if I confessed everything to Mum, she would wave some sort of magic wand and make me feel better, tell me it isn't as much of a disaster as I think, but no, looking at her practically dying of shame because of me, I realise this is worse than anything. Eventually she stops mouthing the words *oh my God* and just stares at me.

'So you see, it's a total disaster,' I admit. Normally I'd drop the f-bomb here, but it's my baby's conception, any which way I look at it, I don't want to say that anything about the baby is a fucking disaster, despite evidence. 'There's no point in waiting, because a paternity test won't prove anything. And anyway, I think John Harding is going to tell Zac before I can.'

'What? No, he wouldn't.' Mum shakes her head ferociously.

'You don't know anything about him, Mum. How do you know what he would or wouldn't do?'

She looks at me, dazed. 'No parent would do that to their child. Break their heart in that way.'

'He's not the same as a regular parent.'

'True,' she sighs.

'And he might think he's protecting Zac.'

'Protecting him?'

'You know, from me.'

'Yes, I see. I see everything. It's all making sense now.' I think she might be in actual medical shock. Her speech is slow, almost slurred.

'You mean the lunch and how he behaved is making sense?'

'Yes.' Mum pats my hand heavily but is gazing through me as though she can't see me in the room. The lunch was excruciating. Like a new level of hell. She's mumbling something about 'moral fit'. What is she talking about? Then she finally snaps to. Something flickers across her eyes and it's as though she's just put on a new coat. She's my mum again, resourceful, helpful, in charge. Slightly bloody bossy. 'Did you know he was Zac's dad?' she demands.

'Of course not. Mum, what do you take me for? Zac stood me up. Turns out he stood his dad up too. He had this dumb idea that the very first time he was going to meet his biological father, he wanted me there, so he'd arranged for us all to meet in a bar but didn't tell either me or John Harding to expect the other.'

'It's very natural to want the support of your girlfriend on something like that.'

'I've told you, Mum I was not his girlfriend at that point.' I can't keep the indignation out of my voice. She rolls her eyes at me, clearly exasperated, but it's the salient point. 'Anyway, he bottled it. Idiot. Didn't turn up to see his dad, left me stranded too. Even the next day, when we made up, he didn't explain that he'd been planning on meeting his father. You know, if he had, then maybe, just *maybe* I'd have made the connection. He just said he was a no-show because of family stuff. I had no reason to expect his bio dad to be at the bar. He only told me all this the other night when I got him to walk through his relationship with John Harding in detail.' I'm careful to say John Harding. I like to keep the man at a distance. 'I thought I was simply revenge-fucking a stranger.' Mum looks pale again and I regret my choice of words, 'Sorry,' I mutter.

'But despite all of this, you maintain you want to be with Zac?' Mum asks.

I love and admire my mum in this moment more than I've ever loved or admired her in my life, and secretly she's always been my favourite human being. It's the biggest deal that her head goes to that space. What I want.

'I do,' I mutter, quietly. 'But it's a fairy tale imagining we can be together, right? After this.'

'Did he force you? Trick you? John Harding, I mean. Were you sober?'

'Three negatives on that, Mum. He didn't trick me or force me, although I wasn't sober.'

'How drunk were you? You can tell me anything.'

She's clutching. I get it, she's looking for a way to hand me a get-out-of-jail-free card. A way to make me less bad. But she's always taught me to own my shit. 'Not drunk enough not to know what I was doing. It was an equals thing.'

I've recalled the night over and over again. It's like I'm on a carousel; fun at first but eventually making me feel sick. Of course I have. I've considered it from every angle. Did he coerce me? Did he ply me with alcohol? Did he abuse his position as an older person to intimidate me? I can see many ways that this situation could be presented to reflect badly on him and somehow excuse me. Offer me a loophole. But it wouldn't be true. Or fair. Yes, I was drunk and not thinking clearly, but he was also drunk and not thinking clearly. And yes, he bought the drinks but I wanted him to.

'I wasn't tricked into it. I jumped into it. Neither of us discussed the matter at all. We just went at it. Sorry. That's a bit much, I realise that, but it is what it is.' I shrug, and Mum looks at me with an expression that I've never seen her use before. A massively complicated mix of pity, understanding, acceptance, but also – and this kills me – like maybe a shiver of fury. I wanted her to be herself, but wow. She's a lot when she has all the feels. I think I know what's bothering her. 'It's pretty disgusting if you think about it.' I try not to. 'How old he is, I mean. I didn't realise at the time. Obviously I knew he was way older than me, but I didn't think he was like Dad's age. Barf. He doesn't look it.'

'Or act it,' chipped in my mum.

'I don't make a habit of sleeping with older men.' I want her to know that. 'I was so confused about everything that was going on with Zac. He's pretty intense, Mum. You've seen that, right? Things between us had moved so quickly, he was talking about love and stuff. I panicked about that.'

My mum looks sad when I say that, and I guess it is pretty sad that this mess and confusion came on the back of a declaration of love. Love should be easier. Love is badly designed. It should be impossible to hurt because of love, but it's the opposite; it's literally easier to inflict pain and damage if love is part of the equation.

'I realise now that we got together at a super inconvenient time. He was working through his Darth Vader/Luke Skywalker stuff and the eternal question that boys seem to get all het up about. Who is my father? Am I as good as my father? Am I as bad as my father?' Hell. This will add years of therapy to Zac's roster. 'If only he'd told me that he'd arranged to meet his biological father at that bar, I'd have been on alert. I wouldn't have had sex with a random man because he reminded me of Zac in some way. You can see that, right?'

'Yes, they do have similarities.'

I was more asking whether she believed that I wouldn't have done this if I'd known who he was, but I don't clarify. I just say, 'Ironic that I picked him to blow off steam with because he looked like Zac. How bloody Oedipal is that?'

'No, sweetheart. Oedipus slept with his own mother.' Ever the educationalist.

'Oh good, by comparison I'm an angel.'

'Yeah, you are.' She smiles at me. My mum. She lets me make a joke, despite everything. She holds her arms wide and

I sink into them. For the first time in ages, I feel something like OK. Silly of me to get comfortable. I should know that she always hugs when she delivers the tough love. 'Are you absolutely certain you don't want to be with John Harding and that you never will be?'

'Of course.'

'You don't think that at some point you'll feel attracted to him again, further along the line, if somehow this manages to work out with Zac? If you're with him and you see John regularly and he's part of your life?'

I can't imagine ever getting to that scenario; it's like a world where there are unicorns, and tickets to Taylor Swift gigs are abundant. Zac is unlikely to forgive me or his father. I can't see us playing happy intergenerational families. But the hardest part of the idea she's conjuring is imagining me ever being attracted to John Harding again now I know he's Zac's dad and basically a very old man. I'm *done*. 'You're safe on that,' I assure her.

'Are you sure?'

'I told you, Mum, I was drunk and very mixed up.'

'Well, honey, I have news for you. You are likely to be drunk and mixed up again. Probably many times.'

'Are you telling me this adulting doesn't get easier?'

'It's peaks and troughs.'

'It's never going to happen anyway. Zac will never forgive me.'

Mum kisses my forehead and then sighs. 'You're going to have to get ahead of John Harding. You're going to have to tell Zac yourself now.'

'You think honesty is the best policy?' I bet she can feel my body turning rigid in her arms; I'm sick at the thought.

'Sometimes. Not always.'

That's not especially helpful. I'm looking for something more definitive. 'In this case?' I probe. 'You still think I have a chance of keeping him?'

'I don't know.'

'Gee, thanks, Mum.'

'Come on, sweetheart, you're old enough to know I don't have all the answers.'

'No, I'm not.'

'Then let me think about it.'

'Great, Mum, take your time. It's not like we're on a ticking clock.' I'm being a brat and we both know it. I should apologise. Instead I say, 'I feel like shit.'

'What do you want from him?'

'From Zac?'

'From John Harding.'

'I just want him to disappear,' I blurt. 'He hasn't been in Zac's life for this long, why must he be now? Can't he just vanish? If he moved on, maybe Zac and I would have a chance. Honestly, I think it would be our *only* chance.' Mum doesn't respond, which confirms to me that she also thinks it's my only chance. John Harding not being part of the picture, vanishing before he's exposed me to his son. 'Will you talk to him, Mum?'

'Me?' She sounds pretty weirded-out at that suggestion. Repulsed, in fact.

'Well, yes. You're his age and I thought you'd be able to get through to him. Find out what's on his mind, see if there's any chance you can persuade him not to tell Zac about . . .' I stumble. 'You know, everything.'

'I don't know,' Mum mutters.

'Could you try? You were talking to him at the lunch. Could you ask him to leave, to move on? I can't ask Dad to speak to him.'

'God, no, you can't.'

'I wish he'd just vanish.' I know it's stupid to keep saying it as though wishing hard for it might make it happen. I'm not eight years old, but I say it again. 'I think it's my only chance with Zac. If John Harding disappears.'

'You know there's honestly nothing I'd like more,' murmurs Mum.

'So you'll try.'

She looks like she's just emerged from a battlefield, or maybe is going into one, but she says, 'OK, I'll talk to him.'

31

Zac

As he dropped off the package at another skanky party, a house packed to the rafters with kids his age who were hell-bent on finding expensive ways to ruin their lives, he thought about the fact that he was a total loser and it was no wonder she wouldn't agree to marry him.

The music was loud and thrashy. He didn't recognise it. He used to really know music, recognise bands and beats and lyrics. But in this last year he'd developed an aversion to everything he associated with the drops. The music didn't exactly trigger him, but it certainly didn't lift him. He remembered a time when he liked to go to clubs, get drunk, dance. He was a pretty good dancer. Obviously it wasn't a thing he could say, that he was shit-hot at it – not without sounding like a total dick – but it was a thing that had been said by others. He was a shit-hot dancer. He felt confident that his limbs found the beat, that he looked cool.

They had never been to a club, he and Fran. That was weird, if you thought about it. He'd have liked to see her dressed up, wearing something skimpy, and he'd have liked to dance with her. He thought they'd look good together, he thought they'd move well together. She'd most likely be the sort to have a laugh on the dance floor, not take it too seriously; she'd probably take the piss out of him, but she'd like it that he could dance well. She'd wear that secret little smile she wore when she was proud of him. The one that made the left-hand side of her mouth move a little faster, rise a little higher than the right. Her smile sort of acted independently, like being happy was out of her control.

They had never been bowling or played mini golf together, they had never gone to a comedy show. They'd never been on a beach together. Suddenly all the things they hadn't done together stormed into his mind. They had never painted a wall; his parents were always doing DIY stuff around the house. They had never been abroad together, they hadn't even been to a festival and shared a tent. They hadn't had much time, not if you counted it on a calendar, and that was the way most people did count time, he admitted sort of reluctantly. They had been together five and a bit months, but with the baby and everything, in some ways it seemed a lot longer. A lot more. It felt like they'd been together for ever. He couldn't quite remember not being with her. He didn't want to imagine not being with her. They were right together. They would grow together, learn and . . . what was that old-fashioned word his mother loved? Flourish, yeah, they would flourish together. They'd have time to visit art galleries, go axe-throwing if she felt like it. They had time. He was sure of that.

Although apparently she wasn't.

The thought of her reaction to his proposal stung. No, that

didn't describe it. A sting was painful, irritating, it might even throb. This feeling he had was way bigger than that. He was in agony. It was like someone was slicing the skin from his bone. Torture. He wanted to lie on the wet pavement and never get up again. Just lie there and stop.

Once he'd dropped off the package, he didn't know what to do next. This Christmas holiday – if such a word was even vaguely appropriate – had been a series of pin drops that he'd hurried to and from, fearful that being slow would cause problems, have seriously nasty repercussions. Those journeys were always weighted with a sense of fear and dread. To think he used to get stressed about submitting a uni assignment late. He used to think that was the end of the world.

There was a temporary sense of respite after he handed over the gear and could dash back to the Bakers' house. He sometimes ran there, keen to savour the moment when he closed their heavy black front door on the disgusting world that he had been drawn into. The relief of being in their warm, bright home was immense. He relished being immersed in the sound of old guys crooning about white Christmases and being home in time for them, high on the smell of food being cooked, or the scent of cinnamon that came off candles – the house always smelt of one thing or the other. It never smelt damp or cold, or of puke or sweat, like the drop-off dives did. Temporarily he could hide behind a wall of funny, clever conversation; open, confident, honest people, and for short periods of time tell himself he was if not safe, then at least safe for the time being.

Now what? Could he even go back to Fran's house? He'd proposed and she'd practically recoiled in horror.

So no, he couldn't.

It had been raining hard, the sort of rain that drilled down relentlessly, not as drops but as sheets, promising nothing other than bother. A shame on this night that was supposed to be all about the party. But fitting, considering everything.

This year needed to be grieved.

Now it was just a damp, hopeless, persistent drizzle. Precariously heeled girls screeched and laughed as they hopped over puddles, their party outfits offering negligible protection. Hair was already beginning to sag and frizz; it would only be a few short hours before their carefully made-up faces looked sloppy and smudged. Since meeting Fran back in his second year, he'd never looked at other women and fancied them, but since being involved with Bear, he couldn't even see the joy of a night out reflected in their faces. He thought people were reckless, lazy, stupid, disappointing, and he was all of those things and more.

The slick streets were pocked with puddles that acted as mirrors, doubling the chaotic tangle of heaving traffic and crowds. Zac began to feel a vague sense of claustrophobia, so he stood still and fought for his space. People jostled him, irritated by his inertia when they had places to be. Twice he was poked by the spokes of an umbrella. Shopfronts still boasting fairy lights and other Christmas decorations seemed to be pushing him into the glare of the headlights from cars, buses and bikes that were crawling along the tight roads. He closed his eyes. The blaring of horns, thrum of engines and hiss of tyres screamed in his head. He couldn't breathe properly. The air was thick with the smell of fast fried food, exhaust fumes and occasionally a waft of someone's perfume or aftershave. Too heavy to be heady. The burden of being who he was weighed down on him. Then it occurred to him.

Might she know?

Did she know who he really was? The thought made his legs go weak. He stumbled forward, placing his hand on the bonnet of a barely moving car, in the hope of steadying himself. The driver opened his window and swore at him. 'Don't you dare fucking puke on my car, you drunk bastard.' Zac nodded, held up his hands, stepped back onto the pavement.

He replayed the proposal, such as it was, back in his head. The things she'd said were weird.

Is there a speech to go with it? Her tone, cold, distant. Almost incendiary.

Was she waiting for him to confess? If he had, what might have happened next? She'd have dumped him, obviously, but . . . An idea nibbled. Could they – the Bakers, with all their money and connections and confidence – could they help him? No sooner had the idea mooched into his brain than he rejected it. No. He shook his head. They couldn't. No one could. Anyway, he hadn't confessed, he'd told her of his love for her and their baby, but all she'd said was, *Falling in love is a fucking disaster.*

What did that mean?

Was she in love with him and hating herself for it? That would track if she knew. Oh fuck, it was over. She would never be with a drug dealer, of course not. He pored over her words. She'd said something about rules and expectations. Her family were all so straightforward, so upright and honourable. So unlike him. What was he thinking, imagining a world where he could be part of that, have access to that? He was a *criminal*. He was the lowest of the low. He had left another man to die. He had no right to ask her to marry him.

How could she know? He ran through the ways she might have discovered his crimes. She might have followed him on one of his late-night dog walks, seen him talking to Bear's men, perhaps followed him to a drop. She might have got hold of his burner phone and read the texts. *Not enough parameters or consequences*. He hadn't understood what she was saying, but he got it now. And he'd just joked with her. Made light of it. Oh God, what must she have thought of him? She was waiting for him to confess to this horrendous situation and he'd joked about chemistry. *Chemistry*, of all things. She must hate him.

Zac slammed his hand against his skull, hitting it forcefully, two or three times. An old woman stepped onto the road to avoid passing him on the pavement. She looked terrified, would rather find herself under a bus than risk being close to him. That was wise. He was an idiot. An idiot and he was disgusting. He hated himself.

What did she know exactly? That he delivered junk? That he'd left Rob to die? Did she think he'd chosen this life? Did she imagine he was paid for it? Oh my God! Another thought hit him like a wave knocking him off his feet when all he wanted to do was stand upright near the shore. She might think he'd bought the ring with drug money. No wonder she didn't want to put it on.

It was as though he was being dragged under the sea now, water in his ears, his nostrils, his mouth. He was drowning. She'd known when the text came through that it was from them. That was why she'd offered to go with him. As if. So naive. He couldn't let her near them. But she must know that too, which was why she'd thrown him a lifeline. She'd asked him to stay in their smug and safe upper-middle-class home, where the 1950s crooners and the scented candles offered a sense of protection. But he couldn't accept it. He wished he could.

He forced himself to take deep breaths. He plundered his head for any other explanation.

Maybe it wasn't that big, that wild. Maybe it was simply that Sophie had said she'd seen him at that party the other night. Fran might think he was boning someone else. Could that be why she was so distant with him? He brightened. That was something. That would be better. At least that way she was safe. He prayed that was the case. That Bear's people were nowhere near her space, that she knew nothing at all about drugs and gangs and death. What a world he lived in that being suspected of infidelity was his best bet.

Where could he go now?

32

Connie

Connie knew with a sudden calm and crystal certainty that she had reached an age when she no longer wanted to be complicated. She didn't want to present herself as a fascinating puzzle that someone should solve; she didn't see the fun in people stripping back her layers to get to know the 'real her', as she had when she was a more romantic, younger person. Now, she was aware of wasting time, of ticking clocks, of the importance of clarity. She thought it was wise to be straightforward and precise. It had taken many years, but she had finally learnt that asking for what you wanted was the best way of getting what you wanted.

Nevertheless, even if she no longer wanted to be complicated, she simply was. And even when she was not, it appeared that her life arranged itself to be so.

There were a thousand thoughts in her head. She sent him a WhatsApp.

We need to talk.

She watched the grey ticks turn blue and then she waited.

And waited. She thanked her lucky stars that WhatsApp was not invented when she had been younger; when she had been with him or any other boy or man, come to that. As someone who had obsessively used the 1471 facility on landlines to see if she'd missed calls from anyone significant, she was aware that she would have been overwhelmed by the multitude of modern ways to communicate and track communication, which somehow only ever ended up with poorer communication anyhow. Knowing he knew she was waiting for a response was a form of torture, torture by technology. God, young people's lives were hard now. Everything had changed. Then she had a still bleaker thought. Some things didn't change. There was a pregnant girl. She might end up doing this alone. That was an age-old story.

She had decided she did not want to face her husband or parents just yet, so she had left the house before they returned and found a bar to hole up in. She reasoned that if she saw Luke and failed to tell him about this latest bomb that Fran had dropped, then she was without doubt betraying her husband. However, if she did not see him, she told herself that she wasn't actively betraying him. She wanted to delay the moment of revelation, at least until she had dug her way to a conclusion. If she could persuade John to disappear, did Luke even have to know this latest complication? Connie thought that telling him that his daughter had had sex with John Harding might kill him. For real. The shock might break his heart. He would not be able to stomach the thought. It had taken a year of separation for him to accept that the man had slept with his wife. Luke hated John. *Hated* him.

Or, if she told him, he might not die of a broken heart but he might very well kill John. The thought made her shudder. She told herself she was getting carried away, that she was being stupid and extreme. People didn't actually kill one another over this sort of thing.

Except they did. She knew they did.

What to do? Because if she didn't tell him, it was worse. Another secret. Another betrayal. That was how he'd see it; he would not accept that her silence was a result of her absolute desire to protect him and Fran. If he ever found out that she'd tried to keep this from him, she'd be fighting for her own relationship. Tooth and claw. A new thought jabbed her. If he somehow found out at a later date, he might kill *her*, not John Harding. She shook her head. She was being really silly. Luke wouldn't hurt her. She sipped her gin and tonic, slowly. She absolutely must not order a second drink. She needed to try to keep a clear head.

After fifty minutes, she received a message from John. One word.

Apology?

WTF. He expected an apology from her? She felt fury flare through her body. True, she'd called him a wanker this afternoon in a coffee shop, but he'd once almost ruined her life and now he had ruined her daughter's too, so on balance she didn't feel the obligation of fault.

Quickly disregarding her promise to herself, she ordered a second G&T.

She wanted to send him a string of more choice insults and vivid expletives. She'd always known that they'd end up here in this chaotic swamp of anger and name-calling. She had tried not to, on so many occasions. Back when they were... whatever they were. She'd say lovers, he'd say a fling. Throughout that intense ball of fire she'd managed never to name-call, to insult. It hadn't turned bloody, at least not between them. She'd borne all the pain, regret and shame alone. And again, when he'd inconveniently reappeared when the girls were young and tried to rock the boat for a second time, she had remained poised, on course.

Every time he was in her life, she had forced herself to resist the urge to yell and scream at him or about him; to call him a bastard and tell him she hated him. She'd wanted to avoid all that predictable, embarrassing anger and to cling to some level of dignity. She'd had an affair and that was grubby and gory enough, she accepted that. But, she'd reasoned to herself, if they ended up hating each other, indulging in a low-brow mud-slinging match, it would completely and irretrievably void any love, or delicacy, or depth that she'd ever thought she'd felt. Once upon a time. Way back when. And if she allowed the final residue of value to their encounter to be obliterated, then she wouldn't be able to stand a single thing about herself. Because everything would have been for nothing. She needed to believe with a very deep, far-buried atom of her being that what she'd done with him – no matter how bad, or mistaken, or foolish or just plain wrong – was at least meaningful.

Now she didn't give a fig about meaningful.

She hadn't thought there was another way this man could wound her, but here it was. However much upset he'd ever inflicted on her was now quadrupled because he was hurting her daughter. Her child. Her baby. Every cell in her body was in revolt. Loathing erupted from every pore. Her head pounded with utter horror that he was on the planet. She hated him for bringing chaos to her girl's life. She really did.

Her focus was no longer on maintaining her dignity or on upholding a vision of herself or their encounter; now her focus was on protecting Fran. She needed to stay smart. Cool. Collected. These were not things she generally was when around him. She was impressed by her daughter's practicality. Her ability to embrace compromise, loll in it. Fran would try to keep her relationship with Zac on course if she could. She was prepared to accept things as they were and find a way of working with it. It seemed more adult than Connie had ever managed to be. Fran didn't care who the baby's father technically was; she had decided who she wanted to be the daddy, who would be the better daddy to her son. Could it work? Did Connie have it in her wheelhouse to persuade John to walk away, to leave them alone? If not that, could she at least persuade him to be the grandfather, to stay quiet about the possibility that he might be anything other?

So she sent another message.

I am sorry I lost it in the coffee shop. I shouldn't have called you a wanker.

She couldn't bring herself to say that he was not a wanker, because he categorically was. The message did the trick.

Where are you?

She was embarrassed, but she replied.

In the bar in your hotel.

When she'd thought of finding a bar, this had been the first place that came to mind. He'd told her he was staying at the Portobello, and as ever, she'd had to make this easy for him. If he simply had to get in an elevator to come and talk to her, he might just do it. If he'd been required to travel any distance, he might have been put off by the weather or the thought of busy Tubes. Any obstacle in his path would trip him up. It always had.

Coming down.

She let him get a beer from the bar and settle into the seat opposite hers before she said, 'What the actual fuck? You slept with my daughter.'

'Ah, she's finally told you.' He took a long slurp of his beer, directly from the bottle. After he'd swallowed and wiped his mouth with the back of his hand – just stopping short of belching – he said, 'I didn't know she was your daughter at the time.'

'That hardly excuses it. She's less than half your age.'

'I didn't realise she was so much younger than me,' he offered.

'Well, how old did you think she was?'

'I don't know. Twenty-eight, maybe thirty.' Fran didn't look especially old for her age, so Connie doubted this. He shrugged. 'Honestly, I didn't really think about it. Are you able to age young people accurately?'

'No, but I don't make a habit of sleeping with them,' snapped Connie.

'Look, I was single, she was single – or at least as far as I knew, she was. I don't feel my age and I don't always sleep with people my age. I didn't think there would be so many consequences.' He made an audible gesture that hovered between a shrug and a sigh. It was too easy to comment that he never thought of consequences. Easy and inflammatory. She stopped herself. John apparently was not so bothered about minimising aggro. 'She's over the age of consent and not exactly an innocent flower. So let's not go down that path.'

'Excuse me?'

'She's trapping my son into being with her, even though the baby might not be his.'

'It might be *yours*. Have you heard yourself?'

'It's unlikely, isn't it? On balance. Considering my age. Zac is likely to have the stronger swimmers.'

He was so matter-of-fact that Connie felt blindsided. He had a point, though, and she was happy to accept he was right – she prayed the baby was Zac's – but it didn't really scratch the surface of this problem. She studied him. How was it possible that he was so cavalier about the situation? Was he really? The hotel bar was busy and noisy. It was a stroke of luck that the tables were set out with a decent amount of space around each. Glamorous, youthful groups were standing about, congregating to take photos to prove they were having a good time before their Ubers arrived and took them on to clubs, or dinners, or other bars. Connie was glad that most people were self-absorbed most of the time, and even more so on New Year's Eve, when the acceptable mood was determined hedonism. No one was paying the middle-aged couple any attention. She was able to talk freely.

'Why didn't you tell me today when we met for coffee?'

'I tried to.'

'No, you didn't.'

'I did. I asked you if you were honest with your daughter. If she was honest with you. You seemed pretty certain on both accounts, so I didn't think it was my place to highlight the fact that both of you are lying bitches, and you in particular are a delusional lying bitch.'

'Lovely. Thank you.'

Him calling her a bitch, calling her daughter one, made her feel filthy. She had an urge to fling her drink at him. She imagined it arcing satisfactorily towards him, then soaking him, shocking him. She slid her hands beneath her thighs, sat on them to restrain herself. She clamped her mouth tightly closed to stop her articulating a retort either. As she'd got older, she'd noticed that her previously straight and balanced teeth seemed a little large for her mouth, her gums were retracting, exposing the roots. Her teeth felt sharp and jagged, and she pushed her tongue up against the roughness, clenching down so hard that a tang of iron slithered around her tongue. Blood. She could taste blood.

'Sorry,' he muttered. Which surprised her. 'You're not being a bitch. Well, you are, but I get it. It's a real mess and I don't know what to do for the best.' Just when she thought he couldn't ever surprise her. There it was. Amazing, a touch of sensibility and understanding, something she could relate to. Vulnerability. He looked at the table as he said, 'This whole thing, it's just too much. I didn't know how to talk to you about it. I've been in shock since you opened the door when I came round for lunch. I figured you'd both tell each other what you needed to eventually, and you have. I doubt you're going to believe me, but by keeping quiet for a day or so, I was trying to do the right thing for Fran, even though she's a bitch and cheated on my lad. I thought I'd give her the benefit of the doubt. Time to get her head around it.'

Connie realised she didn't care what he thought of her any

more. Delusional bitch was as good a label as any for him to pin on her. She didn't care one iota. But she cared what he called her daughter. Yes, she had to avoid a row as she had a job to do here. But she wouldn't allow him to trash Fran. She swallowed the blood she'd drawn. 'Stop calling my daughter a bitch. She's not. If you think you're confused, can you imagine what this is like for her? She's a child.'

He turned red. She used to think his blushing was a charming show of defencelessness; now she thought it was an ugly mark of shame or guilt. 'She's not a child, Connie. I mean, trust me, I know.'

Connie held up her hands, as though she could push his words away. She thought there was a genuine risk that he'd give details of the encounter. The last thing on earth she wanted was details of the sex her daughter had had with her lover. Ancient lover, yes, but still, one of the most important men in Connie's life. A defining man. She wasn't ready to hear that. She never would be. Everything had changed now. For ever.

He continued. 'I realise she's your kid, but she's an adult, a fully grown woman.'

The expression he'd picked horrified her. *Fully grown* sounded too overt, too fecund and blooming. Thoughts of taut thighs, legs intertwined, full breasts and peachy bottoms pushed into Connie's mind. She fought her brain, not allowing it to bring the images into sharp focus. It was best they stayed smudged and general. She didn't want to attach her daughter to the imagined legs by seeing a small cluster of birthmarks on the thigh. Fran had such a mark, and Connie and Luke had always told her it was a constellation; not a blot of any kind, but a cluster of stars. She had a tattoo on her shoulder blade, a tiny kitten. Connie wasn't especially fond of the tattoo, never had been, but now her blood revolted, boiled in her veins at the thought of his fingers trailing across it, his lips honing on it as though it was a target. She mentally started to sing 'Ain't No Mountain High Enough'. She had no idea why that particular song had leapt into her mind. She had never imbued it with any particular significance. It was just loud enough, maybe, to block out the thoughts that were festering in her imagination.

She forced herself to stay on track. Helping Fran was all that mattered. Sticks and stones only, his words couldn't hurt her. 'Fran is dealing with a lot,' she reiterated.

John nodded. 'OK, so I'm guessing now she's totally freaked that we used to know each other?'

'What do you mean?'

'I was trying to be polite. I mean screw. I assume Fran's freaking out because we used to screw.'

Connie recoiled. 'What? No. Obviously I haven't told her we slept together.'

'Oh, I see. Obviously.' John raised his eyebrows, making a point of looking confused. It was an act. 'Hang on, why *obviously*?'

'I'm married to her father, who she loves, and I was then too. I don't want to hurt her. Destroy everything she's ever believed in.'

'Right, I see. So by your account, I'm the only bad guy here.'

'Well, no, but you are the most recent offender.'

'Nope. That's Fran. I was single.' He took another long slug of his drink. He just wanted to make her sweat, make her accept the caveats on her claim at being honest, make her acknowledge her daughter's part in this. She just wanted to blame him for everything, but she knew that wasn't fair. Not really. After a while, he leant towards her, his elbows on the table between them, his breath in the air. 'I get it, Greenie, I do. It's super complicated with kids, isn't it? You have no idea how relieved I was when you first told me she didn't know about us. Up until then, I had thought she'd targeted me for some creepy competitive daughter-mother thing.'

'No, God no.' Not for the first time, she wondered how his mind worked.

'You know, thinking about it now, she reminds me of you in a way.' He leant back in his chair and took another slug of his beer, then smiled, either at the recollection or the thought that he was delivering a compliment. Connie felt horrified. Under any other circumstances, being told that there was a resemblance between her and her daughter was a source of joy. If anyone ever said that they had similar smiles or eyes, the same expressions, she lapped up the flattering remarks. Not just because her daughter was acknowledged to be extremely pretty, but because there was something primal and delightful about seeing yourself reflected in your kids' faces. It helped you learn to like yourself more. It felt like you'd left a stamp, you had a place in the world. Right now, she thought she might vomit. She didn't want compliments off John Harding ever again. Which was useful, because the next thing he said was, 'Not you now, obviously. But something about back then.' He turned his intense gaze from her and stared off into the distance, musing, 'I guess I have a type.'

If so, she hadn't noticed when they were younger. His only criteria as far as she recalled was that the people he slept with had to be female and awake, hardly discerning enough to develop a type. Sadly, this realisation had arrived too late, after she'd fallen for his nonsense about her being special and different.

'So what happens now?' he asked.

'I don't know.'

'Is she going to tell him?'

'I don't know.' A pause. 'Are you?'

'I don't know.'

Connie sighed. 'It appears neither of us knows much.'

'Why did you come here, Greenie? Really, what do you want?' His blue eyes, wide and intense, pierced her. As they always had. She used to think he could read her mind, that they were so in tune, connected, that they had an intangible cerebral energy between them. But then she discovered he just had good eyes. He'd never had a clue what she was thinking, unless she spelt it out. It was time to make her pitch.

'I want to ask you to be a father.'

'What?' The aforementioned gorgeous eyes widened in shock.

'Not the father of Fran's baby. I want you to walk away from Zac. I want you to disappear. It's the best thing you can do for him. Doing your best for him is being a father.' Connie used the argument her daughter had articulated. 'You've barely been in his life. He doesn't need you. He has Clare and Neil. You've only known him a very short time, but you must be able to see how much he loves Fran. Knowing what happened between you and her would kill him.'

The room seemed to still, like a tide going out and a shore being left quiet and empty. The surrounding chatter was muffled, the background music dipped. In fact, it was still as buzzy and loud, but Connie and John were so immersed in their own world, their own chaos, that everything else fell away. The laughter, the song lyrics, the clinking of glasses, their history, their hopes, their love, lust and lies all faded. 'If you stay around, it will come out further along the line. Irrespective of whether the baby is yours or not, it will destroy them. Destroy your son. You should walk away. It is the kindest thing you can do for him.'

'And it's the cruellest thing to ask of me.'

'I know that.'

33

Connie

'No. No way. That's not right. How can you even ask it of me?' He banged his hand down on the table between them. The flame on the tiny tea light flickered and then went out. 'It may not have crossed your mind, but Zac is my *only* child. I just found out about his existence six months ago. I was hoping to develop some sort of relationship with him.'

'Well, the chances of that are slim if he finds out you slept with his girlfriend and that you might be the father of the baby he considers his. Don't you think?'

'Jesus.' John started to blink rapidly. He looked as though he was going to cry. She hadn't expected that. 'It all happened before I met him.'

'It doesn't matter.'

'She meant nothing to me.'

'That will just hurt him more.'

'I'll keep quiet. I don't have to give him up. I can keep this secret.'

And this was new too. Feeling absolute and total pity for

John Harding. She wanted to reach out to him, touch his arm, offer some level of condolences, but she could not. She faced the facts, placed them carefully in front of him. 'You won't be able to keep this a secret. Even if you try. You'll give it away somehow, in the way you behave towards Fran or when the baby comes. You don't know how you'll feel then. You might want to claim him.'

'It's a boy?' John still had tears in his eyes, but his face broke into an astonishing beam. She knew he was already imagining wrapping a Liverpool football scarf around the little boy's neck, taking him to the game. Two generations or three wearing the red and white? Connie wanted to kick herself. It didn't help revealing more about the baby, making him more real and present. It was better if the tiny being stayed in the abstract for John.

'Slip of the tongue, they don't know the gender yet. But you see how you felt in that moment. You wanted to be involved. It's better to cut ties now.'

'But you're asking me to sacrifice such a lot. Everything.'

'Yes, I am. Because it's the best thing you can do for Zac. I'm sorry, but that's being a parent.' At that moment, Connie's phone flashed. It was Luke, ringing her. She wished she could tell everyone to shush before she picked up. She answered awkwardly, as though she'd been caught doing something she shouldn't. In fact all she was doing was what she must.

'Where are you?' Luke sounded fraught.

'In a bar.'

'Where?'

'Just around the corner.'

'Where exactly?'

'The Portobello.' The exchange was at speed. She'd had thousands of phone calls with her husband over the years. The leisurely, flirty, investigative ones were long gone, but sometimes if his work took him away from home, they still enjoyed reasonably lengthy, relaxed chats, although naturally, most often their exchanges were short and to the point: can you buy some milk? Will you pick up cash to pay the gardener? Sometimes, one or the other of them had made a call to pass on bad news. An accident, an illness. Worse. Connie immediately judged this call to be in that bracket. Bad news. A panic, a problem. Did he know about John? Was he coming to find him? Then her thoughts went to her parents. After all, Luke was with them. That seemed most likely. She stood up from the table and walked away from John, already heading to the door before she really knew why.

'Is it Mum? Dad?'

'No, no, they're here with me.'

'Is it the baby? Is Fran OK?'

'Fran's fine.'

'Luke, just tell me.' Obviously, he was trying to. He probably wanted her to stop cutting across him so he had a moment to ready her. Fear made her sound angry, but he'd understand that, he'd forgive her.

'It's *our* baby. It's Sophie. She's in hospital.'

'What's happened?' Her body itched as goosebumps erupted up and down her arms and legs.

'We need to get there straight away, Connie. There is literally no time to lose.'

'Which hospital?' Her voice didn't sound like her own and it certainly wasn't all that she wanted to say, but she didn't dare ask for details. Couldn't bring herself to. *There is literally no time to lose.* This was the call every parent dreaded from the moment they gave birth. The worst nightmare. The last thing imaginable. 'Was there an accident? Is she . . . What do you know?'

'She's taken something. She's not conscious.'

'Taken something? No, she doesn't do drugs. Our girls don't do drugs,' Connie responded firmly, as though stating as much might change something.

'Connie, just get in a taxi.'

'Tonight? The streets are packed.'

'Just get to the hospital. I don't care how you get there, Tube, taxi, run. Just come. We don't know how long she's—'

She cut him off before he could finish the sentence. She couldn't hear what he had to say.

34

Fran

I've never been so scared in all my life. I can't move or think or speak.

My baby sister is not moving, not a millimetre, not a flicker. She is lying in this weird, sterile place and she looks like she's dead, all grey and covered in wires. I don't want that thought in my head, of course I don't, but it's there anyway. Sophie is never still. This is all wrong. The baby in the family, she's generally the embodiment of activity. Always laughing or talking or arguing or screaming or having an opinion on something or other. On everything. Her vibe's sort of sturdy and present.

Normally.

Usually, as she moves around, her hair is falling into her eyes and she's constantly brushing it away with impatience. If she's carrying something, like her phone or a tennis racquet, a cup of tea, a can of Diet Coke, she just blows her fringe out of her eyes. Her silky hair flutters easily, like the pages of a book being flicked through, because her breath is a storm.

But now there are machines helping her breathe. She can't do it on her own.

If she's not talking, she's humming, singing or even whistling. Who still whistles any more, other than Sophie? Right? The only thing whistling and humming now is the steady beeping of monitors and the soft hum of medical equipment. I hate the tubes and machines, recoil from them, but at the same time I'm praying to them, like they're gods, not tech, because they are all we have. They are keeping my little sis alive.

She's the noisiest of the three of us and that's saying something, because we're all verbose. Mum always says that when she was little, Sophie had to shout to be heard, she had to fight to get a word in edgeways. A thought flashes into my head and it's terrifying. Why can't my brain be more filtered? I'm thinking, *We should have listened to her while we had the chance.* And I hate that thought, I really do, with every bit of my body, because it's admitting the chance has gone.

Oh my God. My God.

I don't know what to say to Mum or Dad, so I haven't said a word. Mum hasn't said anything to me either, barely glanced my way. Her eyes are one hundred per cent focused on Sophie. I don't even know if she knows I'm in the room, or if Dad is, even though he's rubbing her back. A constant, circular motion as she bends over Sophie's bed. I check my phone to see when Flora will arrive. I need her here. She lost it when Dad called her. Just instant meltdown. I know she's on a train already. I don't know who she's travelling with. I wonder if any of her friends might have left the party or bar they were at. Did she have time to pull on a jumper and a pair of jeans or is she shivering somewhere in whatever little sequinned number she chose to wear tonight. I'm sad for her. Brighton must feel as far away as the moon right now. At least I'm here with Mum and Dad. But I find I can't feel too much for Flora. Like Mum, I must focus my energy on Sophie.

I follow the tubes, the wires from the machines to veins in her hand. Some chase up her nose, one is in her mouth. They seem tangled and frail. I worry they are not up to the task. Mum is holding her hand, but I can't bring myself to touch her. I feel scared, squeamish. What if I disturb something, knock out a vital tube? I imagine the beeping machine flatlining. It's bloody terrifying.

'Do you think she forgot to take that cap thing with her?' Dad asks this. His voice is not his usual low, calm murmur, which normally fixes everything. Tonight his tone is drenched with something like dread or frustration, even anger, but over all that, just deep, deep sorrow.

'What?' I ask, because Mum didn't seem to hear his question, or if she did, she's not bothering to acknowledge it.

'You know, the thing girls are given at school on Drug Awareness Week. The drink spiking protector cap. Do you think she left it at home by mistake?'

I feel so sorry for him. He's so unaware and therefore exposed, which makes me feel as though I'm in an elevator that's just dropped twenty floors. I don't want to think of my dad as clueless and vulnerable. I want him to put things right, like he always does. I don't know how to tell him about real life. Do I start with the fact that it's not only girls who are advised to use drink protectors because guys can be drugged, robbed and raped too? Or do I tell him that hardly anyone ever remembers to take them out after like the first two weeks of owning one? Or do I tell him there's a chance that Sophie took something voluntarily? This might not be the result of her being spiked. Kids do experiment. I have. Just once. It wasn't for me. I just felt tired and, like, nasty. Maybe this was Sophie's just once. I keep thinking about the moment when she took whatever was offered, by whoever offered it, flicked it onto her tongue. A beat, before she swallowed it. A split second that has changed everything. One moment happy, crazy, messy, whistling Sophie. The next this – a threat of brain damage, paralysis, death.

Because fucking hell, there's that. That's why I'm scared to my bones. These are the things the doctors have said in front of me while talking to Mum and Dad. Mum took my hand, but no one asked me to leave the room, no one warned me that what I was going to hear would horrify me. My parents normally try to hide the worst shit from us. Not that we've had much shit, but a few years ago there was some serious stuff about their friends Daisy and Simon. He was an alcoholic, ended up running over his own child when driving drunk, went to prison for it. All that was only ever talked about in hushed whispers and behind closed doors that my sisters and I listened at. But they didn't think to protect me this time. Either they're not thinking about me at all or they don't think I can be protected. Maybe this situation, and all its horror, all the consequences, will be revealed and so I better get used to it.

They're not making us stick to visiting hours. That scares me. They are giving us all the time she has, and I think that's because they don't know how much time that is. I've messaged Zac. I know we are in a terrible place right now, but

I don't care, I just want him here, by my side. That would be something. His phone is off. The messages go unread.

Besides the doctors and nurses who have been in and out the room, the police have been in here too. They tell us they have closed down the party. No one mutters anything about it being too late, but I think my mum and dad must be thinking as much. There's a search. People, other kids, are being asked if they saw anything, took anything, if they bought anything, is there a tablet that can be analysed. 'No one is likely to offer up the illegal drugs they're taking,' says Dad. 'They'll be too scared.'

'We're offering immunity, just for tonight, to give ourselves the best chance,' replies the officer.

Dad shakes his head. I don't know whether he's disapproving, disagreeing or despairing. Mum makes a little squeak sound that could mean anything, certainly means she's aware of what's been said. Although it's nothing good.

Their pain is so obvious and raw, I think I can touch and taste and smell it. Their horror so profound it's choking me.

35

Zac

It was 3 a.m. before Zac found himself outside the Bakers' house. He was tired. That didn't cover it. His muscles and even his bones ached with a complete and utter weariness. His feet were sore from pounding the streets. After the drop-off, he'd just walked and walked. Going nowhere. He had a blister on the back of his right ankle; there was blood on his trainer. He had skinny ankles, he always got blisters. He'd thought about sleeping in a pub or shop doorway, just stopping, but with it being New Year's Eve, the doorways were fuller than normal. The usual homeless and helpless had bedded down there, but in addition, there was a larger quota of drunks and hooking-up couples taking up residency. The streets were littered with condoms and glass bottles, cans and cigarette butts. Twice he'd slipped on discarded tacos. It was disgusting. But besides the off-putting smell of pee and discarded fast food, he couldn't sleep in a doorway, he couldn't allow it. Because it wasn't just about him, not any more. He was going to be a dad. No kid would want to be fathered by a man who slept in doorways, not if there was a choice, and there was in his case. He had options. He just had to be brave enough to take them.

The Bakers had given him a key as though he was in fact one of the family. They'd done it quite casually, and at the time, he'd accepted it with the same nonchalance. Now, he valued their generosity more. Connie had said, '*Nuestra casa es tu casa.*' He'd thought it was a bit pretentious. The fact she'd even bothered to change the saying from singular to plural, to be technically and grammatically correct. Now he thought more warmly towards her. She'd offered him a home. He realised he could slip inside, get a hot shower, get a decent night's sleep, rethink everything tomorrow. His baby needed him, even if Fran didn't want him. They had more to discuss. They had things to work out.

There were no lights on and the house's darkness was strangely reassuring. Everyone being in bed was just what he needed. Space and time to think through his life. He planned to sleep on the sofa downstairs, avoid Fran until the morning. Then they could talk. Things always seemed better in the morning. His mum often said that.

He gently pushed open the large front door and breathed in deeply, expecting to inhale the smell of whatever delicious dinner they had shared that evening, but the house smelt unusually neutral. No suggestion that food had been cooked or candles lit.

'Christ!' He nearly jumped out of his skin. 'Why are you sitting in the dark? I thought you'd be in bed.'

Fran leapt up from the sofa and rushed to him. She flung her arms around his neck and clamped him so tightly it was uncomfortable. He didn't care, it was just such a relief that she wanted to hold him. That she wanted to be near him. It was going to be OK. He honestly almost pissed himself with the relief of it. She'd been crying. Still was. He could feel her wet tears on his neck, and for a fraction of a moment he had a totally inappropriate sense of satisfaction at such obvious evidence that she'd had an awful night too, that she had missed him as much as he'd missed her and their row had upset her as well. Her tears allowed him to feel like he might climb back up to something closer to an even footing.

Then she said, 'Sophie's OD'd. She took something tonight.'

'What?' He'd heard the words, despite her tears, but no, that couldn't be right. No.

'Mum and Dad are at the hospital with her. She's in ICU. Flora and I were there for a while, but we came home. There's nothing we can do, and anyway there's no room to sit, let alone stay over. We're just in the way. She's unconscious and we don't know if . . . we don't know . . .' She started to sob again, and then chose to finish her sentence by saying, 'It's so awful, Zac, she might not wake up. She might die.' Her eyes were wide and wet. Her thoughts and words unfiltered, unguarded.

'Hey, no. Don't say that. Don't think that.' It was childlike to think that saying the bad stuff aloud made it more likely to happen, as if keeping quiet could keep you safe. 'Everything is going to be OK,' he said. Not because he necessarily believed it, but it was the thing people automatically said.

'You don't know that,' snapped Flora.

Zac was startled again; he hadn't realised she was in the room too. He was embarrassed, because she was right, he didn't have a clue. Plus, he was dismayed because even the usually pragmatic middle sister hadn't thought to put on a light or make a hot drink; she too had sat in the dark and done nothing to try to calm or comfort. They both looked so young and scared. Clueless.

As they waited for the kettle to boil, he pulled mugs and tea bags out of the cupboards. 'So what's the situation?'

'She took something. A lot of something or a bad something. No one knows. She can't tell us,' Fran replied.

'Was it a club? How did she get in? Don't they ID kids any more?' He asked this with some trepidation. It was stating it too strongly to say he was hopeful. Hope was not a word that could be applied to this situation. It was too clean and pure when everything was disgusting and rotten. But if there was a possibility of another route, some way that didn't land this horror quite so squarely with him, it would be something. Not enough, but something.

However, his sliver of the thing that was like badly damaged and bruised hope was slashed when Flora said, 'She wasn't at a nightclub. The police were saying that there's a thing happening where nightclubs are losing their licences because their searches for drugs are too brief or they don't check ID at all. As a result, they've either cleaned up their act and so it's harder to get the drugs in there, or they've closed down. Kids don't go to clubs for their drugs any more, apparently.'

'Right.'

'Gangs have moved into private parties,' Flora stated bluntly.

'I see.' Zac swallowed.

'There's no search at all on people arriving at these parties, but they're not simply wild parties that are getting out of hand. Kids buy tickets to go to these places, knowing they'll get drugs there. It's an underground thing, but everyone knows how it works.' Fran shrugged, not accepting exactly but admitting that it was pretty simple if you thought about it. There was a market. Where there's a will, there's a way.

'These parties are advertised on locked Facebook sites,' chipped in Flora.

'The police said they're working on it, trying to close the sites down, but as soon as one goes, another pops up. The policeman told us about it, he said it's all "very speakeasy". What the hell? As though there's some level of Gatsby allure. She was at a crackhead party.' Fran was outraged. Stunned.

Zac realised the sisters were still processing, swapping information between themselves that they had no doubt pored over many times that night but still couldn't understand. Their incredulity, their shock was hard to witness as it changed them from the giggling pair they usually were around one another to dense blocks of pain. He gleaned what he could, but each fact gathered punched him in the gut, making it harder to flick on table lamps and dig out honey to sweeten the herbal tea. All he could think was no, no, no, no, no!

'The police said that there's a lethal batch of drugs circulating the city. Something new, or badly mixed. I have no idea. The doctors said maybe people with asthma are reacting especially badly. They shut down the party she was at and two others.'

Zac caught a glimpse of his reflection in the kitchen window, which had been made into a mirror by the black night. He looked ill. Ghostly. As bad as Fran and Flora. He forced himself to look past his own gaze. Somewhere in the distance a firework sprayed into the air. Pink and green against the night sky. Hideously joyful. He couldn't imagine anyone having a good time. He made himself move, turn his attention back to tea-making.

'They gathered up some stuff at the raids and are running tests to try and find out exactly what she took.'

'I'm not sure why it matters, though,' sighed Flora.

'I guess so they can treat her more particularly and effectively. I don't know really,' replied Fran.

'How do they know it's a lethal batch? Why are they calling it that?' Zac asked.

'Someone else has already died.'

'Shit.' He wasn't looking as he added boiling water to the mugs, and he poured it directly onto the back of his hand.

'Jesus, Zac, run it under the cold tap.' He could tell Fran was concerned, but she was also exasperated, irritated by him. She didn't need him to be messing things up right now. She needed him to be looking after her, not the other way round.

He let the cold water gush soothingly onto his scald. While it was under the flow, the pain was neutralised. Fran told him to keep it there for five minutes, but he didn't bother. He moved away from the tap after only one. As soon as he did so, it stung like hell.

'It will scar,' she warned. He didn't care, he deserved to scar. He continued to make the drinks and then slid the mugs towards the girls. Fran blew on the hot camomile tea. He'd never understood herbal teas, never really got them, but now he wanted to believe in their healing properties. He wanted to believe in something.

Someone was dead. Sophie might die.

He swallowed, then asked, 'Who is dead? Is it someone Sophie knows?' He thought of another silly teen, keen to seem grown-up and stopping their chances of that ever happening with one bad choice.

'No, some guy in his twenties. The police have said there'll be a post-mortem, but they're tracking down his next of kin first. They think there's a connection.'

'They think Sophie knew this guy, that he gave her drugs?' Zac thought of the lout who had pushed his hands onto Sophie's body, his tongue down her throat when he found her in the hallway.

'No, the dead guy was at a different party, a few miles away. The connection is the supplier. They think the city has been flooded with these tablets.'

'Flooded?'

'Their word.'

'They said there might be more cases during the night.'

'They told you all of this, the police?'

'There were no filters in that room.' Fran sounded regretful. As though she'd have preferred to know less.

'They also said no arrests have been made,' chipped in Flora.

'What does that mean?'

'I don't know, Zac. I suppose it means they're expecting to arrest someone.' Fran sighed. 'Or maybe they're not really expecting any such thing. Maybe they're saying this sort of shit happens so frequently no one ever gets arrested. I don't know anything. I just wish she hadn't gone out.' She dropped her head in her hands. 'You know, she came to me and asked if I wanted to see her dress, and I said I'd see it later.'

He could taste her regret in the air. He understood, because he had regrets of his own. Massive ones. He needed all the facts. 'Tell me about Sophie. What exactly are the doctors saying?'

'Not as much as the police,' commented Flora heavily.

'You should go to bed now,' Fran instructed her sister. 'It's really late and we'll want to be back at the hospital tomorrow morning, early.'

'I won't sleep.'

'Well, try.'

Flora kissed her sister and hugged Zac, then she trailed upstairs, dragging her feet as though they were dumb-bells.

When they heard her bedroom door close and Fran was sure her sister was out of earshot, she said, 'The doctors have talked about brain damage. If Sophie does wake up,' she hiccuped on this sentence, the enormity and awfulness of it, 'she may well be changed. Flora wasn't there when they told us this. I don't want her to know. It can't help anything.'

Fran wanted to protect her sister, even though no one had thought to be as careful with her. It broke his heart. She'd be a good mum, a great mum. But in the instant he thought that hopeful, wonderful thing, he was crushed by the disgusting reality of how different he was. Fran continued to talk in the way people first hit by catastrophe did. They reiterated the same facts, however few they had, they regretted, rewound, reimagined. They blamed. 'I just can't understand why she was at a party where there were hard drugs. I thought she might be sneaking vodka, but Christ, this. None of us had a clue. That makes me feel so bad. We weren't taking better care of her. Who the fuck gives a child drugs?'

Him. He did.

This was his fault.

His world spun, so fast he thought he might be flung off it. He could have prevented this; he knew Sophie was going to wild parties. He could have told someone that he'd seen her the other night. If not Fran, then Luke or Connie. They were her parents; if he'd told them, they could have done something parenty, like ground her. But he hadn't said a word because he hadn't wanted to explain what he was doing at that party. He could have spoken to Sophie directly about the dangers, the damage that drugs caused. He hoped to hell her spotting him at the party hadn't led her to believe he endorsed drugs. He didn't. He hated them. Was that where his portion of blame stopped? He had to know.

'Where was the party?' he asked.

'Somewhere near Latimer Road. Why?'

Momentarily everything turned black. Zac blinked once, twice, a third time until his vision fizzed and resettled. Was he losing consciousness? He had before, once when playing football and he'd taken a boot to the skull in a dirty tackle, another time when he'd fallen off a wall he was climbing as a kid. But no, this was not that. He was getting a moment of horrific clarity, and that didn't happen when you fainted.

'Fuck.' He slammed his hand onto the kitchen cupboard. 'Fuck, fuck.' He punched it once, then twice more in very quick, angry succession. On the third punch the door split. He winced with the pain; his hand was already scalded, now it was badly bruised. Fran yanked at his top, tried to stop him doing any more damage.

'What the hell, Zac. You're not helping. This isn't about you. We don't have room for your upset.' She was shaking, and he knew she'd just pushed him outside the Baker inner sanctum.

And if she hadn't yet, she certainly would in no time. 'How am I going to explain that damage to Mum and Dad? Like they don't have enough on without your big-man-wrecking show. Those cupboards came from Italy. For God's sake, Zac.' It was clear she was pissed off with him but didn't have enough emotional energy to give him the attention of a row. She simply shook her head and said, 'We're all just praying she wakes up. Keep your energy for that.'

THREE DAYS BEFORE THE END

36

Zac

1 January

It made the early-morning news next day. Not the main news, because it was the start of a new year and there were loads of stories about how people across the globe had celebrated the flip of the calendar. Zac had watched people living it large, climbing into Trafalgar Square fountain at midnight, and wondered how many of them were high or drunk. How many got home safely. It was on the London news, second story. There had been another death. A thirty-two-year-old woman. He couldn't comprehend it. He didn't understand how women in their thirties were doing drugs. Wasn't it something you should grow out of, get wise to? He wasn't being judgemental, he was desperate. He just wished people would protect themselves, be careful. Be careful of people like Bear. And like himself. Because he couldn't help them and he had hurt them, this woman, the man in his twenties, Sophie. It was savage to think that the woman would not grow out of anything now. It was all done for her. He scoured the internet for information about her. Then he wished he had not, as he discovered she was a mother of a two-year-old. He cursed and swore aloud. The press reported that a neighbour had revealed that she'd left the kid at home with a fourteen-year-old babysitter.

'Apparently even dying a tragic death doesn't protect her from condemnation,' said Auriol, who had arrived at the Bakers' at the crack of dawn, keen to keep the girls company for the short spells when they weren't at the hospital. 'Are we supposed to care less because she was a regular clubber? There is no mention of the father of the kid,' she added.

But neither Fran nor Flora engaged with Auriol's outrage. Usually vociferous feminists, alert to the bias of sexist journalism but they did not care less about this woman because she was a clubber; they didn't care at all, because she wasn't Sophie. They had no capacity to grieve beyond their own tragedy. Zac thought of the toddler who had lost its mother and didn't have the sort of father that was mentioned in the press in any shape or form. He wanted to be sick.

Maybe there were people yet to be found or reported. No doubt there would have been the usual stomach-pumping situations that regularly occurred on any night, let alone New Year's Eve, let alone when the city had been flooded with a deadly drug, but as it stood, the count connected to the lethal batch of pills had stagnated at two dead and one in intensive care. That was how the journos reported it. Numbers. Names withheld. Sophie was a minor, so her name would never make the papers unless Luke and Connie decided to release it. The dead bloke, well, Zac assumed they were still waiting to tell his mum and dad. Happy new year to them. Fuck.

They were all glued to the screen as Detective Inspector Elizabeth Gianella, Metropolitan Police, said, 'These nimble response raids are part of a rolling programme of action against drug-dealing. There is no safe way of taking illegal drugs. We urge anyone who bought drugs in or around the Latimer Road area to dispose of these substances as soon as possible. Anyone who becomes unwell after taking an illegal substance should seek medical advice immediately. There is an anonymous, untraceable hotline for anyone who has any information about the incidents.'

The police officer was being interviewed outside the party house, most likely following the raid. She looked determined, honest, capable. Weary. Zac wished he could talk to her. He thought that if he could, things might be better. Not everything, but something. Was there a world where he could call the hotline and it would lead to an arrest, many, many arrests, so that he could safely walk the streets? He considered 'anonymous, untraceable'. He didn't know if he believed that such a thing existed. Even if he did, the police tracing him was not his biggest fear.

Bear was.

He thought of Rob curling like a caterpillar as the boots stomped on him. He thought of how they'd discovered Zac himself was in the city within hours of him arriving, plus the fact they knew where Fran lived and where he'd start working as soon as he graduated. No, he couldn't call the DI, no matter how capable she looked. Of course not. He turned away from the screen, asked if anyone wanted anything to eat.

Someone had pinned the baby scan picture to the fridge.

The black and white image mocked him. The tiny, hard-to-map swirls of pixels showed a head, a spine, legs, all curled up like a cute little alien, but growing, getting ready to become his boy. A fact. There in black and white. His son. But everything was so far from black and white in life. Even so, something about seeing the image made him impulsively turn back to the TV, pull out his phone and snap a photo of the hotline number. Then he turned away for a second time and pushed his phone into his back pocket. He wasn't sure why he'd done that. He wasn't sure of anything much, other than that when he thought of the baby, he wanted to hope for . . .

Well, for something.

37

Connie

My darling, my darling, my beautiful girl. Mummy is here. You're OK. You *will* be OK. Please God, let her be OK. I'll swap, God. Take me. If it is that world after all, if there are deals to be done. Take me. She's just a baby. What were you thinking, Sophie? Drugs? Drugs? I told you, I warned you. We warned you *all*. Why would you take drugs? Were you bored? Did someone make you? Were you showing off? I'm not cross, darling, no, not that. Just sad, so, so sad. It's just a mistake. We all make mistakes. You don't deserve to be this unlucky. How could you be so unlucky. Well that's it. This is *enough*. You have been very unlucky, but now you need to get lucky. You do. Do you hear me? You need to get well. Because we need you, Sophie. We love you. Our home needs you. You know that, don't you? Just because there's a new baby coming – and yes, I've been distracted – but that doesn't mean I'd forgotten about you. I'm sorry about the revision timetable. I will make you one. Or not. It doesn't matter. The exams don't matter. Not really, do they? You'll do fine anyhow. And I'll let you into a secret, we just tell you that they matter because we want to think there are some guarantees, some way of stacking the cards in your favour. So you might get on in life, do well. But they don't matter. Nothing matters except you getting well. You hear me? You understand? You know you are everything to me, don't you, baby? Take me, God, don't take her. Please, please God. Don't take my baby. She's just getting started.

'Connie?' Luke moved closer to his wife. 'Did you want something?' Connie shook her head. 'You were mumbling. I thought you asked for something.' She just shook her head again.

THE DAY BEFORE THE END

38

Zac

3 January

The Baker family had stayed suspended in the no-man's-land of emergency. Regular mealtimes were abandoned, everyone managed on tasteless white-bread sandwiches bought at peculiar hours from the corner shop nearest to the hospital; clothes were worn from one day to the next as no one had the energy to open a wardrobe and choose something fresh; showers were only irregularly taken; sleep was fitful and rarely took place in the comfort of a bed. Instead it happened in snatches, on hard-backed hospital chairs around Sophie's bed or on the sofa in the Bakers' sitting room, while waiting for someone to come back from the hospital with news.

They waited. That was all anyone could do. The family, friends, the doctors and nurses, the police and Zac himself, they all waited for Sophie to wake up. Even though he wasn't family, he had been allowed to go into her hospital room. He hadn't asked, he wouldn't ever have, but Fran wanted him by her side. That was something. He'd take it while it lasted. He knew he was on borrowed time. They all clung to an expectation that this change of state *would* happen. They didn't allow for the reality that it might not, at least not outwardly. Zac thought about the fact that she might not wake, so he supposed others might be thinking about it too, but no one gave breath to that scenario; they all behaved as though they believed she could be willed back to consciousness by the sheer force of their love.

The family seemed to instinctually know how to act around her. Connie held her hand, kissed her forehead, murmured gently in her ear. Soft, low things that the others didn't always catch. One time, he heard her mumble that she'd trade places with her daughter if she could.

He would too. If he could, really, he would.

Luke talked about a summer holiday. Apparently it was a Baker joke to start planning the summer holiday as soon as the party poppers from New Year's Eve were swept away. He asked Sophie if she wanted to go to Venice this year. 'You've always liked the idea, what do you think?' They'd all waited a few beats, hoping for a nod. It didn't come. 'We should really go for it. Get a hotel by the Grand Canal, splash out. Excuse the pun. Dad-joke privilege.' Zac had no idea how Luke managed to keep his tone upbeat; to look at him, he was a dead man walking. Of course, Sophie couldn't look at him. That was the point.

Flora gently brushed her sister's hair; she'd asked the nurse if she could paint her toenails. At one point, mindful of the tubes and medical machinery, Fran managed to carefully manoeuvre herself close to Sophie's hand, which she then picked up and placed on her bump. 'Can you feel him kicking?' she asked. 'It's a boy, Sophie. I should have told you earlier.

What do you think of the names Arlo or Luca? Which do you like best?'

He admired the fluidity and purpose that they maintained around her. From the moment he'd walked into her room, he'd felt harnessed, restricted, as though he was wearing concrete boots. He was sure to drown. He fought to hold onto thoughts of the kid who'd argued for a later curfew on Christmas Eve and who looked gleeful when she won a worthless bit of tat out of a cracker. He tried to think of her buoyantly chatting to his own sister, their unchecked excitement at the thought of becoming young aunties together. He even wanted to recall her defiant and vulnerable in her skimpy dress at the party he'd dragged her from. But it was no use. When he looked at her, all he saw was a slab of biology. Inert. Finished.

This was his fault.

Her condition had stabilised, and so she was moved from the intensive care unit to a supportive care room. The Bakers had private healthcare, so both rooms were single occupancy, but Zac really didn't understand the difference. They still had her linked up to the machines that monitored her heart, her blood pressure, her breathing. They had circumnavigated her lack of ability to swallow; nutritionally, she was being catered for through drips and tubes, and they'd ensured she wouldn't choke on her own saliva. Now she was stabilised, she apparently wasn't likely to suddenly die of a heart attack or the poison of the drug as they had feared in the first few hours. Was he the only one that noted that 'likely' and 'suddenly' were surely both important caveats. There was talk about the Glasgow Coma Scale. They used it to monitor for signs of improvement or deterioration. Sophie scored poorly, but a doctor said that didn't necessarily mean severe brain damage or that she was less likely to recover, as it was early days. The words were carefully chosen. Zac wondered about the word 'severe'. Did the poor score on the test mean there was some level of brain damage? He reached for his phone. The doctor smiled briefly and tiredly, advised the young adults to stay away from Dr Google. 'That goes for you all, in fact. A little bit of information can be dangerous or disheartening. Ask us anything you want to know.'

'Thank you, Doctor,' said Luke. He turned to Fran and Flora. 'It's great news that she's stabilised and out of ICU. Let's focus on that.'

Was it great news, though, or had they sort of given up, accepted that this unresponsive state, this eternal deep sleep, was as good as it got?

The questions Zac asked himself were so awful, so wrong that he was ashamed they even entered his head. He'd rather cut out his own tongue than articulate them to the doctor, and he had the sense to know they'd shatter Fran and her family. As they swirled determinedly around his head, he wondered what sort of person he was now. Why did he doubt, expect the worst, wait for more misery to pour onto the already horrific situation? But he knew why. That was one question he could answer. Bear and his men had shown him things didn't always get better. Often, things got considerably worse. This was all his fault.

A big part of him just wanted to tell the Bakers as much. Or the police. He wanted them to arrest him and take him away, throw him in jail. He thought it would be a relief to be punished for his crimes, locked up so he couldn't commit any more. But did he deserve to feel any sort of relief? And anyway, was going to prison more of a punishment than watching the family go through this? No, it wasn't. It would be easier to do time, and he didn't deserve easy. Besides, confessing would just make things worse for Fran. She'd be devastated, distraught that her boyfriend had done this to her sister; she might even start to blame herself for bringing him into their world. How would that help things? He was holding onto the sliver of sense that instructed him to keep it together for Fran. To stay quiet for Fran.

Or maybe he was just a total coward and was reasoning his way out of jail. He didn't know, but he hated himself. He wondered whether the world might be better off without him in it.

They said Sophie couldn't feel pain. He wanted to ask how they knew for sure, but realised it was best to take that one at face value, for everyone else's sake. He wanted to believe it, but he wasn't sure what they really knew for certain. The family had been given instructions to play her favourite songs – Ariana Grande and Swiftie – on a loop, and spray her perfume around the room in case either thing triggered a sensory response. Miss Dior fought against the smell of disinfectant, hand sanitiser, coffee and anxiety. They were told to be careful what they said around her, in case she could hear them. The doctors spoke of cases when patients woke up and reported feeling enormous reassurance from the presence of a loved one. Zac wondered if they were simply telling the family this stuff to give them a sense of hope.

The staff were doing their best to be kind and considerate under truly miserable circumstances. But they kept swapping in and out, depending on their shifts, and the family rarely saw the same face twice. When alone, Fran whispered to him that she resented that.

'The fact they can walk away blows my mind,' she muttered. 'I get it that they have to stay professional, not get too involved, but how do they do that? You know, I'm almost jealous that they can move on to the next tragedy. That they can walk out of the room and leave us sitting in this state.' She shook her head. 'Don't listen to me, I'm not making any sense.'

'You're tired,' he said. He was sorry he'd resorted to such a dull platitude when she was scratching at something deep and important. But he couldn't go there with her. Back in the late summer, lying on her skinny student bed in her grungy accommodation, they'd enjoyed how deep they'd wanted to dig with each other. But the existential questions that they playfully chewed over no longer seemed thrilling and fascinating. He couldn't remember simply feeling the bright electric charge of discussing emotional responses to theoretical situations and finding a soulmate who understood the nuance you were grappling with.

They'd enjoyed asking one another things such as 'You're at your best friend's wedding, the ceremony is in one hour's time and you find definitive proof that your best friend's spouse-to-be is having an affair. What do you do?'

'You get to save one life, your brother's or the man who will discover the cure for cancer.' They'd decided to ask the question with 'brother' as neither had one. They were playing. Scaring themselves without any risk. The emotional equivalent of getting on a roller coaster.

They were subterranean now. Something real and dreadful.

He couldn't let her see inside his head, where black thoughts lingered: Sophie never waking up, the family spending an eternity around this hospital bed. It was too dark, guilty and filthy. He couldn't tell her he understood and that he too was having angry, irrational thoughts about the fairness or otherwise of outcomes, the various capability of humans.

His skin felt tight, uncomfortable. His head, back and shoulders ached. He told himself he was just sore from lack of sleep. He also considered the possibility that his entire body was revolting against his mind, his soul, core, whatever. It was like it wanted to leave him. Split in half. He was tight, awkward. He supposed this was Guilt 101.

The strange thing was, while Sophie's world had ground to a halt and the Bakers were now crawling along at a glacial rate, the rest of the world kept turning at a pace. On the evening of 3 January, he received a text with details of a pickup. Business as usual for Bear, then.

'Fran, my mum has just messaged. I'll go and take this call outside. She'll want a full update.'

Fran nodded, aware that news had to go from one person to the next even though it was bad news, even though there was nothing to be done. That was the nature of these things. He'd been glad to leave the oppressive heat and stillness of the hospital room, but the cold January streets shocked. People tore around, going about their business. They seemed annoyingly occupied and irritatingly unaware.

He followed the instructions on the text, did the pickup as usual. He did not ask any questions. It was the man who'd stabbed his hand on Christmas Eve who handed it over. An incongruous padded manila envelope. But a large one. The biggest he'd ever carried. Why? Was this some sort of sick unwanted promotion? Was he considered trustworthy now? Or were they trying to move things quicker? He didn't open it, he never had, but he shook it and heard tablets rattle against each other. His best guess, at that weight, was there might be as many as a thousand tablets. They sold at about £10 each. He was carrying £10,000. One thousand lives. Stabbing-hand man seemed agitated. No doubt the raid and police interference in their operation had made Bear's people jumpy. Zac avoided eye contact. He accepted the details of the drop-off. The obedient little foot soldier.

He kept walking.

It took about fifty minutes to reach Hammersmith Bridge, a few miles away. Zac wasn't hurrying, he wasn't ambling. He was steady. As he made his way to the river, as usual he thought of nothing other than Sophie's state. He was tired, he'd barely slept these past few days as the grim thoughts of the future he'd stolen from her followed him into his nightmares too. Even before this, over the past weeks, months, he'd only managed to sleep fitfully. He couldn't think clearly. He didn't plan to make a big performance of it. He wouldn't stop and lean over the railings, stare longingly into the water and wait for someone to stop him or ask him what he was up to. He knew what he had to do. There was only one answer. He noted the green sign placed by the Samaritans. It read: *Talk to Us, if things are getting to you*. There was a freephone number: 116 123.

He swiftly chucked the package, let it drop into the Thames. The water swallowed it up silently. The passing traffic was heavy, and he was too far away to hear it plop. For one second, he felt something like relief. He was free of, it the dead weight.

The weight that caused death. Then he giggled to himself, imagined the fish nibbling the tablets, partying, maybe hallucinating. In his mind, they turned into cartoon fish. Most likely his reaction was triggered by some sort of nervous hysteria, a release of tension.

He turned and started to walk, but suddenly, before he was even off the bridge, the laughter turned to sobbing. Oh God, he was crying in the street. Like a child. He rubbed the sleeve of his jacket hastily over his face, smearing snot and tears. He must look a state. He would attract attention. He thought of the fish, dead and cold. Not the dancing cartoons that had been in his mind a second ago, but lifeless blocks, like you saw at the fishmonger's, gutted. Then he thought of the man who had died. Not gutted exactly, but there was an autopsy. A grown man able to make his own decision as to whether it was a good idea to swallow a tablet a stranger had just sold you – not Zac's responsibility – but also someone's son, brother, partner. So maybe, maybe yeah, his responsibility. He thought of the mother and her toddler. Why had she chosen to go out? He just wished she'd stayed in. Even if she was old enough to make her own decisions, be accountable for the consequences, the toddler wasn't, was it? And Sophie, still hanging on, but maybe she'd stay that way for ever. Maybe she'd never return to them and be the snarky, funny kid they all loved.

It was his fault. He was a killer.

The thought stopped him in his tracks. He looked back out onto the dark, glassy, gloopy river. The tablets had been swallowed. They were no more. He didn't know what to do, where to go or who to speak to.

He just wanted this to end.

39

John

John was packing. He was due to check out tomorrow. It had been a lousy start to the new year. New Year's Day itself had been a washout. One of his worst, and he'd had some stinkers. Many had been bad because he was so hideously hung-over from the night before; the one six years ago was awful because he and his second wife had finally agreed to divorce after months of disappointment and discontent. So he had a low bar to plummet through. This year it was especially dreadful because he'd let himself think it might be rather good, and the discrepancy between the hope and the reality had been enormous. Hope could be a bastard like that.

He'd been so moved when Zac had first asked him to join the Christmas party, to meet his girlfriend and her family. He'd been blown away by the thought that this lad of his wanted to include him, that he was proud of his bio dad (or if that was going too far, at least not ashamed of him) and that he wanted him to be part of the family. He'd hoped he was at the beginning of a process. When he first booked the trip down south, he'd thought there would be the initial meet-and-greet with his son's girlfriend's family, at which he would be amiable, everyone's friend. He expected to find common ground with the girlfriend's father (sport could usually be relied upon) and to charm the girlfriend's mother (because he was usually liked by women); he'd mend bridges with Clare and tread carefully with her fella. He'd thought he'd get to know the girlfriend a little bit, see if she was up to scratch for his lad. He'd planned to grow much closer to his son.

He imagined he'd then offer to return the hospitality. Obviously he wasn't at home and so couldn't cook for them, but he had thought he'd invite them all out to a restaurant for lunch. He'd even made enquiries. They were a big party and he was trying to book for New Year's Day, so the choice had been limited. He'd put down a five-hundred-quid deposit at an Italian around the corner from his hotel.

Once he met Zac's girlfriend and her family, he'd tried to get his deposit back.

This trip had far from delivered what he'd hoped. It was another dead end in his life.

He'd screwed his son's girlfriend. And she was pregnant. She thought John himself might be the father. What a disaster. Connie was right, there wasn't a reasonable route through this.

Oh yeah, Connie. The other complication in this drama. He'd screwed his son's girlfriend's mother too. Imagine a world where that was the least of your problems.

The manager of the restaurant hadn't been too obliging re the deposit. John had eaten there alone on New Year's Day. He had antipasto, primo, secondo, insalata, dolce and a digestif, but still, he was out of pocket and he'd left uncomfortably stuffed.

'A *depositare* is a *depositare*,' the chubby, no-nonsense manager had said with a shrug. Fair enough. John asked if he could take a couple of bottles of wine home with him.

He'd spent the last few days hoping Zac might call and they'd at least spend some time together, just the two of them, but he hadn't. No word. John wondered what that meant. It was odd to be so intrinsically involved with this family but also very firmly on the sidelines. He didn't like it.

He'd been managing work emails remotely and taken a few business calls, but it was time to get back to the office and back to his new but straightforward, fairly promising relationship with Nicky, the divorcee he'd been on holiday with this Christmas. She was easy company, a laugh, independent, and she rode a Harley-Davidson, which he found quirky enough to be intriguing. He was looking forward to it. Going home, sleeping in his own bed, re-establishing his routine. He liked coming to London well enough, but he also liked leaving it. It was a laugh and then it wasn't.

He carefully placed his Belstaff T-shirts and Burberry wool sweaters into the Maxwell Scott case. They all pleased him, these things he owned that confidently said wealthy, sorted, made it. He paused and wondered whether he had, though. Considering everything.

He didn't know what was going on in Connie's world that had made her run out of the bar on New Year's Eve in such a hurry after taking that phone call. Some drama. Another one. He hadn't heard anything more from her since. He was unlikely to. She had said her piece, she had presented the solution as she saw it, she would think the ball was in his court. Was it? Should he just disappear? Absent himself from Zac's life for ever? Something had to be done. He realised that. From the moment Connie had opened that door and he'd seen Fran peeking at him from the back of the hallway, he'd known something had to be done. He just didn't know what.

Why was his life like this? A series of crazy intense events, one thing after another. His mum often said he went looking for trouble. Sometimes she yelled that at him, furious that he'd got himself in the wrong at school. Other times – when it was a girl knocking at the door while another sat in the front room and a third was ringing on the telephone – she'd say it with an indulgent roll of the eyes, a smothered laugh. Truth was, she quite liked it about him, his mischievousness, his success with girls. She hadn't seen the harm. She was indulgent because she loved everything about him. He missed her. Really badly. She'd died of breast cancer three years ago. There wasn't a day went by when he didn't think of her. That had been one of the things that upset him most about missing out on all his time with Zac: his mother had missed out too. She would have loved to have known her grandson. John's sister had three kids, but he knew Zac would have had a special place in his mother's heart.

When he initially got the email informing him that he was a father, his first thought had been 'I've been expecting you, Mr Bond.' Silly really, but he sometimes fell back on daft little quotes from old movies and stuff when he needed to find the right words and couldn't. Not that he'd expected Zac per se and not from Clare exactly, but he'd always thought it was a possibility that a kid might pop up. It was something he and his mates had joked about from time to time over the years.

Considering the life he'd lived, the time he'd lived it, there was always a chance. He wasn't actively careless as a lad, but he wasn't always careful either. Not completely. He always chose to believe a woman if she said she was on the pill, as he liked the feel of no-condom sex, although he obliged if it was requested. Sometimes he would start the night using a condom, but if they went at it a second or third time, he might not have enough with him. Put it this way, he never let a night be rained off even if he lacked a brolly. Yes, he was aware that he'd had STIs now and again and should have had a different attitude, but all the lads were on and off various courses of antibiotics back then. The past, it wasn't all good and it wasn't all bad.

Look, he was a total prick, right. He knew that. But everyone was in the 1990s. First, he was young. Second . . . Actually, he didn't have a second, and the first was null and void since he'd had unprotected sex with Fran just a matter of months ago, when he was categorically far from young, careless and carefree. Truth was, he was a total prick. Plain and simple.

He was sorry he couldn't remember Clare exactly. That was awkward. But he wasn't sorry that Zac had knocked on his door. Or, to be precise, that he'd sent the email. In fact, the truth was, he'd been delighted, because whenever he'd joked with his mates about some offspring appearing out of the blue, he'd not just seen it as a possibility, he'd seen it as a chance. A hope.

John had a good life. He'd worked hard, starting out from a working-class home that reeked of ciggies and chip fat, not quite covered up with a squirt of air freshener. He rarely encountered that synthetic, sickly smell nowadays – everyone he knew had room diffusers and scented candles – but when he did, he thought of his mum's desperate grasp at respectability and it made his heart ache a little. He went to a local uni that had just changed status from a poly. As a student, he'd only worked moderately hard because he was cleverer than everyone else around him and didn't need to exert himself to be the best. But then he'd lifted his game, got serious, decided he needed a big job in a big firm that would pay big money. So he'd competed against posh Oxbridge types who spoke old-school BBC English and had generations of protection and privilege to give them a leg up the corporate ladder. He'd succeeded with his Liverpudlian accent, comprehensive education and the enormous chip on his shoulder. This, even before accents became acceptable, let alone cool and desirable. He earned a healthy six-figure salary now and had done for years. He'd come a long way.

Yet sometimes he did wonder what the point of it was if he didn't have anyone to share it with. He'd been married twice. No kids from either marriage. A myriad of reasons and also just one – it wasn't to be.

His mum would have said Zac was a blessing. In fact, she'd probably have said 'a godsend' and really meant it from her deeply Catholic core. Obviously, it was special that the lad looked so much like John himself. And it seemed he was a decent kid. Clever, good-looking, funny, honest. He must have got that last thing from his mum. The small joke rolled into John's head and he laughed to himself at his own gag, made at his own expense. He was used to being the butt of jokes about a range of subjects – honesty, morality, responsibility, the Peter Pan syndrome. A lot of his mates made that sort of crack a lot of the time. John didn't mind much; he had a thick skin. He knew blokes often showed affection by taking the piss and he knew that his mates were sometimes a little bit envious of his responsibility-free lifestyle. He'd occasionally thought that his middle-aged mates laughing at him was a way of them avoiding seriously considering the option of leaving their wives. By being a parody – which made them feel safe and scared them off single life – he was doing a public service of sorts. As the jokes were going to be cracked, he always rushed to crack them first. It was fine. He really didn't have a problem with it.

He did have a good life, although it wasn't as carefree and careless as his friends liked to imply.

John and Zac had been taking things slow but steady; they hadn't rushed into this new father–son relationship. He wanted it to be that, but Zac already had a dad, so John had to find his own place. He just wanted to get to know the boy. They'd only met up about half a dozen times, but they messaged each other almost every day. Some days, several times. Nothing heavy, just chat about Zac's studies, or a film, sport or what they had eaten. Zac liked to take photos of the meals he cooked and send them to John. He wasn't exactly Jamie Oliver, but his student dishes – mostly variations on tinned beans, tomatoes, tuna and dried pasta – looked good enough. John liked cooking; he sent pictures of his chicken pot pie and his apple and sausage bake. A couple of winter favourites. He'd offered to make both dishes for Zac. He was waiting for the lad to take him up on that.

A little joke had developed between them, to do with extraordinarily bad or funny shop signage. It started when Zac noticed a hairdresser's called Curl Up and Dye. He'd taken a photo and sent it to John. It had cracked John up. Really, he'd laughed a disproportionate amount, so much so that his EA had had to bring him a glass of water.

'For a minute there, I thought you were crying,' she'd said.

And for a minute, he'd thought he was too.

Because it was so good to have a son who sent you a picture of a crazily named hairdresser's. Then John had been in Darlington on business and spotted a cake shop called Top Bun. It had a life-size cut-out picture of Tom Cruise in the window. That demanded a photo. Zac followed up a few days later with a picture of a chippy called the Fishcotheque. John had wanted to keep it going, so googled and found a flower shop called Florist Gump, but he decided it was against the nature of the exchange. They had to organically find the signs in real life, stumble across them; the implication was it would be their thing, an ongoing joke, over years maybe. The thought had made John feel great and he'd deleted the try-too-hard Google option. They had time. He'd wait. He sent his thoughts on the footie instead.

Besides the texting, they spoke once a week. John always called Zac. The first time he'd done so, Zac had been panicked.

'What's wrong?'

'Nothing.'

'What do you want?'

'Nothing.'

'Then why are you calling me?'

It was quite the commentary on their relationship, closer to a condemnation, actually. John had felt awkward, but he'd pushed through it. 'I was just wondering what you're doing tonight. You know, I was curious as to what it is that Gen Z kids get up to on a Friday.'

'Well, I can't speak for the entire generation, but I'm reading a book.'

'On a Friday. It's not even termtime.' John hadn't thought to hide his shock. 'Are you sure we're related?'

'Ha ha.'

'Haven't you got friends?' The question came out brutal; it wasn't supposed to. He was trying to make a joke.

'Cheers.' John could hear from his tone that Zac hadn't taken offence. He had a sense of humour. He had friends. He added, 'Actually, I'm going out later.'

'With a girl?'

'Yes.'

'A date?'

'Yes.'

'Good, that's really good. Is it, er, serious?' John squirmed to hear himself ask the very question his mum used to ask him, as it had sounded dated and intrusive even back then. It wasn't any of his business and it didn't matter anyway whether it was serious or not. John didn't really care. He was just trying to make conversation.

Zac replied, 'First date. We were mates before I went to London, but we lost touch. Bumped into her today. She's cool.'

The first call lasted one hundred and twenty-six seconds, John knew because he checked his phone. He knew he needed to do better.

He gave the parameters of his second phone call a lot of thought. He wondered whether he should ring during the day, but he imagined it would be stilted, his tone and questions constrained as he'd have to call from his desk in his open-plan office. Sidebar: he hated open-plan, always had; his lifestyle consistently leant into a need for privacy. So an evening then. He considered which might be best for Zac. He didn't want to call at an inconvenient time and hand the lad a reason to cut him off before they got into their stride. Assuming his son had inherited his gregarious nature, surely it was still reasonable to assume Fridays and Saturdays were obvious nights out. Thursday (he'd read) was the new Friday, so that left him Sunday through to Wednesday as best bets. But as soon as term started, Wednesday afternoons at uni meant sport, which inevitably (although paradoxically) led to heavy drinking, so Wednesday evening would definitely not be a good night to call.

John called Zac for the second time on a Tuesday; that time Zac wasn't so surprised to hear from him. Nor was he reading a book. He was cooking a meal, which he continued to do while chatting with John. It meant the conversation had to be held at a volume that rose above the clanking of pans and the hiss of frying, and it was inevitably interrupted by the occasional utterance – 'Who's used up all my rice?' 'Ouch, crap, that's hot' – but John didn't mind. He liked being rolled into his son's everyday ordinariness. The not-too-special fact that he prepped food and ate it was still incredible to him.

On the third occasion, Zac suggested they FaceTime, and as he cooked, his housemates wandered in and out the kitchen. A stream of young men wearing earbuds; listening to the anthem of their own lives. Karl was scooping food from a bowl to his mouth in a manner that suggested he'd never eaten before, Vic was bare-chested and carrying weights, Jorden had his hand in an enormous bag of crisps. With each name offered, Zac said lightly, 'This is John, my bio dad.'

John had felt giddy.

So he'd taken a punt. 'I've got some business near York next week. I was thinking of stopping over. Might you be around? I thought we could grab a bite to eat.' Grab a bite to eat. The words sounded wrong; he wasn't trying to casually move a Tinder match on to the next stage. But he didn't know what would have been the right thing to say. 'Might you be around? I thought we could catch up on the last twenty-two years that I've missed out on.' Probably Zac regretted putting John on FaceTime, because he clearly didn't like the suggestion. The panic on his face was patent. John had backtracked immediately. 'Don't worry about it. I'm sure you're busy and—'

'Yeah, no, we should. Good idea,' Zac had said.

John was so happy. He'd wanted to believe the boy thought it was a good idea; he chose to ignore the look of shock (terror?) that Zac hadn't been able to hide quickly enough, but he shouldn't have ignored it. He should have acknowledged that Zac was freaking out. Despite all the texting and the three phone calls, Zac bottled it. Just got cold feet. At the time, John had been bitterly disappointed. He had been so scared that there was only one shot, that Zac might never again agree to meet. He had needed comforting, cheering up. Obviously, he turned to casual sex. Situation normal. It was a fresh sort of hell to think of that evening now. The boy had become part of his life. The biggest part. What was he going to do?

The phone in his room rang. The trill prodded him out of his fug of indecision. He picked it up assuming it was something about checkout times or his bill.

'Mr Harding?'

'Yes.'

'So sorry to disturb you, but there is a young man here in reception who is insisting he wants to speak to you.' The word 'insisting' conveyed some level of disapproval. 'He's very . . .' the receptionist paused, searching around for the right word, 'agitated, sir.'

'Zac Knight?'

'Yes, that's the name he has given. He says his phone is flat and he can't call you himself, which is why he asked me to call you.' The receptionist sounded sceptical. A Gen Z with a flat phone was about as suspicious as a man in a balaclava demanding you empty the safe. Agitated. John considered what that might mean. Could it simply mean Zac was annoyed about the inconvenience of having a flat phone? No, that was too much to hope. More likely he was enraged because he'd heard his father had shagged his girlfriend. Yeah, that would agitate him. John felt a sinking in his stomach. 'Are you comfortable with us allowing him up to your room, or would you like to collect your guest?'

Comfortable was not the word he'd use, but John said, 'Send him up, send him straight away.'

40

Zac

'Drink?'

John was already holding a decanter of whisky, hovering over two very fancy heavy-looking glasses. Zac didn't really enjoy spirits, but he nodded. If ever there was a moment for Dutch courage – or any sort of courage – it was this. John took his time to pour the whisky. Zac assumed he must have ordered an entire bottle from room service, which he considered unusual. Most of the hotels he had ever stayed in had empty fridges, there just so you could chill any booze you bought at the supermarket. This room was really posh. Dark walls with heavy print wallpaper of birds and animals and stuff, a bit like the old-school Hollister stores, but better. The wooden furniture gleamed, the duvet was thick, the lighting dim. He was glad of the gloom. He didn't want to be seen. Fran would love to stay in a room like this, Zac thought, and he wanted to cry.

'What brings you here?' John asked as he handed over the heavy glass, a third full of neat whisky, no ice, no water, no concession to Zac's youth or inexperience. Neither thing had likely crossed John's mind. They sat opposite one another in dark green velvet chairs that were shaped like seashells, a small table between them. Zac felt the contrast of this exotic, expensive room with the sparse, functional hospital room where Sophie lay still and the grimy, obscene party rooms where he had collected and delivered packages for Bear. He wanted to close his eyes and he wanted to stay here for ever.

He was glad that John had not tried to bother with small talk. If he had, it would have been far too easy to avoid saying what he had come to say. He was shaking. He couldn't hold the glass steady. He took a large gulp. It singed his throat. 'I'm in trouble. Really bad shit.'

John's face and body changed completely in that moment. He went from looking tense and rigid to looking something close to relaxed. That confused Zac. Whenever he told his mum and dad bad news, they sort of sprang into action, became alert and anxious. The stress of such an announcement would make his mum brittle; she might snap or shatter. It made his dad bullish and demanding. Was it John's lack of experience as a father that allowed him to react in the opposite way? Zac didn't know, but he felt grateful that John hadn't looked stern or worried or judgemental. It helped him start talking.

'Sophie, Fran's little sister, is in hospital. She took something at a party.'

'Christ. How is she?'

'Not good.' Then Zac admitted, 'Really bad. She's in a coma and they don't know when, or if, she'll wake up.'

'Bloody hell. When did this happen?'

'New Year's Eve. Fran's in bits.'

'They must be desperate. Her poor family. How is her mum?' Zac noted John's surprisingly thoughtful question. He had identified the person who was likely feeling this most acutely, after Sophie herself.

'They're all in shock, obviously. I didn't know what to say. Or do.' Zac shrugged, helpless.

'Right. No, course not, this is huge. It's hard to know what to say.'

Zac wanted to stop there. That was enough, but there was a reason he'd come here tonight. He had to tell someone. Or else . . . well. The alternative that had started to play in his mind – taking this secret to his grave – that thought was scaring him. 'Two other people are dead. The police are saying it was a bad batch of drugs.'

'Is there such a thing as a good one?' asked John with a slow sigh. Zac was pretty sure John Harding had developed this POV later in life. He'd probably taken stuff when he was young, when he'd been reckless and stupid. Perhaps that was why Zac was here and not on a train north to talk to his mum and dad, who wouldn't understand the risk Sophie had taken, who would silently condemn it even while pitying her and praying for her. He knew their draconian views on drugs. The irony was he'd always heeded their dire warnings, he'd caught their fear and caution. He'd never so much as puffed on a joint, let alone tried coke, ket, molly or meth. No, entry level for him was straight in as a pusher.

The thought made him feel sick.

They'd be so disappointed in him. They'd never forgive him. John Harding didn't have any expectations about him, so he couldn't let him down as badly. They'd only spent a handful of evenings together, mostly in pubs, sometimes going out for food. The last time they'd been in one another's company was that weird lunch at the Bakers'. A week ago? A lifetime ago? John hadn't messaged much since then. Kept his distance. Zac had thought about that just briefly. Was his biological dad going to be more than a biological grandfather? Did he have the interest or capacity to step up? But he hadn't given him a great deal of thought; he'd had a lot on his mind this past week. The fact was, John was sitting opposite him now and Zac needed to talk.

'I know something.' He stared at his trainers.

'What, son? What do you know?' John's voice was low and calm. *Son*, a northern term of endearment, not exactly a claim but Zac leant into it mentally. He was, after all, this man's son.

'About where she got the drugs,' he muttered. It was a starting point. He explained about the ticketed parties, the scale of them. He confided his fears that the police would never be able to suppress them, let alone incarcerate the people who ran them.

'Why do you say that?' asked John gently. He hadn't interrupted up until that point. He'd actively listened. Nodded his head, murmured encouragement, sounds not words.

'It's impossible to stop it.' Zac's voice scratched out, desperate and lost. 'Because people want the gear and so money can be made. A lot of money.' He thought of it, the vast amounts of cash he'd witnessed spread out on the bed in that dark party room; he knew enough to realise that would be a drop in the ocean. Further up the food chain, yet more would be made, obscene amounts. He thought of the associated unharnessed violence, sex trade and deadly weapons that accompanied dirty money. He thought of the vicious, anarchic people and their extraordinary, immeasurable greed that stomped on all the values Zac had been brought up with, stomped on actual people. Kicked them to death. Shot them, knifed them. There were countless ways to dispatch the uncooperative, the people who got in the way. 'You know, the police told the Bakers it was like the speakeasies in the Prohibition years. But without the charm, I guess.'

'I'm pretty sure the mobsters who ran the speakeasies were unlikely to have been charming,' commented John carefully. 'The charm was brought by the nostalgic movies made by Hollywood.' Zac heard something in his father's voice that sounded like compassion. Did he know, or at least somehow sense, what Zac was going to tell him? Had he guessed that his offspring was embroiled with the limitlessly vicious?

'I've really fucked up.' Zac dropped his head into his hands, overwhelmed. 'It's my fault Sophie is in a coma. I delivered the drugs to the party that she was at.'

John got up out of his chair, backed away. He was still clutching his drink, and the forcefulness of the move meant whisky spilt down his sleeve, splashed onto the floor. 'Jesus, Zac.'

So apparently he could disappoint his bio dad even if he hadn't developed expectations over twenty-two years. John's face was curled up in disgust. Of course, how else would anyone ever look at him from now on? Zac started to cry. The tears came fast. He sniffed, clenched his fist, blinked over and over again, but he couldn't stop them. He felt worse for crying – he didn't care if he looked weak or pathetic, but he didn't want to look like he was trying to get John to feel sorry for him.

'If she dies, I murdered her.'

'You're a drug pusher?' John's voice was full of disbelief.

'No. Yes. I don't want to be. I have no choice.' The caveats and attempted clarifications hiccupped out of Zac's mouth. John edged a fraction closer; he reached out and put his hand on Zac's shoulder.

'OK. You better tell me everything, from the top.'

Zac shook his head ferociously. The room felt hot, the walls seemed to be edging closer to him. The wallpaper didn't look posh or cool any more. The animals depicted were vicious. Talons, beaks, claws, teeth. It was a jungle out there, and in here too. Nothing was safe. Nowhere was. He shouldn't have come here. He shouldn't have said anything. How could it help? He felt dizzy, sweaty. 'No, no. The less you know the better. They use it. They trap you if you know stuff.'

'Who are "they"?' John asked. Zac shook his head again. 'Trap you? How?'

'I'd swap places with her if I could. You have to believe me when I say that.' Honestly, the thought of just being numb, beyond reach, was bliss; he really should be the one in the hospital bed. A new wave of distress hit him, nearly turned him inside out with anguish. Was he saying he envied a girl in a coma? What sort of monster was he? That was a terrible thought, selfish and wrong. He literally hated himself for having it. He deserved to be there, motionless, out of it, but Sophie didn't. She was innocent, she deserved consciousness and vibrancy. The things she would feel if she were conscious would all be good, not like him. He was being ripped apart with guilt and grief. He was disgusting. 'I did this to her.'

John squeezed Zac's shoulder, a slow, strong, determined grip. 'Hang on. Take a deep breath. That's not quite true. She took the pill. You didn't force it down her throat like you were giving a cat a worming tablet.'

'She's a kid,' Zac sobbed.

'I get that, and it's a tragedy that she is where she is. It's a tragedy that she took the drugs, but that's not on you.' John had now placed both his hands on Zac's shoulders. Most probably it was supposed to feel like support, but the gesture added to the sense of claustrophobia. It was condescending. He wasn't getting it.

'Aren't you listening! I delivered them!' Zac yelled; his spittle landed on John's right cheek, but John didn't move his hands to wipe his face.

'Yeah, that is on you. *That* you own. But son, if you are ever going to take a piece of advice from me, it's this. You are not responsible for other people. It's enough to be responsible for yourself. You've messed up, obviously. But let's break this down. We can sort it. Look, kid, since it's the first bit of advice I've ever offered, might you try to take it on board?'

Zac stared at him; it was so weird seeing his own blue eyes flare back at him with such intensity. He wondered whether he could believe this man. If there was a world where this was sortable, salvageable. But then John said, 'We need to go to the police.'

Zac was disappointed by the conventional response. His entire body deflated, drooped. But what had he expected? What else would ever be said or offered by people outside of this nightmare – and everyone was outside but him. 'No. I can't. They'll hurt her. Maybe kill her. Really. They do that shit. I've seen it.'

'Kill who?'

'Fran, I dunno, maybe my mum or dad, maybe Celeste. Anyone I know is in danger.' The tears started again. This time he didn't swallow or blink to try to suppress them; this time he leant into the despair. He let out a loud growl, a groan, like a wounded animal. He couldn't control the tears and howling; he no longer had control over himself. He hadn't had for a while. 'Maybe even you. They could be watching me right now. They could have followed me here.'

'I'm sure that's not the case.' John was sort of shaking Zac now. Not roughly, but with definite determination. Trying to snap him out of it, shake some sense into him. Whatever. It didn't matter what he tried to do, this situation was irredeemable. 'Look, obviously you've got yourself mixed up with something proper nasty, but we can sort it out, Zac. We can. I'll come with you to the station. We can go right now.'

'If we go, they'll arrest me.'

'You've just said you're in danger, that other people are; there are worse things than being arrested. You *have* to talk to the police. I'll get you a good lawyer. The best there is. I'll be right with you.'

'You know I wouldn't mind doing time.' John looked doubtful, but Zac meant it. 'I deserve it, but that won't fix anything. They could still hurt Fran even while I'm on the inside.'

'But why would they? If you're just a runner? They must have loads of people to drop off this shit. You can't be that important to them.'

Zac shook his head fiercely again, and then, in a whisper because he could barely say the words aloud, 'I stole from them.'

'What?'

'That's the way they'll see it. I threw away one of the deliveries. A big one. I don't know what it was worth, but it was a lot. I owe them. And when I'm inside, he'll send someone. Bear has people everywhere. *You* can't help me at all.' It was a desperate accusation. He wasn't angry with John; he was angrier with himself for thinking anything could help. For hoping even for a fleeting moment. 'No one can,' he added firmly as he pulled away. 'I think everyone will just be better off without me.'

John started to gabble. Zac could hear his bio dad's fear and panic pushing in a different direction now. 'No, absolutely not. That's bullshit. What about your mum and dad, your sister? Fran? Do you think they'd be better off without you?'

'Maybe. Yeah, and they'll probably think so too, once they know what I've done.'

John was saying more stuff, but Zac's head was swimming, he couldn't take it in. He fled from the room and down the stairs, tore through the little foyer and out of the big wooden door onto the street. He didn't know exactly where he was heading. As he slipped through the black night, all that mattered was that he disappeared.

41

John

'No, absolutely not. That's bullshit. What about your mum and dad, your sister? Fran? Do you think they'd be better off without you?'

'Maybe. Yeah, and they'll probably think so too, once they know what I've done.'

'No. Are you listening to me, Zac? You're a kid too. Like Sophie. You're just starting out. I know what you've done and *I* love you. I do. I don't care. We'll sort it.'

John wasn't sure if Zac heard his words. He certainly didn't heed them if he had. He darted out of the door like a dog at the races. He was out of the room and down the stairs by the time John located his shoes. Sockless, he roughly, speedily thrust his feet into them. The leather scratched his ankles as he chased his son. But Zac was too fast, fuelled by desperation, he was out of sight by the time John reached the street. He flicked his head left and right; he strained his eyes in the dark to see which way his son had run. But he'd vanished. Frustrated, John swore into the night.

THE DAY IT ENDS

42

Fran

4 January

I don't know where Zac is and I know that's not good. He didn't come home last night. I guess he stayed over at a friend's, but I don't know which one or why he'd choose to do that when I need him here with me for support. 'He could have at least sent me a text to let me know his plans,' I grumble to Flora.

'Maybe he just doesn't want to be in the way. This is family stuff,' she mutters as she leaves the room.

She's trying to help, but I glare at the back of her head, irritated. He *is* family. Why doesn't she see him that way, and worse, is it possible she's right and *he* doesn't see himself that way? Is this about the proposal? We haven't spoken of it since New Year's Eve. Obviously I've had other things on my mind. I've discreetly moved the Tiffany bag out sight. It's in the bottom of my wardrobe. I still haven't tried on the ring. Will I ever?

For whatever reason, it's pretty obvious that Zac doesn't like being around Sophie's bedside. The first hint of an excuse to get out of the room, he takes it. He's always volunteering to nip to the hospital canteen or the corner shop to buy chocolate and sandwiches, even though no one is hungry; he goes out to buy magazines no one reads; to make update calls even though there's nothing to report, and anyway, he doesn't know her friends. How many updates does his mum need? He's up and down like he's doing the TikTok House of Pain challenge. It's making me feel weird. Weirder. Isn't his job to make me feel better? No one wants to be here, I get that, but we *are* here. We're family and Sophie needs us. He needs to buckle up, but I keep getting the feeling he's not coming along for the ride. He's got one foot out of the door. I guess I can't blame him, given everything.

I put my hands on my stomach and tell the baby not to worry. I only tell him in my head because I can't say the words out loud in case my mum hears. Microscopic chance, as her focus is on Sophie, but I can't risk it. If Mum drags her gaze up from Sophie it's to throw it on me or Flora. She pulls her face into an approximation of a smile; it's so strained that it's macabre, but it lets me know she knows we're still here. The thing with Mum is you can never tell when her mothering radar might turn on you. We've all felt that over the years. It might seem she was only concentrating on, say, Flora's school report, and then, as I'd be sneaking out the door, hoping to visit Auriol to watch a YouTube make-up tutorial, thinking I was going under her radar, she'd pivot. Not even physically; it's as though she really does have eyes in the back of her head, as she's often insisted. 'Fran, how is the cello practice coming along? You've got your Grade Four exam on Wednesday and I haven't heard a note.'

I sigh and try not to overthink the idea that the baby can

read my thoughts. I need to believe he can't unless I specifically direct them his way. The stuff that's swilling around my mind unchecked, well, I just don't want it on my little baby's radar. Not *ever*. Most of my thoughts are too much, they're too sad and confused.

Sophie.

Zac.

John Harding.

A total clusterfuck of problems. I have tried to think positive thoughts but am stumped.

When Dad and I are alone together for a couple of minutes at the coffee vending machine, I mention to him that Zac is acting oddly. I'm vague, I don't tell him Zac didn't come home last night, I just say he's sort of jumpy, unsettled. I don't know why I say it really. The last thing Dad needs is something else to worry about. It's habit, though, to tell my dad my fears. He always gives a solid perspective.

'Maybe he's squeamish around medical stuff,' he says with a sigh.

I feel bad for bringing it up and don't comment that if that's the case, the birth is going to be tricky. I'm selfish to be thinking of these things when my sister is lying there in a coma; she should be all I'm thinking about. Mostly, she is. But I've found there's apparently a limit to how many hours I can sit still and internally mutter, 'Wake up, Sophie, wake up, Sophie.' If all I think about is Sophie, then quite soon I want to cry or scream or something. I am in a peculiar alternative reality to other girls my age. A place where imagining my boyfriend thinks my family is too much drama and wants to leave me is almost healthy in comparison to thinking my sister is never going to wake up and is going to be trapped in some sort of weird Sleeping Beauty nightmare for ever.

Mum doesn't seem to have a limit as to how long she can stay hunched over Sophie's bed. When I look at her, I think of those petrified bodies in Pompeii that we saw in a museum years ago. I read that when the volcano erupted, there was a pyroclastic flow that hit hundreds of people, and then they were covered by layers of ash that calcified, so the result was they were preserved in their moment of tragedy for eternity. Sophie was about ten years old when we went to that museum, and the casts frightened her. She cried all afternoon; Mum said that for the rest of the trip we had to eat more ice cream and visit fewer cultural sites. Flora and I were so pleased with our baby sis we gave her a much-coveted glow-up. The thought of being calcified in tragedy is too much.

Mum smells. My beautiful, stylish, immaculate mum reeks. Her hair smells greasy, her body stinks of stale sweat. It's as though some small rodent has died inside her mouth. I have to turn my head from her on the rare occasion she speaks. I'm almost glad none of her questions are directed my way; they are all pushed out to the medical staff. I have seen her clean her teeth in the hospital loos, so I think the stench comes from the fact that her stomach is churning. We've only once persuaded her to go home for a shower, but as she was part way through doing so, she lost it. According to Flora, who was with her, she leapt out of the shower – almost slipping, still sudsy – and dashed for the door, convinced she'd felt Sophie regain consciousness. Full menty B. Flora said she had to more or less physically tackle her to get her to put on some clothes; she was somehow unaware of her nakedness. Poor Flora. It was a lot to deal with. I know Dad wished he'd been with Mum when she had this meltdown, but she wouldn't have even agreed to leave the hospital in the first place if he hadn't promised to stay with Sophie. Anyway, in the end what she reached for was the clothes she'd just taken off. The whole exercise in trying to persuade her to get cleaned up and get some rest was aborted.

Of course when she got back to the hospital, Sophie had not woken up.

You should have seen Mum's face. Or not, because it was hellish to look at. Heartbreaking.

'We'd have rung,' Dad said simply. 'If she'd woken up, we'd have rung.' Mum flung him a look that made me think of supervillains in Marvel movies who have laser eyes and can raze houses to the ground at will. 'When she wakes up, we'll ring everyone,' he added calmly. Providing the reassurance she was looking for. Technically his tenses had not been at all incorrect, but Mum had just panicked at the 'if'. She settled down next to Sophie once again, folded over the bed, tucked up into the tragedy. Eyes trained on my baby sister, only breaking her gaze to occasionally glance at the monitors. To check they were beeping and whirling in the necessary rhythms.

For about the millionth time today, I check my phone, hoping for a message from Zac. I search through all the possible ways he might have contacted me: text, WhatsApp, Insta, Finsta, Snaps, etc. The entire range. Nothing. I realise I'm crying again when I see a drop splash on my phone. The tears just keep leaking out. Mum hasn't cried. Not once. I can't decide what that says about her state of mind. About Sophie's condition. Is she waiting to grieve?

I'm in the loo stall when my phone finally beeps. Zac! My heart lifts a little and my irritation about him going AWOL instantly evaporates, I just want to talk to him. I open the message.

It's a photo. I don't understand what I'm looking at.

It's him. I recognise his jumper first, but this is nothing like I've ever seen him. I don't get it. He's slouched on a wooden chair. At first, I think he's like out-of-it-drunk. But at this time of day? His arms are tied behind his back. Legs spread, tied to the chair legs. A drinking game? But it's not. I know it's not. I just want it to be because the alternative, the reality, is horrifying. His face is so swollen I can't see his eyes. It looks like he has a small balloon attached to his face. I zoom in and then want to hurl. He's cut, bleeding. It looks like he's in some sort of garage or warehouse. I can see corrugated-metal walls around him. There's something on the floor that I think is oil and then I realise it's more blood. His blood? I'm shaking so hard I drop the phone onto the tiled floor. What the fu— I don't understand what I've just seen.

The phone pings again. I pick it up quickly. Another message from his phone, although clearly it's not him sending them.

He'd be dead by now but he owes us $$.

Gt £15k from ur rich mummy and daddy or we'll finish him.

My thumbs dance a reply.

Who are you?

Blue ticks but no response to my question. I don't know why I asked it. It doesn't matter who. They – whoever – clearly think the same, as they add another message.

Your on a deadline.

Despite the incorrect grammar I understand the message. And the next one.

No police. Will drop pin. Don't be a silly girl.

Then there are two emojis. One the zipped face, which I get means to keep a secret. The second is of a teddy bear. Not an emoji I use myself. It makes no sense. Is it a reference to the baby? I put a protective arm around my bump. Or maybe the sender is hinting something about my own youth, or Zac's. Silly girl. The usually cute emoji sends shivers through my body. I want to be sick.

This can't be happening.

43

John

Her number was not programmed into his phone. She knew that, so she helpfully signed off her text.

Where are you?? This is Fran.

He wondered what this might mean. A showdown with the girl was not something he was looking for, but he wouldn't swerve it either. If she wanted to meet, he'd speak with her. Of course. He owed her that. He wondered what she knew about Zac's situation. His son a drug pusher? He just couldn't get his head around it. No, there was more to it. Zac had thrown away drugs. He wasn't a bad lad. Or if he was, he wasn't the worst lad. John had to find out who was. Zac had been terrified. He'd talked of violence, death threats even. He had to have that wrong, didn't he? John recalled his words; he'd been definitive. *Maybe kill her . . . They do that shit. I've seen it*. Hoping he had it wrong was wishful thinking. The truth of it was, there were some proper bastards out there. The trick was avoiding them, finding a way to share the geography of the streets but operate on separate planes. The trouble was, these sorts could from time to time punch through to your sanitised, carefully controlled environment and pollute it. Ruin it. What had Zac got mixed up in?

Obviously John wouldn't betray his son's confidence by disclosing the mess he was in, but maybe if they met, Fran would reassure him simply by commenting that Zac was at home with her. That would be great. That would be everything. He needed to find his boy.

John had called Clare this morning, pretending he was just ringing to say it had been nice to meet her family and to wish them all a happy new year, as though he was a regular sort of ex that made that type of social call to the mother of his son. He'd tried to sound casual as he'd asked if Zac was knocking about.

'He's in London, John. Still staying with his girlfriend's family.' She'd sighed, exasperated. 'Honestly, you should know these basics if you want to build a relationship with him.'

He got it. Clare was guarded, worried that he'd disappoint her boy, play with him, here one moment, gone the next. John felt sorry for her; she had no idea how much more she had to worry about. He'd given it some thought, but in the end decided not to tell her anything. *The less you know the better. They use it. They trap you if you know stuff.* John had never protected Zac or Clare. What with him not knowing about one's existence and forgetting about the other's, the occasion hadn't arisen. But now, he thought it was perhaps time. The lad had come to him, he hadn't wanted his mother to know about all the trouble he was in. John wanted to respect that for as long as he could. No doubt, in time, Clare would have to know everything, John put that off because his first concern was finding Zac and persuading him to go to the police. Telling his mother about the mess wasn't a priority.

He had checked out of the hotel, left his bag with the concierge because he couldn't pull it around after him all over London, like some lost tourist, and he wasn't leaving London until he located Zac. His plan, such as it was, was to spend the day trying to track down the lad; he'd find somewhere or other to sleep tonight. Maybe it wouldn't be as smart as the Portobello, but whatever. When he received Fran's text, he was outside the police station on Ladbroke Road, debating whether to go in and report Zac missing. He hadn't been gone twenty-four hours yet and he probably had half a dozen mates he might be staying with, he was probably fine; John wanted to believe this more than anything in the world.

But.

He hadn't slept a wink last night. He'd been plagued with nightmares that Zac would do something really stupid. Something irredeemable. He'd run through the streets towards Hammersmith Bridge. He was so very glad to get there and see it quiet, a regular amount of traffic and pedestrians crossing; no flashing blue lights, nobody raising an alarm, screaming or crying. He went to the Tube station after that. Made himself. The stillness was eerie compared to daytime, when you had to shove your way through crowds, salmon upstream. He asked the question and the guard on lates looked at him suspiciously, most likely thinking he was some sort of ghoul to be interested in such things.

'I'm just looking for my son,' he explained.

The guard softened at that. 'No jumpers. Not here, not anywhere tonight. We'd have heard. There's always a backup if that happens and everything's run like clockwork tonight.' John thanked him. Then he'd walked the streets for hours, hoping to catch a glimpse of Zac. Maybe huddled shivering in a doorway. He longed to find him smudged into the tableau of urban desolation, under makeshift cardboard shelters or a filthy sodden blanket. He didn't. He checked in countless pubs, late-night cafés and bubble tea bars (what the hell?). He opened doors on the good times, letting the chatter and heat out and the cold, wet blackness in. A quick scan around the boozy or rosy faces was all he needed. When there was no sign of Zac, he turned and was on his way to the next place, not stopping to warm up.

It was past four in the morning when he finally returned to the hotel. He fell into bed allowing himself to hope Zac had found a warm bed too, that he was perhaps already asleep, oblivious to the crippling worry John had absorbed. It was ridiculous to think he could feel – sort of sense – his son on a molecular level; after all, he'd only known about his existence for a matter of months, but John believed a lot of ridiculous things. He *did* think he could feel Zac's fear, his danger, his pain. He was shot through with all three things. He dreamt he was walking with Zac aged about three years old; they were holding hands and Zac was hopping and skipping along the pavement, tugging at John's arm. He kept waking up and rubbing his chest, trying to ease the pain. It was as though Zac was tugging at his heart.

He suggested he and Fran meet in a coffee shop. He only knew one by name, the one he'd met Connie in. Fran seemed to know it too, she'd most likely been there with her mum. This whole thing was so knotted.

The only free table was at the back of the café. He was informed that he couldn't sit there and order from the bar, that it was table service only in that area. He didn't want their conversation interrupted so he ordered them both a flat white. The coffees arrived before Fran did. He had no idea what she drank, other than negronis. As it happened, it didn't matter; she didn't touch it.

She hovered near his table, for a moment he wasn't sure she was going to sit down. 'I got your number off my mum,' she muttered, as though disclosing this annoyed her.

'Right.' He wasn't going to say more than he had to. He waited to see what she knew.

'I know she spoke to you about . . .' She trailed off and dropped her eyes to her belly. 'But that's not why I'm here.' She suddenly sank into the seat opposite him, committing to the conversation, swallowing whatever reservations she had about talking to him. She held out her phone. Arm straight, almost challenging. Her arm was skinny, her elbow knobbly. She looked like a tiny kid with a beachball up her dress, play-acting at being pregnant. 'It was sent from his phone. But his phone is off now.'

44

John

John's eyes fell on the image of Zac. His boy.

This was categorically the worst-ever moment of his life. His body realised it before his mind could process as much. Until it happened, he had not been fully aware of how perfect and trouble-free his life was. Dealing with prick bosses and managing uncooperative, uninspired underlings; knuckling down to earning constricting alimony; even taking the call from the hospice where his mother had spent the last few weeks of her life, none of this was as cruel and narrowing as this moment. His stomach roiled, he tasted vomit in his mouth, just managed to swallow it down. His hands and head felt clammy, his heart beating so quickly he was struggling to breathe. What he was looking at was incomprehensible but made absolute sense considering what Zac had told him; considering that he'd allowed the boy to fly out of his room last night, a sparrow going out into a black and perilous world.

He let out an unchecked sound. A sort of strangled squawk, as though someone had their hands around his neck and he was struggling to breathe. He'd seen some shit over the years. Lads getting into fights. Giving a punch, taking a punch. But *this*. This floored him. He read the message. Understood everything. 'We need to go the police. Right now.'

'Which is as predictable as fuck and a hundred per cent unhelpful. If I'd wanted that response, I'd have spoken to my own parents.' Fran looked like death. He couldn't see a shadow of the young woman he'd cheerfully shagged. There was nothing playful or careless or even seductive or adventurous about her right now. She looked bleak with terror. So she wasn't stupid, she was right to be afraid. He wondered what it was about him that made kids think he was the one to come to if you didn't want to play by the rules. But also, he knew exactly what it was; something he should look at later, not now. Now, he had no time for anything other than Zac.

He leant across the table to be closer to her. He wanted her to listen and be convinced by him. 'We have to go to the police with this photo and threat,' he repeated firmly. 'This isn't a job for the Famous Five. This is real shit and we need the police. They might be able to trace his phone or something and find him.'

'I'm not going to the police. Whoever has him told me not to.'

'Of course they did, they're criminals. But we *must*. We should. Look at him.' He didn't need to ask this of her. She hadn't taken her eyes off the image scarred onto her phone since she sat down.

'They say he owes them money. He might be a criminal too.' She whispered this, and John was touched as he knew that she was trying to protect Zac. He had a nanosecond of hope that she and Zac could have a future together one day, that they might have one another's backs, but then he remembered her sister was in hospital in a coma and Zac's actions had led to her being there. Once all of that was revealed, there wasn't much hope for the two of them. Not in reality. Anyway, first they had to get through this hell. If they could.

'That doesn't matter,' he muttered. His mind was whirling, piecing it together. These thugs, these bastards had done this to Zac because he threw away their gear. Zac had said they would. Why hadn't he listened? He should have locked the door, wrestled him to the ground, tied him up himself, *anything* to stop him running away and into this. His failure to prevent this happening seared. It was like swallowing a flaming sword but without the circus training.

Fran finally dragged her eyes away from the image of beaten and broken Zac and up to meet John's gaze. 'I think they'll kill him if we call the police.'

'What? No. They won't do that.' John very much thought these twisted, ruthless criminals could kill his boy; they were probably planning on it. He'd spewed out the vapid reassurance simply to comfort her and maybe himself. He didn't want it articulated, that particular Armageddon. It was too much to hear.

Fran looked at him pityingly but also with disappointment; she no doubt had expected him to treat her like an adult, considering their past. 'Oh, so you're some sort of expert on the London criminal underworld, are you? You know what they might or might not do.'

'Well, no, but—'

'You think this looks like bluffing? You think this looks like people who are scared of the police? People who have limits?' She shoved the phone towards him again. He wanted to look away, but didn't do so because he couldn't let his son down like that. If he looked away, he'd be somehow abandoning him.

He sighed. 'I just think the police have resources, tactics, experience. We have none of those.'

She pushed her chair away from the table, making to leave. 'I thought you'd want to help,' she snapped.

He couldn't allow her to leave. He'd failed Zac last night; he couldn't let her go out there too into God knows what. He reached for her arm. 'Look, Fran love, don't go.'

She snatched her arm out of his reach and glared at him, hissing, 'I'm not *your* love.'

He felt eyes swivel in their direction. How was it that everyone was as nosy as hell, overcritical and interfering, but no one ever offered genuine help? The world exhausted him. 'I truly meant it in a fatherly way. You know, like I'm almost your father-in-law.'

'Oh my God, my life.' She rolled her eyes skyward and stared at the café ceiling as though it was fascinating. He thought most likely she was blinking back tears. The prying, judgy types they were surrounded by were young people with endless inks, topknots and multiple piercings, sipping on matcha oat milk lattes and engaging with Reddit debates about some existential question Taylor Swift had presented in the lyrics of her latest song. It wasn't fair that Fran was so far from what was usual for young people. He knew he was going to help her in any and every way he could. Of course. They wanted the same thing, Zac safe and home. He tried again at nudging her down the route he thought was most likely to achieve that.

'The police are all we've got.'

'Not true. We could pay the fifteen grand. You could, I mean.' She flushed a little at that. No doubt embarrassed at having to ask him for anything, let alone money. It wasn't about the money. He'd pay it in a heartbeat, but would that guarantee Zac would be extricated safely? Did these people make deals and stick to them? Fran continued. 'Don't you read the news? The police are basically as corrupt as the people they lock up. *If* they ever lock anyone up, that is; the rate of solving cases isn't exciting, incarceration rates worse still. The crims rule the streets.'

'Well, I don't believe all that. I believe there are more good guys in the force than bad. I believe they want justice and will help.'

'It's really sexist that you call them good *guys*; there are women in the force too, you know.'

'Right, and that should encourage you.' His heart cracked. My God, she was just a child. If this wasn't so absolutely horrifying, he'd laugh at her talk of crims and this soapbox she'd jumped on. So opinionated and entitled, yet so inexperienced and naive. He knew she wasn't going to listen to him. She'd probably never listened to anyone in her life but instead existed in a shroud of utter confidence in her own vision of the world; a vision that concurrently terrified her.

He had to pivot, because they had to do something. They were wasting time here. He began to calculate how much money he could gather today. He had a few credit cards and a couple of current accounts. He had no idea what the daily cash withdrawal limits were on any of them because he didn't live the sort of life where cash was needed. At least, not usually. Was the limit a few hundred pounds, or maybe a couple of thousand? He could raise £15k, but not in one day; it would take a couple, maybe three. They didn't have that time. Would it be quicker if he sold shares? Was a bank transfer possible in this situation? Would these people give him details of their banks?

'Right.' He was about to tell Fran to text back and say they would raise the money for the debt as long as Zac was released immediately. He was ruminating on the reality of that negotiation. Who would he enlist to help pick the lad up? Who did he trust? He could ask Neil maybe. He'd go alone if he had to, but he was thinking about what was most likely to get the result they needed, and going alone wouldn't be as forceful as going with backup. But when he looked up, he caught an expression on her face that declared he'd failed a test he hadn't even been aware he was taking. Once again, she oozed an intricate, dense mix of frustration, disappointment and anger. She did not believe he'd help. He drank in the flash of disdain, but then she was a blur. Fran was streaking through the café and heading for the door.

Shit.

Why did these youngsters run away when they had initially come to him for help, when they *needed* help? Why were they so knee-jerk and impetuous? Cursing, he jumped to his feet and grabbed his coat off the back of his seat. The sleeve was caught under the leg, and his tugging upended the chair. The clatter ricocheted through the café. Social convention or habit or something equally constraining and pathetic made him pause for a fraction to right the chair. Then he swiftly moved towards the door, chasing after her.

It wasn't like it was in the movies. He had no cash to fling on the table to pay for the coffees. He was up and off, but a burly barista noticed as much and followed him out the door, grabbing him by the arm, marching him back into the café and demanding payment. An inquisitive crowd immediately surrounded him, so he couldn't slip loose. They weren't exactly making a citizen's arrest, more full-on rubbernecking; still, they were a barrier. John dug about in his wallet. He would have thrown the card at the disgruntled staff, just left it there and not wasted time waiting for the cost of the coffees to be run through the register and for the tap of the card on the machine, but he knew he needed it if he was going to make cash withdrawals that day.

He drummed his fingers on the counter top, dying of impatience. He already hated himself for letting Zac slip away last night. The kid had vanished so quickly. He was fast. Sporty. John felt something complicated as he acknowledged that maybe Zac got his sporting ability from him – he'd always been fast on the footie field – but the flash of pride was pummelled when he thought of the picture Fran had shared. Zac bruised and broken. Not sporty, not able to walk, let alone run. He wanted to scream at the jobsworth idiots who were asking him to tap again.

'The machine's been slow today.'

He bolted out of the shop for a second time, jerking his head left, then right, as though he was watching the fastest of tennis matches. And, oh God, the relief, it wasn't quite like the nightmare of yesterday. There she was. Right at the end of the street, but in sight. She was hurrying but not running. He hadn't lost her. Thank God. He broke into a run.

45

Fran

I thought once I showed someone the photo, you know a fully fledged adult – his father, for fuck's sake – that things would get sorted in some way, shape or form. That *he'd* sort it. So it wouldn't all be on me. I just needed him to give me the money. He must have it. He rakes it in, no kids to spend it on, I bet he has an absolute pile of ready cash. That's why I went to him, not Clare and Neil. I don't think they have much of anything overspill. My mum and dad are swamped with the whole Sophie horror, how can I possibly ask them for help? Besides, John owes me and he owes Zac, right? And although I hadn't quite thought through exactly what would happen next – how we'd get the money to the mental, scary bastards who have Zac, or how we'd get him back – at least it wouldn't be just me working it all out alone. That was the point.

But the moment I showed him the picture, I knew that wasn't what was going to happen. He looked unbelievably terrified. His face went sort of silver-white, like quicksilver, fast and mercurial. It was as though someone had just flicked a cool blue filter over him. I could see through his skin. I mean, obviously not for real, but I thought I could see his skull. I felt sick. Thoughts of the baby scan erupted in my head. Skulls are so vulnerable. I don't want to think of Zac's skull split, brains and blood spilling out. But I saw that too. It's a stupid drama-queen thought, but I had it anyway. John just kept banging on about calling the police. I was surprised by his conventionality and pissed off by it.

John is not going to fix this. He isn't a fully fledged parent. He's not willing to go all in, to dredge up the necessary self-sacrifice that my mum and dad are always banging on about but, to be fair, offer up as simply as breathing. He's a useless, hopeless man. I'm embarrassed I ever did what I did with him. I put my hand over the baby and tell him, 'He's not your daddy. Zac is your daddy.' Technically it might be a lie, but I'm going to be a parent and tell this baby that Father Christmas is a thing.

I don't want it to be John. I hate the thought. I want it to be Zac. I want us to be a family. Most of all I want him to live. And I'm as scared as it's possible to be because that might not happen. So I got up and left. Accepting I'd have to find someone else, someone who is actually willing to help. I didn't explain myself. I don't owe John Harding that, or anything.

I walk quickly, concerned that he'll try to stop me, insist again that I call the police, but I didn't have to worry. He didn't even follow me out of the café. He's such a quitter. I don't run, that would attract attention, but I slip quickly between the clusters on the streets, people with nothing more to worry about than taking an unwanted Christmas gift back to the shops without a receipt. It's a wet, windy day. The worst. People are bent over themselves, clasping their coats against their bodies, pulling their hoods and hats low down over their eyes. It's Orwellian, every man for himself.

The wind pushes against me, lifting the litter from the streets. A page of the freebie newspaper, the *Metro*, wraps around my ankles, like shackles. I pick it off and let it go, and it flutters down the street. I think of Sophie, the story of the drugs that are flooding the city being reported and so important to everyone for exactly twenty-four hours and then just scattered by the wind, trodden into puddles. Beneath notice. I wonder how much more bad luck can I expect. I might lose my sister and my boyfriend. One or both. I might have already done so and I just don't know yet. The thought causes me to stop; I send a quick text to the family chat, asking if there's any news on Sophie. Rationally I know there isn't, because they'd have called if there was, but still.

I wait a minute, chewing my thumbnail, then Flora replies. *Same*.

On our private chat, she writes:

Where r u?

I don't respond. I don't want to have to lie to her. I stand still for a moment longer, because where can I run to next?

My dad? I guess we have the money. There's always money when I ask for it, when I need it. But I've never before asked for anything more expensive than the dosh for the uni ski trip. The thing is, Dad believes in order, rules, fairness, the state, king and country, all that stuff. Although maybe his belief in fairness has taken a bashing as he's spent these last few days wrapped around Sophie's bedside. He must be wondering whether it's fair that she swallowed a tablet to chase a high and has been brought down so low. But yeah, he will insist on taking my phone to the police. Mum might be more flexi about this. She's more of a rule-bender. Thinking of my mum makes me ache. I miss her. She's out of reach right now. I wish I could talk to her about all of this, but when I think of her solidified with pain and shock, I know I can't add to that, no way.

Suddenly I'm frozen with indecision. Maybe John is right, maybe the police could track Zac. His phone's off now so there's nothing I can do, but they could talk to the phone provider. I allow myself to believe in a world where Vodaphone have a what3words reference that would reveal Zac's whereabouts, then the police could do an armed raid, shoot up the bastards that took him. Just do some spy-thriller shit. But then what? I think of the big shoot-outs you see on TV. They're always chaos, there are always casualties. Stupid word, casualties. What's casual about death? I bet they wouldn't even care if Zac got killed while they were trying to round up whoever took him in the first place. I'm not an idiot. I understand he's in with a bad lot. Maybe he *is* a bad lot. Certs that's how the police would see it. I think about the times he's left our bed at night. The times he's said he was taking Asti for a walk. I know now that wasn't the case. He lied to me about where he was going. The question is how much more did he lie to me about?

I whisper on the wind, 'What have you done, Zac?'

Here's the thing, though. I don't care. I don't care that he lied to me or that it looks like he's a criminal or that he's in debt. I just want him home. I'm not going to call the police. The crims said I'd get instructions. I'm not usually especially good at taking any level of instructions, but I'll take this. I'll do this. I'll know where he is soon enough. They'll send me a pin drop, and when they do, I have to be ready. I must raise the money without John Harding or my parents.

I can sell my jewellery; I have nice things that people have given me for birthdays and Christmases and I have the ring Zac gave me too. Or at least tried to give me. Obvs there's no point in taking it back to the store, the refund will just go back on whichever card he flexed to buy it in the first place. I can take the whole lot to a pawn shop. There's one just near us, specifically for designer brands. The area we live in is pretty boom and bust, it's not unheard of for bankers' wives to have to relinquish anniversary presents to get their kids through to the end of the year at private school if hubby's bonus wasn't all that. I browsed in the shop once. I thought it would be like an upmarket vintage outlet and that I'd get a deal on a handbag or something, but the prices the pawnbroker was charging were mental. Even so, I'm pretty certs they'll offer me something insulting for my Tiffany stuff. That's the way it goes, isn't it? People get rich off other people's desperation. I can get some cash from my own current account, and there's Mum's emergency credit card that she insisted I have for when I'm at uni. I think I can get about five hundred cash out on that. I remember her saying it would be useful if I ever had a leak in the flat or needed a locksmith in a hurry. 'Tradesmen respond faster if you offer cash.'

Dad had been irritated that she told me that. 'We don't want to encourage tax avoidance.'

'I'm just telling her about the real world,' Mum had replied. That was back when she had life lessons to teach me. Back when the worst thing my dad wanted to protect me from was the slightly dodgy practice of cash-in-hand. Yeah, I've well and truly leapfrogged.

Doing the hard maths, I know I won't be able to raise enough money on my own. I'm way off. I wonder whether I can go to Lucy. She's loaded and she is my godmother. If ever there was a time for her to sprinkle some fairy dust, it's now.

With what my mum would definitely call renewed purpose, I set off in the direction of home. I can stop off at cash machines on the way, then collect the jewellery, text Lucy, drop in on the pawn shop. I feel better having a plan. Doing something at least. I round my shoulders, head down against the rain. Determined. I've only taken about ten steps when some moron barrels into me. He's huge and I'm nearly knocked off my feet. I feel punched in the chest. I whirl around, ready to lash out at whoever wasn't looking where they're going or – as I'm short on time and too frantic for that sort of shit – to at least throw out a withering look.

'Sorry, love didn't see you there.' The wind whips up my unfastened jacket and my face is obscured for a fraction of a moment. Then I feel a second impact. This time from behind me. Unexpectedly, I'm on my knees. What? What did I trip on? I look up and am face to face with an enormous, ugly bald bloke. He's covered in inks. Least, his head is. He looks bloody scary. He reaches for my arm and starts helping me up. I don't want his help and try to pull away, but his grip is unnecessarily forceful. I can't shake him off. Panic grips me as hard as he is.

'Oh, so sorry, love, in your condition too.' His voice is loud; is he being sarcastic? No, it's performative. Then, in an instant, someone else is on my other side, his hand firmly on my left upper arm. Another man. Huge, powerful, brutal.

And I know what this is.

It takes just a moment, not even that. Lots of women fear

this in general; since receiving the photo of Zac, I should have been expecting it in particular, I should have been aware. I'm being hoisted between them with the sort of ease that a toddler is swung between her parents. I stamp about at the air beneath me as I realise my feet can't touch the ground; it's as though a rope is around my neck and the stool has been kicked away. There are hands all over me. Abrupt and forceful. Lingering, intrusive. The inked man clamps his hand over my face and pulls me close into his neck. From a distance it might look intimate, sort of affectionate, but in fact he's gagging me. I wriggle and struggle. I do. But I'm held so fast and tight that my resistance barely registers.

A step or two and they bundle me into the back of a Transit van that is parked next to the pavement. The doors are open, enormous jaws waiting to swallow me. They fling me like a sack of soil; I land on my side, my shoulder taking the impact. Thank God, not my belly. I scramble to my knees and try to scrabble out of the van. Ink Face immediately climbs in after me. He's massive and blocks my exit. He pushes me in the face and breastbone, forcing me to the back of the van with terrifying ease. His actions are calm, cool, and even more horrifying for that. Their entire operation is efficient, fast; no one seems to notice what's just happened. No one intervenes or even takes photos on their phone. Did it look as though they were helping me up?

In a flash, the second man slams the door closed and then dashes around the van, jumps in. By the time he's settled in the driver's seat, Ink Face has wrapped gaffer tape around and around my mouth and the back of my head. I only realise he's doing it when I feel the pull and tear of the sticky tape in my hair. As the engine starts up and we move away from the kerb, I lash out, kicking and flailing. I slam my feet against the doors. My foot aches but the sound is quite loud; surely if someone was passing, they'd take notice. I try to kick, struggle and scratch at Ink Face, I don't just take it, but I'm a puppet to him, the puppet master.

Then I hear it: a gun being cocked.

I've never before heard the sound for real, but I've heard it a thousand times in movies; I recognise it instantly. And freeze. You can't win against a gun. You can't out-scream, out-kick, out-run a gun. He points it at my stomach, my baby.

'Stay still.' It's such a simple command, understated, delivered in a way that announces he has all the control, I have no choice. He zip-ties my hands behind my back and ties my legs together. He takes my phone from me. Opens it with facial recognition by shoving it in front of me, then scrolls. I stay absolutely still and silent as instructed. 'Roll over.' I roll onto my stomach. Not knowing what's coming next but knowing it won't be good. It's a shock, the sharp jab in my arm. I know what has happened. It happens in night clubs, FFS, of course it's going to happen in a situation like this. It's faster than I thought it would be. Almost instantly I feel sleepy, woozy, sick. I want to fight it. But the gun, and besides, I want to sleep too, just sleep.

My legs feel like bricks.

My arms too.

I just want to sleep.

I just want it to stop.

46

Connie

The new year meant nothing to Connie. It didn't offer any level of increased expectation, renewed vigour or broadening prospect. It did not bring promise or hope, or even the torture of the idea of unattainable standards, new goals. She didn't strategise about cutting out alcohol or taking up a new hobby, she had no plans to clear out her wardrobe, casting off bobbled sweaters or finally relinquishing her size 8 trousers that she'd never again fit into. The only thing that could provide her with any hope was Sophie's eyes opening. That was the solitary goal.

Time rolled on. It might have morphed but it still mattered. Each hour that passed was priceless but also punishing, as it brought with it a complex mix of gratitude that Sophie was still breathing and horror that her thin, blue-veined lids had not fluttered open; that they might never again. Connie mentally tiptoed along a tightrope. She could fall one of two ways, into a swamp of overwhelming anxiety or a quagmire of regret. Teetering on the brink of two forms of hopeless despair was exhausting. Her stomach was hollow. Her eyes stung. Her heart throbbed.

The boxy private room had a square window that seemed just a little mean in its proportions. It faced out onto the car park. Due to the time of year and the glum weather, if ever she did glance up and stare out of it, she seemed to be confronted with nothing other than a wall of grey, heavy emptiness. A precise reflection of her mood. Even if it had been July and streaks of sunlight had tumbled into the room, she would not have felt cheerful. Clement weather, long, bright days would have been insulting. Better that the world mourned with her.

Her days were not being segmented by the usual conventions of mealtimes, yoga classes, opening the gallery, feeding the dog, TV viewing or cocktail time, so she had little interest in one hour dragging into the next; all sense of progress had dissolved. Her nights were not being utilised in the usual way. She was not managing to sleep for longer than forty minutes before she jerked awake as a nightmare bit, sinking its torturous teeth into her mind. She dreamt of burying her child, or watching her reach old age in absolute stillness. It was unbearable. Or sometimes she simply woke because she was hideously physically uncomfortable. She refused to go home to rest in her bed. She slept in the seventies-style wooden armchair (possibly an original). The seat was padded well enough, but if she did find sleep, often her head slipped to one side and banged against the hard backrest, jolting her into returned consciousness. She hadn't slept this badly since she'd been nursing Sophie.

Luke had only stayed at the hospital on the first night; after that he'd gone home at about 10 p.m. It made sense. Only one of them was allowed to stay overnight. Connie supposed the rule was in place so that parents would take it in turns to go home, rest and freshen up, rather than exhausting themselves with constant around-the-clock vigils. She did not allow Luke to take his turn. He'd stopped asking for it. He went back to the house and checked in with her parents, reassured Fran and Flora. Connie wouldn't have wanted that job even if she could have found it in her to leave Sophie's side. She wouldn't want to have to play that falsely positive role that was so frequently demanded of parents. She didn't have the emotional resource to pretend that no news was good news or to fake any level of cheer or optimism at all. She couldn't choose happy. She was using every iota of her energy hoping. Praying. She'd bargained with God. Promised she'd be there when her daughter's eyes opened – whenever that was – just as long as they did open. Even Luke was praying, and he had been a staunch atheist since he was a teen, hadn't even hovered around agnosticism. She watched him silently move his lips as he said goodbye to her and Sophie every night, and then again each morning when he burst into the hospital room and found them there still.

You think you won't. You think you're more sophisticated than that. But you do.

She would not leave Sophie's bedside. She knew Luke thought she was being extreme, everyone probably thought as much. She could see that he was exasperated with her by the way his eyes tightened just a fraction when she insisted that she wasn't hungry, didn't want to go to the hospital café, couldn't eat a thing. It was something she'd often been accused of as a mother, being a little too ferocious, a little too protective or involved. What a joke. She hadn't been able to keep them safe. If only she had been more shielding, more immersed. She hadn't done a good enough job. How would she live with that? She honestly didn't care what Luke thought. If she didn't follow her instincts, if she allowed herself to be persuaded into leaving Sophie and something changed, she would never forgive herself. She'd never forgive him. She tried not to let him see that she hated him for being able to leave their daughter's bedside.

Her mother and father had visited twice. They didn't stay long. Not because they weren't desperate to, of course they were. It was just too much for them. They felt intimidated by the doctors and floored by the tragedy. They couldn't understand a world where a child was given drugs at a party. It had been just minutes since Sophie was going to parties where there was cake and goody bags with sweeties, stickers and bubbles. Her mother had said, 'Why don't you come home with us, Connie love, just for an hour or two. Try and sleep in your own bed, that way you'll be stronger for Sophie when she needs you.'

Her father added, 'You won't be any good to her if you make yourself ill.' She didn't even answer them. She felt comfortable ignoring her parents, ignoring her husband, because they were right about one thing: she did have to preserve her energy for Sophie. She sometimes looked up to smile at Fran or Flora when they visited. If she found their hands loose, she would reach and squeeze them. She didn't want them to feel alone and neglected. Hadn't her single-minded focus on one daughter led to this disaster? She'd spent her Christmas worrying about Fran, she'd let Sophie fall under the radar. She'd never forgive herself for that. She hadn't even bothered to nag her about revision, let alone check who she was going out with. For God's sake, what sort of mother was she?

The girls had visited early this morning. Fran had only stayed an hour, then dashed off; Flora had stayed for most of the morning but then left to meet a friend for lunch. Connie was relieved that they had places to go, people to see, that against all odds they were finding a way to stumble through a semblance of normality.

Luke had arrived this morning with a bag of snacks from Waitrose. He had perhaps thought the healthy and tasty goodies might tempt her more than the sugary and fatty ones on offer locally, but she ignored the bag, left it forlornly languishing on the small side table where he had placed it. He paced around the room, his shoes squeaking annoyingly. He spent some time studying the charts and notes that were kept at the end of Sophie's bed. Connie wondered if he understood them, what he was looking for exactly. When her stomach rumbled, he said, 'It's lunchtime, Connie. You haven't had breakfast, for God's sake eat something.' It wasn't said with any impatience or frustration, it was a genuine plea. She realised he needed to feel useful, he needed to think he could help his wife, if not his child. If she ate the food he'd brought her, he would have some sense of achievement and progress. Having this thought was a peculiar sort of development. Connie felt sad that her mind had normalised the situation with Sophie enough to allow her space to think about Luke's feelings, and then she felt ashamed that she hadn't allowed room for him earlier. He looked so unhappy and lost. Not recognisable as her strong and usually stoically untroubled husband. Almost as gone as Sophie. She reached for the grocery bag he'd brought.

'So, Sophie, let's see what your dad has picked out for me. Can you guess?' They'd both been doing this throughout the ordeal, chatting to their daughter, including her. Finding a way to pretend they weren't dying inside. 'Carrots and hummus dip. Lovely. All-butter cheese twists, very nice. Double pack of Scotch eggs.' Connie's voice quivered here, as these were Sophie's favourites, not something Connie ever ate and Luke knew that. She nose-dived back into the bag so as not to allow the upset to overwhelm. 'Oh, look at this. Kefir cherry drink and a strawberry one as well. Both delicious. Which shall I have?' She held a drink in each hand and pretended she was weighing them up. It was as she was doing so that it happened.

'Erry.' The sound was muffled, almost indistinct. Of course it was; she had a tube in her mouth.

Connie froze, but Luke sprang into action. He hit the alarm button that alerted medical staff, he was at the door yelling, 'Nurse. Nurse, Doctor, someone come quickly. She's awake! Come quickly!'

Then he was back by Connie's side, by Sophie's side, and they both saw it: her eyes blinked, just once. And it was as though the air she'd moved had swept over Connie and blown her into action. She felt it in every fibre of her body. It was like the moment she made the final push, after crowning, and her babies slithered into the world. Took a breath.

'Darling, my baby. We're here. Welcome back.'

47

Connie

Connie could not remember feeling happiness like it. Not on her wedding day, not when she drank champagne with friends and art dealers and surveyed her first photographic exhibition, not even when she first discovered that each of the girls had been conceived. The exhilaration pumped through her body like fizzy blood. She floated, bounced, with a level of elation that she hadn't imagined humanly possible. She had never expected to ever again feel anything so sweet and blissful, so unique. Now she was middle-aged, her emotions were usually somewhat anaesthetised with experience and wear.

For days, time had lumbered, smudged and shuddered; now suddenly time zipped. The minutes jumped and she couldn't harness them, even if she'd been inclined. But she was not, it was glorious that things were happening at last. The afternoon was a blur of activity as medical staff buzzed around Sophie, monitoring her progress. Then family arrived, willing to guide her back to the land of the living. Hoping, and now believing, there was that opportunity. Connie and Luke had previously been told that the first stages of emergence from a coma were, generally, decerebration or decortication; reflexes that caused straightening and bending of the arms and legs. In the second stage, localised response might occur, such as response to sound, touch or sight. But they had fast learnt that doctors scattered any dissemination of information with words such as 'often', 'usually', 'it can happen that', 'it isn't unknown' 'there are exceptions when'. No one really knew what to expect as so many factors were at play. How quickly or completely a person might recover was a mystery. However, following the verbal response, demanding comprehension of the conversation that was happening, and the blink of the eye, Connie wallowed in hope.

Sophie was examined and the doctors appeared confident that she was now capable of swallowing independently. So they removed the tube that sucked out her saliva. Connie noticed she blanched during the procedure.

'She's not in pain, but it's good she felt the discomfort of that,' assured one of the nurses as she patted Connie's shoulder. Connie put her own hand on the nurse's and patted back affectionately, because they were celebrating. Sophie hadn't opened her eyes again after that initial flutter, but Connie noted that there was movement under the lids when Flora and the grandparents charged into the room and Flora carelessly flung herself onto the bed.

'Careful, you'll knock out the tubes,' warned Luke. He was being tetchy and cautious, not allowing himself the indulgence of believing it was over yet. But Connie knew her prayers had been answered: her daughter was recovering. Soon Sophie would be capable of following simple instructions and would open and close her eyes when they asked her, she'd stick her tongue out on demand, she'd grip and release their hands. The doctors had explained those were examples of the next steps. Connie felt sorry that Luke couldn't yet commit to believing in the recovery. He still harboured fears of brain damage and had tried to warn her against premature hope. But Sophie had leapfrogged the usual recovery progress markers. She'd engaged with their conversation. She'd said 'cherry', or at least tried to. One of the doctors had cautioned that most likely it was just a sound, not a response, not an articulated word. He'd reminded Connie that the mind could play tricks; there was a suggestion of wishful thinking. Luke seemed to back-pedal a little. He spoke of Sophie 'making a noise' rather than 'saying a word', but Connie knew better. She knew Sophie always chose the cherry-flavoured kefir drink.

The doctors said they needed some space and time to run more scans and response tests on Sophie. They asked the family to give them a few hours.

'It might be a good opportunity for us to go home,' Luke suggested tentatively.

'We could stay,' offered Flora. She was gesturing towards her grandparents. 'We can hang out in the visitors' room until we're allowed back in with Sophie. Then we can call you.' The grandparents enthusiastically nodded. Glad to be of use.

'Yes, OK. Let's do that.' Connie's agreement caught everyone off guard. They'd expected her to resist, but buoyed up on her belief that Sophie was going to be OK, she found it in herself to be generous towards her husband and family. She would give them what they wanted, a chance to make it better for her. She'd never tell them that Sophie was the only person with the power to make Connie feel better, and she had. 'I'd like to go home for a couple of hours,' she admitted. 'Maybe Fran and Zac will roll in. We can tell them the good news in person.' She smiled at Luke and he sagged with relief.

They left the smell of disinfectant, antiseptic and dread behind them and paused outside the hospital doors, taking long, deep breaths, filling their lungs with air. 'London air has never smelt so good,' said Connie with a smile. It was a windy afternoon; litter and leaves were being picked up and swept across the asphalt. She glanced upwards to the patchwork of fast-moving clouds scudding across the sky and felt a surge of joyful, untamed energy. She reached for her phone to see if Fran had responded to her earlier calls or messages. She'd sent a text asking if she and Zac were planning to come home for dinner. *Come! Some news!* she'd typed, and then added a row of smiley-face emojis. Her second thought had been that was too much, they might then expect Sophie to be sitting up in bed giving and receiving hugs, so she deleted all but one smiley face and added a heart. Flora said Fran had 'checked in', but Connie hadn't received any word from her all day. She guessed that she was in a tight clinch with Zac somewhere or other. Making up and making out. She wished she'd come home, because she wanted to share the phenomenal news in person, she wanted to pore over the miracle in the finest detail, but she also accepted that the young couple had a lot to work through too. It was good that Fran had turned to Zac in this testing time and that he'd been waiting to catch her. She reached for Luke's hand and they headed towards the Tube.

The last four days, keeping vigil, had drained her. The adrenalin rush provided by the selection of the cherry drink lasted long enough to get her through the door, prep and eat a cheese toastie and drink half a cup of tea, but then her eyelids began to feel like lead, her body demanded sleep. She couldn't muster the energy to even climb the stairs. She joked with Luke that he'd need to fireman's-lift her to bed, the way he sometimes had to with the girls when they were small and exhausted. However, he didn't look keen; he too was exhausted. She carefully dropped herself down on the sofa, and felt him ease the half-empty mug out of her hand. She stretched out her legs and he tucked a rug around her. She was aware of him collapsing into the chair closest to her, but her eyelids were already closed. She could finally allow herself to give in to sleep. She expected that soon the click of the front door opening would jerk her awake. Soon all her chicks would be home again.

The phone rang a blaring alarm, charging through her home, her mind. She sat up with a start. Blurry-eyed and foggy-headed, it took her a moment to understand where she was, and why. Not in the hospital room. She was home. Yes, the cherry drink. She hadn't slept for long enough. Her brain was still soggy. She stretched her arms high above her head and smiled to herself. She would shower and change and then dash back to the hospital. By now the doctors might have updates. She reached for her phone, sure that it would be Flora with good news. There was more noise: someone was banging at the front door. Luke had jerked awake too. He had a line of saliva running down his chin. He wiped it quickly, pushed the heels of his hands into his eye sockets and then leapt up, rushing for the door.

48

John

'What are you doing here?'

John realised that Luke was unlikely to ever welcome the sight of him, but he thought that was an especially hostile starting point. Rude. It was a shame, because beginning so badly meant this was likely to escalate at a rate of knots; there would be nowhere for Luke's emotions to go, least nowhere good. And that was not helpful. John had been taught that on a negotiation course. He was here to deliver terrible news – things were only going to get worse – he'd hoped that Luke would at least have started proceedings with a pretence of conviviality and civility. It would have made it a fraction easier. But sod him. There was no time for his posturing, his anger or grudges.

'Can I come in?'

'Why?'

'It's important. I need to see Connie. I need to talk to both of you, actually.'

'It's not a good time.' Luke crossed his arms over his chest.

John was pretty sure he was tensing his muscles, showing his biceps. John was generally one to meet challenge and aggression with the same and a pinch more, but it wasn't the time or the place.

'OK. Right, I realise you have a lot to digest. I can only imagine what it must be like hearing that I slept with your daughter, but I think we need to move past that for now at least. Park it. In fact, I know we do because—'

'What the hell did you just say?'

'Oh shit.'

'You slept with my daughter?'

'I was going to tell you.' That was Connie. She was at the door now too. If she had been planning on telling him, it didn't matter, Luke wouldn't believe her. Most likely he wasn't going to believe anything she ever said again. 'I only found out on New Year's Eve, and then with Sophie and everything I haven't had the chance to talk to you,' she added. She looked weary and tiny. John felt bad for her. Worse because he knew that however terrible she thought it was that her youngest daughter was in hospital and that he'd just revealed that choice piece of info about her eldest, he was about to deliver something so much more devastating. An actual grenade. In a matter of minutes she would be begging for the nirvana of simply thinking her grandchild's paternity issue was a problem. Soon she'd accept that one child in hospital, being looked after by trained doctors, might seem OK.

'How is Sophie?' he asked.

'We're hopeful,' replied Connie with a small smile.

'Oh good, good.' That was something.

'I'm sorry, what the hell?' Luke demanded. He was

spluttering, furious. Naturally enraged that he was having to play catch-up. John wanted to punch himself. He was exhausted and overwrought, otherwise he'd never have made that mistake. It was very unlike him to volunteer information to anyone, and he certainly was not in the habit of revealing anything as incendiary or private. Normally he was the soul of discretion.

'Look, I get it, you're pissed off. I'm sorry about that.' The words had come out all wrong. Sort of casual and dismissive. That was not what he was aiming for.

'It wasn't enough that you had my wife, you had to come after my daughter too.'

'I had no idea she was your daughter. Look, it doesn't matter.'

'Of course it matters.' Luke looked stunned. 'What was it, an affair, a one-off? What are we talking about here?'

'Should we discuss this inside?' Connie said as she gently tugged on the sleeve of Luke's jumper and tried to ease him away from the doorstep and into the house. Probably she was aware of the neighbours. That was a Connie thing. What other people thought mattered to her. He had seen her cross lines, follow the beat of her own drum, but that was a long time ago. She was quite conventional now. Luke seemed unconcerned about washing their dirty linen in public. He shook her off with impatience and glared at her.

'The baby might be his,' she muttered.

It might have been funny if it was happening to someone else or just on TV. The man's face. His mouth fell open. He gaped and gasped like a fish on the riverbank struggling for air; John knew he was there to deliver the killer blow. 'You should be locked up.' Luke sprang forward, and for a fraction of a moment it seemed like he was going to throw a punch. Instead he grabbed the lapels of John's coat and shook him. Connie tried to force herself in between the two grappling men. Normally John would have given it back, hard. Unconcerned that Luke was half a foot taller. He was a fighter. He'd had to be. He automatically checked out Luke's soft hands – were they actually manicured, or just naturally perfect, having never had to strike anything other than a keyboard in his life? – and felt a flicker of derision alongside the pity he still cradled for this man. He jerked out of Luke's grasp and took a step down the stoop, away from the door. He held his hands in the air, conciliatory.

'Right, yes, I've heard it all before. I should be locked up. I'm a bastard, it's all on me. Blah blah blah. You are clearly not going to listen to me, so can I speak to Connie alone? Please.'

'Go screw yourself.'

'It's important. It's really important, you prick. I need to talk to you about Fran.'

'Not now, hey, John,' interrupted Connie. 'We're dealing with a lot. Yes, we do have to talk about the situation with you and Fran, but can we just get through this with Sophie first, please?'

They still believed they had the power to draw a line under the conversation, to say when enough was enough. Fran was the same. She had a naive belief in what she could control. He and Zac were cut from different cloth; they knew that there were many, many things in this world that were far from manageable. Cruel, unwieldy things that rolled out of control. The image of Zac bruised and bloody had been swimming in his head all day long.

Luke went to close the door, but John quickly rammed his foot in the gap.

'They have our kids,' he yelled at the top of his voice.

It wasn't the way he'd planned to deliver the news. He'd wanted to tell her calmly. Shield her a little. As much as he could. He expected that when he told her everything, she'd fall to pieces. He had. In the police station this afternoon, they'd brought him hot sweet tea, and after the lengthy questioning, they'd asked if he needed anyone to come home with him; they'd said he could be assigned a family liaison officer. He'd stumbled at that. Suggested that that person, whoever they were, would be better placed visiting Clare and Neil and their girl. They were a family. He was just him.

'Well, actually the role of the FLO is a point of contact between families and investigation teams. They gather evidence and information to contribute to the investigation. You saw Zac Knight and Frances Baker last, so you're important in this investigation.'

'Then just send the regular people round. Don't waste the resources of one of these FLOs. You don't need to treat me with kid gloves,' John had replied.

Now, he stared at Luke through the crack: just a couple of inches of his face. It was enough. He hated the smug bastard. He was a total arsehole and always had been. Privately John had long thought that Luke was not enough of a man for Connie. She deserved better. She should have left him years ago, but even so, he wished he didn't have to tell the bloke what he was about to. No one should ever have to give or receive this news. The police would be here any minute, he imagined. Connie and Luke would need a FLO, they'd expect one. Whatever he thought of Luke, he was Connie's choice and they were a family. John had come here straight from the police station because he wanted to tell her personally. Answer her questions directly and honestly. Because, dear God, this might kill her.

Connie was a weird mix of all sorts of things. Capable of an entire gamut of emotions and actions, some of which he understood, others . . . well, they were beyond him. She was impassioned, cold, honest, a liar, loyal, capable of betrayal, often hilariously funny, sometimes bloody mean and rigid. But there was one thing that was always steady about her, and he'd seen it the moment he stumbled upon her with her kids outside the school that day years ago. She was a good mum. It was obvious that she'd do anything for her girls. She would grow old and lose her looks – honestly, she already had to an extent – but the most beautiful thing about her was she was a good mum.

'Who has our kids?' Her voice cold and clear. Alert.

'Some drug gang. I don't know exactly.'

'What are you talking about?'

'I realise this sounds insane, but this morning I watched as your daughter was bundled into a van and taken. I don't know where.'

Luke opened the door. 'No. What? You're making this up.'

'What the hell, John. Call the police. Call them now.'

'I went straight to the police. I've been with them all afternoon. My guess is they'll be coming here any minute now.'

'Wait, what, you said they have *our* kids?' said Luke.

John turned to him and nodded his head once. 'Yeah, they already had Zac when they took Fran. They've both gone. Fran had a photo of him. They sent it to her. Oh my God, Connie. The state of him. I don't know if he's dead or alive.' John swayed as though saying the words aloud had sapped all his energy.

'This isn't right. This can't be right,' muttered Connie. 'We've just been at the hospital. We've been with Sophie.' She shook her head.

There was a beeping announcing that one of them had received a message; all three reached for their phones. Connie looked momentarily triumphant. 'Ha, look there's a text. I bet it's from her. You see, you're wrong. She's fine. She's . . .' Connie fell silent. John knew what she was looking at, or at least he could approximate a guess.

49

Fran

'Sit up. I'm gonna untie your legs.' The words echo. My head hurts so much. Worse than any hangover I've ever had. I've been asleep. Such a deep sleep. Where am I? What's happening here? I think for a moment maybe I'm still asleep. Classic it's-a-nightmare-I'll-wake-up-soon stuff. But then I start to remember and realise, yeah, this is a nightmare. But I won't wake up from it.

Zac, the photo, John Harding hopeless, a man, two of them, a van, they jabbed me. The moment the last thought slots into place, I go full menty B. Then I feel the end of the gun jab into my back, reminding me how stupid it would be to do anything other than follow instructions.

'Get up, don't try running.' That's a ludicrous command. I can barely move. My feet and legs feel like huge weights. The sort boys at the gym try to get you to pick up knowing you won't be able to, so they look tough. I'm tied at the hands and that, and the effect of the drug leaves me desperate and uncoordinated. I loll. They think I'm being uncooperative. I'm not. I'm just a mess. They roughly drag me out of the van.

It's dark. A pitch blackness that could place me any time after 5 p.m. but before 7 a.m. at this time of year. The cold relief of outside air lasts just a minute, before I'm shoved inside a huge semi-derelict building. Is it an old factory, a warehouse? The walls feel close as I'm pushed through various doors and led down corridors that smell mouldy and abandoned. They move at a pace and I keep stumbling because it's disorientating and I'm shit scared. One foot in front of another is a massive task. Panicky, disappointed with myself, I try to stay upright so as not to show my fear or make them angry by slowing them down. The third time I stumble, Ink Face mutters, 'Stupid bitch,' and forcefully grabs my upper arm. His knuckles are close to my breast. He was handsy as he hauled me out the van too, I can just tell he's enjoying the freedom he's getting with my body.

Prick. Scary fucking prick.

I try to shake him off, but the more I struggle, the tighter he holds me. What did they give me? I think of the baby and I want to cry. I want to kill. They put something in my bloodstream, in *his* bloodstream.

I'm led into a large, dimly lit room and pushed hard into a chair. I clock three faces. Ink Face and two others, one black, one white. The black face is insolent, detached, cold. The white one is skinny, vicious, possibly high. All three are terrifying. I can feel their breathing as they peer at me. The white guy ties my legs to the chair legs; I'm splayed and feel a new level of danger and exposure. This man pretends to be checking how secure his binding is but takes the opportunity to run his filthy hands up my calves, my thighs.

He mutters, 'What a slut.' I have no idea why this is said. Is there ever a reason?

Just take a look around you, sweetheart. I hear my mum's voice. Not for real. She's not here, I know that. But this is the advice she has always given me, that I have always followed. I look past the eyes that are boring into me and try to take in my surroundings. I've already decided this is not a place I want to be, so following Mum's age-old advice I'm looking for an exit.

It's some sort of warehouse or storage facility. A lock-up. A big one. Three of the walls are corrugated metal, one is bare brick, no windows. The ceilings are really high up. I'd guess four metres. There are tin tiles and unpainted beams above me. The space is segmented by impermanent panels that look like something you might use for backdrops in a school play. They're made of cork tiles and stretch approximately from one metal pillar to the next. Cork? Soundproofing. Why? I don't want to answer that. Especially as I see that part of the room is draped in plastic sheets. The sort you might use if you're painting a ceiling and want to protect the floors. No one is painting a ceiling in here. The thought causes stars to flicker into my head. I think I might lose consciousness. Part of me wants to. But I can't. I wiggle my toes to try to stay conscious and focused.

There is a lot of junk piled and scattered about, barrels, boxes, crates. *Stay curious, darling.* More parental advice comes into my head, but I think in this case it's best I don't know what is in the boxes. Guns, drugs, tools that could be used to hurt people. WTF, I have no idea. It's unlikely to be a music box holding a tambourine and a glockenspiel. My nose feels blocked as panic and claustrophobia threaten to overwhelm me. I hear my mum's voice again. *It's not scary if you know what's in all the corners.* I think she might be wrong about that this time, but I force myself to be thorough. To keep looking and not give in to the tears or the fear. Then I see that in the right-hand corner, as far away from where I am as it's possible to be, there is another door. I quickly look away because I don't want the men to see I've noticed it. I drop my eyes to my lap.

'Say cheese.'

I can't say anything, obviously, but I look up at Ink Face. He's holding a phone. He snaps a photo of me and then types something. I suppose it's going to my parents. They'll receive it the way I received Zac's. I feel so sad for them. Sorry that they are going to have to deal with this along with Sophie's coma. How will they cope? My emotions must show in my eyes or my demeanour, because Ink Face taunts, 'Cheer up, we have a surprise for you.'

The white guy laughs, sort of manic-snidely, the black guy looks icy and bored as they lift one of the dividing panels and show me what is hidden behind it.

When we set eyes on each other, it's unclear which of us takes it the most badly. The sight of one another – usually so healing and happy – is now the worst thing ever. He looks horrific. The photo didn't prepare me. He looks like he's been through a windscreen. Like me, he is tied to a chair so he can't leap up or lash out, but when he sees me, he simply slumps, falling forward like he's been shot. I haven't been beaten, but I suppose the shock of seeing me here is enough to floor him. He knows better than anyone the danger I'm in. It says a lot that he doesn't struggle, not even as an instinctual reaction. He knows we've lost this, whatever *this* is. Why am I here, Zac? What have you done?

Might I be dead soon?

I've never thought much about death, but these past few days, since Sophie OD'd, I've thought of little else. Sophie could die. I could die. Zac could die. My baby boy has never even had the chance to live. The thoughts cascade and clash. It's too much to deal with. My poor parents, poor Flora, middle child to only child, what a nightmare for her. We're all so screwed. I have not ensured my pop-up pool stayed full; it's so far from overflowing, gushing, a deluge. That idea – my previous life philosophy as shared with Zac – seems arrogant, childish. What was I thinking? My basic goal now is to stay alive. I start to cry, sob. The sound is muffled by the gaffer tape across my mouth, but any hope of appearing brave or defiant vanishes. I don't want to die. I don't. I don't. I'm not ready to. The tears stream down my face, my shoulders judder up and down, my whole body is quaking. It's proper hysteria.

Ink Face gives me a sly, nasty smile. 'Hey, don't get upset. Daddy's rich, Mama's good-looking.' He leans close to me, places the muzzle of the gun at my throat. I can feel the cold metal on my skin, like a cut. He trails it down my neck, pokes at my shirt to open it a little wider, expose more cleavage. Then he slowly continues his exploration, over my blooming stomach, lower so that the gun rests between my legs.

Seeing Zac slump forward, give up, accept defeat was so scary, I thought I'd never see anything worse, but now he starts to struggle as though he thinks he can get to me. I know what's going to happen before it does. The bloke next to him thumps him, not in the face as I expected, but this odd sort of chop movement between Zac's shoulder blades. Zac cries out. I jump my chair towards him. I want to put myself between him and the next blow. I make just a couple of inches of progress before Ink Face kicks over the chair and I fall onto my back. Pain slams through my body; my hands are trapped by my weight and they throb. I'm stranded like an upside-down beetle, kicking my legs in the air. I've seen cruel boys mindlessly poke insects with sticks, pull off their legs or wings, just for the hell of it. The three thugs surround me. They are laughing. I'm an insect to them.

50

Connie

'Come in, come in,' murmured Connie on autopilot as she listlessly trailed into the living room.

John followed her as Luke muttered his objection. 'You are literally inviting a vampire into our house.'

'Luke, not now. Please.' Connie pushed her phone into her husband's hands. He glanced at the message she'd just received, gasped and then handed the phone to John. They exchanged a quick look, and for the first time in their convoluted twenty-five-year history, they were united. They had total empathy with one another's position. They were in fact standing in the exact same spot. Both wished to hell it wasn't the case.

'We need to call the DI on the case, the one I've been talking to today. If she's not already on her way, this will bring her quickly.'

Connie as a parent had experience of assessing professionals such as teachers and those in health care to work out at lightning speed if they were good at their job; friend or foe when it came to answering her children's needs. Within minutes of

Elizabeth Gianella arriving, she had ascertained that the DI was no-nonsense, she didn't lean in too heavily to her position as a woman, or Connie's as a mother. She just started talking facts, asserting what they knew, what they didn't. What they were doing to discover the whereabouts of Fran and Zac. This was exactly what Connie needed. She didn't need emotions. She had legions deep of her own to keep in check. She listened carefully as the inspector revealed details about first Zac's abduction and then Fran's.

How could anyone expect them to cope with this latest disaster? Connie thought this amount of bad luck should be divided up between different, unrelated families or spread out over time. *It isn't fair.* The words pushed their way into her mind. They came in the voice of one of her daughters. She couldn't discern which one was pricking her memory right now, as all three girls had repeated this particular phrase on many an occasion. It didn't matter which of them had said it, her response had always been the same, delivered with a cavalier cheerfulness or her last gasp of patience: 'Life isn't.'

But honestly, hers had been. In fact her life had been better than fair; she'd been lucky, her life had been *glorious.* Why hadn't she revelled in that? She was ashamed to think she used to make a virtue out of 'choosing happy'; why the hell wouldn't she have been happy all the time? Back then. In the past. When her kids had been safe and healthy. A different world, let alone country. She couldn't remember why she might have thought an unexpected pregnancy was anything other than brilliant news; her family growing was a wonderful thing. Far better than this threat of it shrinking.

Disappearing.

Was she being punished for her smugness? Was she being shown just how 'not fair' life could be? Her eldest daughter was being held hostage by God knows who. They could do God knows what to her. Connie found it literally impossible to think of what they might do to her. Fran was tied up and gagged. Connie could only see her eyes, but she looked terrified. Small.

The policewoman had briefly taken the phone off her so she could forward the image to different departments. They had a record of the demand now. The photo was part of the investigation. John had said £15,000 was demanded for Zac; now they were asking for £35,000. Connie didn't think it was a lot of money for her child. She'd give them ten, a hundred times more if it brought Fran home safely. Give everything she owned. But that didn't seem to be the point. No one had said where the money was to go, how Fran and Zac would be returned, whether delivering one thing guaranteed the other. Connie wanted someone to say it would all be all right, but no one was saying that. The DI had placed the phone on the table between them. Connie itched to pick it up, cradle it like she'd cradled her children.

'Luke, will you contact the hospital, or text Flora, my parents, see if there's any news about Sophie? Don't tell them about this.'

'I won't, not yet.'

Connie didn't like him adding 'not yet'. It had a ring to it that suggested that sooner or later they would have to tell the rest of the family about this latest horror. She didn't want to think that. Surely things could be resolved, restored before she had to spread this news.

As the DI had revealed what the police knew, Connie and Luke kept shooting John looks of shock and incredulity, but every time they did so, he sadly nodded a confirmation. Debt, gangs, death threats, ransom messages. What was Zac involved with?

'Mr Harding taking a photo of the van's registration plate was useful. We're tracking who it's registered to and there are thousands of cameras positioned up and down the country's motorways. We are already searching through footage.'

'So there's a good chance that you'll spot the van, know what route it took?' said Connie.

'Well, providing they didn't remove or change the plates. Depends how thorough they're being. And the cameras are only on the main roads. So even if we do pick it up, we won't necessarily be able to track it to an exact location. But it's a start. A lead.'

'We have Fran on Find My iPhone,' said Luke. He scrambled for his phone. Her last position was exactly where John had said she was abducted. 'I suppose they turned it off straight away,' he said with a sigh.

'So what now?' Connie asked. She was waiting for someone to have answers, solutions. Someone had to.

'We've contacted Fran and Zac's phone providers. We're asking for their records to be released, see if there's anything else to be gleaned. We'll trace and analyse everything we have.' It didn't sound like they had much. The DI added, 'In an effort to establish a wider picture, what can you tell us about Fran and Zac's recent movements?'

'What do you mean?'

'Anything about their general behaviour recently that seemed out of character, out of the ordinary.'

'We don't know what his ordinary is,' spluttered Luke. Normally a patient man, he was now tapping his foot against the floor. This was all taking too long for him. Connie was usually the impetuous one; he seemed to be filling the space she had vacated. She was simply too flattened to have the energy to be outraged, angry, even regretful. She just longed for this not to be happening.

'This visit is the first time we've met Zac,' she explained to the officer.

'And Fran's behaviour, anything notable there?'

'Everything has been very up in the air. Her behaviour hasn't been easy to measure.'

'How so?'

'Well, the pregnancy. It was unexpected. That dominated.'

'His fault,' muttered Luke darkly. Connie wondered whether he was referring to Zac or John.

'And then with Sophie being in hospital . . .'

'His fault.' This time there was no doubt who Luke was blaming.

Connie couldn't believe it either. Zac had delivered drugs to the party Sophie was at. Why? Why would he do that? She considered herself quite a good judge of character, and Zac did not seem like a drug pusher. He'd seemed like a perfectly pleasant young man; someone she might have actively delighted in if he hadn't reminded her of her ex-lover.

But what did she know? She had no idea what a drug pusher might be like. Zac obviously was one, John had told the police the boy had admitted as much. It was unbelievable.

The DI asked more questions. She wanted to know who Fran and Zac had spent their time with over the holidays and where they'd hung out. Connie and Luke gave names, addresses, phone numbers. They grasped at the hope that they were doing everything they could to help, all the while fighting the feeling that nothing could help other than a message from the kidnappers.

'Have you seen anyone hanging around the house? Think carefully about any tiny incidents that might seem like nothing or might seem unrelated. They could be relevant.'

Connie and Luke fell silent and diligently dredged through their recent memories. 'There was one thing, on Christmas Eve.' Connie described the night she had stood by the bedroom window and watched the youngsters walk home from the pub. She gave as good a description as she could of the two men she'd thought had been following Zac. 'I'm not sure I can offer much more. It was dark and fleeting. So much has happened since.' She paused and then added, 'I think maybe one of them was getting up in the night, leaving the house.'

'One of them?' DI Gianella probed.

'One of the kids.' Always kids to her. 'I was worried it was Sophie or Flora because I found cigarette butts in the garden. I ruled out Fran, because of the pregnancy.'

'Sophie was getting up at night to smoke and you didn't mention it?' Fury sparked like a lit match on Luke's face. 'She's *fifteen*.' As though she could have forgotten. 'If I'd known she was smoking, I'd have grounded her. She would never have been at that bloody party in the first place.' Connie tried to ignore his accusation, his blame-laying. He was scared. Scared people said rash and hurtful things.

'I didn't know for sure it was her, so I didn't mention it. I didn't want a row over Christmas. I was watching out for other evidence as to who it was, but I've never smelt smoke on any of them, so I sort of let it slide.' Connie couldn't decide now if that was normal parenting or neglectful parenting. She'd always done her best.

It was just sometimes so difficult to know what that was. 'Now I'm thinking maybe Zac was meeting someone.'

'Can you show me where you found the cigarette butts?' asks DI Gianella.

Connie led the detective to the back door, a little way along the path into the garden. There was a cigarette stub in the usual place and the police bagged it.

'What might that prove?'

'Maybe nothing, but we have a lead as to which gang might be at the root of all this. Some of them are known to us, they're on file. We might get a name attached to the DNA on this and know who visited here.'

The idea made Connie shiver. A London gang member at her back door walking up her garden path. 'Should we start raising the ransom money?' she asked.

There was a beat. 'It's not what we advise.'

'Well, what, then?'

'It depends on the next message. We'll have a clearer idea once we understand their demands.'

'The demands are here. Thirty-five thousand in cash. That will take some time to raise. We can't waste time waiting for their next message, we must start collecting it now.'

The policewoman eyeballed Connie. 'We don't recommend paying ransom money. The UK's position on payment of terrorist ransoms is very clear: we do not pay, on the basis that providing money fuels terrorist activity and encourages further kidnaps.'

'But this isn't a terrorist group,' said Luke. 'It's a drug gang.'

'We don't know exactly who or what we are dealing with yet. One thing doesn't exclude the other,' said the officer firmly. She closed her notebook. 'OK, that's me done here for now. I need to get back to the station.' Connie felt panic surge through her body once again. She couldn't understand it. They were going? They were abandoning her? They weren't letting her pay the ransom. What use were they? 'We have Fran and Zac's laptops, thanks for releasing those. We need to start combing through them now.'

'You won't find anything on Fran's,' said Luke firmly. 'She isn't involved in drugs.'

The DI nodded. 'Right, but you want us to be thorough. It's best to keep an open mind. Not to jump to any conclusions. As things stand, we only have one account of what we think is happening.'

'I told you everything I know,' interrupted John. 'I was with you for hours.'

'Yes, and we're grateful for your cooperation, but your narrative was built around what Zac and Fran told you.'

'They weren't lying. Neither of them,' John insisted.

The policewoman nodded in a way that didn't quite commit to agreement. 'Right, but it's possible that something was omitted from their accounts. Inadvertently or otherwise.' The three parents understood that the detective was saying perhaps the kids couldn't be trusted. Considering the situation, it wasn't an unfair theory to hold. They might have told John the truth or just 'their truths'. They might be hiding stuff through fear or misplaced loyalty or for any number of other reasons. They might simply not have had time to reveal everything that was important. 'We know that these people want money. They will be in touch. You'll need to contact us the moment they are.' They nodded. 'I'll put a call out to have the house watched. There will be patrol cars in the street when available, someone will walk by if it's a quiet night. I don't think it's the best use of resources, having someone on your door permanently, but we can if you insist on it. Do you feel threatened? Scared for your own safety?'

'No,' Connie replied hurriedly. Not for her own. The detective was right: resources were better employed elsewhere than babysitting them. She quickly rattled off a text to Lucy. She always felt better, safer, supported when Lucy was in the loop. With her effervescent certainty and conclusive competence, Lucy never let her down.

'It's most probable that they'll text their instructions as communication has started that way. I think it's unlikely anyone will come to the house,' the detective said bluntly. No doubt she was trying to make Connie and Luke feel safer. They didn't, as the thought of gang members arriving at the door hadn't crossed their minds until that point.

As soon as the door was closed on DI Gianella, Luke said, 'OK, we must get back to the hospital to be with Sophie. The doctors need to talk to us.' Connie felt stunned. Torn in half.

'I have to stay here.'

'Why? Just bring your phone.' Luke was already in the hallway, putting on his coat.

'You heard the detective, they might come here to make their demands, give instructions on how to pay.'

'That's not what she said. She said it was *unlikely* they'd come here.'

'But not impossible. I can't risk missing the opportunity to help her. Imagine if they came here and they couldn't reach anyone. It might enrage them. We don't know how these people think. They're not rational or normal.'

'Well, if you think they might come here, I don't want you here alone. I'll stay, you go to the hospital,' said Luke.

'It was my phone they contacted first. I think they're more likely to talk to me. Besides, you'll understand the medical stuff better. I should stay here and you should go to the hospital.' Connie felt this situation was peculiarly like one that had often played out in their lives when they had been forced to split resources to best meet the needs of their children. Connie might take one child to a party, because she was better at making small talk with the other parents, and Luke would take the other two to swimming club because he was the more confident swimmer. Or one parent might attend a parents' evening and take meticulous notes on the teachers' comments, while the other went to a music concert and enthusiastically called for an encore. They had learnt to be pragmatic, efficient with their time and resources.

'I'm not leaving you here alone if there's any chance that one of these thugs might come here.'

'I'll stay with her,' offered John.

Connie and Luke were both startled, almost as though they had forgotten he was in the room. Luke rolled his eyes, swore under his breath. He couldn't stop himself muttering, 'You're the reason we're in this trouble.' Over the years, Connie had often felt John ought to be accountable for trouble or pain, but not in this instance; he could hardly be blamed for Zac's actions. Plus his position wasn't any better than theirs. What was the point in being angry with him? There wasn't time for misdirected blame or rage.

'Thanks, John, that's good of you. Luke, you need to get to the hospital. Call me with any news. Tell Sophie I love her so much. I'll be there as soon as I can be.'

51

Connie

She had thought something would happen quickly. Something else. Something more. Because everything had happened at speed today. But once again Connie found herself waiting. Not crouched around a hospital bed this time, willing Sophie to blink or move, but staring at a phone, waiting for it to buzz or ring. It did not. She was sure an hour had passed, but when she checked, it was just nine minutes since she'd last looked at the clock.

Lucy popped round. 'I've brought some goodies. Scented candles, Ferrero Rocher chocolates, aromatherapy bath soak, that sort of thing. There's everything you might need in there,' she said, handing over a gym bag that she'd bothered to tie with a ribbon. Always stylish; there wasn't a world where Lucy's aesthetic standards might drop. 'Do you want me to come in and wait with you?'

'No.' They went back far enough that Connie didn't need to offer more.

Lucy understood. With a hint of unusual helplessness, she added, 'I'm here for anything you need. Just around the corner.'

'I know. Thank you.'

They hugged, tightly, a gesture so rare for Lucy it was painful. Connie could feel her friend's heart beating against her own chest. Fast. As they pulled apart, Lucy murmured, 'Take care of yourself.' Making eye contact, she flipped the hackneyed comment into something intense. 'Promise me.'

'It's on my list.' Connie smiled weakly. They both knew her priorities.

Alone, Connie and John fell back on the only thing they could do at a time like this: they made and drank tea. She pulled biscuits out of the cupboard but didn't have the energy to put them on a plate. When John polished off four in a matter of seconds, she offered to make him a sandwich. 'Or soup? I could warm a carton of soup.' It was obvious she was saying she didn't have it in her to make anything complicated. Sometimes a distraction was a good thing, other times it was an impossibility.

'I'm starving, can I have both? I'll make the sandwich.'

She shrugged and let him rummage in the bread bin and poke about the fridge. She stretched past him and retrieved a carton of leek and potato soup. It wasn't that they were comfortable around one another exactly, it was more that they were too worn out to be uncomfortable. 'It's three days out of date,' she admitted, noting the Best Before printed on the packaging.

'I think those dates are more of a suggestion,' he replied.

She poured the soup into a pan. They didn't talk much as they prepared the meal. Connie realised that this was unusual for them, quietness. There had always been an abundance of noise and chatter between them: flirtatious comments volleyed, light banter bounced, passionate thoughts swapped, a never-ending string of complex compliments and cruel words to tangle and disentangle, tangle once again. They perched at the breakfast bar, him eating the simple meal they'd prepared, her pretending to. Her eyes kept falling to her phone and the image of Fran tied to the chair, gagged, vulnerable. Of course she couldn't eat.

Eventually he said, 'Thanks for letting me stay.'

'I'm glad you're here.' He nodded, understanding. It was more than the potential threat of a gang member turning up here; neither of them wanted to be alone. 'What was the photo of Zac like? Was he tied to a chair too?' John nodded, dipped the last of his ham sandwich into his soup and then stuffed it in his mouth. Manners wouldn't let him speak. Connie wondered what he was avoiding saying. 'You said he was beaten up,' she probed. He nodded again. 'That must have been horrendous to see. I'm sorry.'

He swallowed. 'Yeah, Connie, it was. Whatever he's done, he's paying for it.'

'We all are,' she said with a sigh.

He stiffened. 'Hey, this isn't a competition over who's having it the worst. I know you have two girls in desperate trouble right now because of Zac, but it's not like that's double my pain. He's all I've got, so we can't rank each other's anxiety.'

Connie thought that maybe they could, because John had only known he was a father for approximately six months, she'd been a mother for twenty-one years, but she didn't want to get into it. She was almost proud of him for being defensive over Zac. Parents were universally protective of their children. She patted his arm. 'I was just asking about the photo to gauge what they're capable of. Sorry.'

John turned pale. 'God, no, Connie, *I'm* sorry.'

So Connie had her answer. These people were capable of very bad things. Very bad indeed.

They cleared away the pots and then went back into the living room. They flopped down on the sofa, next to each other, facing the TV, but neither suggested they turn it on, or that they listen to music. Connie took a call from Luke. Sophie had blinked again, and this time in response to being asked to do so.

'That's brilliant, Connie,' John said when she relayed the news. His face lit up with joy and relief, all the more notable for its recent absence of both emotions. She noticed he'd finally stopped calling her Greenie. Had they grown up?

'It is, but there's still a long way to go.'

'She'll do it.'

'I thought so too this morning. I was sure of it. That was when I still believed in my own luck and invincibility.'

'Right.' He pushed his hand through his hair and asked the question that was bashing around both of their heads 'Why haven't they got in touch?'

'I have no idea.'

'I thought they'd move quickly. Make their demands before they could be tracked. I keep wondering what's happening to Zac and Fran. You know, right now in this moment. And no word from the police either.' He shook his head.

'I hope they're working around the clock. You don't think they knock off when their shift finishes when they're dealing with a case like this, do you?' she asked.

'No, no, they wouldn't. Every minute counts.' But neither of them knew for sure. Their dealings with the law were limited to speeding tickets and watching episodes of *Slow Horses* on TV. John was just saying that because it was what she wanted to hear. Another first. Him giving her what she wanted. Maybe DI Elizabeth Gianella went home and slept. Perhaps she went out on a Tinder date. Connie wanted to ring her just to check. 'Shall we call them, see if there's any news?' suggested John. It was as though he was reading her mind. Again unprecedented.

He called, but there wasn't much in terms of an update. Not really. The police tried to placate him. Checks were being run; every avenue looked at. The DI said, 'With an ongoing, fast-moving investigation it's never useful to share conjecture about leads until we see how things pan out.'

When John hung up, he said, 'She's at her desk, though, not out on a hot date. That's something. Will Luke head home soon?' It was 8 p.m., not unreasonable to think that visiting hours might be coming to an end. It highlighted to Connie how John had no idea what they had been living through these past few days, what they still had to face.

'He'll probably stay at the hospital all night, I imagine. I have been, these last few days, because you never know what might happen when. But I think my parents and my middle daughter will be home shortly.'

'I'll get out of your hair the minute they're back.'

'You don't have to. You might as well stay. I won't be going to bed. I can't stand the idea of night, and sleep, and another day,' Connie muttered. 'I can't bear just sitting here and doing nothing. It feels like each passing minute is taking her further from me.' She simply wanted time to stop rolling forward. Even if her daughter was in one physical spot and not being moved from A to B and Connie stayed in this house for the rest of her life, every passing minute created an increasing distance. 'I thought enduring each hour of Sophie's unconsciousness was the worst thing I'd have to deal with as a parent, but this is possibly more horrendous still. Not even knowing where Fran is. Imagining a world where I might lose track of her, lose sight of her for ever.'

'I think they'll be together,' said John. 'You know, wherever they are.'

'I hope so. I know Fran would like that.' He grimaced. Unconvinced. The silence in the room felt heavy and hard. Connie now wished there was some background music to hide behind. There wasn't, so she reached for the only thing she knew was irrefutable. 'She loves him, very much. I know you don't believe that, because of what happened with you and her, but—'

'No, no, look, let's not talk about that now.' John waved his hands as though he could push away the embarrassing, inconvenient facts, their history. Perhaps sweep it under the carpet and reinvent a glossy, cleaner reality; something Connie had advocated for not so long ago. 'I believe you,' he insisted. 'She loves Zac very much.' He said it in a way that sounded as though he was latching on to an idea, taking comfort in it. John wanted his son to be loved ferociously and completely. It was a good thought to hold tightly to, now in among all the violence, desperation and degradation that Zac was enduring.

Connie checked her phone again. No message. 'He proposed to her, you know.'

'What? Like with a ring and everything?'

'Yes. She didn't put it on, didn't answer him. But she told me she wanted to say yes. She just couldn't bring herself to because she was, well, you know, ashamed.'

'Where is it?'

'The ring?'

'Yeah.'

'I don't know. Her room, I suppose.'

'I'd like to see it.'

'You would?'

'Yes, just, I don't know, to see what he picked out.'

'OK, let's go and look for it.' It was something to do.

Connie picked up the phone, as she couldn't risk it being out of her sight for a second; it was an actual lifeline. John followed her up to the top floor. Fran's bedroom. As the door swung open, Connie half imagined she'd find her daughter flopped on the bed, phone in hand, propped up on half a dozen pillows, struggling to find a comfortable place to rest. She was ensnared by thoughts of the endless times she'd popped her head inside this room, settled on the edge of the bed, sometimes lain down next to Fran to talk about her day, kiss her forehead and say goodnight.

The usual rubble of youth scarred the room – damp towels, toiletries, hair scrunchies, discarded clothes, odd socks. Yet despite the untidiness, the emptiness of the room was what Connie noticed most. She breathed deeply, hoping to catch the smell of Fran's shower gel, maybe Zac's aftershave; she'd have settled for the disconcerting moist smell that told her, far too forcefully, that they were having regular sex, knowledge she'd been waging war against this holiday season – constantly flinging open windows, lighting candles. The room smelt empty. Cold.

She hunted about for a while until she found the Tiffany

bag propped up at the bottom of the wardrobe. 'This is it.' She carefully opened the box. 'It's beautiful,' she admitted as she stared down at the princess-cut solitaire on a gold band. 'He's got great taste.'

'I can't think how he's been able to afford that.' John looked colourless.

'It's probably on a credit card somewhere.' Connie wondered if this was why he owed money to the vicious gang. It was an unbearable thought, impossible to digest. Cruel to articulate.

'The debt, he said it was because he'd thrown away their gear after what happened to Sophie,' John said, understanding the leap she'd made and wanting to convince her his son has been honourable. Ultimately.

'Oh yes, I'm sure,' she said. She wanted to believe him.

'He was really serious about her,' mused John.

'Please don't talk about them in the past tense. I can't stand it.'

'Sorry, I didn't mean . . .'

She placed her hand over his mouth. Anything he said might hurt. They were both sitting on the bed. Connie couldn't remember choosing to sit, couldn't remember John joining her there. They'd just sort of stopped moving and ended up there. They had never before sat on a bed and not wanted to tear one another's clothes off. They were older, wiser. If not exactly old or wise.

'I can't remember everything,' she said softly. She suddenly became self-conscious that her hand was still on his mouth. His lips. Awkward. She pulled it away quickly.

'What do you mean?' he asked.

'Everything she said or did. Has done so far,' Connie

corrected. 'I keep trying to remember it all, but it hasn't stuck. Least not hard and fast enough. Not everything.'

'Well, no, that would be impossible.'

'I've been careless. I've always thought there would be more. More chatter, more laughs, more tantrums, more casual "love yous". I didn't pay attention to every single one of the things she said or did, every single moment of her being here. You know, with three of them it's often an accomplishment if you just get them out the door, dressed and hair brushed.' Her tears dropped on the duvet cover between them.

'Hey, now.'

'I should have known nothing lasts. I should have written everything down. Everything, every feeling, word exchanged, view expressed. I should have kept a record the way some people keep baby teeth or locks of hair from first haircuts. I didn't even do that.'

'Thank fuck, Connie, that sounds weird.'

'No, no, it's not weird, it's very commonplace. People do it. But I didn't because . . .' she smiled through her upset, and admitted, 'yeah, OK, because it felt weird. I just wish I'd tried to capture and hold tightly to everything it meant, being their mother.' He handed her a handkerchief. She was amazed. She didn't know anyone still carried cotton handkerchiefs around with them. She thought her father was the last man alive doing that. 'Are you ever aware of your mortality, John?'

He coughed. 'On a Sunday after a big night. Every time. I feel like I'm dying then.'

She sighed. She wanted to tell him to be serious, but there was no point. He was not serious. Never had been. Never would be. If even now he was resisting an open acknowledgement of depth and sincerity, he was putting a very definite stake in the ground. This was who he was.

The joker.

The one who tried to ease tension.

She was the deep one. She realised she was embarrassing him, creating anxiety by articulating things he'd like to skate over, avoid generally. She'd thought they were connecting, understanding one another, finally bonding, even if it was over tragedy, but he'd only ever disappoint her because the intensity of her scared him. It had scared most men she'd ever been involved with. Only Luke revelled in it. Luke was not as deep as she was, but he liked her constant questioning, the way she challenged and probed and felt things.

She missed her husband so much and wished he was at home. Most of all, she wished there wasn't a need for him to be elsewhere. By their daughter's bedside.

Her phone buzzed. They both pounced on it. Connie was first to reach it. 'It's them.'

52

John

Keep the fuckin police out of it. We're watching.
£35k.

And a pin drop. John pinched the screen, zooming in. 'They aren't far. Just off the M4. It's an industrial estate, I think. Looks like warehouses, storage units. We need to call the police.'

'Yes, well, maybe.'

'Maybe?' John stared at her. She was nothing if not surprising. 'You don't think we should?'

'The kidnappers have told us to keep the police out of it, and you heard that DI. She said we shouldn't pay the ransom. So what are they going to do? Go in there with their guns?' Connie's eyes were wide and she looked horrified by the idea.

John was certain the drug gang would have guns. Going in with some of their own didn't seem like a totally ridiculous idea to him. 'What are you saying?'

'We should go, just us two. We should follow instructions. It's the best chance of getting the kids out safely.' She seemed firm, certain.

He didn't know. Possibly. Or possibly they'd all get killed. Wasn't this one of those occasions when you left it to the professionals? He remembered Connie talking to Clare when they went for a walk on Hampstead Heath. She was bragging that she dyed her own hair, painted her own walls, didn't have a financial adviser – she and Luke made all their own financial decisions. She had an allotment and grew her own vegetables, for God's sake. What was the point of Sainsbury's? He'd thought she was trying to appear down-to-earth to Clare, but now he wondered whether maybe she was just a bit arrogant, or a total control freak, certain she could do most things better than most people. But surely this was a job for the police. Wasn't it? He had to talk her out of this. 'But we don't have the money. It will take us a few days to collate that sort of money.'

'Lucy dropped it off earlier,' Connie replied calmly.

'What? The cash? Thirty-five thousand?'

'Mostly cash. Some gold.'

'I'm sorry, what?'

'She and her husband are investment bankers. They're the type who keep gold in their safe.'

John wasn't aware that there was such a type. 'They have a safe?' Even that seemed alien unless you were in a hotel room.

'Yes. Theirs is a different world.'

'And she's just what, like, given you thirty-five thousand pounds?'

'Yes. I texted her earlier. I explained what I needed. She can help, so she has. I'm sure I'll pay her back, or not. Fran is her god-daughter, I'm her best friend. It's just money.'

He nodded. He agreed, in fact. There wasn't a price he wouldn't pay to have Zac and Fran safely at home. 'And Luke?'

'Luke?'

'Is Luke aware of your plan?'

Connie did not blink; she held eye contact. 'No, I didn't tell him.'

'Because he wouldn't agree, he'd want to call the police?'

'Because he has to concentrate on Sophie right now. He's too wrung out to think effectively.' John thought the same could be said of Connie, of any one of them, but she seemed cool, calm and steely determined. Faced with her conviction, suddenly he was less certain about his own path. Maybe she was right. Maybe they should do what was asked to get their kids back. 'Please, John, you don't have to come with me, but please don't call the police. At least not yet. Give me some time.' She paused, and then added, 'It wouldn't be the first time we've kept a secret from Luke.'

He didn't bother pointing out how badly that had ended.

53

Fran

I think the worst is coming. It's a possibility, isn't it? It happens. I know it. Every woman knows it. I have never felt fear like it. My blood is sluggish as the fear claims my mind, breath and body. I sort of drift outside of myself. I can actually see me from above, tied to the overturned chair. Helpless. I close my eyes and just wish for it to be over. Maybe, for a moment, I want everything to be over. But there's my baby, so no, not that. Not for everything to be over.

Just this.

Then the black guy just rights my chair, hardly breaking sweat, like it's no big deal, like I am a toy doll and he can pick me up and play with me whenever. Next, he rips the gaffer tape off my mouth. It's wrapped a number of times around my head, so it really hurts as the tape tears at my hair, yanking clumps out. Once my mouth is free, I say, 'Thank you.' I don't know why I say it, not a ploy or a tactic. Just because I am so relieved that they didn't do anything worse. And on a basic level, I am just glad not to have the blood rushing to my head any more, grateful to be more comfortable. It makes them laugh. Not a friendly laugh, obviously. More of an untethered, excited laugh. Scary. I regret my people-pleasing ways, which are drilled into little girls and which I have been quite effectively eradicating until this. But I am at least upright.

'Don't scream. No point. We're miles from anywhere,' says one.

'And we'll kill you if you do,' says another. 'Got it?'

I nod.

Then they walk away. Sort of saunter, as though I bore them, as though beating Zac is something they can return to later if they feel like it. Which I guess they can. They settle at a scruffy wooden table about eight metres away. I can see crisp packets and Jaffa Cake boxes and a half-empty bottle of vodka on it. I guess there's drugs too, as the white guy snorts something. The black guy pulls out a packet of cards and starts to performatively shuffle the deck. Whenever I see anyone able to dovetail shuffle or riffle or waterfall cards, whatever, I think they're probably not busy enough. I mean, who has the time to practise that stuff? I guess now I have my answer: people like these. People who hang around and wait to hear who they're going to hurt next. Ink Face is talking in a low voice on his phone, but his eyes are on me. It feels odd. I don't trust the space and time they have given me and Zac. What are they waiting for? What comes next?

I flash my eyes at Zac. Where to start? What to say to him? He saves me a problem by kicking off.

'I'm so sorry, Fran,' he mutters. 'I never meant you to get mixed up in this.'

'But *you* are,' I accuse him. Because what the hell?

'No, no. I'm not like them.' He shakes his head and it lolls weirdly. I think it's going to snap off and roll to my feet. 'It's not like that.'

'Then what is it like?' I want him to give me an answer, a real one, a reason. He takes his time. Right, we're not going anywhere, what's the rush? He slowly gathers his words. I guess whatever he has to say is beyond difficult, I guess that's why he hasn't said anything to me until now, when he has to.

'I saw something, something really bad, and since then they've been threatening me. Then I did some bad stuff of my own.' His voice doesn't sound like it usually does. We're whispering, so there's that. And he's beaten and swollen, so I guess talking isn't easy, but I think there's something else on top. Shame? Regret?

I've always operated on a system that it's a duff idea to ask questions unless you really want to hear the answers. I find I do want the answer here. I'll deal with it. 'What bad stuff?'

'I delivered for them.' I can guess what sort of thing he delivered. I think of Sophie lying so still, and a flare of pure hate snakes through my body. It's incredibly confusing. Without having a name or a face to blame, I have wished violence and hate on the person who was responsible for putting her in hospital. Him. He was that person. I wished hurt on Zac. Well, go me, because my wishes came true. Look at him now. Pounded and broken. But my hate is doused by a sting of pity and love. I'm so sorry and sad. 'Then I threw away one of their packages, so I owe them. Least that's the way they see it,' he says.

'You did what?'

'I just couldn't do it any more. You know, after Sophie.

I guess it brought it home that there wasn't just me at risk in this.' He shakes his head, regretfully, and then with more force adds, 'But I should have carried on. I should have done what they asked because then they wouldn't have come for you. I'm sorry. I'm so sorry.' His voice cracks. Actually smashes into shards as he reveals his guilt and regret.

'No, no, don't be sorry.' He's crying now. His shoulders are shuddering and I just want to put my arms around him. 'It's OK, it's OK.' I don't know if it is. I mean, it isn't. We're screwed, but as we are, and as I love him, I rush to lie to him because he's wrecked and I want to soothe him, comfort him, in any small way I can. It's horrible to watch. I'm here because he tried to do the right thing. He threw away their junk. I mean, brave and stupid. He's both things at once. Getting done over for trying to do the right thing is school-kid standard. Happens. But it's not fair.

Life isn't.

My mum's voice again, in my head. Looks like she's going to get the last word. The thought of my mum, or maybe last words, makes me see white. Or nothing. I can't think about it. I can't think about Zac's pain, or what might happen to me, Sophie's predicament or how shattered my parents might be. It's literally too much.

I scratch about in my head for something to say that might help. I look around the cavernous room again, then I blurt, 'If this place was in Manhattan and I wasn't going to die here, it would be almost cool.' Zac laughs, which is what I wanted. I love making him laugh. It's as exciting, powerful and fun as making him come. But I regret it immediately. It's a spluttery, uncontrolled laugh, and I glance to the table and see the card shuffler look up. He catches my eye, bothered about what's making us happy. They don't want us to be happy. I look to my feet. Freeze. I can't forget what danger we're in, even if I want to. Zac seems to be thinking exactly the same thing. He shrinks. Fades.

I smell my own sweat.

One, two, three. I count in my head. Thinking about numbers and breathing. Nothing else. Fighting to stay calm. It takes for ever, but eventually, when I'm sure our abductor's attention has fallen away again, quiet and low I dare ask, 'What did you see?'

I watch his face, which, while unfamiliar now it's battered, is somehow still the face I've come to read best in the world. I see him struggle; he's definitely deciding whether to answer truthfully. 'I saw them kill a guy.' My skin ripples as the hairs on my body stand to horrified attention. Well, I did ask. 'They made it look as though I did it. They have photos that would frame me.'

'What?'

'Then they threatened you. I didn't know what to do. You have to believe me. I was doing everything I could to avoid this. Everything.'

Check. I believe him. What level of mental would you have to be to want this as an outcome? I need to pee, my arms ache, I'm so scared. Normally I blurt every thought in my head; since I've been pregnant, I've given Zac a total minute-by-minute running commentary on my bodily comfort, or otherwise, but now I know there's no point. He can't alleviate anything for me. It's not as simple as nipping out to buy me a jar of pickled cucumber from Waitrose; he can't rub the base of my back to bring me ease and comfort the way he has on several occasions this Christmas holiday. I search around for a way to distract us. 'If we get out of this alive, imagine how easy we'll find parenting,' I mutter quietly.

'What?'

'Well, you know, nothing will freak us.'

'I think parties might. Drugs. Him going out the house,' replies Zac.

'No, we'll be great. We'll be invincible.' I force myself to smile at him. He looks at me for a long time through his good eye, or more accurately, his not-quite-so-bad eye. It's like he's looking at me for the very first time. I don't feel as brave as I'm trying to sound, but Mum is forever advocating 'fake it until you make it'. She used the phrase *illegitimi non carborundum* – don't let the bastards grind you down – even before *The Handmaid's Tale* being on TV made it a thing. She's always going on about us being resilient and self-reliant. She thinks it's bigger than being pretty or even clever. I'm beginning to see her POV. Even if I had got an A star in maths A level, it wouldn't help me right now; dealing with the fact I got a B, probably on some microscopic level, has. Because shit happens. 'They asked for a ransom for you,' I tell Zac. 'And I guess now they're asking for one for me too. We're no good to them dead.' This is rational, practical. I choke down the doubt that these thugs are neither thing. Because it doesn't help. Thinking that, knowing that, it doesn't help.

'You are totally amazing,' Zac says with a slow, sad smile.

'That we can agree on,' I say almost cheerfully, and I really hope he's not the last person to note as much. I want to think I'm just starting out.

54

Zac

She was. She was totally amazing, and Zac just wanted to sit there and think about that. Not even think about it, because his head hurt too much for him to actually think about anything, but somehow just wallow in the absolute certainty of it. Fran Baker was amazing and she was his girlfriend. They'd beaten him a lot, and hard. Kicked him too. The worst of it was that now he knew that pain, he feared it. For himself and more for her. He had to do one thing. He had to keep her safe until help came. Could he do that? He'd messed it up so far. But he had to try again. He wasn't a quitter.

'When we get out of here, we should go on holiday, abroad somewhere.'

It was a crazy suggestion. They had no money for a holiday, it would be term time and they might never get out. Because of all these things, he was grateful that Fran replied, 'Yeah, where are you thinking?'

'Somewhere hot, with a beach.'

'We can lie on sunloungers.'

'And drink cocktails. Negronis. You like negronis, right?'

She looked like she was about to give up on the comforting fantasy. 'I've gone off them.'

'Oh yeah, of course. Our baby. We'll both stick to Shirley Temples.'

'You don't have to do that.'

'I want to. What's in a Shirley Temple anyway?' She didn't reply. Maybe she didn't know. Maybe she was losing interest in his attempt to distract her from their actual situation. He tried again. 'Would you like to go camping. Tent? Baked beans and bacon cooked on a stove for supper.'

'Tent and baked beans. Have you thought that through?'

'Have you ever been axe-throwing?' She stared at him oddly. 'We'll go to galleries, we'll go clubbing.'

'Zac, are you having like an early midlife crisis or something? We'll be going to baby yoga and baby music classes.'

'OK, we'll do that,' he said keenly. She had just agreed, hadn't she? To a future, to another chance. 'I just mean, I'm just saying, we're going to do stuff together, aren't we? We're going to have time and flourish.'

'Flourish?' She was sort of laughing at him. At the word. It was a particular vibe. He waited, and she said it again. 'Flourish. Yeah, OK. I could be into that.'

'We just need to stay quiet. You know? We need to fall beneath their notice for a while. Just sit it out.' Their conversation had been at a low level, the voices people instinctually used in churches or libraries. They needed to be less than that. They needed to disappear if they were to ever have the chance to shine. He was reminded of their telephone conversations, where neither of them ever wanted to hang up and they'd say,

'You do it', 'No, you do it', 'Love you', 'Love you more' for ages. He wondered if she'd understand that today was not the day for that kind of romantic indulgence. Today was more real, more urgent than any other day. She nodded at him.

Relieved, he settled into the silence, wondering how long they'd have to wait until the police came, or their parents, wondering exactly how help would present itself. Because now she was here with him, he not only dared to believe help would come, he absolutely needed it to. Fran and his baby had to be rescued.

'YOU FUCKING GRASS.' The words roared across the space, filling it, bouncing like shrapnel into his being. What was happening? Ink guy was storming towards him. Zac's body began to shake and quake as he anticipated what would come next. Ink Face kicked his chair and threw a punch. Zac's head snapped back and blood sprayed from his nose. Scarlet teardrops arced through the air.

'No, no, stop it,' Fran yelled. 'Stop, please.'

'What is it?' The guy who had been shuffling cards was now up on his feet, hopping about, clearly wired. Dangerous.

'Look what I found on his phone. A photo of the number for a hotline for squealers. So what did you tell her, you fucker?' Ink Face roared his question just inches from Zac's face. Spittle and blood and fury flew.

'Nothing, I didn't call,' Zac insisted.

Another blow landed on him, then another. He had no idea how many times a person could be hit. How many times he would be hit. Each blow felt like the last one he could take, but they kept coming. He was glad Fran had closed her eyes, but my God, what was she doing? She had opened her mouth and let out a scream. He understood the term bloodcurdling for the first time. She mustn't scream. She mustn't draw attention. They'd hurt her too. But her mouth was a black oval, and from it poured a siren of sound. A long, continuous alarm. She kept screaming and he didn't think she'd ever stop.

'Shut her up. Shut her the fuck up!'

55

Connie

It was impossible to see inside the building, but inside the building was where they needed to be. The night had an endless depth about it, and unusually for anywhere in London or the surrounding suburbs, there were no street lights or car headlights, not so much as a window lit up with the grey-blue glow from a screen. The bulk of the building was just about traceable, a wet brick dense silhouette on black sky.

'You sure about this?' She was annoyed that he'd spoken unnecessarily; stealth mattered, but she was also irritated by the question because she didn't want to have to face facts or consider carefully. She couldn't be sure. Like so many things about parenting, she had to be just sure enough. She needed to be propelled forward. This was a gut thing. In fact, a womb thing. She didn't need his hesitation, his doubts. Even his logic or reasoning was a distraction.

They silently pulled open the heavy wooden door. Connie noted that a pane of glass was broken, maybe deliberately to access the lock, maybe through neglect or age or accident. The fact that the door opened suggested they were in the right place. While simultaneously being in a very wrong place.

The corridors smelt institutionalised and musty. Perhaps it was as long ago as the 1980s that this place was last used for any sort of respectable industry. The floors were covered in tacky, dusty lino, the walls were painted magnolia and scuffed. They stayed close to the walls and carefully edged forward. They couldn't go back.

Connie heard signs of life before she saw it. If you could describe what she heard as a sign of *life*. It was Fran screaming. A sound so full of horror, revulsion and shock. There was no doubt it was Fran. Connie thought two things simultaneously. Her daughter was alive. Alive! But she was in agony, in danger. She started to run towards the screaming. John just as instinctually and with equal speed and greater force grabbed at her. She'd insisted on carrying the bulky gym bag of money and gold; it was that he managed to lay his hands on. She knew she needed to deliver the money, so she pulled at the bag and it acted as a lock between them. He slammed her against the wall, using his body to pin hers. One of his hands was now over her mouth, the other still clasped around the handle of the money bag.

'Let's think about this. Jesus, Connie, we can't just charge in there.' For just one moment she let herself note the power and forceful certainty that he exuded. Part of her wanted to let someone else take control, take responsibility. She wanted to surrender to a plan. He whispered into her ear, 'We need the police. We should at least look around, understand the entrances and exits.' What if he was right? What if running in there with a sack full of cash was just going to get them all killed? But the wild and impossible screaming continued; Connie knew she wasn't going to listen to him. To anyone. She had to do what she must.

And then he ran.

But not in the direction of the screaming. Away from it. It happened so quickly, she struggled to process it as she watched him dart back into the black corridor and vanish. He'd left her. It was unbelievable, but, of course, also very him. She stood stock still for a shocked moment, but only a moment. She didn't need him. Or even if she did, she didn't have him. She never could depend on him. She ran too, towards her daughter.

The screaming became louder, reassuring her she was heading in the right direction, but as she drew closer, she heard something else too. A dull thud, a muffled cry. Vomit tickled her throat as she realised someone was being punched. Not Fran, the scream was too consistent. Zac, then. Jesus. She ran faster, her lungs and legs punching, performing, never before more definite or powerful.

She launched into the room and towards Zac and Fran. She skidded, glanced down at her feet. My God, she'd slipped on blood.

'Hello, and who do we have here?' The voice came from behind her. Someone had followed her into the room. For a moment, everyone fell silent. The screaming stopped; the punching stopped. Thank God.

'Mum! Mum!'

'It's OK.' Connie instinctually headed to her daughter, who was tied to a chair, and flung her arms around her. She hugged her, kissed her head over and over.

'It's far from fucking OK, lady.'

The man who said this was holding a gun, so Connie thought he probably knew best.

56

Bear

Bear had barrelled into the room, slowly coming up behind the crazy, flailing woman. What was going on? Fuck, his men were morons. This was obviously louder and messier than ideal.

His size, stature, beard and broadness must have announced his importance to this pathetic little gaggle of give-it-a-go, middle-class fuckers who were causing him problems right now, and if not that, then certainly the attitude of his three men broadcast how serious he was. How terrifying.

His three men all had their eyes on him, agitated, desperate to charge in any direction he pointed them in. Desperate to do anything he told them to, no matter how degrading or vicious. No questions asked. The blokes who worked for him were, without exception, lousy, contemptible little shits who could be bought or sold or scared into doing anything, and it was all sort of fucking boring at times. Most of his men bowed and scraped when they saw him, or they went to the other extreme, puffed up their chests, strutted like little cocks. Whatever, they all hung on his every word. He wouldn't have had it any other way. They should be scared shitless of him.

He glanced about. His men had been trying to manage this on their own, but they had not. That was clear. Just fucked it up more. Some little twat kid had sold his gear, although he claimed he'd thrown it in a river. Neither option permissible. The kid had stolen from *him*. Bear. The kid *owed* Bear. Not happening. And now there was this whole circus.

This was Ink's fault. He'd been shuffling, jostling for more power, more of a cut. He'd got above himself. He'd thought he could clean this up, get the money back. Got it into his head that the parents would cough up. But he'd fucked up everything. Kidnapping. It wasn't what they were into. A clean-out. Yes. A knifing, an occasional shooting, a too-severe beating, that shit happened, but all this stuff – abduction, blackmail, hostage-taking – required a level of planning that Ink and his idiots were not up to.

This was a fucking mess. First it was the boy. Scrupled, not quite scared enough. Then his girl. Pretty, the sort to attract media attention. Now, apparently, the mother. Determined, the type that could pay for expensive lawyers.

Fuck.

They were not even blindfolded. He couldn't believe that. Idiots. His first thought had been to back out the room the minute he'd charged into it, but the mother had instantly clapped eyes on him. Drilled into him. She wasn't letting him go, she knew he was the one to watch. He couldn't have dashed out to find a balaclava and then come back in once she'd eyeballed him. He'd have looked weak. But now they'd seen him, and that . . . Well.

'There's been a lot of noise today. A lot of screaming.' Bear said this in a way that communicated he found it wearing, irritating. He walked around the room. Assessing what had gone on. He had to give his lads a bit of leeway, couldn't oversee everything, but it was important to him that the rules were followed. The boy had taken it good and proper. That much was obvious. Fair enough. But they knew never to mess with girls. He wasn't into that. It was unpleasant and unfocused. He was who he was to make money. He didn't mind being violent, in fact he considered it the only effective way, but he didn't see a need to rape women. That was for sick fuckers, not serious ones. You could get it so many ways; even paying for it was better than taking it. Most of his lads were too high or stoned to bother most of the time, which was convenient, but just to be sure, he'd once shot a man in the bollocks for not understanding his stance on the matter.

'I have the money. I haven't called the police.' That was from the mother. She was folded over the girl. Not tied up herself yet. He hardly thought it worth the bother. It was obvious all she wanted to do was hold her daughter; he thought she might as well. She didn't have much time left.

'No, I don't imagine you have.' He wanted to laugh. It was funny really. They had no idea. He knew they wouldn't have called the police. This type always thought they knew better, were stronger, cleverer, different. They thought they were above the law and sense and rules. They were wrong. They were small. When it came down to it, everyone was small, except the one with the gun. That thought prompted him to walk to the table. This place was a disaster zone. Sloppy. DNA everywhere. He scanned for a gun, expected them to have left it lying around, discarded on the table, like an ashtray or a set of keys. No respect. It wasn't there. One of them had it. Which one? That was the question.

He had a quick mind. His mother always insisted he'd have done well at school if only he'd applied himself. She'd wanted him to be a mechanic. Good woman his mum, but did she know any mechanic that owned eight Rolexes, who drove the cars he did? He'd applied himself all right.

So now there was a maths problem of sorts. Three bodies to lose was too many. He had no building work going on at present, so cement foundations were not an option. It wasn't even easy to drop a single in the Thames nowadays. Always someone about, not just party people, bloody joggers, the homeless, whatever, eyes everywhere. Three was an ask, especially as this was a hot case. Even though the mother had not called the police, his unreliable, lazy twat gang would undoubtedly have left some trail that even the pigs would pick up on. They were too high to be reliable. Bear didn't touch drugs himself. Drugs were for losers. Clear heads won the day. He'd once done an online quiz and scored an IQ of 152. Mensa genius official. He was also 98 per cent psycho, according to another online test. There wasn't a printable certificate for that one.

He weighed it up. He needed to finish off at least five of them, maybe all six. Give the pigs something neatly tied up.

So what order? Mother, daughter, boy. Had to be that way. The mother wasn't tied up, so it was safest. The girl would start screaming again, he'd need to shut that up. The boy had, after all, caused this, there was some justice in letting him see it to the end. Well, if not justice, a lesson, and you should never stop learning, should you?

The question of which of his men had the gun, though. That played. He couldn't ask outright and take it off them, that would look odd, put even these pricks on alert. Best idea was a bit of theatre first, with the hostages. He was known for it. His lads would be all over that. They'd get excited, chaotic. Most probably they'd reveal the gun at that point. They'd likely as not pull it out, pull the trigger. They'd want him to see them seeing off the captives. Criminals were often basic show-offs.

So, Ink, Mick, Ekon or Ink, Ekon, Mick? Ink was the best shot and by far the most vicious, so made sense to take him first. There was a chance the sixth might get away. He had to consider it. It wasn't wise to be arrogant. So who was the weakest link? Who would do him the least harm if they did slip loose?

Institutional racism would mean that if Ekon avoided a bullet and spoke up about Bear, anything he said would be ignored. The pigs would be all too happy to send him down for a long time. But on the other hand, Ekon was more on the ball. He might just get clean away. Not land in the hands of the pigs at all. That would be a loose end. Better he take out Ink, Ekon, Mick. Mick was off his tits, wasn't likely to remember anything that clearly, and whatever he said would be met with doubt.

Anyway, that was just the safety net. His plan would be to finish them all, wipe his gun, put it in Ink's hand, make it look like a shoot-out, leave the money with one of the others. Least half of it. No point leaving without covering his costs. He'd do a few minutes' chat, distract his lads, then get down to it.

'OK, they've seen us all. Let's finish this.' He swung round to face the hostages, waved his gun in a lazy manner in their direction.

'No, no, no,' the boy begged. He wasn't more or less than anyone else. They all begged in the end.

'Do you have the money you owe us?' Bear asked him.

'No, but—'

'Then you are no fucking use.' Bear straightened his arm, pointed the gun directly at the lad.

'I have the money.' This was the mother. He turned to her. 'Don't shoot him. Please. I have your money.'

'Where?'

'My bag.' She looked around her, frantic. 'Where's my bag? The money's in the bag.' Bear couldn't see a bag. A good show, an attempt at a distraction? Or real panic that she'd mislaid thirty-five k? He wasn't sure. He almost didn't care. He'd kill everyone, then look for the bag.

'I could just shoot you in the leg. People think that's a kindness, a chance, but they're wrong.' He liked seeing them flinch. Pull back from him, acknowledge their limits and his superiority. 'See, if I hit the giant artery that runs down your leg,' he paused, waved the gun to indicate the length of the artery, the target, 'then you're dead in a matter of minutes. Even if I just nick the femoral artery but don't apply a tourniquet, there'll be a rapid drop in blood pressure, and combined with the inevitable blood loss, again, you'll be dead in minutes.' He paused and added, 'I'm not gonna apply a tourniquet.'

Ink sniggered, he'd seen this show before. Bear couldn't do anything out the ordinary, in case they guessed he was planning on cleaning them out too. One of them was packed, he couldn't forget that. He needed to lull them.

'Or, I could shoot you in the arm. The brachial artery. That takes a bit longer. I'd watch you go into decompensated hypovolemic shock. Ugly, that. It's a lot of money.' He shook his head, almost regretful.

'I can pay it back.' The boy was sobbing now. Some of them pissed themselves at this point.

'Can you, though? Because now I'm looking at you and I'm thinking, cheat or liar? You see, if you can pay it back but haven't when I've asked, and asked so nicely, then you're a cheat. If you can't pay it back, liar.' He paused. 'I don't like cheats or liars.'

57

Connie

Connie had started to move across the room. Fast. Faster. Fastest. She could see the bag now, the gym bag that held the cash. It was flying. Flying in the direction of the man with the gun. That didn't make sense. Where had it been when she was looking for it and needing to prove she had the money? It all happened at once. It was impossible to track chronologically or even emotionally. She was between Zac and Fran. She had expected the talk to go on. To buy a little more time, to get her thoughts together, to act, but the bag hit the arm of the thug, then *bang*! Sudden and irretractable. The sound of gunshot ricocheted around the warehouse. Bang, bang, bang. Three more shots. The tattooed man was shooting too. Bang, bang.

One moment there was something – hope, possibility, a chance. The next, there was a lot of blood and screaming and a sense that ends were looming. Ends had happened. She pressed her hands over the wound. An actual hole, in flesh, it was inconceivable. She couldn't think, she couldn't breathe. The blood spluttered through her fingers. She thought she was going to be sick or lose consciousness. Her vision began to sway, she felt sweat prickle up all over her body from the soles of her feet to the crown of her head. Her body felt like liquid but was also convulsing; a jarring, jerking electric solidness. Someone turned down the volume, dampened it, stretched out the tape recording of her life. The seconds lengthened and struggled. How long did she have?

She thought of the blood that she had encountered in her life to date, all of it to do with her children. Her periods, their births, their childhood injuries, their periods. Now this. A gunshot wound.

'I thought you'd left me.' Her words stuttered out.

'No, no. I just went round the other door.' He was panting, barely able to speak. 'Surprise attack.' His big, blue, unfair eyes held her gaze; she only broke it as she looked around to locate the kids. Both still tied to their chairs, but both alive. All four of the criminals bleeding on the floor. Three were still; they looked like they might be dead. The other was dragging himself to the door, leaving a bloody trail, pulling the bag of money behind him. The gang leader had shot his own men, but who had shot him? It made no sense to her. It was all too much. She couldn't take it in. She could hear wailing, a siren; she didn't quite understand that. Was there a marksman? Had the police shot the gang leader?

John mumbled an explanation. 'I called the cavalry.' An old reference that only people of a certain age might get, and she felt awash with gratitude that he was trying to reassure her, that he was still being him, that they understood one another's references, that they had been on the planet at the same time in history and somehow found each other. Despite the fact that they were born and lived in different cities, despite the fact there were millions of people in those cities, despite the fact she was married to another man, they had found one another. Since Christmas Day she had been obsessing about the theory that she couldn't peel him from her life. She had allowed words like fate and destiny to flirt with her thoughts. She'd trembled at the idea. Retreated. She had wanted to believe she was more in control of things than that. Yet here they were. He had found her and he'd stood in front of a bullet for her.

'I always thought I'd die in your arms,' he murmured.

Connie's mouth twitched to smile. Because, oh God, the bravery of him. Making a joke now. In this. This dark, long moment. She knew she had to meet him with the flirty, playful banter that had always been theirs. 'Liar. You absolutely did not,' she replied, through her tears.

'That's your takeout on that sentence?' He was breathing heavily. 'You're not going to refute that I'm dying?' He laughed and winced, and Connie was gripped with panic. She pushed harder on the hole in his chest. He'd been shot in the thigh too. So much blood. She didn't know what to do. She thought of all the things she'd said to him, some of the things she hadn't. She felt the joy and the shame of him. The pleasure, the disrespect, the excitement and fragility. All the emotions rushed through her simultaneously. She didn't understand this man, he did not belong to her, he'd often ruined things for her, but she felt intense, undiluted, unapologetic love for him.

'Dad, Dad! Is my dad OK?' Zac yelled. Frantic.

John smiled. 'I'm OK, son,' he said, but Zac was unlikely to have heard him. He couldn't project. Connie wanted him to conserve his energy. He must, so he could have a chance;

the ambulance, with its trained medics, would be here any moment. The sirens were getting louder, tantalisingly close. They'd take over. It would be OK.

But she also wanted him to keep talking to her.

She wanted to drink up everything, something, anything, because what if? What if he was not OK? Dear God, dear God. She repeated the words on a loop in her head. Dear God, she felt so inadequate. Why didn't she know exactly what to do to help here? His eyelids fluttered closed, shutting her off, and she was ambushed with a crazy desire to hold them open. He was losing consciousness and it was too much to stand. 'It's always been you, Connie,' he murmured.

'Should you risk lying if you're going to die? One more charge to answer at the pearly gates.'

He managed a weak laugh, as she'd hoped he would. As he did, blood spurted out of his nose. She didn't understand. What the hell was happening? 'I don't believe in all that,' he replied. She had to put her ear very close to his mouth now. She felt his breath. His words were barely audible. 'It's all been here. Heaven and hell. On earth.'

'I was joking, you're not dying.' He was, though. She thought he probably was, and the thought pounded in her skull, in the base of her back.

'Tell her I had a vasectomy. Tell her the baby can't be mine.' He blinked open his eyelids once again and stared at Connie with those eyes that had haunted her for years and would haunt her for ever.

'It's not true, is it? You're just giving her peace of mind.'

'Just tell her,' he murmured. 'Bye, Connie, it's been a ride knowing you.'

There were other people around them now. Medics, thank God. People who knew what they were doing. The police had surrounded the skinny white guy, the only gang member still alive, cuffed him even while others were attending to his gunshot wound. They untied Zac. He limped and crawled to where his father lay bleeding, dying. 'You, you, you,' he hiccuped through tears and pain. 'You jumped in front of the gun. Wrestled it right out of his hands even while he was shooting. You came from nowhere. I thought we were all going to die.' The boy was nothing but tears and blood and snot and love. He bent over his dad and kissed him.

Connie felt someone move her away from John. Her bloody hands trailed down his body, found his hand, but then that fell out of her grasp too. Someone placed a tinfoil wrap around her as though she had run a marathon. Then Fran was clinging to her. Tight, all limbs and bulk. She was sobbing. 'I thought it was you. I thought it was you they'd shot.' The medics were trying to get close to John, so they pushed Zac away too. Connie spread open her arms, and Zac, although taller than her, fell under her wing.

EPILOGUE

John-Luca Neil Baker-Knight was born on St George's Day, 23 April. One of the nurses suggested George was a great name to include, but at 6 lb 8 oz, it was agreed he already had a pretty long name for a fairly tiny being. He didn't need to be named after a martyr who was famed for slaying dragons. He was named after his grandads. The two who would have the privilege and joy of seeing him grow up and the one who'd died saving the lives of his father, mother, grandmother and the tiny namesake himself.

By making the series of split-second decisions to call the police, then enter the room from the opposite door to the one Connie had taken, to throw the bag, to get in front of the bullet, John had saved all their lives. John had slain dragons.

He had once told Connie that he struggled to commit to anything, anyone, that he was easily distracted, and she'd believed it for too many years. She'd resented the memory of him for a long time. Now she knew that people changed, they grew and reprioritised. John had committed to his son and the new young family-to-be. As a middle-aged man, no one could describe him as fickle, lazy or selfish. The press, and those who spoke at his funeral service, used words such as committed, brave, selfless. Connie cried for him; the church was in fact packed with women crying for him. She hoped he was wrong about all of heaven and hell being here on earth; she hoped that somehow he could be watching from somewhere above. He'd have liked to have seen the disproportionate amount of heaving, grieving bosoms. He might even have remembered some of their names.

The funeral was beautiful. There was an abundance of white lilies and a surprisingly traditional, magnificently moving all-boys choir; copious amounts of champagne and bite-size chicken pot pies and apple and sausage bakes were served. They were made from John's recipe, which was in fact a *Good Housekeeping* recipe. The winter favourites he'd wanted to make for Zac. Far from resenting the memories she held of him, she now cherished them. Had learnt lessons from them, become a better person herself because she had them.

There was no doubt in Connie's mind that she would have put herself between the gun and the kids too; she'd entered that room prepared to take a bullet. As a mother, it was a decision that would never have to be considered or weighed up, it would just be a given. But she was grateful he'd beaten her to it. That sounded flip and minor, considering his sacrifice, but it wasn't meant to be. She understood the enormity of what he'd done. Thoroughly. There just weren't always words. Sometimes there were only actions. She was sorry, so sorry, that he would not see his small blue-eyed grandson grow up.

Fran had quietly accepted the news of John's vasectomy.

nodded when Connie had told her. Luke had let out a sigh of relief and muttered just one word, 'Good.' Connie didn't imagine the matter would ever be discussed again. Some secrets were better buried. More than anyone ever imagined probably were.

Sophie was released from hospital by the end of January. Her speech therapy and physiotherapy lasted until May. As she'd missed so much school, it was decided that she should delay her GCSEs for a year. She seemed thrilled to spend the time at home, and revelled in her position as most hands-on aunty, always available for cuddles and to assist at bathtime. It was apparent that she believed she was being an indispensable help and as such manifesting a level of adultness; Connie thought that watching her youngest daughter play with John-Luca was like watching her play with a doll. She saw the child, not the grown-up that Sophie kept surging towards becoming. Connie felt total gratitude every day for this second chance they were all being given for Sophie to have a childhood.

On Thursdays, Connie looked after John-Luca while Fran concentrated on her uni work, now confined to online studies. Last week, Connie and Sophie and the baby had spent almost three hours in the park, chatting, eating an M&S picnic and blowing bubbles. Connie tried to sing a song to her grandson that her own grandfather once used to sing to her, 'I'm Forever Blowing Bubbles', but she soon realised that the lyrics were pretty sad if closely examined. Like old fairy tales and nursery rhymes, there were a lot of things that were best left behind.

Zac had moved in with the Bakers and Fran wore his Tiffany ring, although there was no talk of a wedding date. They could afford it, or at least would be able to soon, as he was to inherit the bulk of John's estate. Sometimes Fran said they were waiting until she was her pre-baby weight before they made wedding plans, other times she said she wanted to wait until the year was out.

'This year, you mean?' asked Connie, not quite following.

'A year since . . . you know, everything. Like an old-school minimum grieving period.'

'That seems oddly formal,' commented Luke.

'Does it? I think it seems like not quite enough.'

Connie didn't have a view on if or when the young couple should marry. She had never heard report of Zac's proposal speech, but if she had, she would have agreed with him. It came down to one thing. Zac and Fran were in love with each other and they were in love with their baby. Everything would be OK because they were a unit. They were just beginning.

ACKNOWLEDGEMENTS

So this is my 25th novel in 25 years and that means the credits due are longer than ever. Strap in, hunker down, here we go . . .

I want to start with saying thank you to Kate Mills, my wonderful publisher, who is fabulous fun; so positive, persuasive and persistent. Thank you for continuing to understand and accommodate weird, mercurial me. For trusting me, encouraging me and gently reeling me back in when needed! You are so clever and a joy to work with. Thank you, Lisa Milton. Every author at HQ benefits from the fact we have such a determined, creative, enthusiastic force at the beating heart of HQ.

I believe the tone and ambition of a team is set by the leadership, so thank you Charlie Redmayne for being a remarkable, pioneering and inspiring CEO. I'm very proud to be published by HarperCollins.

I'm so delighted to be working with such a lovely team – the sort of people who make me look forward to meetings and opportunities to spend time with you. I am utterly appreciative of every single person involved in this book's existence.

Thank you, Philly Cotton, you are a wonder! I'm in awe of your can-do attitude, your persistence, creativity and organisation. I think you are super special and I'm so lucky that you joined my team. Thank you, Kate Elton, Anna Derkacz, Emily Scorer (newcomer and already making your mark. I adore your energy and your results!), Joanna Rose (stalwart and so valued!), Sophie Rosewell, Abigail Soddy, Laura Daley, Angie Dobbs, Halema Begum, Aisling Smyth, Lucy Vanderbilt, Kate Oakley, and Stephanie Heathcote. I can't possibly detail everything you all do (it would be another novel in itself) but please know, I'm aware and truly grateful. Also, shout out to Graham Bartlett who, as well as being a writer, works as an advisor to authors about police matters. Graham is responsible for making me aware that some drugs cost less than a glass of wine! Important plot point.

I want to send massive thanks across the seas to the brilliant teams who publish my books worldwide. You really are making my dreams come true. My North America team are absolutely tremendous and it's such a joy to be finding readers in America and Canada. Thank you, Craig Swinwood, Loriana Sacilotto, Margaret Marbury, Leo McDonald, Sophie James and Rebecca Silver. I know there are many, many more people on this team and I appreciate every one of you. Thank you to Sue Brockhoff in Australia. There are many other publishing teams, who I have yet to meet, but I am so grateful that incredible professionals across the globe are giving my books their love and attention. It's so ridiculously exciting finding readers in so many countries.

Thank you to all my readers, bloggers, reviewers, retailers and librarians who have supported me throughout my 25-year career. That's wild! I know many of you have been with me from the beginning when Connie first stumbled into existence. Thanks for coming on this journey with me. I realise some of you reading this will have just discovered me; that's so exciting too. Think of the backlist! I say it time and time again, without readers, there really would be no point in doing what I do at all. You are, by definition, the entire point of my career. I love meeting you at my events throughout the year. Do follow me on social media or sign up to my newsletter if you want the best chance of getting to say hi in person.

A reader I'd like to say a particular thank you to is Cathy Kaburara Nyarwa. It could be argued that this woman is responsible for the entire creation of *Our Beautiful Mess*. Cathy, thank you for being so passionate and excited by my tentative ideas of a plot to reintroduce Connie and John. Do you remember chatting about how you'd like to see the story unfold? Your youthful, beautiful energy was so inspiring and just the encouragement I needed to bring Connie back. I hope you loved this book and that it lived up to your expectations. Another reader I'd like to acknowledge is Joanna James. It's been an honour to find a way to keep the name Elizabeth Gianella rolling on.

Thank you to all the wonderful authors who I have had the joy and privilege to meet throughout my career. Many have inspired me; many have supported me. I really am fearful of starting to list names as I will leave someone out, but you know who you are. You big-hearted, enthusiastic, funny, clever people who I have partied with, shared panels with, been endorsed, celebrated and consoled by. I'm glad I'm in your tribe. #LivingTheDream.

Despite resisting a list, I am going to drag one person into the spotlight. Tasmina Perry. For the past decade our put-the-world-to-rights brunch, lunch, dinners and theatre trips have often counted among the most important, fulfilling, uplifting, hilarious dates in my calendar. Thank you. Here's to you being your clever, kind, optimistic, curious self.

So, 25 published novels along the line a HUGE thank you must go to my mum and dad for nurturing a love of reading, for valuing my imagination, for encouraging me to believe that as long as I worked hard enough, nothing was out of reach. My mum is always asking: 'Where does she get it from, Tony?' I'm proud to say, I'm a definite mix of the two of you and I am who I am because of you both. You taught me so much.

Thank you to my sister, Andrae Dent, who listened to my stories before anyone else ever did. I think you are possibly the only person who ever guesses all the twists. Brilliant you!

Thank you to Jonny Geller, who first ensured Andrae wasn't destined to be my only audience.

Finally, obviously, forever and always thank you to Jimmy and Conrad. My husband and son. My North Star and inspiration. My good sense and salvation. You are such incredible men. I love you both. I've written millions of words throughout my career about love and life and learning. They are all for you.